WIND SWEPT

-THE HIGHTOWER TRILOGY-

BOOK TWO

JADIE JONES

The Parliament House Press Edition, May 2018

Windswept

ISBN: 978-1719478830

Cover & Interior Design by
Shayne Leighton | Parliament House Book Design
machoviprods@gmail.com

Edited by
J.D. Castleberry
and David Rochelero

Published by The Parliament House
www.parliamenthousepress.com

Printed in the United States of America.

WIND
SWEPT

PROLOGUE

I have lost myself.

My blood is no longer my own. What now pumps through my body is a thousand years old and not human. My soul has memories of another life neither my mind nor my body experienced. If blood and soul and memories are what make a person, I no longer belong to myself. If they aren't, then what else is there?

I once heard our bonds are what make us. I hope that's not true. I don't have any left. My father's body was swallowed by the river. My mother's spirit was smothered by whiskey. My friends are not my friends, and I am not even myself—not really. A thousand-year-old soul has made a home inside this body. They say she's me, that we are one and the same—not two souls fighting for territory. One. So why does that girl—her life, her loss, her love, her sacrifice—feel more like a bedtime story recalled from childhood, and nothing like something I once lived through? Something I once died for?

I used to think having something to fight for made a person strong. So I fought. I fought against the belief that my father was dead—the dive team never found him, after all, and even magic couldn't recover his body from the water. I fought for my mother, forfeited Wildwood and college, the world beyond the walls of our house, and every ounce of my happiness for her, and she still abandoned me. I fought for Vanessa. I trusted her. Trusted Dana and Lucas, and all of them betrayed me. Over and over I fought and fought, and I didn't gain strength. I didn't win. I broke.

All this time, I've been wrong. Dead wrong. Having something to fight for doesn't make a person strong. Our bonds, our empathy, our very *humanity* . . . they're vulnerabilities. Weaknesses.

We become most dangerous when we have nothing left to lose.

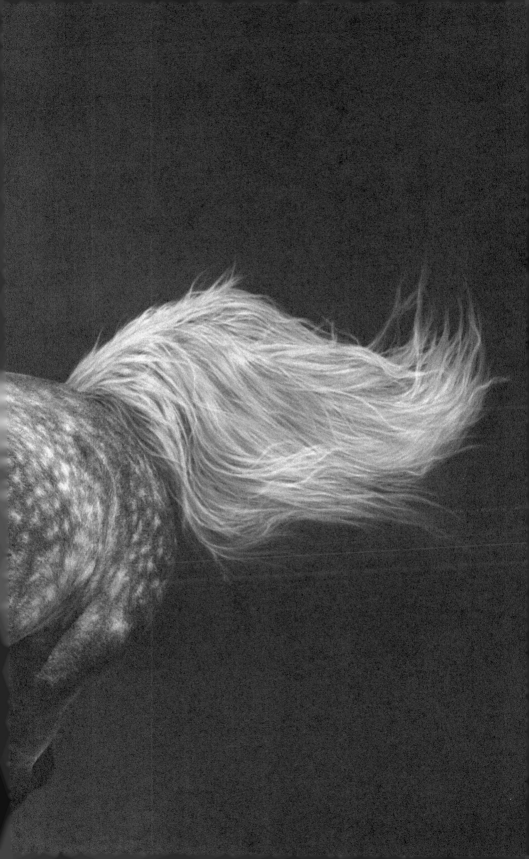

CRY WOLF

"Tanzy." My mother murmurs my name without reaching for me.

My hands tremble at my sides. I should meet her gaze, but my focus is drawn to her throat. I want nothing more than to cradle my cheek against the soft curve of her neck, to feel safe in her embrace. To feel like her *child* again. How many times over the course of this past year have I wanted to feel exactly the same way?

A girl steps between us—a girl I met moments ago. Her name has already escaped me, incinerated by the shock of seeing my mother come through the cloak of fog and trees. Whatever else she said, mere seconds ago—something important—has scattered from my mind like ash in the wind.

My mother. My mother is *here*. Here, in the woods lining Vanessa Andrews's house. Vanessa, who's been playing mind games with me for months, who knows what I'm going to do before I do. My mother wouldn't, *couldn't* be on Vanessa's property without her knowing, could she? If she knew what danger she was in, she'd never have come. But she's here. . . . *She's here.*

What if this isn't my mother at all? What if it's an Unseen creature borrowing her face? A chill pricks my thudding heart, slowing it in my chest.

"Who are you?" My voice falters, and I withdraw behind a line of shadows. The taste of metal floods my mouth, and everything inside of me begins to hum. I mean the question for my mother, but the girl answers instead.

"I'm Jayce, remember?" she says. "We're here to help you, Tanzy. Both of us." Her fingers are strangling the strap of her messenger bag. Her white-blonde hair frames her narrow face. The ends are dyed pink, a shock of color against her alabaster complexion. Faint lines of darker pigment zigzag across her exposed skin. Two bright stripes descend from the inner corners of her eyes, tapering to a point at either edge of her mouth.

I recognize those markers immediately—the stain of Vires blood flowing through her body, which means she's met Asher. If the pattern on her skin is any indicator, he transfused her with the blood of a tiger. Fresh suspicion prickles my spine, and I'm suddenly comforted by the knowledge that I'm one of the strongest mortal creatures on this side of the veil.

Jayce may have the stripes of a tiger, but the deepened hue of my skin, my long lashes and dark, wild hair, all of it emerged after my transfusion in the hospital. Asher completely siphoned my blood and replaced it with the Vires blood of a wild horse—the horse Spera saved from death a thousand years ago. The horse who laid down its life for her, and for her future incarnations, apparently. The horse now rendered to porous stone in Vanessa's magnificent mansion, not a hundred yards from where we stand.

Vanessa, who I trusted. I wonder if I'll ever trust blindly again. I hope not. I clinch my hands to fists and step out from the shroud of shadows.

"Who are *you*?" I say, staring hard into Hope's eyes this time so there will be no misunderstanding.

"I'm your mother," she says meekly.

I close my eyes and steel myself against the rising memory of the letter she left in my empty room:

Tanzy,
This house is no longer your home. I am no longer your responsibility, and you are no longer mine. Don't look for me. You won't find me. Our paths will not continue unless we walk them alone. Leave, Tanzy, and don't come back.
Hope

She signed it with her name instead of her role. Perhaps that hurt worst of all. Not my stripped belongings, the bedroom she left bare save a lantern and a pathetic scrap of a note. Not the days I spent in the hospital wondering if she was okay, when she should have been worried about *me*. Not the hundreds of unanswered phone calls.

She locked up the house. Our home. Abandoned it. Abandoned *me*. She isn't my mother anymore. She's just . . . Hope.

"Even if you are my mother, I'm no longer your responsibility, remember?" I say through my teeth, my eyes brimming with tears.

"Please, I don't have much time." Her hands dangle at her sides. I catch myself staring at them, willing them to reach for me. They don't even flinch in my direction. I could die a day from now; an hour. Or worse, I could be taken by Asher and kept alive for an eternity. If today is any indicator, it's a matter of when, not if. She can't possibly understand what I'm up against, but shouldn't a mother recognize when a daughter needs her most?

In a way, her distance confirms her identity. An impostor would've tried to hug me by now. This shred of proof is sharp and hot.

The pressure in my chest creeps up my throat. "You're wrong." My voice cracks. "I'm the one who's running out of time." I turn away from her and move deeper into the trees. I can't think in a straight line with my world so categorically flipped on its side.

"You have to stop her," my mother cries out, choking on a sob.

Keep walking, I tell myself, but my stride slows. My pulse soars. I strain to hear the note of desperation in her voice—desperation for *me*. As if . . . as if she actually cares.

Footsteps, too light and quick to be hers, scurry in my direction.

"Hear Hope out, Tanzy," Jayce pleads. "If you don't, you'll regret it. Trust me." She steps in front of me, blocking my path, and hugs her arms to her ribs.

Regret. Trust. Those words make me want to laugh. Or vomit. I glare at her, but the sight of her stripes stirs something inside of me. Sympathy, remorse. Do those feelings belong to me, or to Spera? Does it matter?

I remember Jayce now, and who she once was a thousand years ago—*Cavilla*. I saw her in Spera's memories. Another soul marked by Asher. Guilt creeps around the base of my throat and draws tight. A thousand years ago, my first incarnation ended hers.

Does any piece of this life belong to me and me alone? Or is my every move and relationship colored by the decisions Spera made during her existence? Is anything in this life really, wholly mine? Is even my mother a piece of this puzzle? A pawn like me? Or something else . . . something worse?

It should have been you in that river. Her words come clawing to the surface in my mind, the words that drove me back to Wildwood and into Asher's carefully laid trap. And yet, she repeatedly warned me away from Wildwood, tried to forbid me from ever returning.

"Why is my mother here? What's she doing with you? What's her part in all of this?"

"She needs to tell you good-bye." Jayce toes at the ground with her sneaker.

I press my hand against the ache in my chest, stunned there's any piece of me left intact enough to break. *I am no longer your responsibility, and you are no longer mine.*

"She already told me good-bye," I mumble, turning away. I can't take anymore. I can't endure another blow and be able to keep walking, keep fighting.

"Fine," Jayce calls at my back. "Don't talk to her. But don't run away, either. Please, Tanzy, you have to stay with me." Her footsteps punctuate her words as she follows behind me, and I have to stop myself from taking off at a run. "We need you, and like it or not, you're going to need us, too. If not for her, if not for yourself, then do it for Lucas. He's going to need all the help he can get."

Lucas. My heart lurches against my sternum. My face snaps to the side, where Vanessa's stone house is peeking through the trees. In my head, I hear myself calling Lucas a killer. I see the agony painted on his face, feel the burn of his eyes on my back as I turn away and leap through the window, leaving him in Asher's murderous hands.

"I forgot . . . How could I . . . ?" Freeing Lucas is my plan. At what moment did I lose focus?

"Hey, you didn't forget him. For ninety seconds, you got distracted."

Jayce touches my elbow. The slight contact makes me crash back into the dreary woods, gray and slick with mist. I yank my arm from beneath her fingers.

She lifts her hands in a show of surrender, then lets them drop.

"Lucas is part of one life for you. Your mom is part of another. When one showed up, the other took a back seat. I get it. What you need to square with is that Hope and Lucas are very much a part of the *same* life. The same world."

"I highly doubt it." But doubt has made a home in me, its reach consuming and breathtaking. My mother is the last piece of the world I once knew. Lucas is everything else, a lighthouse in a sea full of teeth. He was there when lightning struck me. When I died and was resuscitated. He was there day after day, sitting beside my hospital bed, filling that stale, white room with wild flowers in mason jars. Turning me into the light of the sun.

He was there when I woke in the hay shed after my trip through Spera's memories. Guarding me. Always guarding me. And where has my mother been all this time? Even before she left, she was leaving me, more and more every day. Leaving me for a *year*, when I needed her most.

"Let Hope explain it to you," Jayce is saying. "Please. This is the one lifeline you're going to get. You can try to survive on your own, and we won't stop you. But if you come with us, we might be able to save your soul."

I wrestle with her words, indecision gnawing within. No one has mentioned saving my soul, only the price I will pay for living, and the price I will pay for dying. The prophecy of the Vessel is horribly simple. If I choose to open the door between our world and the Unseen world, I will live forever as Asher's queen and deliver the Novus, the one Unseen child in all of time. The Seen world will not survive. If I choose to seal the veil, I'll die, my soul never to return, and Unseens will be trapped on their side of the veil forever. I can't decide what's less likely: the possibility of some kind of ancient loophole, or the idea that my mother is somehow involved in all of this.

I work my lower lip between my teeth as Jayce returns to my mother's side.

Always look a gift horse in the mouth, Tanzy. Always. My father's voice echoes in my head, and I close my eyes, absorbing the warmth from the memory of him. If I'd heeded his advice, if I'd examined Vanessa's friendship more closely, I might not be in this mess.

At last, I raise my gaze and stare at my mother. She's thinner than I've ever seen her, pale as wind-driven snow, and just as shaky. I would know her face, her hands, her laugh among a million. But in this moment, I realize I know absolutely nothing true about her aside from two facts: that she loved my father, wholly and unwaveringly, and once upon a time, she loved me too.

I armor myself with these truths, and ascend the hill.

Jayce steps to the side as I approach. My mother visibly swallows. Her face is a canvas of desperation. A blue sheen ripples beneath her ivory skin. Sweat collects along her brow. Her lips move to form a word, but the lines around her mouth blur. She looks sick, dangerously sick.

13

My tears come, hot and disobedient and all at once. "What's happening to you?" I take a step closer and reach for her.

"No!" She recoils from my touch. Her movements are weak, shaky.

It doesn't make them hurt any less.

I stagger back, doubling the distance, and gulp in air as if I've been struck.

"I can't, Tanzy. I want to. You have no idea how much I want to. But I can't. What I wrote in that letter, I had to." She struggles to catch her breath. "I couldn't help you as a human. I had to . . . to turn back."

Jayce's earlier words return like the melody of a song: *What you need to square with is that Hope and Lucas are very much a part of the same life. The same world.*

The Unseen world.

"You're an Unseen," I whisper, as ringing floods my ears and the world around me blurs.

"Yes."

I press my lips together to keep my chin from quivering. The final layer of foundation crumbles beneath me. She was in on this the whole time. She knew one day Asher would come for me, and she never said a word. I've been little more than a pawn from the moment I was born—reborn. *But how was I born at all?* Unseens can't have children. It's impossible. The prophecy of the Vessel states there will be one Unseen child in all of time— the Novus. I am not the Novus; I am destined to be its mother.

Hope draws enough strength to continue. "I am an Unseen, nothing but a piece of wind and sky. For a short while, I became human. Not a masked Unseen. A true, mortal human."

"How? Why?" I nearly choke on the questions, their weight and velocity a most damaging combination.

She shakes her head, a tremor rocking her body. "The kind of help you need now . . . I can't give it to you as a human. I found a way to change back, but nothing comes without a cost."

"What price are you paying?" My voice breaks.

"You." Tears roll down her face, taking strips of color with them. "The price is you. I've been given this time to tell you good-bye. Then I can never appear to you again. You will not see me after this. We cannot exist to each other. I promise I won't leave you . . ."

"How long do we have?" I whisper. *Please don't go. I have so much more to say. Don't you? How am I supposed to do this without you?*

"A few minutes. Maybe less."

"Haven't I already paid enough?" I cry out. Everything inside of me quakes as whatever binds me together threatens to explode.

"I will find some way to make this up to you one day. Stay with Jayce. Stay alive. We'll find a way to save us all." She closes her eyes.

"Wait! How do I save Lucas?" I plead.

Her form brightens, glowing white at her core. "He doesn't deserve saving," she says. Her voice is like air, but her gaze is heavy and sad. She knows I'll try to save him anyway. Spera would save him, and Spera and I . . . we're two different people. But we're also the same. "The less they have to use against you, the longer you can hold them at bay."

Save yourself, Tanzy, she means to say. But I can't. I won't.

You've taken care of people for so long, you don't even see when you're the one who needs help. That was Dana, Dana who knew me well enough to betray me. But she was right. I tried to save my father from the shadows on the ridge. I tried to save my mother from herself, tried to save Harbor from those beasts, tried to save Vanessa from Dr. Andrews. Saving people . . . that's who I am. Me, Tanzy.

It's who Spera was, too.

My mother's skin is fading. Becoming translucent.

"Don't go," I rasp.

Her face falls. A wind sweeps through the trees, distorting her form into wisps of light.

"I love you," she whispers. Her voice hangs in the air a moment longer than the traces of her body. Then even her words are gone, claimed by the damp gray.

I reach for the space she occupied a heartbeat ago. The wake she's left is cooler and charged. I curl my trembling hand, trapping the sensation in my fist. The chill of her slips through my fingers, and is swept into the fog.

SKIN DEEP

"We need to get moving," Jayce says from behind me.

I blink away the sting in my eyes without answering or turning around. Once I can see clearly, I focus on Vanessa's stone manor, which is visible in slivers. My mother's second abandonment has undermined her warning. All I can think about is freeing Lucas, of having someone by my side who will not leave me.

I take a step forward.

"Wrong way, Tanzy," Jayce cautions.

I keep walking. "I left him in there. I will bring him out."

She pulls alongside me. "Slow down. I promise I'll help you save Lucas, but not right now."

"Why would you help me? You don't think he's worth saving." My insides clench. Didn't I make the exact same decision when I left him to die less than an hour ago? Lucas's expression, hollow and stricken, appears in my mind's eye.

"Your mom might think he's not, but I do," Jayce says.

"You answer to her, don't you?" Frustration blurs the edges of my vision.

"No," Jayce counters. "And for the record, I don't agree with her. Take you, for instance. She's kept you in the dark this whole time. She might have considered it best, but it's not how I would've played it."

"Oh really? How would you have played it then?" I stop and turn to face her.

"I would've told you the truth. Given you as much information as possible. Let you make your own choice. Right now, the best way you can help Lucas is to understand who everyone thinks you are and what you're up against."

"Thinks I am?" I snap. I know exactly who I am. I witnessed my first life and my purpose as the Vessel less than twenty-four hours ago.

"You are Spera reborn. No arguing there. She was the only candidate Asher ever branded in the front." Jayce nods at Asher's signature brand of interlocking circles burned in the flesh above my heart. Spera earned three of them in her short, brutal life, and they appear on me now exactly as they were inflicted upon her a thousand years ago. "But no one has ever been able to prove that the match of your soul and the horse's Vires blood creates the true Vessel." She assesses my face for a reaction. "Do you *want* to be the Vessel?"

"No." The answer is a reflex, words jerking from my mouth like a knee from the prompt of a doctor's hammer. My blood isn't so quick to reject the question, carrying it from limb to limb. A life absent of this constant mortal fear is more tempting than I'd like to admit.

Jayce holds my gaze for a second longer, and then frowns as she considers Vanessa's house from our closer vantage point.

"I don't envy you," she starts. "When it comes down to brass tacks, you really are alone in this. I promise I'm on your side. Lay low for tonight. I'll get help, and I'll tell you everything I can. At sunrise we'll go for Lucas. You have my word."

Indecision swells in my chest. I am alone, once again, and desperately so. I trusted the person who reached out to me last time, and it was one of the worst mistakes I've ever made. Yet I find I have little choice. I have no money, no shelter, and no identification. I don't have anywhere to go from here.

Jayce could lead me straight into a trap. I half expect her to. At the same time, the horse's strength filling my body makes me more powerful than any human I might face. Unfortunately, none of the creatures holding Lucas captive fall into this category. I will need all the help offered to me to stand a chance of rescuing him.

I scan the side of Vanessa's house one last time, committing each detail to memory so I'll recognize any changes between now and dawn. Vanessa never does anything by accident. Her every move is a message.

"Okay," I say, consent bitter on my tongue. "Let's go."

"Follow me." Jayce turns down the hill. "There's someone here to help us."

The woods grow thicker as we descend into the valley. What little light manages to filter through the fits of rain, the lingering fog, and the canopy of naked branches overhead diminishes further as evening settles around us. Every few minutes, Jayce turns her chin a few degrees to the side, ears straining for proof I'm still behind her. I don't offer her any kind of verbal confirmation. In fact, we don't talk at all. There's entirely too much to say.

I am acutely aware that my body is covered by nothing more than a tattered linen dress—the dress I woke up in after I was guided through Spera's memories. She was wearing this dress the day Asher cast her into a pool of fire, which destroyed her body while preserving her soul.

That day, the sun was high, the sapphire sky cloudless. The earth was flowering in the warmth of a thousand-year-old Egyptian spring.

Now, winter throws blades of wind through the forest, whistling as it carves a path down the mountain, rattling the naked limbs, snapping my tangled, black hair like the tail of a whip. Bursts of freezing rain claw at my exposed skin. The wind shifts, and the precipitation pelts my cheek, but I am numb to the pain, awash instead in the memory of Lucas's scars and how he came to have them.

Lenya.

Vanessa.

Shivers begin at the base of me and spider-web through my body like a growing crack in a pane of glass. Slow at first, and then fast. I am moments away from shattering to pieces.

At last, the mountainside levels off. A fifty-foot swath of manicured lawn is rolled out in front of us like an emerald carpet. At its end, rose bushes, still flowering despite the season, mark a boundary in front of a new section of woods. Beyond the roses, the crooked boughs of trees grow too close together. Some lean unnaturally far. Others twist around each other. Blackberry vines, rope thick and covered in thorns, spiral around the trees and blanket the floor.

Adrenaline pours into my veins, sending up flares of heat in my chest.

Jayce strides across the grass, her gaze fixed ahead. I stall behind a tree and watch her slide between two bushes, waiting for a rush of sound or for a blitzing shadow to descend. Neither comes.

I exhale, shake my tingling hands, and peer harder into the woods ahead. The pink streaks in Jayce's hair are barely visible from here, but I can see them well enough to know that she's standing still on the other side, probably waiting for me. In the gap between us, tendrils of mist and vapor somersault in the wind and bend in bursts of lingering rain. It is impossible to tell shadow from fog, wind from warning. I have no choice but to follow, to walk into the living gray.

I step into the open. The grass is soggy. Puddles of frigid rainwater chill my bare feet until they burn with numbness. I dash across the open green, slowing just enough to turn sideways before maneuvering through the hedge. Thorns tug at my dress. The sound of fabric tearing spurs me through faster, and I trip into the clear. Jayce stands beside a tree bent so low it runs parallel to the ground. She regards me in silence, an eyebrow raised.

"You know, for the strongest, most fierce, chosen soul, yadda yadda yadda, I wanted to believe you'd be . . . you know, strong and fierce," she says, her expression deadpan, and then she hops over the tree trunk without waiting for a response. I stare after her, mouth open, emotions spinning.

Spera. Spera was strong and fierce. Spera would be leading Jayce through these woods, not the other way around. The sooner everyone realizes Spera and I are different people, the better.

"I didn't choose this, you know," I say, nearly spitting.

"Oh, and I did?" Jayce retorts over her shoulder. "You aren't the only one inconvenienced by this whole nonsense, princess."

"I'm the only one who has to die for it," I bark before I can stop myself.

Jayce spins around. "Don't act like you're the only one who will suffer or die before this is all said and done." Her pale eyes darken. Silence hangs between us. Her jaw is clenched, her ivory skin drawn tight over her small knuckles.

"I never should have agreed to follow you." I heave a sigh.

She glares at me, gray eyes narrowing to slits. "I'm going to pretend you didn't say any of that just now. You have no idea how big this picture is, how far the reach. And that's not your fault." She whirls back around, hair whipping over her shoulder, and strides through the trees.

I mutter a swear and hasten to her side. Ahead of us, a tangle of brush grows in a wall. Jayce steps up to it and reaches through with her hands, prying twigs and brambles apart. She fights her way to the other side. I limp behind her, my raw feet screaming in protest as I tread over broken limbs.

We emerge along the slick edge of a swollen creek. I hang back while Jayce brings a finger to the surface of the churning, murky water and draws a spiral. The current stills under her touch, casting a wide circle across the surface. The wind ceases all at once. Loose leaves, tossed wild a moment before, fall limply to the earth.

Turquoise flashes erupt beneath the surface along the outermost band of the ripple Jayce created. They race to the center of the circle, gaining speed and brightness the closer they come to impact. They meet, and the turquoise turns silver. A woman's head emerges from the glow. Tendrils of silver hair frame her weathered, blue-black face. A robe of azure velvet is draped over her shoulders, and is bone dry the moment it appears. Her waist breaks through the water, and her eyes fly open, their bright silver centers leaping from the dark canvas of her skin like they're lit from within.

Maris. My mind splits down the middle. Vanessa introduced me to Maris, which does very little for the fragments of trust I have left. Maris also gave me a way to travel a thousand years into the past to witness Spera's life. Whether doing so made me more or less vulnerable, I haven't decided.

Asher knows my face.

I know what choice I was born to make.

Am I safer, knowing?

Or less safe, being known?

"Are you sure this is a good idea?" I hiss. I quiver with readiness, nearly unable to stand still. My weight shifts to the balls of my feet.

"Why wouldn't it be?" Jayce asks.

"She knows Vanessa."

"As do you," Maris interjects, leaving no wake as she glides to the bank.

"I didn't know Vanessa was working with Asher!" I counter, defending myself, wishing my teeth wouldn't chatter. The information sounds strange in my ears. Vanessa was my friend, an incarnate of Lenya—who drowned herself moments after Spera was killed. She saved my life, I saved hers. We saved *each other*, just like our previous selves. Our fast, deep connection made so much more sense once I realized what we'd already been through together. How could our friendship mean nothing to her now?

How could it have meant nothing all along?

"Vanessa had us all fooled," Maris says. "We learned her true identity yesterday when Jayce saw her cross the veil. Since then we've been trying to find where she took you. I'd hoped Lucas might be a step ahead of us. I see he was not."

She casts a wary glance up the long hill, and then her eyes climb skyward. I follow her gaze, wondering what she sees, and if I should trust anything she says.

"I do not ask for your trust." She returns her gaze to me. "Only for your hand."

I cringe, remembering she can read every thought, every secret, and make a mental note to keep my mind empty in her presence.

"Why do you want my hand?" I ask, balling my fingers to fists.

"Our enemies are close. Too close. If we all join hands, I will be able to seal our sounds inside so we can speak freely," Maris whispers.

"How do I know you're not an enemy, too?"

"You don't." She flexes her fingers, but waits for me to decide to make contact.

"For Pete's sake, Tanzy. This isn't The Bachelorette Candidates' special edition. You're not getting married. You're just casting a damn spell." Jayce grabs my arm with one hand and Maris's arm with the other, and joins us together. "There. Hashtag let's-do-this-already," she says, clamping her palms in ours to complete the circle.

Maris suppresses a smile and closes her eyes. I deny a shudder of nervousness and force out a long, slow exhale.

"May I begin?" Maris asks, barely tilting her face in my direction.

I open my mouth. Close it. Yes, I mentally project, and Maris squeezes my fingers. It takes every ounce of self-control left inside me to not jerk away.

"Air and water join us here, use our light, and make a sphere. Seven colors round and round, shield our circle, hide our sounds," Maris commands. She repeats the incantation two more times. The air warms and thickens. A growing charge pulses through my arms like an electric current.

Maris falls silent. Everything does. The mist continues to drizzle, blanketing the muddy earth and barren trees, but the steady hiss has vanished. Even though we sit within a few steps from the creek, I can't hear it. With a start, I realize it must work both ways. *No sounds in. No sounds out.*

"We are safe to speak, but it won't last long." Maris slips her hand from mine. Her charcoal skin is pale in places where I'd unwittingly tightened my grip. Will I ever learn how to use the horse's strength deliberately?

I rub my clammy, filthy hands together, trying to make them warm enough to stop shaking. They're sweaty with nervousness, and the rust-colored film on my hands rolls into beads. It's not gritty like the dirt I clung to when I climbed out of the ravine at Wildwood. It's smooth, and presses flat into tiny flakes wherever I push down.

This is not earth.

This is dried blood.

David Andrews's blood, caked in the webbing between my fingers and crusted beneath my nails.

The sound of his last, sputtering breath echoes in my brain. I let out a cry and wipe my fingers violently against my dress. Copper streaks the wrinkled white linen within seconds. The color leaves my hands, but there's no relief from its weight, its smell.

"What's wrong?" Jayce's voice is an octave too high. "Is that blood?" She sniffs at the air. Her pupils dilate as she arrives at her own conclusion.

I can't summon the focus to answer—can't stop trying to make my hands clean. From the expression on Maris's face, she's seeing the memory of me strangling Vanessa's husband. The image of life leaving his eyes. The nightmare I can't wake from.

Her gaze trains on Asher's mark, and she brings an open palm to the brand. Heat crawls across my chest, but I'm frozen in place. My arms don't heed the mental command to bat her hand away. Two of the circles turn black, shimmering like the coming night, and then fade back into the appearance of an old scar.

"When did this happen?" She regards me with new distance, studying my face like I'm a complete stranger.

"Vanessa tricked me into believing her husband was attacking her. She told me he would kill her. She set me up. She made me believe . . . I thought he was Asher." The confession tumbles from me, heavy and slipping.

"You've killed someone?" Jayce asks, her throat constricting around the words.

"She has taken two lives. Two of these rings belong to her now," Maris says. Her fingers curl. She stares past me. I risk a glimpse of Jayce, whose face falls from brazen to defeat within a single second.

"Tell me about the first," Maris orders, her mouth forming a grim line.

"An Unseen attacked Vanessa in the woods. I got between them. He picked me up by my throat and I . . . exploded," I whisper. "I didn't want to kill him, but he kept coming." The memory plays in front of my open eyes. "If I hadn't killed him he would've killed me."

"Doesn't matter. She's useless." Jayce shakes her head and mutters under her breath.

"I'm not useless." My fingernails dig into my palms.

"Yes. You are," Jayce growls.

"Enough," Maris says. "This is Hope's fault. She chose to keep Tanzy in the dark, and this is the price. Tanzy, you can't kill anyone else, Seen or Unseen, for any reason."

"A third kill, and you belong to Asher," Jayce adds, focusing her icy glare on my face.

All the air is sucked from my lungs. I was under the impression the three circles had everything to do with Spera. How could I have missed this? A mental path quickly links the two lives I took, and arrives at one common denominator: Vanessa. She's masterminded every move I've made since waking with the horse's Vires blood coursing through my veins. She must know what will happen if I take a third life.

It's an insurance policy, I realize. If I won't use the strength for Asher, I can't use it at all.

"This changes everything," Maris says. The note of worry in her voice makes my muscles flood with preparation.

"What do we do?" Jayce asks, straightening.

"Tanzy can't be trusted to defend herself, so a possible confrontation must be avoided at all costs. It is not safe to move far in the dark, especially with no strategy. For tonight, stay close to the riverbank. I can cast a shield to make you harder to find. The best time to move while this close to Asher is at first light. Hope will send word to Reese to arrange for emergency transport for dawn tomorrow. We will meet you here with word of how, and then Tanzy will go directly to Reese. Tanzy will be safest among other candidates, and Reese is best at teaching control, which Tanzy needs more than anything." Maris speaks to Jayce as if I'm not present and don't have a say.

"I'm not going anywhere." Heat erupts in my middle. I may need Jayce more than I'm willing to admit, but I will not play the pawn in anyone's agenda again. "I'm not leaving without Lucas."

"I strongly suggest you reconsider." Maris's eyes bear into mine. "Lucas is the perfect bait. He will live as long as you do. Staying alive is the best way to ensure his survival, and the best way to do so is to stay out of sight. Lucas would not want you to come for him, not with this high a risk."

The truth of it is nearly crippling. How can I save Lucas if I can't kill whatever is guarding him? I chose to follow Jayce in order to keep my options open. In less than an hour, I've lost them all.

"If anyone can keep you hidden, Reese can," Jayce says, softness returning to her voice. "She has a safe house for candidates in the Outer Banks—Carova, specifically. Where the wild horses live."

"How many candidates are there?" I ask, even though my mind is still fixated on the house up the hill instead of the safe house.

"Seven, at present. Including you."

"Doing what, exactly?"

"We research and train. And mostly, we stay alive," she answers.

I imagine us around a table, taking tallies over breakfast of who killed who in our past lives. How will they feel about me? About Spera, who never lost, who was burned alive beneath Asher's fiery touch? How are we all supposed to live under one roof when we've been molded to kill one another?

I swallow. "And everyone gets along?"

"We have a common goal and a common enemy. Sometimes that's all it takes." Jayce shrugs. "We try to recover any newly awoken candidates before Asher does. We want to find the rest of the Artius Six before they do."

"The Artius Six?" I ask.

"The six candidates from Spera's life. You, me, and Vanessa are all we've identified so far. There are three more out there."

"What's so special about the other five?" I ask.

Jayce quirks a brow. "Hey, you might be the Vessel, but Reese says each of the Artius Six has a part to play in finding and opening the veil. We're still figuring out what. We're searching for the ritual scrolls. The more information we find, the better chance we have of figuring a way out," she says.

"There's no way out." I stare at my hands, at the remnants of dried blood I can't completely pry from beneath my fingernails.

"There might be," Jayce says.

I roll my eyes.

"Regardless, the longer you stay out of Asher's grasp, the better," Maris interrupts, and then turns her attention to me. "Spera, I have something for you."

"My name isn't Spera," I murmur. Spera knew what to do, who to trust. I've spent the last eighteen years of my life as a puppet, and I'm still not wholly sure who holds the strings above me.

"Spera is so much more than a name," Maris answers. She reaches a hand inside a fold of her cape and pulls out a black cylinder. The tube is made of stone, and is colder than the winter night.

"What is this?" I inspect the tube on my palm.

"Purified Tenix. Do not open it here. This is for you alone. Open the vial after you've reached the safe house."

"How do I use it?"

"It's not a matter of how. It's a matter of why. You'll know what to do when the time comes," she says. "Now, I need to return to my element, and you need to rest."

Maris raises her hands, and Jayce mimics her. I clutch the stone vial, bite back a line of questions, and elect to stay silent as Maris begins to speak again. "Seven colors wove the spell, elements you served us well. Return you now from where you came, with thanks until we call again." She repeats the chant twice more. The prism barrier dissolves into mist, and fades into the clearing night.

Maris walks into the heart of the creek. Submerged to her waist, she twists at her hip to look back to me, regarding my face for a full second before speaking. "She is around you all the time. Don't forget it."

My mother, bound to air. Now a piece of wind and sky once more. Ever present, ever invisible. In truth, not much about our relationship has changed. I wrap my arms around myself, rebuking a sudden chill, determined to blame it on the winter air, which has plunged ten degrees now that the storm has passed.

Maris slips into the water until she completely disappears under the surface. A turquoise flash erupts from somewhere below, and the creek resumes its steady melody. In Maris's absence, the night is considerably darker. A nearly full moon peeks out from wisps of clouds, casting enough light to discern solid from sky, and to betray the worry in Jayce's eyes. I ignore it, my gaze instead traveling up the long hill—to Vanessa's house and Lucas.

"Don't even think about it," Jayce warns.

"Too late." I glance down at the stone vial. Can I use purified Tenix to save him? I wouldn't even know how to start.

"If you go barging in there right now, all you'll do is kill again or be killed, and then Lucas is as good as dead." She pauses and lets out a hard sigh, which vaporizes in front of her face. "I'm with you. We can't just leave Lucas here without trying to get him out at least once. But our best bet is to make our move just before dawn. We'll need to be in and out, and back here in time to meet Maris again. I will give it one shot. One. But you have to wait until I say go."

Heavy silence follows in the absence of my answer, testing the weight of our fragile bond. I look away from her and to the creek. Moonlight shatters against the moving water, splitting everywhere it lands. My path forks here, too. If Jayce helps me rescue Lucas, will I owe it to her to travel to the safe house?

"Well you're not running up the hill. Does that mean you're going to wait?" she asks.

"I don't know."

"Just promise me you'll tell me when you do," she says.

"I don't make promises." The thought escapes me before I can rein it in.

"I appreciate the honesty," she answers with a snort. Jayce moves closer to the wall of brush and bramble, and gathers a pile of leaves and sand into a bed.

I don't know how to get back to the house, other than heading uphill. My feet are bloody. My limbs tremble with fatigue and the aftershocks of too much adrenaline. What good would I be alone against Asher, Vanessa, and Dana? The weight of the day, of what I've lost, of what I've done, sinks me where I stand. It takes every ounce of remaining strength to maneuver the few steps to drier ground.

I find a softer place along the foot of the wall and take a seat on the dirt, tucking my numb, torn feet beneath my legs. Feeling comes back like the blade of a knife, and draws a howling line up each arch. I clasp my hands over my toes and rub the sting away.

Jayce kneels and rummages through her bag.

"Here." She tosses me a sweatshirt, and curls up like a cat on the bed she's made, using her canvas bag as a pillow. I prop myself against the wall and watch the water flow downstream until I hear Jayce's breathing slow. My forehead finds my knees. The burning trapped for hours in my eyes becomes liquid. I am in no frame of mind to beat it back, and the black of night will cover my tears if Jayce wakes.

Where do I go from here? Will Lucas still be held hostage in Vanessa's house come daybreak? What else will they try to use against me? My mother is invisible. My father is dead. They already have Lucas. I'm forgetting something. I can feel it stirring in my skull. My brain is too spent and scattered. I can't fit enough pieces together to find the remaining holes.

The stars fade and the night sky purples. Light is still at least an hour away, but all I can think of is yesterday's sunrise; of the hope I clung to, convinced and painfully naïve. I can practically feel Lucas's calloused hand and hear his promise to keep me safe. Above all else, I can't shake the fact that I failed him the very first time I was tested.

I peer at Jayce. I may be safer in her company, but she is not safer in mine. Her strengths appear to lie in hiding, in gaining close proximity to an enemy undetected. The enemy knows I'm here, there's no changing that. We can't stay out of sight and free Lucas at the same time. If she comes with me to save Lucas, she might help, but it's a bigger possibility that she'll be hurt, captured, or worse. Accepting her help is akin to putting a target on her back.

I stretch my legs out in front of me. Nearby, Jayce stirs, drawing a hand over her heart as she rolls to her back. She'll wake soon. The softening night bathes her striped face in lavender. Her skin is smooth with youth. I doubt more than a year or two separates our ages. I can imagine her walking down a high school hallway, her book bag slung on one shoulder, a devil-may-care expression on her face, the laces of a sneaker untied. I cannot imagine her walking into the doors of Vanessa's house with any chance of leaving alive.

She can't come with me.

I rise to my feet. Soreness lingers, but the biting pain has passed. I step to the wall of bramble and reach a hand inside. Pausing, I glance back at Jayce. If I wake her, she'll come no matter what I say.

I pick up a twig from the ground and tiptoe to the bank. I write Lucas's name in the dirt, and then underline it with the stick. I stuff my hands inside the sweatshirt. Maris's vial rolls into my fingers, and my attention returns to Jayce. She bares her teeth in her sleep, and I squeeze the bottle of Tenix. I am 100 percent sure Jayce will try to find me the moment she sees where I've gone, and if she's going to survive it, she's going to need all the help she can get. She probably knows exactly how to use Tenix. She seemed less phased by casting a spell on the beach of a creek than a pop quiz. She might know more about the Unseen world and the Vessel prophecy that I do, but when it comes to Vanessa, she has no idea what she's up against. At least with Tenix on her person, she will have some sort of bargaining leverage if she can't conjure some kind of way out.

An exterior pocket on her bag is accessible, and her head is turned the other way. I ease the vial into the opening, move further downstream, out of Jayce's earshot, and pass through the wall alone.

DAWN

A row of trees stands between Vanessa's house and me. The window I leapt through yesterday has been replaced. No shards of broken glass sparkle from the wet lawn below. Nor is the grass crushed flat where I landed. In true fashion, Vanessa has erased every sign of my temporary victory over Asher and her.

Maris said first light was the best time to move, but standing here waiting for the sun to rise, I disagree. A cloak of pale gray settles around me, shifting as the swaying trees cast their long, dark trunks across the lawn. Any one of those shadows could be Asher, who can fade into the same transient black as easily as he can breathe. What if he's hidden Lucas the same way, demanding he change into the black blur of an Unseen? Hiding him from me in plain sight, in any corner of Vanessa's unlit house? I might walk right past him and never know it.

I pace from tree to tree, and dash my gaze from one window to the next, searching for movement, for the flicker of a light. Suddenly I realize I'm wincing, bracing myself for a scream to slice the approaching dawn in half.

Lucas, where are you? I wonder. *Where are the others? What's waiting for*

Should I charge inside? Should I stay away?

uncertainty is maddening, my thoughts traveling unaided to the deep end of a dangerous pool. Without exerting any effort, Asher and Vanessa are gaining ground.

My toes curl into the dirt with the effort it takes to keep myself from running back to the river, to Jayce. Or even farther. To Wildwood. To my mother's house. The places I once felt safe. But nowhere is safe for me anymore. Wildwood is in ashes. The home I grew up in is bare.

Wherever I go, Asher will find me. I'm sure of it.

I choke back a sob. *Dad . . . Daddy, I'm scared.* A single image fills my head, a memory of my father coaxing me back onto a horse after I'd taken a bad spill. I told him I was afraid. His answer: he was scared sometimes too, and if I didn't have a speck of fear inside of me, I had no idea what kind of risk I was taking every time I climbed on the back of something ten times my size.

I would give anything to have a horse to climb on right now—the speed, the height, the confidence. In Spera's memories, I witnessed Asher pale in the presence of horses, the only time he ever showed a sign of being afraid. I don't need Jayce, Maris, or even my mother. I need *Harbor . . .* I need my horse.

My breath catches in my throat as I realize where she might be at this very moment: here. *We have hundreds of horses to match . . .* Vanessa's words from yesterday come roaring back. Dana and Vanessa must have stolen all of Wildwood's horses the night of the fire, including Harbor. They have to be keeping them somewhere close, and Vanessa has an empty barn with state-of-the-art security. It would be the perfect place to stow part of a stolen herd.

I stumble from the trees and into the open. I inhale, wanting the earthy scent of hay and horsehair to fill my lungs. But all I smell is the ice in the air, the promise of snow in the days to come. I can't smell Vanessa's barn at all.

I inch toward the crest of the hill, glancing back at the house every few seconds to make sure I haven't given away my presence. Ahead, where a small, spectacular farm stood hours before is now nothing but a slope of grass still slumping from yesterday's storm. The barn is gone, vanished off the rolling lawn.

There has to be some kind of mistake.

Disbelief floods through me, accelerating my heart and urging my feet down the slippery hill. I break into a run, even though I'm sure the empty field is an illusion and I'll slam into something solid any second. My foot catches on a slick patch and sends me sprawling to the ground. My knees take the brunt of the hit, meeting a hard surface before I can get my hands in front of me to break my fall.

I stifle a cry and roll to my side. There, sunk in the ground like a gravestone, is the blank metal name plate that once hung over the entrance to Vanessa's barn. It's not blank anymore. She's engraved the plate with Asher's brand of three interlocking circles, and three words: "High Harbor Farm."

"No," I whisper. My pulse roars in my ears, even though my heart has shuddered to a chilly stop in my chest.

High Harbor Farm. The name I'd chosen for my own farm, one day. Vanessa knew. It must be a message, and it can only mean one thing. Either the horses are dead, or they will be soon.

I stare at the plate, heaving and empty. My mother's words drift back: *the less they have to use against you, the longer you can hold them at bay.* Vanessa knows how much Harbor means to me, and she's an artist when it comes to using Tenix. She could probably turn a rock into a horse. Even if Harbor were to gallop up to me right now, I wouldn't wholly believe it was her.

Harbor trusted me. *Only* me. When Lucas came along, she trusted him too. No one else. But if I saw her now, I wouldn't trust her. Wouldn't chase her. I'd let her go. I'd have to.

I have to let her go *now,* before that moment comes. I have to let her go while it's still my choice.

My mother was right: there's one way to fight back. I have to leave the idea of retrieving Harbor behind.

I bite the inside of my cheek to keep from crying as memories of Harbor flash behind my eyes—seeing her for the first time. Our first ride, and how quickly she threw me off. How I forced myself to climb back on, terrified and tear-stricken. The flood of victory when she began to respond to me instead of fight. The power of our first jump. Our first show, our first win. The first time she nickered a greeting upon seeing me. The scent of her coat—warmth and earth and cedar.

"Good-bye." I barely whisper the word. A staggering breath leaves me. *It has to be this way. It has to.* If I allow her room in my heart, Vanessa will take it and use it to inflict another wound. Even if Harbor is alive, I don't have the first clue how to find her, and if I did . . . I would deny her. I imagine her approaching me, soft, copper eyes lined in black skin and rimmed with long white lashes. In my mind, I see her black-tipped ears prick with recognition, nostrils flaring with breath, with my smell. She would stride to me, recognizing me, sensing safety, sensing home. And I would have no choice but to turn my back on her and walk away. Finding her . . . finding her may be a more painful fate than staying apart.

I want to hit something. I want to lie down on this piece of metal and never get up. I want to run until my lungs give out. I want to walk off this piece of godforsaken property and find some town full of people that don't know me, that have never heard of Spera, that see the clear air all around us and don't have any idea how full it is, how deadly. I want . . . I want . . .

The thoughts in my head blur to sound, the drumming of my heart roars above it. In my mind, I hear the river, I watch Dad and his horse plummet over the edge of the cliff and into the water below.

I throw my head back and scream. The sound of it is shrill and deep at the same time, propelled by the emotions and memories coming to a boil within the cauldron of my ribs. My blood responds, and heat floods my limbs. My fingers tingle. My legs beg for movement. My chest rises and falls faster with every heartbeat. I can feel the horse's wild blood within me, driven to riot . . .

And baited by Vanessa.

This realization blows the fight and panic from me like breath on a candle flame, and I am left shaking and hollow.

The Vires blood must be taking over. I am a human soul in a human body, but nothing else about me feels familiar. The blood is the captain, my body the ship. The black stallion's will is more tiring to suppress each time it assaults my self-control. There will come a time when I will lose my grip on its reins. I will break, and it will break *free*. When that happens, I have to make sure that it counts.

I cast one last glance at the empty meadow and mentally let go of every piece of what I used to want and who I used to be. This is my truth now.

Awareness washes over my body like waking from a dream. The ground is beneath my feet. The sun is moments from the horizon, casting a platinum glow along the edge of the earth. Spera's white dress from a thousand years ago, tattered, blood-stained, and wrinkled, is plastered to my body.

And something that does not belong is on my hand.

The telepathic ring Vanessa gave me rests on my finger, dull under a film of her husband's dried blood. Is Vanessa wearing the matching band? If so, can she still hear my thoughts?

My pulse rises, spooked by the idea that she's been lurking in the shadows of my mind. Listening in.

Vanessa, I think, hissing her name, and listen to the silence within, daring her to answer. The buzz is there, the line between us open, but she doesn't acknowledge me. I glance down at her ring, wondering if she can see through my eyes, or if she's already seen this coming in one of her psychic visions.

Watch this.

I twist the ring off and heave it downhill, turning away before it lands. I take a step. The nameplate shimmers in the grass, bringing me pause. I lean down, tempted to trace the word Harbor with a finger, and then quickly close my hand to a fist. A tear rolls from my eye, down my face, and strikes the plate, mixing with the sheen of old rain. In the east, the sun breaks the horizon, announcing the new day, and at last I have the light. I exhale hard, force my gaze uphill, and leave everything I thought I knew behind.

David's car sits across the driveway, silent and awkward, the driver's side door flung wide on its hinges. I catch myself staring at it, speculating how long the dashboard protested the open door before the battery gave out. My hands tremble at my sides, and bile laps the back of my tongue. I imagine him springing from the low-slung car, sprinting for the doors, taking the stairs two at a time, all to find Vanessa . . . to save her . . . from me.

I close my eyes, shuddering, and then fling them open again the moment I remember where I am. The black Ford truck Vanessa bought for my use waits on the other side of the circular driveway. She must've moved it overnight. I'd bet money the keys are in the ignition, meant for me, but I won't leave without Lucas.

I ease into the open and cross to the front of the house. The fountain's been cut off. Yesterday, the copper statue of a woman spun in a glowing pool. Flames and water dripped from her raised hands. Now, she is still and dry, allowing me to see the unbridled terror carved into her face. Her wide-set eyes search the sky. Her fine jaw hangs open, suspended from the peaks of her cheekbones, and her wild hair fans away from the fiery pool at her feet. Recognition strikes me center: Spera's image burns eternally in Vanessa's front yard.

The muffled squeak of rubber soles on polished stone spins me around, the creature within me alert and ready to fight. Jayce is a step ahead of me. She backpedals when I whip in her direction.

"Sorry," I mutter, and drop my fists.

"I shouldn't have come up behind you. My fault." She moves to my side and stares at the fountain. "That chick is evil." She shakes her head. "And you are dead wrong if you think you're going in there to face her and Asher alone."

"No. This is my fight." I stare her dead in the eyes. "You're here. You kept your word. If you go in there, you probably won't make it back out."

Jayce follows me to the cover of one of the stone pillars lining Vanessa's porch. "You think I'm a liability," she scoffs. "I can take care of myself."

"You don't have to prove it to me. You've camped on Vanessa's property without anyone finding you, pink hair and all."

"What, you don't like it?" She smirks.

"No, it's very bold. Very you." I scan the entryway. A sliver of the grand foyer is visible through the gap between the French doors. Vanessa's house is enormous by any standard. Searching it won't be a simple task. Several rooms have balconies and other places for ambush. Neither one of us should set foot inside this house, but it's becoming clear neither one of us is leaving.

"It's your call. Just don't get yourself killed," I concede.

"I was about to tell you the same thing," she retorts.

We creep onto the porch. A new welcome mat has been placed in front of the doors.

"Just in case we didn't realize that we're walking right into a trap," I mutter under my breath.

"Wait," Jayce hisses, and pulls me to the side of the door frame. She steps in front of me, slides her hand into the opening between the doors, and flips open a compact mirror in her steady palm. Her face twists as she considers the foyer's reflection. "We're good," she whispers and tucks the mirror into the front pocket of her bag.

"Stay behind me," I order. She tucks her small frame neatly inside my shadow and follows me in.

We creep into the maze of hallways. Most of the doors are closed. I don't bother opening them. Vanessa does everything on purpose, and she's obviously leading me somewhere. Ahead, the hallway opens into Vanessa's favorite part of the house, a circular room with a forty-foot ceiling. Half of the room is rung with balconies, and the other half is striped with floor-to-ceiling windows. Sunrise glares bright and traitorous through the panes of glass, and casts a blinding glare on the polished floor. I pause just shy of the threshold. Once we exit the hall, we'll be completely exposed. Anyone could take aim at us from above, and we won't even be able to see them.

—

"I don't like this," Jayce whispers beside me.

"Me either," I admit.

"Let's go back to the staircase," she says in my ear. Instead of answering, I draw in a breath and step into the light.

—

Too Late

Nothing happens. No rush of sounds or sudden movements. I shield my face from the glare and scan the open walkways lining the interior wall of the room. They're empty and still. If an Unseen is waiting up there, they've had plenty of time to make a move. I wave to Jayce. She hurries to me, lips pinched in a line.

"That wasn't smart at all," she growls.

"Probably not," I retort. A familiar scent sends up a flare in my memory. *Lucas.* My stride lengthens. I have to fight to keep from breaking into a sprint.

"What is it?" Jayce asks, keeping pace with me as we cross the atrium and turn down a darkened hallway.

"He's still here. I . . . I can smell him." I glance over my shoulder, but Jayce only nods, gravely serious. In the dimmer light, her stripes darken, gouging her skin. The surfaces of her eyes reflect stray rays of sunlight with an iridescent glow.

Witnessing her sudden change encourages more adrenaline into my veins. My pulse roars. My body begs me to action, yanking each limb at the socket.

I force myself to a stop, curling my fists against invisible shackles, re-membering Spera—cuffed and dragged into the arena at the matching cer-emony. Commanded to kill.

She made her own choice that day. She overpowered the Vires blood. So will I.

Jayce stalls a few feet ahead and stares back at me, her face a question mark. I hold up a hand, signaling her to wait, and force my heart to heed my brain. My pulse pounds so loud I can barely hear my own thoughts as I mentally move ahead, down the path Vanessa has laid for me thus far. I've been this way before. If memory serves, Vanessa's towering study lies directly ahead of us. At its center stands the horse who gave his Vires blood to save Spera, the same blood that is now fighting for control of my body. He is nothing but a statue now, preserved by Asher, turned to porous stone.

Is Vanessa trying to make me choose? The wild horse or Lucas? My heart lurches over a beat, leaving me searching for my next breath. Spera risked her life for that horse, and for Lucas. I can fathom the reality of Jayce and I being able to carry Lucas out of this house, even if he is unconscious. But how can we move a life-sized, stone statue? It must weigh thousands of pounds, and if what Vanessa said is true, no one can lay a hand on it with-out causing it harm. Why is she leading me to it, then? What will happen if I touch it? Will the stallion burst to life? Will he crumble beneath my fingertips?

My nose tips to the air as the sudden scent of horses rides in on a breath. A surge of longing makes my heart pound in my chest. "This way," I whis-per, and sprint ahead, the horse's blood taking charge of my legs.

Something dark and wet glistens on the floor ahead. I can't skid to a stop in time. My gait is too long and swift, my feet chopping over the marble floor.

I slip, and catch myself on my hands and knees. Liquid splatters my chin. I sink onto my haunches, bowing my thighs, and massage my aching wrists, one and then the other. My hands are matte and sticky with . . .

"Blood."

"You okay?" Jayce whispers, hurrying to me.

"Blood." The word rasps over my tongue. "It's blood."

"Are you sure? It doesn't smell like blood." Jayce steps into my trembling shadow.

Her shoe makes a wet squeak and she recoils.

"Because it's not human." I sputter. "I'm too late." Bitter cold peals through my veins. The blood inside of me throbs in place, as if it's too thick to move, and my muscles strangle my bones. I quake at the center. I am ten feet from the study door, and I may shatter where I kneel. "They killed him."

Jayce treads across the soaked hallway and crouches by my side. I stare blankly ahead, my vision blurred as my mind conjures every other scenario, every other way I could've saved Lucas. Worse still: that he wouldn't need saving if I had never left his side.

"I hurt someone with every step I take," I whimper. I don't blink. Don't scrub the hot tears from my face.

Is this what you wanted to show me, Vanessa?

Jayce pushes her thumb over the smear of blood on my jaw. Lucas's blood. My gaze drops to my lap. To my sopping dress, my painted thighs. I am covered in it. I raise my stare. The river of his blood is widest at the open doorway. What have they done to him beyond that door? What gruesome scene have they orchestrated for me to find? I can't stop my brain from guessing, as if to prepare my eyes for what they might witness. What all was in that room? A desk. Floor to ceiling book shelves. A chandelier draped in razor thin slices of jade. The statue of the horse. What if they pinned him to the desk, directly beneath the chandelier, and then cut it free? It would explain the blood . . . hundreds of punctures . . .

A broken cry escapes me. *Lucas, I'm sorry. I'm so sorry.*

"Come on." Jayce tugs at my arm. "Let's be sure."

I'm sure already. He's dead. I know he's dead. I've been through this before. I don't need a body. There's too much blood on this floor for him to have left this hallway alive.

"Tanzy, come on!" Jayce pulls on my elbow. I draw my wobbling legs beneath me and steady myself on the stone wall. Jayce tiptoes ahead. The open door to the study is a few feet away. Something flares in my chest. A warning. I want to tell Jayce to wait, not to step in front of the door, but I'm not fast enough, and my voice is still buried somewhere beneath the muscles squeezing my throat.

The nearly inaudible twang of thread drawing tight sets the wild blood within back into motion and forces me to the present. In a single motion, I catapult from my crouch and tackle Jayce to the floor as an arrow rushes silently into the hall and buries into the stone wall. I roll to my knees and scurry away from the door. Jayce follows, and we hunker together in the corner. A new thought floods me with hope: why would someone guard a dead body?

"I didn't see that coming," Jayce hisses. "Do you think it's Vanessa?"

I shake my head, unsure. A bow and arrow doesn't really feel like Vanessa's style, but she's surprised me before.

Jayce shoves her hair over her ear. Blood from her fingertips makes scarlet streaks against the pink. She tilts her head to the study, listening. I mimic her movements, straining to hear something. Anything. Asher seething. Vanessa chuckling. Lucas breathing. But there's only silence.

I crane forward, but Jayce pinches my arm.

I glare at her. She rolls her eyes.

"Use this." She shoves the compact mirror into my hands.

I crouch outside of the open door and slide the mirror past the molding. A flash of red hair gleams across the glass. I narrow my eyes, and angle the mirror to a tightly bowed elbow. Further, to freckled cheeks and—

Swish.

Another arrow flies, shooting the mirror right out of my hand. Reflective glass rains down on the floor, and the casing skitters down the hall in several pieces. I duck away from the entry, and clutch my stinging fingers to my ribs.

Jayce practically throws herself between my body and the open door.

"Did you see Lucas?" she asks. Demands, more like, something desperate in the hushed pitch of her voice. My eyes dart to the arrow rolling away from us, across the floor. I'm risking both our lives now, and for what? If Lucas isn't in there, if Lucas is already dead . . .

I imagine him bleeding out on Vanessa's polished tiles. Shaping his last breath into the sounds of my name, still looking for me, still loyal.

I shake my head. "All I saw was a girl with red hair. Sorry about your mirror."

Jayce shrugs. "She's a good shot. Is she alone?"

"As far as I could tell. Do you have anything else in your bag we can use?"

"What? Scared of a few arrows? You've got *super strength*. You're like the Hulk. And she's Hawkeye. Hawkeye sucks."

I lower my brow and wonder what in the world she's talking about. "You said it yourself," I say. "She's a good shot. Too good." Frustration builds in my chest. "And that super strength of mine . . . I can't use it."

Jayce purses her lips. "If you think you can't control yourself enough to take on *one chick* with a bow and a couple of pointy sticks, then we need to call this a day and pack up."

"Tell me what to do," I hiss.

"I'll do you one better." She grins. "I'll show you." She springs up and dashes into Vanessa's office.

"Stop!" I leap in front of her. The redhead is perched atop Vanessa's antique desk. Her shoulders jerk, tight and precise, as we burst in.

She takes aim.

Instantly, everything slows down. Every fiber of thread makes its own distinct sound as she draws the bowstring back. A short whoosh of air exits her mouth as her finger depresses the trigger on the crossbow. The arrow shudders as it's released, and sails in my direction. Its movement is slow, lazy even. I watch it approach, bewildered, and pluck it from its path the moment it comes within reach.

The instant I make contact, the humming under my skin quiets and the world around me returns to its normal speed. A new arrow clicks into the shaft, drawing my gaze.

"Do you really want to waste another one?" Jayce chirps from behind me. The girl's eyes dart between us. I take advantage and make a quick scan of the study, ready to put myself between her and Lucas.

There's no one else here, and the statue of the black horse is gone. I need someone to rescue, a good decision to make, a way to set any piece of this right. How can I do that now? Why did Vanessa bring me here if there's nothing to save?

My senses converge into a laser point, focusing on the girl. Her green eyes press wide as she takes me in. A tangy, sickeningly sweet smell drifts from her. My brain names the scent: mortal fear. Saliva pools under my tongue and my temperature rises.

"Tanzy," Jayce warns. "Stay calm."

"I am calm," I snap, but I'm not, I realize. I'm heaving breaths, every muscle craving more oxygen in preparation for extreme exertion. My lungs are shriveling, screaming, with every inhale.

This is why Vanessa lured me here. I'm not supposed to save anyone. I'm supposed to kill again.

I exhale through my teeth and let my jaw go slack. I inhale slow and shallow, though it pains me, my chest constricting for want of deeper breaths.

"One chance. Put the crossbow down," I instruct, my voice low and even. My fingers are flexed at my side. I make them limp. Everything inside me still wants to lunge for her and rip the red hair from her scalp. Instead, I roll my shoulders open and rock weight back onto my heels.

The redhead's knuckles go white on the bow, still angled at us.

"Yeah, I don't think so," she says, eyeing me through the sight on the crossbow.

Can she see the Vires effect thrashing behind my eyes, I wonder?

"No one is dying today," I say as calmly as I can manage. Vanessa won't snare me so easily.

She lifts her chin, but she can't mask her nervousness. Not from me. It wafts away from her, a syrupy-sweet cloud, and fills my nose.

I glance at Jayce, who's leaning into her hip, her expression halfway to a grin, and for the first time I'm glad she's here.

"My sister told me about you," the girl says. "All talk. Just like Spera." The confession quivers over her tongue.

Sister? My mind lights on the word, and a past life memory returns to me: Lenya's first kill in the arena was her sister.

Asher pitched Lenya against her own sister . . . and Vanessa was willing and able to kill her. What would it have been like to be killed by someone you love?

The lingering cloud of rage and fight inside of me dispels on its own. I study her smooth skin, the catlike slope of her jade eyes. She's more willowy than Vanessa, but their statures are similar. Their noses are identical. I realize with a flush of guilt that I can't remember what this girl looked like from Spera's memories in those dark cells or on the arena floor, but she must have been there.

This girl is one of the Artius Six.

I nearly look to Jayce. Even in my peripheral vision, I can see her stiffen. Chances are she's figured out this girl is one of the candidates she's been looking for.

Relax, I think, and wish Jayce could hear me. If only she had one of Vanessa's Tenix rings. *Don't let her know she's important*. The shift in her value helps, though, and it is easier to talk the Vires blood down from the steering wheel in my brain.

"What's your name?" Jayce asks, cocking her head too far to the side, narrowing her eyes too close together. It's a good thing she doesn't lie. Her poker face is terrible.

The girl curls her lip. "Does it matter?"

"We can make a game of it," Jayce says, straightening. Movement helps her look more natural. "I like guessing games."

"Save it," the girl says with a sneer. "My name is Bridget." She tosses her long ponytail over her shoulder. "Vanessa has a message for you."

"Of course she does," I mutter. "I don't do games. So go ahead and . . ." I trail off, my senses besieged with a flood of stimulus. There's blood masked in the red of Bridget's hair, and her black pants are streaked with something dark and crusty. Iron floods my mouth. I can smell Vanessa's sister—I can *smell her*. Not just the lavender soap residue heating on her skin, or the bursts of jasmine that her hair emits each time she swings it back and forth. I can smell the warm, salty beads of sweat collecting along her brow. Above all else, I smell Lucas. I smell him all over her. The scent of his skin, like freshly cut wood and smoking embers, mixes with the tang of fresh adrenaline spilling from her pores.

Jayce's gaze snaps to mine, as if she can sense the Vires power unfurling inside of me again.

I suck in a breath. *I am Tanzy. I* choose to be *Tanzy. The wildness belongs to Asher. I belong to myself.*

I grind my teeth. Humanity flushes through me, ice cold and heavy. It sets my hot blood to steam. It *hurts*.

"Where is Lucas?" I say. I inch closer, one step, then two. Bridget clamps her jaw shut. She lurches, attempting to swing her crossbow to my throat, but I'm faster. I seize her wrist and squeeze. Twist. My gaze whips to her fingers, white and blue in my grasp. I can feel her twiggy, birdlike bones beneath my thumb. So delicate. So easy to break.

Bridget bares her teeth. Rage and fear collide on her face and glisten in her green eyes. A whimper scrapes out of her throat.

"Where is he?" I demand. *Where is the black horse?* I want to add, but my mother's final warning makes me reconsider. It's safer for the horse to seem unimportant to me. They may leave him less protected if they don't think I've figured out what the statue really is.

"With Asher," Bridget sputters.

"Alive or dead?"

She pinches her lips shut.

I squeeze, and she cries out.

Beside us, Jayce steps closer, her fingers open, stretching for me.

"He was alive when they left," Bridget says. "He was alive . . ."

She trails off. My heart leaps. "And now?" My fingers have completely curled around Bridget's wrist. I yank her to me, nearly toppling her from the desk, so we're nose to nose.

"He lost a lot of blood. I'm not sure," she whimpers.

"Tanzy," Jayce hisses.

Slowly, painfully, I release her. Each of my fingers lifts away, one after the other. "They left you here to die," I say. "*Your sister* left you here to die. She wanted me to kill you. Something tells me she won't be relieved to find you alive. And Asher . . . he'll be furious."

Bridget's cheeks blanch white. Even Jayce is stunned to silence.

I tremble where I stand. The very fiber that holds me together, that holds this blood within, stretches to the point of agony, and every inch of me howls. Before this rage can become music, beautiful and inspiring, I turn my back on all of it and bolt through the door.

SINKING SAND

I storm back through the maze of corridors, my mind spinning, my blood racing. Each breath comes faster than the last. What was the point of this? I know why I came here—for Lucas. But what was Vanessa's goal? She's more careful than this, more exact. Leaving her sister alone in her house had to mean more than just a weak opportunity to lose my self-control. And why would she put her own sister up as the bait?

Only when I pass under the curved, jade staircase leading to the second floor do I feel the need to slow down and take stock of my surroundings. Vanessa has proven catlike in her every move, her every thought. Glowering silently from on high probably comes quite naturally for her.

I press against the far wall and track the stairs with my eyes, and then scan the catwalk that looks out over the foyer. It's empty. I'm not sure if I'm relieved or disappointed. I can't kill anything, but I can hit something. And I would love to hit something. Plus, I don't think Vanessa would let me kill her as a matter of pride. But there's also a chance David Andrews is still there, cold and stiff on the carpet, eyes open and unseeing, surrounded by blood, crusty and thick.

A flash in my periphery evokes a backfire in my tingling nerve endings. Jayce appears from the shadows, her jaw set, her pale eyes ablaze even in the dim light.

"Thanks for that," she says with a growl. "You left me in there with crossbow Barbie and no weapons."

"I thought you said you could take care of yourself," I say over my shoulder as I stride across the foyer and through the front doors.

"Well I got out, didn't I? Besides, that's not the point. We're a team."

"We aren't anything!" I rebuke, nearly shouting. "I did what you said. I waited until dawn. And look what it gave me: nothing. Lucas is gone. Probably dead." The weight of the words strikes me center, and I have to catch my hands on my knees, heaving in the middle of Vanessa's sunstone circular drive. The morning light turns the flecks of mica embedded in the red marble into tiny mirrors, which does nothing for the wave of nausea overtaking my stomach and climbing my throat. Jayce approaches from the side, but I wave her off.

"Go home to your safe house, Jayce. Just, just go," I mutter. "You kept your word. I kept mine. Let's call it even."

"We're not even. We're not even close," she says with a scoff.

"I'm not going with you, Jayce," I reiterate. The world around me feels like it's spinning. I just want it to stop, to get off this terrible ride.

"Fine. Then I'm going with you." She plants her hands on her hips.

"No, you're not. I don't even know where I'm going yet. I can't be responsible for you and me and the whole world and a plan I don't have all at the same time." I stand upright, and place myself face-to-face with Spera's statue. It looks like she's glaring at me, furious and disgusted. *Well then, you shouldn't have gotten yourself killed.*

There's something dark on her cheek that wasn't there before. I step closer, reaching out a finger. The scent of decay rides in on a breath. I recoil, clutching my hand to my chest. Blood is pooled in the corners of her eyes, and more of it is pooled at her feet where flames once tore at her copper-colored limbs.

The strange, coppery smell of Lucas's blood is faintly present, but this blood smells older . . . and much closer to the blood I wiped on my dress. I backpedal, clutching my churning stomach. The smell is too strong for this amount of blood, and seems to be sieging from all sides.

Beyond Spera's statue, red lines come into view, tracing a pattern around the perimeter of her circular driveway. My mind hums. My heart accelerates.

I turn in a slow circle. The lines closer to me are easier to distinguish, and the patterns become letters. Words. Someone has finger-painted on Spera's statue and written words in blood on the driveway. There's just one person—one creature—who comes to mind: this must be Vanessa's message.

My breath catches as I follow the words to the foot of the stairs. I'd stepped right over them and hadn't even noticed.

"Jayce," I whisper, suddenly hoarse, but she's already pacing along the letters. Her expression is void of emotion, reminding me of a human calculator as her eyes track back and forth, her lips moving the slightest bit, mirrored by the slight rise and fall of her brow. She frowns, crosses the driveway, and starts again. I am rooted in place.

"Here." She points. "It starts here." She continues, reciting the words as she walks. "*Two little Vires girls called on a turquoise whirl. They all drank some most delicious blood. One walked into the pond, but all the water's gone. Now there are no more Vires girls.*"

She looks up. "This wasn't here before. Someone painted it while we were in the house."

"Vanessa," I manage to say. Jayce nods. She chews on her lip. Her shoulders, relaxed and round, make me want to shake her. How can she stand there, hands soft, her face contemplative, when we are standing in a ring of blood?

"Maris," Jayce says on an exhale, snapping me out of my train of thought. "This is referring to Maris. The turquoise whirl . . . all the water's gone . . . They're going after Maris. They set us up."

I stare at the words, determined to see something else, something that makes sense in the bigger picture, and not just another string in Vanessa's hand, taut and waiting to be pulled once we step within the loop of another invisible snare. What if Maris is another one of Vanessa's puppets . . . holding us by the creek overnight . . . drawing us back . . .

"What would she want with Maris?" I ask carefully.

"It doesn't matter," Jayce replies, and plants her hands on her hips.

"It matters! You don't know that much about her. None of us do. She deals in Tenix for goodness sake. She deals in *death*. That doesn't bother you?"

"She's an Unseen. It's different for them," she replies. Her entire being is relaxed. Her freakish serenity makes me want to pinch her or shake her.

"Yes, it is. It's very different. They're different. The way they operate, what they're willing to do, how far they're willing to go, who they're willing to fool . . . to sacrifice." I pause, my throat suddenly raw with emotion. "They *are* different." I lower my voice. "I can only head in one direction, Jayce. One. I don't know what that is yet, but if we go chasing after Maris, who may or may not be in trouble, who may or may not even be in this dimension, I am turning my back on everything else."

"Oh, so you're suddenly the classic hero, stalwart and true?" she asks so quietly I almost don't hear her. "You lead a charge somewhere and come out victorious? I haven't seen it go down that way for you yet, Tanzy. Honestly, what I've seen has been a whole lot different than what I thought I was going to see from the strongest soul in two worlds. I thought when we finally found you . . ." She trails off. Red touches Jayce's cheeks and the tips of her ears, masking her stripes, and revealing the teenage girl beneath.

"We came back here to find Lucas, they knew we would," she begins again. "Bridget wasn't there to bait you, she was there to delay you—to keep us out of the way. Maris is a lot of things. She's not physically strong like they are, like we are, and I'm sure it took everything she had to shield us from sight all night. She could be up against the devil all alone right now, and that's my fault. I chose you. I followed you, because I told you I would. I made a promise because I make promises, Tanzy. And I keep them. But if I had been there instead . . ." Jayce blinks fast and works her jaw from side to side, and I realize she's trying not to cry.

Heat blooms behind my eyes, and in looking plainly at Jayce, I see myself: scared, desperate to do the right thing and having no clue what the right thing is. We aren't a team, but in this moment, we are one in the same.

"Okay." I nod. "I'll go. But if we find Maris, and something seems off . . ."

"It won't," she says.

Jayce turns on a heel for the trees and breaks into a run. I cast one last glance at Spera's statue, at Vanessa's fortress . . . at David's grave, and possibly the place where Lucas lost his life. I clamp my teeth together and sprint to catch up to Jayce.

We retrace our path through the woods without speaking. Vanessa or Asher could be waiting for us at any place along the winding path to the creek. My ears are piqued, my head swiveling from one side to the other every few steps. I catch myself analyzing every shadow, fitting the shape to its source. The twisted woods beyond the roses seem even thicker, and by the time we reach the wall of bramble I am sweating.

Thorns claw at my skin as I shoulder my way through. Ahead of me, Jayce emerges and draws up straight and stiff.

Something is wrong.

I burst through, barely feeling the resistance. Jayce stands on the dry bank, which slopes down hard in front of her. The creek is half the width it was when we left it, and shallow enough that I can now see the rocky floor through what's left of the silty water. The rush of the creek has a higher pitch to the melody, as the thinner veil of water crashes over newly exposed stones and tumbles white as it plunges down the changes in elevation.

"Did we take a wrong turn?" I scan up and down the creek, and then spy the pile of leaves Jayce made last night, the indention her bag left in the sand. We are exactly back where we started, but nothing else about it looks the same. "Something is clearly off," I mutter.

When I turn back to the water, Jayce is staring at me.

"Yes. Maris *clearly* ran. Or she was *clearly* taken." Jayce rolls her eyes.

"Well if it's so clear, then which is it?"

"It's clear she's in danger."

"Or it's clear she left."

"We were supposed to be here an hour ago, Tanzy. If she chose to leave us, which, for the record, is not what I think happened, she had every right to."

"Then why would Vanessa write a message about it if she isn't involved?"

"Because she took Maris. Duh."

I shake my head, staring past Jayce and to the line between water and earth. The border of wet dirt is wide. I tilt my head. The bank is a rainbow of tans and browns, paling in perfect succession from dark to light.

"The water didn't drop all at once," I say, and walk along the creek's edge, opposite the current. "It's still dropping."

I stare upstream, where the creek bends to the right, disappearing from view.

"Come on," I say, striding upstream, but Jayce is already on the move. We walk side-by-side up the bank. Beyond the bend, the creek is even thinner, reduced to puddles and slender ribbons of moving water. A small fish flops on its side. I scoot it into the biggest puddle I can find, wondering how much longer it will have with the dwindling water and the sun soon to be high overhead.

"Check it out." Jayce points further up the empty riverbed, which ascends a sizeable hill. A giant silver wall glitters at its crest. Jayce grabs my arm and tugs me closer to the wall of bramble, which has followed the creek the entire way, and we hopscotch run up the rocky shore.

We reach the top of the hill, panting. The silver wall is about four feet high and made of metal wires, which are braided and looped so tightly around themselves that no daylight shines through. Apparently, the water can't pass through either, save a few, meager trickles.

"What is this?" I whisper. The wall is at least twice as thick as it is tall. I can't see the other side from where we stand.

"Looks like Caro wire," Jayce says. "Unseens use it to hold other Unseens hostage. Don't touch it. If it's Caro, human contact will make it explode."

"Don't we want it to explode?" I ask in a hiss. "Free the water? Free Maris, if she's in there?"

"Not while you're standing close enough to be roasted like a campfire marshmallow." She snorts at her joke.

"Stay here. I'm going to go check the other side." I tiptoe around the width of the wall, expecting to find the river swelling on the other side of the wire dam. Instead, the dry bed continues, littered with glass bottles in every shade of color, necklaces strung with ornate pendants, and an open metal chest flung on its back. About twenty yards upstream, another wall of silver wire extends the width of the river. Brown, frothy water pours around the edge on the lower bank and spills into the woods.

Across the basin, someone clears their throat. My gaze snaps up. Dana is standing on the high side of the river, towering above me. My mind flashes back to the day my father died, the hope I felt when she came from seemingly out of the blue, riding along the edge of the river . . . how sure I was she would save us. My heart feels too heavy for my chest, too heavy to beat, and sinks against my lungs, making it hard to breathe.

"Hey, Tee." Dana says. "Lucky you. This river is all dry." She grins. I am silent, unable to respond. The years I've known Dana McDaniel, barn manager, the right hand of my late father, pitted against the hours it's been since I learned she's an Unseen who works for Asher, who just made a joke about the day my father died and the hours I spent soaked and shivering beside the river at Wildwood.

"It really didn't need to go this way, you know." She leaps to the flat part of the bank, and walks to a heap of blue glass jars. "Vanessa only stepped in because she had to. If you'd come to work for me a year ago, this would've all gone much smoother. I could've saved you a lot of confusion. A lot of . . . mistakes. We could've used those powers of yours for good, you know? Killed someone who deserved it, not a doctor who saved people. You could've felt good about it. Do you have any idea what you could accomplish, what kind of life you could have? It's not too late, Tee. You can still come with me."

"I don't even know you," I whisper through the strangled sensation in my throat.

"Tee. We're practically family. Who came to your graduation? Who was there for you when your dad died? Who made sure Harbor got back to the barn after you left her on the ridge?"

I flinch at the mention of Harbor, wondering if she's trying to make sure the nerve stays struck so I'll react more from emotion should Harbor miraculously appear. I flex my hands at my sides to dispel the rush of adrenaline.

"You chased us through the woods. You nearly killed me. Harbor is probably dead because of you."

"She's not dead, Tanzy. I can take you to her. You belong with her. With us. We know you. The real you. You wouldn't have to deny it anymore." She steps closer and places a hand over her heart. "I can't imagine how hard it is to have that stallion's blood inside of you. The instincts. The impulses. Flight or fight. They will attack anything to defend their herd. Stallions are even known to fight to the death if neither backs down, and that stallion . . . he never backed down. Those traits all belong to you now. There's no way to turn them off. You just have to learn how best to set them free."

"I can turn them off," I say, my tongue dry, my throat squeezing. My pulse whooshes in my ears. I can feel the rushing current growing by the second. Even the best-trained, most experienced, most domesticated horse will have moments where the wild breaks through. The blood inside of me is born of a stallion, untamed, unbroken. Proud and defiant. His instincts and his reactions would take months or years to manipulate and quiet.

I swallow, blinking slowly, and turn my human mind inward. *Easy, now. Be easy.* I force my muscles to unclench, my breathing to slow, and am rewarded with a full-body ache of restraint.

"For now, maybe." Her expression softens. "It'll get harder. Every day, every time you or someone you love is threatened, that blood will answer louder, stronger. And one day, it'll win."

"Is that what you're doing now? Threatening things you think I care about?" I try to keep my voice and expression neutral. "Are Lucas and Maris trapped inside these wire walls?" I reach out to my side, my finger an inch from the downstream dam.

"Don't touch it!" Dana cringes away.

"Why not?" I don't move.

"Because you're no good to anyone if you're dead," she says, confirming

Jayce's suspicion about the wire.

"Help me find them, Dana. Show me you still care about me, that you are the only family I have, and maybe I'll go with you," I say, motionless. I don't mean it . . . I don't. But I can't deny the whisper of longing inside that wants to be with someone who remembers me before this all started.

"This picture is so much bigger than a tall, dark, and broken Unseen and a water witch. You're wasting your time and your heart on them, Tee," Dana says gently.

"Don't call her that," Jayce snarls, moving to my side.

"Oh, good for you, Tee, you got a pet," Dana says, and her expression hardens. Her eyes flash as she takes in the sight of Jayce, and then narrow like a lion focusing on something young, fumbling, and isolated. In this moment, I see point-blank that the Dana I once thought I knew was nothing but an act. Anger, hot and electric, floods every limb. I step away from the wall and in front of Jayce. Dana blinks, and I watch her face work back to something close to neutral and passive.

"Those are Maris's things." Jayce scans the exposed floor. "Where's Maris?"

"Don't know. Don't care," Dana says without taking her eyes off me. "I have something for you, Tee."

"I don't want it. Tell Vanessa I don't want any more of her sick little gifts or messages. If she has something for me, she needs to deliver it herself."

"I think you might want this one." She slides her hands in her pockets, and strides toward us, confident and casual. Jayce moves to step in front of me. I let her. I can shove her to the ground and jump over her if need be.

"I am a lot less likely to hurt Tanzy than you are," Dana says, stopping in her tracks.

"I highly doubt that," Jayce responds.

"Time will tell." Dana stops a few feet short of us and tosses something silver in our direction. I reach out for it, but Jayce shoulders me back, and we let whatever Dana threw land on the wet bank.

Spera's horseshoe pendant glitters from the sand, and the rest of the world falls away. I drop to retrieve it. Jayce is faster, blocking my hand with hers.

"No," she says. "Let me check it first. If it's a trap, it's meant for you, not me." Reluctantly, I rock back on my heels, wondering with morbid speculation what kind of trap Vanessa could create from a necklace when she could use a ring to hear my thoughts, and how Jayce would be able to tell. Furthermore, what could Dana mean by Jayce being the larger threat? Vanessa has prophetic visions. Could she have seen something coming? Although I don't want to admit it, I already trust Jayce enough that I don't think she'd launch some kind of direct attack against me. The thought is barbed, and shreds every other thought it touches.

Jayce plucks the necklace from the ground and inspects it, her fingers running the length of the chain. I glance up at Dana, who's smirking at Jayce. The expression, so foreign on features so familiar, makes her face look like that of a stranger.

"It's clean." Jayce hands it gingerly to me. I don't know what she means by clean, but I don't want to put it on yet. I clench it in my palm, finding relief in how solid it feels, how real, when everything else about my reality is akin to smoke and mirrors.

"Of course it's clean. Who do you think I am?" Dana scoffs. "I care about you, Tee. That safe house and the traitor who runs it, they don't care about you. They just want to control you. We want to set you free. You have one last chance to come with me, Tanzy. Otherwise, things are about to get harder for you. I don't want that. No one wants that."

"She's going to take a hard pass," Jayce quips.

"I can answer for myself," I say, and stifle a growl. A smile plays on Dana's mouth, revealing pointed teeth. "But like she said, I'm going to take a hard pass," I say.

"I want you to remember this, Tee. Remember that this is the path you chose all on your own." She pulls a cellphone out of her pocket, dials a short number, and holds it to her ear. "Dr. Andrews has been murdered. 5858 Foxfield Lane. I think the killer is still here. There's blood . . . there's blood everywhere. Please hurry," she whispers into the receiver, her voice ragged and panicked. Without hanging up, she tosses the phone into the woods, and turns and smiles at us. I am rendered speechless, stunned at the double pivot in her voice. Not because of the here and now, but because of every moment before it. Who knows when her betrayal began? She can take on any face, any voice, any emotion within the blink of an eye. Everything about her is an act. Our friendship. Her loyalty to my father . . . to his memory. It was all an act.

"Who are you?" I ask, my voice shredding. "Was there ever a time when you were really just Dana . . . *my* Dana?"

"I wouldn't waste your time or your breath here, Tee. The police will be here very soon, and poor Dr. Andrews is very dead. If I were you, the person who killed him, I'd be running. I'm still trying to look out for you."

"It's not my fault Dr. Andrews is dead. I was the weapon, but Vanessa pulled the trigger," I argue, a buzz growing in my brain. I regret the words as soon as I hear them. This betrayal of humanity is exactly what Asher wants. To deny fault here furthers his goal and his control.

"I agree with you," Dana shrugs. "Too bad your handprints are all over the house, on his body. Is his blood on your dress? Doesn't look too good for you. Anyways, I have some horses to move. Best of luck. Run fast." She gives me a parting wink, and dissolves into the shadow of an Unseen before vanishing.

The horses . . . My conviction divides. Dana may have given me more information than she intended. If her transition is any indicator, they're keeping the horses on the Unseen side of the veil. There's no way to get to them without Lucas's or Maris's help, if they're still alive. Their mention could also just be another attempt to manipulate the stallion's blood within.

"Come on, Tanzy. You're covered in blood, and even if you were a good actress, which you're not, we don't have time to deal with police."

"Maybe they can help us," I say in a rush.

"Police?" Jayce nearly laughs. "Best case scenario, they'll want names, Tanzy. Details. Information. They'll want to take you down to the station and get a statement. What are you going to tell them? They'll be able to tell when Dr. Andrews died, and they'll know you went back inside. Even if you didn't kill him, which, by the way, you did, you look guilty as hell. We need to get out of here. Now." Jayce jogs to the wall of bramble and disappears through the tangle of sticks almost instantly.

My body moves, but my mind is stunned to silence, all words and thoughts replaced with a razor sharp note, the memory of Dr. Andrew's face blooming within, his eyes bulging and desperate and scared, his teeth clamped together, clawing at me, still trying to defend himself . . . to defend Vanessa. I clamp my eyes shut but the vision plays on until his face goes slack, his mouth opens, his tongue goes limp in the bed of his teeth. And that note . . . the note with my name on it, covered in my fingerprints and his blood, is on the floor right next to his body.

"Tanzy!" Jayce shouts. I crash from my head and jerk to attention. I bolt through the wall of bramble and vines, finding relief in fighting through something tangible.

"You okay?" she asks, her expression condensing with alarm as she takes in the sight of me, heaving and stricken.

"There's a note on the floor. Vanessa used it to make Dr. Andrews think I was threatening her. It has my name on it . . ." I trail off, panic swelling in the place on my tongue where more words should be.

"If she wanted you to be caught for this here and now, she would've called the police while we were in the house," Jayce says, matter-of-factly. "She's moved us like chess pieces all morning. She wants us off the property, and I'm happy to go. You want to go try to play on police sympathies, I wish you all the best of luck. But I won't be going along. I don't know how you plan to save Lucas from a jail cell."

Lucas. His name is cool rain on the wildfire within.

"Okay." I plant my hands on my hips, forcing myself upright. I search the woods, looking for some sign from Vanessa, but all I see are trees and shadows. "So where do we go?" I ask, my voice breaking, my heart shuddering in the cage of my ribs.

"We just need a way off this property." She pivots on her heels. Her eyes are wild and unseeing.

An invisible snare is drawing tightly around where we stand. If we could get to the truck, we could probably be gone before the police arrive. Jayce is right. Vanessa seems to want us off the property. She also wants me alive for now, which brings me comfort, albeit chilly.

"I have a plan." I turn uphill.

"Does it involve the police?" Jayce asks through her teeth.

"It involves outrunning them," I reply.

"I'm following you," she says, and we take off at a dead sprint.

As expected, the doors to the truck are unlocked and the keys are waiting in the ignition. A change of clothes and a new pair of correctly sized boots sit neatly on the driver's side floorboard. I glimpse at Jayce, this candidate I have known for less than twenty-four hours, who is about to see me completely naked, but there's no time for modesty, and she's turned away from me. It's as much privacy as I'm going to get.

I toss Spera's necklace into the truck, listening for confirmation that it's landed. Then I rip off the stained, wet dress and pull on the jeans and sweater. I shove my feet into my boots and crank the engine.

"Nice truck," Jayce says as I punch the gearshift into drive. "Is it yours?"

"In theory."

"Is it Vanessa's?" Her eyes narrow.

"Technically."

"What if it has a tracking device or something? She'll see where we're going." She wraps her hand around the door handle.

The faint wail of a siren draws my ear. The stallion's blood feeding my brain takes over my senses, and my head swivels in the direction of the siren. My mind tracks the source like a heat-seeking missile, specifying the location and calculating the distance. They're coming from the west. They'll be here in three minutes, maybe less. This truck is our sole option, another step orchestrated by Vanessa down to the second.

"I'm sure she already does." I wipe the blood from my face with Spera's stained dress, toss it out of the truck, and floor the gas.

In the East

The tires squeal as I make a hard right turn out of Vanessa's driveway. Jayce swears and clutches the dashboard to balance herself.

The sirens wail behind us, gaining volume. I glance at my rearview mirror, certain I'll see flashing blue lights in our tread. Cops. Human cops, with guns. Maybe they won't notice the skid of our tires, the smog left in our wake. The obvious signs of a hasty getaway.

Maybe.

I flatten the gas pedal beneath the ribbed sole of my new boot and floor it.

The rearview mirror remains empty. The sirens fade, their sounds disrupted by trees and elevation. I let out a hard breath and adjust my hands on the steering wheel.

"Close call." Jayce peers behind us. "Vanessa couldn't have planned that any better herself."

"Vanessa did plan it," I mutter, and focus on the road.

Jayce tilts her gaze to me. I can feel her staring.

"We need to get to the safe house," she says. "It's the only place she can't touch us. Don't roll your eyes. She hasn't found us yet. We can be there in four hours. Maybe three with the way you're going." She nods at the speedometer. I lighten my foot on the gas until the meter drops to the speed limit. "Where do *you* think we should go?" she asks, sarcasm ripe on her tongue.

"Let me think."

"Think all you want," she says. "Just keep driving east."

She starts rifling through the console and the glove compartment, piling anything worthwhile on the dash.

"Whoa," she mutters. I flick my gaze to the side and catch her fanning through an envelope full of cash.

She tucks it between her thighs, and peels up the mat beneath her feet.

"Looking for loose change?" I grumble.

"I think this is yours." Jayce rights herself and extends Spera's glittering necklace to me.

I hesitate, but just briefly. The necklace calls to me somehow. Beckoning me to touch it, to take it. If Lucas is dead, this might be all I have left of him.

"Thanks." I pluck it from her palm and latch my fingers around the cool metal, sighing as it digs into my skin. "What did you mean when you said it was clean?"

"Unseens are fond of turning pieces of jewelry into instruments. You take someone with Vanessa's kind of abilities, her artistry with Tenix, and there's no telling what she might do. I bet she can create siphons, portals, you name it." Jayce settles into her seat and props up her sneakers, smearing the pristine surface of the dashboard with mud.

"You can tell if she's done that?" I ask, and immediately think of the ring I left in Vanessa's yard.

"Yep. An Unseen can use Tenix to charge any piece of metal with purpose. I can tell when something's been altered. Usually. That's my gift. Not so useful if you're fighting to the death in an arena, but it's been pretty useful in this life."

I catch myself nodding, and rein back the awe in my throat. "I know what you're doing," I mutter.

Jayce arcs a brow.

"You tell me your secrets, I tell you mine. I made that mistake with Vanessa. I won't make it again."

"First of all, we're on the same side whether you like it or not. I am not Vanessa. That hag couldn't look this good if she tried. Second, I don't believe in secrets."

"Well I do." I chew my bottom lip to keep from baring my teeth.

Jayce shrugs. "I'm an open book," she says. "That's who I am. It's not a bargaining chip. I have one secret. One." She holds up a finger. "And it has nothing to do with you. If you're keeping secrets from me, fine. Keep them. Just don't get me killed."

I bite my tongue. I'm not just keeping secrets from Jayce, I'm keeping everything from her. There's a difference.

Jayce nods at my fist. "You should put that necklace on before you break it. It's pretty."

I tuck it into my pocket instead.

A sign for the interstate looms ahead. East or west? Do I continue alone or fall in with Jayce's ranks?

Jayce drums a rhythm on her knee, eyeing the sign. Waiting for me to make a decision. My mother's parting words echo in my mind: *Stay with Jayce. Stay alive. We will find a way to save us all.*

I move into the eastbound turn lane. Jayce exhales. We merge onto the interstate and roll down the next few miles in silence.

Minutes pass and we say nothing. After everything that's happened, sitting still and quiet feels absurd. We could be coasting to Wildwood for a trail ride. Instead, we're speeding toward a house filled with girls bred to slaughter one another.

A *safe* house. I almost snort at the irony.

"What are you thinking about over there?" Jayce says. Her voice is low, careful. Against the overbearing silence, it feels loud.

"Just drifting," I say.

Jayce studies me. I can almost feel her biting her tongue.

"Do you need directions?"

I shake my head. "Not yet. I'll need your help once we get to the coast."

Her gaze warms the side of my face. "I have something else for you." She hesitates. "Something to read. A letter."

"It's from my mother, isn't it?"

"Yes."

I bite the inside of my cheek, releasing when I taste metal. What more could my mother have to say to me? My throat swells. I'll never see her again, never speak to her again. Whatever's in that letter . . . it won't be enough. It will never be enough.

My gaze wanders to Jayce's bag. Then to her lap, where she's laid one palm, face-up, over the other. She wriggles her fingers and squeezes them to a fist.

"I don't think I'll ever get used to it," she says. She uncurls her fingers slowly, as if there's some tiny winged creature inside that she's reluctant to let fly away.

"What are you talking about?" I pretend to watch the road.

"You know exactly what I'm talking about. Your mom is an Unseen. You see the elemental marks. You don't have to deny it in front of me."

"Hope was human when she had me," I say.

"Well, duh. If Unseens could procreate whenever the hell they wanted to, we wouldn't be in this mess." She laughs, and her face softens. "We might be freaks," she says, and peels one of my hands away from the steering wheel. She turns it palm up. "But we're in this together."

"Do you really see them? The elemental marks? Vanessa said she did . . ."

"Oh, I'm sure she does." Jayce drops my hand and returns her own to her lap.

"Every candidate can?" I glance at her fist. Once, I would've seen a vibrant light threading through her loosely bound fingers, emanating from the horseshoe-shaped mark stamped into the center of her palm. Now all I see is skin.

What's happening to me?

Jayce shrugs. "As far as we can tell, just the Artius Six can see the marks. That's what makes the final six from our candidate generation so special. Supposedly, we were all born from one parent who began life behind the veil, and then became human."

"What color is my mark?" I ask her. "I've never been able to see my own."

Jayce creases her brow, gaze darting back to my hand. "Purple," she decides. "But kind of silver, too. The color of lightning. It makes sense."

"Spera," I say, and she nods.

"Unseens can tell what a Seen is made of. You know, the elemental makeup; ratios of earth, water, fire, air, and Tenix. Your soul's ratio balance must resemble lightning. Mine is the color of the ocean because I'm made mostly of water." She shows me her empty palm. "Does it make more sense now?"

I nod, and imagine a sunlit turquoise.

I commit the color to memory in case she asks me again.

WE PULL ONTO THE SHOULDER in Richmond and switch seats.

The shift in speed is jarring. Jayce sticks to the limit, her eyes constantly gauging the speedometer. I didn't realize how fast I was barreling over bridges and roads. We're lucky I didn't flip the truck or smash into a tree.

Jayce motions to her messenger bag, now on the floor between my feet. "The letter is in the left side pocket," she says. "Just in case you're interested."

I unzip it, and pluck out my mother's note. It's folded into a tidy square. I try not to feel disappointed at how thin it feels between my fingers. How could a mother's last words to her daughter fit neatly on a single sheet of paper?

Jayce turns up the radio and starts singing along. I suppose there's not much else she can do to give me space. I glance at her out of the corner of my eyes, and unfold the note.

The handwriting belts back at me. Wrong. It's all wrong. The letters are sloppy and leaning, and the margins are clean. *This doesn't look like hers at all. Could this be a fake?*

My heart sinks. I search every word for a sign that my mother's last words were penned by Vanessa, or Asher, or Dana.

Every *T* is double-crossed, every word beginning with *R* is capitalized. My mother's quirks. My mother's hand. Relief whistles through me. My heart pounds in my ears, muffling the radio.

I start to read.

Dear Tanzy,

I Received word you're back from witnessing Spera's life. I hope to the heavens I find you in time to say good-bye. If not, please believe I love you, no matter what I've said in the past. I have so much to tell you. I wrote down as much as I could in a few leather journals. You'll find them in your Room at the safe house, should you choose to go. You have an independent streak a mile wide, and I admire it, but please consider joining Jayce, Reese, and the others.

Should you decide to travel alone, there are a few things you must know. First, no Unseen creature can cross the veil below sea level. If you need to hide or sleep, do so underground. At least then you'll be able to see them coming.

Second, when an Unseen crosses the veil, we must take on the guise of something Seen. Something recognizable to human eyes. The strongest among us can mimic any form, any person. Learn something small and insignificant about the people you choose to trust, something difficult to fake or Replicate.

Third, nothing in your world now is a coincidence. Pay attention to every detail, every sign. Asher may have an army, but you have an army all your own, even if you can't see us. We will try to light your way from the other side. Any Unseen can die while on your side of the veil, but please, please do not go up against Asher alone. Not yet. He is the First. Many Unseens believe he alone can sire the Novus. He is unimaginably strong in any form.

Lastly, stay away from Lucas. Asher is the First. Lucas is the third. His elemental makeup is nearly identical to Asher's. There was a time when they worked exceedingly well together, to the detriment of all who crossed their paths. Lucas is strong, cunning, and dangerous. Perhaps he means well now, but I feel certain, with time, Asher will turn him against you. Sever your ties with him, and with anything and anyone of value. Any loyalties you keep are liabilities, plain and simple.

I love you, Tanzy. I'm so sorry it has to be this way.

You are mine, and I am yours, forever.

~ Mom

I reread the letter once, twice, committing her advice to memory.

My eyes burn. I duck my chin to my chest, blinking back my tears, and work to refold the paper until I've lined up the creases exactly.

Jayce shifts in her seat. She keeps her gaze on the road. Maybe she's read my mother's letter already. Maybe she hasn't. Maybe she's waiting for me to tell her what it said.

"Asher's the first," I say. The fact that it's easier to talk about a mortal enemy than linger in my mother's voice isn't lost on me. I blink my eyes clear and keep my gaze aimed straight ahead, the note pinched between my fingertips. "What does that mean?"

"Unseen creatures were created from the energy it took to make this planet's parts stick together. Call it cosmic or big bang or divine or whatever. When the process started, the very first moment when random parts were given new purpose, Asher came to be. Other Unseens were formed soon after—just seconds apart. I think all of them rose from the energy in less than a couple of minutes. But Asher was first."

"And that makes him special?"

"It makes him perfect. He's pure energy. Pure purpose."

Perfect. I sink into my seat. A shudder runs the length of me. "So why are other Unseens afraid of him? They can't die."

"At Asher's hand, they can. He's the only creature who can end the life of any Unseen behind the veil."

"Whose brilliant idea was that?"

"The way the story goes, when the world was created, the Powers had to adhere to the law of balance. Asher is pure energy, pure life force. So they had to create in him the capability of pure death. He has the power to destroy everything in his world, but it's his responsibility to keep his realm functioning. Reese says it's why so many Unseens are bent on keeping him happy, and why those who believe in the prophecy of the Novus think Asher has to be the father. Some of them just want easy access to Tenix. Apparently, the only one who can kill Asher on the Unseen side of the veil is the Last Unseen, and no one can prove which Unseen was created last."

He alone can destroy his world. I alone can destroy mine. We are more alike than I care to admit. Guilt slips through me, slick as oil, and my mind shifts to Lucas. His scarred face appears in my head. I wish I recognized myself in him instead of in Asher.

"What can you tell me about Lucas?"

"You probably know more about him that we do, so congrats on that." She flicks her eyes at me and her lips curl in a smirk. "When we witness our lives as candidates, we only get to see our own paths and the choices we made. Reese said the Unseen side calls these journeys down memory lane an "Origin." To all of us in our Origins, Lucas was just another guard. Reese had heard through the grapevine that he'd broken rank with Asher and was searching for Spera, but no one realized he was still alive or how important he'd turn out to be, until . . ."

She trails off. *Fill in the rest,* her silence says.

I buckle my lips.

Jayce shrugs. "Maris and Hope probably filled in as many gaps as they could when they met with Reese. I'm sure she is preparing an updated lecture on him as we speak."

"A lecture?"

"Part of our training," she explains. "Reese thinks we should know as much as we can about everything, and *everyone*, involved in this War of the Worlds."

Her gaze flick in my direction. A grin quivers at the edge of her mouth. I gape.

"You've had a lecture on *me*?"

"Like you're *so* fascinating," Jayce snorts. "Spera, horses, blah blah blah. Don't worry. You're not the chosen one when it comes to lectures. Reese debriefs us on every candidate. At least, every candidate we've identified so far. She's going to be very interested to learn about Bridget. She has to be one of the Artius Six." Her look of speculation presses into a smirk. "You should've heard *my* lecture," she boasts.

"Cavilla," I say, remembering. "The lecture was probably pretty short. If memory serves, Cavilla didn't last long." I peer at her from my periphery, eyebrow raised, the first resurgence of humor tugging at a corner of my mouth.

Jayce laughs, and dances her fingertips over the steering wheel, practically preening.

"Honey, Cavilla's got nothing on me."

SOLID GROUND

We leave the mainland and cross bridge after bridge, which link for several miles across the Atlantic. At last, the island stretches before us like a rib bone, long and skinny. As we travel further north, hotels and strip malls give way to high-end condominium complexes, gift shops, and restaurants. Nearly all the parking lots are empty. Most of the businesses display signs relaying the same message: closed for the season. The Outer Banks is effectively hibernating for the winter months.

Jayce pulls over into a vacant lot in front of a closed gift shop.

"What are we doing?" I ask as I scan our surroundings, resenting the painful prick of alarm as it courses through exhausted, sore muscles.

"Reese will pick us up here." Jayce gathers her things and tucks them into her bag.

"We're leaving the truck?" I ask.

"There's no way Reese will let this thing any closer to the safe house than it already is. I'm kind of shocked it hasn't blown up or something." She slowly cuts the engine and withdraws the keys from the ignition. "I mean why would Vanessa give you a car? Doesn't she want to keep you close?"

"I'm sure she's still close enough," I mumble under my breath, and the truth of it sends a shiver dancing between my shoulders.

Jayce frowns, studying me, until movement somewhere behind me draws her eye.

"Reese is here," she announces as she watches a black jeep whip into the parking lot. Its windows are tinted and its collapsible roof is drawn tight across the roll bar.

"Dana called Reese a traitor," I murmur. "Why would she say that?" I regard her from my peripheral vision, watching for any hint that Jayce is editing an answer.

"I mean, at least she didn't call her a friend. Dana is probably calling you a traitor right about now. That's a vote of confidence in my book."

"How did Reese know where to find us?" I ask, one suspicion breathing life to the next. Jayce hasn't been out of my sight since I left her on the creek bank, and we hadn't followed evacuation orders. When could she have called Reese?

"Hope probably told her. She wants to help you home however she can," she says.

Home. The word unsettles me. I'm not sure if it's because I want to belong or because I fear it. I don't have time to decide. The Jeep brakes to a stop next to Jayce's side. The window rolls down and a young woman's face, I assume Reese, appears. Her smooth skin is a shade darker than the shadowy interior of the car. The lower half of her gaunt face plummets from the ledges of her cheekbones. Her black hair is pulled back in a neat bun. Worry lines are stitched across her brow. They deepen as she moves to speak.

"Claire will get rid of the truck," Reese says. She nods to a girl in the passenger seat, who immediately steps out of her side and rounds the front of the Jeep. "Don't leave anything behind you want to keep."

"You ready?" Jayce asks, shouldering her bag.

I squeeze the strap of my seatbelt, the rest of me unmoving. Vanessa may have bought this truck or made it out of Tenix or whatever, but it's the only thing I have that's mine, and not at all theirs. They will want me to stay inside their walls, eat their food, march to their proverbial drum.

Jayce glances back at me. Her focus moves to my hands, and her face falls.

"Give us a sec, Reese," she says. Reese purses her lips and steals a glimpse over her shoulder before giving the faintest nod. Out of the corner of my eye, I see her step out of the Jeep, her lips pressed in a hard line. I haven't even formally met her yet, and I already feel like I'm disappointing her. I expect to feel a pang of regret, but instead, I feel nothing.

Jayce rolls up her window and turns to me. "You don't have to stay," she starts. "Learn as much as you want and walk whenever you want. That's the way it works. No one is a prisoner here." She waits. The keys are in her open hand. She won't try to stop me if I move to take them. But I am not enough on my own. Not yet.

"Let's go," I say before I can talk myself out of it.

Jayce slides out of the truck. I slip out of my door and gingerly close it behind me. Reese and Claire are posted on either side of the Jeep, watching up and down the road. They meet us between the two vehicles the second I exit the truck.

"Tanzy, Reese, Claire," Jayce leads introductions. Aside from being identical in height, and both wearing all black, Claire and Reese are polar opposites in appearances. Reese is compact, thick muscles roping her arms. Her legs and upper body seem even for length, while Claire, lithe as a ballet dancer, is all legs. Her long blonde hair is braided over her shoulder, and her bright blue eyes twinkle despite the gravity of her expression.

"Sp—Tanzy, it's an honor," Reese says succinctly. She straightens her black sunglasses on the bridge of her nose. Claire nods, but it turns into more of a bow. The pressure in my chest squeezes down any response. I manage a nod and a pained smile.

"There's bottled water in the Jeep if you're thirsty," Reese continues. "We'll get you something to eat at the house. Claire, you know what to do. Make sure you're home before dark."

"Yes, Reese." Claire takes the keys from Jayce and hops into the truck. It roars to life the instant her door slams shut, and she rumbles onto the two-lane road, back the way we came.

"Hop in," Reese says, and slides back into the driver's seat.

I cast a glance at Jayce, fumbling for something to say to her. She's already climbing into the back seat by way of the console, so I slip into the passenger seat. As soon as I shut my door, Reese locks every opening to the vehicle and punches the gas to the floor.

"Did you see someone coming?" I twist to see through the rearview window. The road behind us is empty.

"We're not safe out in the open. I always feel better when we get back to the house," Reese explains.

"We're not safe anywhere." I don't mean to say it aloud, but there it is.

The whole truth in four words.

Reese clenches her jaw. She flexes her fingers on the steering wheel. "We stand a fighting chance at the house," she says.

She shifts the Jeep into four-wheel drive. Ahead, the two-lane road crosses a flat, iron cattle guard, and the asphalt turns to sand. I cling to the handle above my door with one hand, and steady myself on the dashboard with the other. The flat terrain quickly gives way to a bumpy trail that carves through rolling hills of packed sand. Shallow, brackish water spills from surrounding, low-lying marshes, and pools in the deeper troughs of the path. Lone, scraggly trees and clusters of wind-whipped, dry grass checker the landscape. Sea gulls trill overhead, kiting in the ever-present wind, which rocks the vehicle each time a hard gust blows inland from the gray Atlantic.

Reese accelerates down a hill and around a tight bend, startling a cluster of wild ponies grazing on the rise above. My entire being reacts. My lungs ache to draw a breath with their scent on it, and a need to stand among them takes hold of every nerve ending. I turn in my seat and watch them until they disappear into the marsh, wondering why horses elicit fear from Asher. My guide in Spera's life said their freedom, their unique ability to cross the veil in their true forms, troubles him most. I think there's more to it. But if Reese believes a few wild horses will scare off Asher, she has no idea who we're up against.

"You really think these wild ponies are enough of a deterrent?" I ask. Jayce stiffens in her seat.

"To keep you from Asher long enough to let the window pass, yes," Reese whispers, her lips barely parting enough to let the answer through. I furrow my brow.

"Window?" Jayce asks, echoing the question in my head.

Reese doesn't answer right away. She scans the rolling terrain and checks her rearview mirror. More horses dot the sand dunes cresting both sides of the road. They look up as we rumble past, their eyes following the car as long as we're within sight. Part of me is certain the horses watch every car passing through. The other part fears their attention is for me alone. My teeth trap the inside of my cheek.

"Not yet," Reese says, and gestures through the windshield. Ahead, the open terrain meets with a tangle of thin pines and twisted scrub oaks, and the bright sand turns brick red with the presence of clay and soil. The roots of the trees are covered in a blanket of copper pine needles. Other dirt roads branch off from this main artery. Further into the woods, little houses lifted on stilts are barely visible from the road, tucked in tiny, cleared alcoves.

We make several quick turns. No one speaks. We go a hundred yards or more without a single house in sight. The trees grow closer, and their canopy overhead thickens, nearly snuffing out the gray winter light filtering in from above. My pulse shifts up a gear. Beside me, tension slides from Reese's shoulders, and she exhales through rounded lips. Then, she turns up the volume on the radio and clears her throat to speak.

"We found a piece of the ritual."

"Finally! Where was it?" Jayce wraps her fingers around the back of Reese's chair.

"Hidden in a book of nursery rhymes," Reese continues with the same caution. The corners of her mouth pinch with restraint. "Abby found it last night."

"Brilliant." Jayce shakes her head and sinks back into her seat.

I turn over my shoulder and give her a curious glance.

"She doesn't know anything, Reese. Like, at all," Jayce announces, drawing a line along the center of the car. I shrink away from the invisible boundary, and press my back into the corner made by the edge of my seat and the car door.

"Hope said as much. We're almost to the house. As soon as we get there I'll answer anything I can," Reese says. "The others can help us fill you in, too."

I nod, staring ahead, and imagine what a safe house might look like. In my mind, it's bare and clinical, metal tables and chilly floors. An air of quiet, disturbed every now and then by hushed conversations I'm not privy to. Will the other girls ask me questions? Who will they expect me to be?

"A horse has never given us a welcome before," Jayce murmurs. I follow her pointed finger out of her window. A shaggy, muddy pony jogs alongside the car, ears pricked toward the front of the vehicle.

Reese scowls. "We don't need this kind of attention."

"That's not normal?" I ask. I've never been around wild-born horses before. It's not uncommon for domestic horses to recognize cars, or even follow them down a driveway.

"No, and everyone around here will know it," Reese grumbles.

I peer harder through the wall of trees and search for anyone interested in our car. While I have seen a handful of houses, I have yet to see a living soul. The longer we drive on these nameless, sand streets, the less likely it seems we'll encounter one.

Reese makes a hard right, maneuvering the Jeep between a narrow gap in a grove of low, twisted trees. They grow so close together their limbs make a wooden web. It's impossible to see the road we left moments ago.

The horse does not follow us into the brush. I do my best to ignore the squeeze of loneliness.

A modest, brown house appears in the trees, raised above the sand by a row of concrete pillars. Brown tarp lines the back and sides of a makeshift garage.

Reese steers beneath the house and cuts the engine. She plucks the keys from the ignition and slips them into a compartment I hadn't noticed below the radio.

Jayce trails Reese out of the driver's side, and helps her drop another brown tarp, covering the way in. I climb from the car and let my eyes adjust to the dim light. Another tarp hangs down from the center of the ceiling, walling off a corner of the space.

"They're blackout tarps," Jayce says, following my gaze. "The material is actually metal hammered into paper-thin sheets. Unseens can't see through it from their side. Reese had the same material embedded in the walls of the house. It's not impossible for them to find us here, but it's a lot harder." She drops the last tarp, which triggers a light positioned above a flight of weathered wooden steps. They are narrow and steep, positioned between two cement pillars, and end at a plain brown door.

Reese steps to the landing and gestures Jayce and me ahead of her. I hesitate, strangling the hand rail. Jayce skips ahead of me. Reese presses close to my back, and suddenly I am too hot.

"I need to reach that string," Reese says quietly, and points to a string dangling from the ceiling above my head. I duck my chin and move up a couple steps. Reese tugs the little rope, which releases a narrow flap of identical brown tarp. It settles between the pillars, masking the entrance to the stairwell. The immediate darkness is a total, solid thing. It threatens to swallow me. I let out a breath and chase Jayce up the remaining stairs.

Jayce swings the door open and light floods the narrow passage. I blink, disoriented. The inside of the house is surprisingly typical. Bright, printed fabrics are stretched over a set of wicker furniture, which is situated around a low, oval table. An oversized picture of a palm tree hangs on the longest wall, right next to the entry to an unlit hallway. In one corner, a clunky television sits on an entertainment center, which is warped by the constant humidity. Windows, cloaked in venetian blinds and floral drapes, stripe the back wall. A long bar separates the living room from a galley-style kitchen. Books and laptops are stacked on nearly every possible surface, but there's not another soul in sight.

"I told the other girls to give us some space," Reese explains, following my gaze around the room. "We'll do introductions later."

"Thanks." I step further inside and glance down at a book lying open on the back of the couch. I trace a line of foreign text, wondering what language it's written in, and who in the house can read it.

"What did the ritual say? How close are we?" Jayce asks.

"I'll show you." Reese points to a laptop on the kitchen counter. She types in her password and opens a file marked "Six."

Jayce reads the rhyme aloud: "Sing a song of six souls, one body full of fate; four and fifteen candles burn on a cake. Before the candles burn out, a choice must be made; a choice for death or a choice for life, all for the king of greed." Jayce leans closer to the screen.

"How can you be sure it's a piece of the ritual?" I ask.

"We can't be absolutely sure, but we believe it is."

"Hidden in a book of nursery rhymes, though? I figured they were on scrolls or something."

"Rolled up inside a glass bottle buried on a remote island?" Reese says, her features becoming playful for nearly a full second.

"Well, yeah." I flush at the idea, childish and obvious.

"When an immortal being is searching for something, the safest thing to do is to keep it moving and changing," she explains. "There's no telling how many forms the pieces of the ritual have been in so far."

"If they want to make it impossible to find, why not destroy it?" I ask.

"Balance."

"It's easy for them to say. It's not their lives on the line," I argue.

"In a way, it is. The members of the Unseen council charged with keeping the prophecy hidden are truly immortal. They cannot be killed on either side of the veil. The one way they can die is a lack of purpose." Reese raises an eyebrow as if to question whether or not I'm following her.

"So, if the ritual is ever fully uncovered, they die," I summarize.

"Exactly."

"There's no way this ends well, is there?" I mutter.

"If we're right, the ritual must occur before you turn twenty. All we have to do is keep you from Asher's hand until your next birthday. Then you're safe—everyone is safe—for this lifetime, anyway."

I swallow, digesting the idea of ten months in this little house on this narrow island, dropping tarps and learning how to discern one unmarked sand road from another. How and when will I search for Lucas if I'm hiding here?

I should be grateful, I remind myself.

I should be a lot of things . . .

"So, what does the poem mean, exactly? How can you tell when the window will end?" I ask, turning back to the screen.

"The differences in the real rhyme and this one are the most important parts. The second line changes 'black birds' for 'candles,' and changes 'pie' for 'cake.' We believe those are references to a birthday cake," Reese continues. "The numbers are also different. In the original, it's four and twenty. This one says four and fifteen, so obviously the total is important."

"So that's it, then?" I ask, my head swimming, the pieces of a puzzle she sees so clearly refusing to fit in my head. "I wait here?"

Reese nods. "For now."

"What if you're wrong?" I push, folding my arms at my front. "Vanessa wrote a weird rhyme on her driveway to drive us to Maris, and it absolutely worked. What if this is her work?"

"I don't think so." Any remnant of humor evaporates from her. "I think that's why Asher is noted as "the king of greed," here. It doesn't exactly rhyme, and it's a swipe at his character. No one who is devoted to Asher would discredit him in any way, and, from what I've learned of Vanessa, she would've made sure the rhyme was exact."

"I have to agree with you there." I stare at the carpet, teal and faded in spots. Reese's idea sounds simple and impossible at the same time. Why does the idea of waiting make me feel like we're playing straight into Vanessa's hand once again?

My eyes move to Jayce. Her nose nearly touches the screen as she scrolls through search results. Her foot taps a rhythm on the leg of the bench and her fingers absently twist at the pink ends of a lock of hair. She's home. The recognition is bittersweet. I'm glad she has somewhere she belongs. I wish I could say the same.

I move to the window, anticipating Reese will stop me. When she doesn't, I take the curtain between my fingers and let in a sliver of light. Beyond the back porch, the sand piles into dunes, and then drops to a wide stretch of beach. Patches of dry grass are blown flat by the steady wind coming off the frothing Atlantic.

"I can't go out there, can I?" I ask.

"For about ten minutes," Reese answers, and joins me at the window. "Hope can create a temporary shield for you. She's here, you know. She won't leave you again."

My heart flutters against my ribs. "How will I know when to come in? I can't see her." The admission is heavier than I feared it would be, and makes every inch of me sag beneath its weight. At least she'll be on the beach with me. Somewhere.

"I'll tell you," Reese says, and then points to the first door visible in the dark hallway. "That door goes to the other side of the carport. It's where we train. I think you'll appreciate it. The walls are the same tarp system as what you saw in the garage. Unhook a couple of the latches and you should be able to slip out to the beach. Once you're outside, don't go farther left or right than the sides of the house."

I nod. My insides hum, and I don't know whether it's knowing I'm about to be alone in the wide open or Reese's growing list of restrictions that is prompting the reaction.

I hurry through the door and down the stairs, shoulders hunched to my ears, guarding my neck. The lights are on in the training room, even though there's no one in it. Blue training mats are stacked in the far corner. A rope ladder dangles from the ceiling. Several punching bags hang in a neat row. Free weights run the length of one wall. I run my fingers across the metal bar of a weight bench. It's still warm from recent use.

A pang of unexpected envy makes my chest constrict. How might my path have changed had I met Reese instead of Vanessa? How far along would I be now? This is how you educate someone like me. My kind of strength needs a leash and the instincts controlling my body need discipline.

The enormity of my circumstances stretches in front of me, a canyon's worth of missing pieces between what people expect of me and how little I understand. I challenged Asher, made a promise I would see him fail, but I have no idea where to begin. Standing in the center of a room created to prepare me, I am face-to-face with how little I can help myself, much less Lucas. The silence hovering in the training room seems to agree with me.

I unhook a line of latches, slip through the gap between two tarps, and jog onto the empty beach. A breeze kicks up and tosses my loose hair around my face. I catch a lock of it in my hand and let it run through my fingers. The black strands are a stark contrast to my skin. I marvel at how much more I resemble my mother than I did at the start of all this. We have both become entirely different creatures. I'm hanging on to my humanity by a thread, and she's invisible to me forever more. Yet for the first time in a year, I feel like she's paying attention.

"I don't know what to do," I whisper into the wind. It wails off the Atlantic. Currents of sand sweep down the beach. I clasp my elbows and stare across the sea, wishing there was some way my mother could show herself. I'm not sure why I miss her now. I taught myself how to live without her a long time ago.

The sensation of eyes on my back creeps down my spine. I ease my chin over my shoulder. The scruffy brown pony from the road studies me from a cluster of trees high on the ridge. *What do you want?* My insides quickly divide, half of me desperate to climb the hill and see if it would let me touch it. The other half of me shrinks away, sure it's just one more thing I can let down.

"Tanzy!" Reese calls through a crack in the door. I turn, catching her gaze, and she slips back inside the house. I hustle up the stretch of sand and to the gap in the wall, pausing as I reach a hand between the tarp sheets.

Out here feels more like home, the wind, the surf, the freedom. I breathe in deep, and steal one last glance at the ocean. There, standing fifty yards from me and still as stone, is the wild pony. It screams at me. The sound rallies my blood, quakes in my bones. I grit my teeth, hating the fear and longing that ripple through me by turns, and force myself back inside the house.

CLARITY

I jog to the top of the staircase, my boots clacking beneath me. Each step echoes, urging me faster.

I reach the top, and pause. A jolt of awareness ripples through me, lifting the hair on my arms like hackles. It seizes my limbs and renders me completely still.

My hand is half-raised to the tarp that separates the staircase from the living room. My fingertips graze the waxy, brown vinyl. I draw them back.

Something feels different.

The air has thinned. A new energy buzzes over my skin. I tilt my ear to the flap and hear murmurs. Sneakers pacing. The whisper of a page being turned.

My hearing sharpens, and I imagine fingernails sifting through hair, heartbeats even and slow.

Jayce giggles. Suspicion wafts away from me on an exhale, evaporating into the black.

I push through the tarp's frayed seam and open the door. Eyes fly to me, rooting my feet to the ground. The spacious vacancy of the living room has been replaced by bodies. Two girls are perched on opposite ends of the wicker couch. The one nearest to me has a short cap of white-blonde hair. She uncrosses her legs and tucks them beneath her, parts her lips and slaps them shut again.

At the island, both barstools are occupied. Two more girls. One clutches a leather-bound book, the one with the foreign text. The other sits with her fingers poised over the keys of a laptop, the cursor of a search engine blinking back at her expectantly.

Reese stands just beyond the island in the unlit kitchen. Just the shape of her body is visible in the shadows. She's still wearing her sunglasses. She leans one shoulder against the humming refrigerator—an easy posture, but nothing about her screams *relaxed*. Her head swivels, left to right, sweeping the room, gauging my reception.

Jayce emerges from behind her. "Seriously, you guys," she says, pink tips whipping back and forth as she scans the frozen faces of the other candidates. "She's not the freaking pope."

The sound of her voice, bright and jarring as the clang of a bell, snips the invisible puppet strings suspending us all in our places.

"Tanzy, candidates. Candidates, Tanzy." Jayce waves the introductions away.

The blonde girl springs to her feet, hand already half-extended to shake mine. "I'm Abby," she chirps.

"Whoa now." Jayce bends her elbows over the island. "Easy, Abs. Don't pounce on her."

Abby glowers and lowers her arm. Someone chuckles as she sinks back onto the couch.

"Back to work," Reese murmurs. Her voice is low but effective. The gazes plastered to me drop back to crisp, white screens and dingy-yellow pages, feigning disinterest.

I still feel like I'm being watched.

"Want a drink?" Jayce plucks a damp glass from a drying rack and crosses to the sink.

"Sure." I cut a straight path to the kitchen, my eyes trained to the carpet. The other candidates steal glances at me. I pretend not to notice.

Jayce flicks the faucet up. "I was telling Reese how you caught that arrow," she says. She downs the glass in three gulps, refills it, and passes it to me.

"You two were lucky," Reese whispers. "You have to be more careful,

Jayce. You don't think anything through." She removes her sunglasses and glares. Her eyes are too yellow to be human.

Jayce scuffs her toe over the linoleum tile.

"She needed to see what she could do," she mutters. "No one's ever bothered to show her."

"And if something had happened to her? To either of you? What then?"

Jayce frowns, and kicks her sneaker against the island, disgruntled but subdued. I examine Reese from beneath a crinkled brow. She's older than us, but surely she's not old enough to *scold* us. To sound so much like . . . like a mother.

"She didn't want to go into the house at all," I speak up. "She said we shouldn't. It was my fault, my idea. I was going with or without her. She was doing her best to keep me protected."

"Then the same sentiment applies to you. What we've all been through will be for nothing if you don't help us keep you alive and on this side of the veil." Reese turns her hard stare to me before excusing herself from the kitchen. She sweeps the dust from a chair placed directly in front of the back door, then settles onto the seat, rigid and alert. She leans back to steal a glimpse behind the blinds, flicks her gaze around the room, then stares straight ahead, her pointer fingers resting like a temple against her lips.

Jayce clears her throat. "Do you want to see your room?" she asks. "You're bunking with me. Hope that's okay. Space is tight."

I hesitate. Abby's awed gaze flutters to me. Panic slices across her pupils when she catches my eye, and she thrusts her book back in front of her face.

I feel another pair of eyes on my back. Less friendly, baring into my skull. Waiting for me to . . . what? Break something? If they've had *lessons* on me, they must know what I'm capable of. On the flip side, I barely know what I can do, only what I've done. Maybe they're not waiting for me to break something. Maybe they're waiting for me to *break*.

I straighten my shoulders. At least Jayce isn't spying on me from behind or peeking at me over the brim of a book. She meets my stare head on.

"Good with me," I decide.

I follow her through the den and down a narrow hallway. I count five doors, and a sixth at the end of the hall.

"Reese sleeps there." Jayce points to the far door. "And we're right here. Third on the left."

She swings inside.

The room is split into distinct halves. Clothes litter Jayce's bed and mark a trail to an open closet. Penciled sketches are tacked to the wall in an uneven row. A single, black-and-white picture sits in a metal frame on the peeling nightstand. It's a younger Jayce, tucked beneath the arm of a woman whose smile is identical to hers.

I avert my eyes, feeling like an intruder.

I shift my attention to the other side of the room and freeze. My gaze darts from the denim bed spread to the poster of Harbor pinned over the headboard. A wooden tack trunk sits beneath the window. My trunk. *My room.*

The image of my old bedroom flashes back to me, the wave of shock at seeing it stripped bare. My mother sent my things *here.* The message is clear. She wanted this to be my new home. But it feels empty and unfamiliar, even with my belongings staring back at me.

A framed photo of me with my parents is perched on the bedside table. The urge to pick it up, to press it tightly against my chest, passes over my fingers. I shove my hands into my pockets instead. These pieces of my past feel foreign, as if they belong to somebody else. Someone with dirt caked underneath her nails instead of blood.

"You've got some clothes in your trunk," Jayce starts. "You should change. Maybe burn the clothes Vanessa gave you. No, don't. They might send up some kind of flare. Leave them in a pile by the door and I'll make sure they get taken out with the next run to the dump. The bathroom is across the hall if you want to take a shower."

"A shower sounds good." I hide my nails in my fists.

Jayce crosses to the narrow closet on my side of the room. The door whines on its hinges when she opens it. She withdraws a towel, ratty around the edges, and extends it to me.

I take it, and return her meager smile. She *wants* me to like it here.

"Thank you," I say. "For everything.

Jayce flushes. "No problem."

An awkward silence stretches between us. I do my best not to squirm.

"Everything's going to be okay, you know," Jayce says.

I arc a brow, as if to say *sure it is*, and she grins.

"I'll fill Reese in about Maris." She takes a half step into the hall. "Don't use all the hot water."

I snick the door shut behind her and rest my back against it. I catch myself staring at the poster-sized picture of Harbor sailing over an evergreen hedge with me tightly bowed on her back. Our eyes are level, focused on the trail ahead. We are one.

We *were* one.

"I'm sorry," I whisper. I shove the glassy sheen of tears from my eyes. Then I stride across the room and tear the poster down. The corner rips, and I pause. *Harbor.* I make my fingers slack. Carefully, I roll the poster into the shape of a tube. I look around the room for a safe place to stash it.

The trunk.

I kneel, and open it gently with one hand. Folded clothes take up half the space. A stack of leather-bound books are piled in the corner. A strange dagger rests in its sheath on a pull-out tray. I pick it up and slide it from its casing. The short handle is crafted from an iridescent stone. The color shifts from purple to green as I flip it over. Slowly, I draw out the blade. My mother's name is carved at the base. I brush my thumb over each deeply engraved letter.

Hope.

This blade belonged to her. Now, it's mine. If my mother left it for me, she must think I'll need it. Even here.

I slip the knife beneath my mattress and return my attention to the trunk.

A familiar pattern catches my eye. Blue plaid. A line of thin, black buttons. My pulse stutters over a beat. It's one of my father's favorite shirts, neatly folded and tucked into a stack of my old clothes.

I clutch the worn fabric and bring it to my face. I breathe in deep. My father's faint scent mingles with cedar and settles like a quilt over my entire being.

Something clatters against the floor, and I jump. My eyes dash to the ground, where my father's dog tags have landed in a heap. They glitter back at me from a puddle of sun. They must have been tucked in his shirt.

I buried these. I prop the rolled poster against the trunk and pick up the dog tags. Suspicion spears through my blood. Could they be imbued with a tracking power? If they've been tampered with, will Jayce be able to tell?

I open my palm and stare at the silver tags. My thumb runs the length of my father's name. *Travis Hightower.* If Jayce suspects something, even if she doesn't *feel* Tenix on the tags, she'll turn them over to Reese.

A defensive surge rolls through my core. *No one touches these but me.* I slip them around my neck and tuck them under my sweater. I refold my father's shirt—tight and square, the way my mother would have done it—and slip it back into the trunk.

My eyes move to the brown leather books. There's no lettering on their covers. Most of them are bound with leather cords. These must be my mother's journals. I reach for the one on top and open it in my lap. Tears surge into my eyes. They blur my mother's loopy handwriting, the spiraled doodles she infamously left on every spare sheet of paper any time she held a pen.

I blink and clear my vision.

The first sentence is short, but I can't read beyond it: *Tanzy, I hope you never Read this.* Her words are too real, this piece of truth too big and too severe at its edges. My stomach bottoms out. She's bracing me for something terrible, I can feel it. My arrival here at the safe house is part of a worst-case scenario.

I command myself to keep reading, but I can't. My father must be in here, his memory preserved by my mother's script.

It should have been you that day! It should have been you in that river!

My lips quiver as my mother's strangled blame echoes in my head. Teague stampedes across my mind, over the ridge at Wildwood, into the churning froth below. My father is on his back, gripping his mane. Vanishing forever.

I close the cover, set the journal back where I found it, and latch the trunk.

My mother could be in here right now, watching me, and I would never know it. Anyone could be here, any Unseen, spying on me from the other side of the veil. Unless Jayce is right, and we really are untouchable here. I recall Reese's position in front of the back door, guarding it. Guarding us. As if she could keep Asher or Vanessa or any of them from getting through.

"Safe house," I mutter. I know it's only safe as long as my presence here remains a secret.

The whole house suddenly feels cramped and overcrowded. I peer at the closet, and stifle the overwhelming urge to crawl inside. To curl up in some small, hidden corner and wait for the storm to blow over.

Could Reese be right? If I camp out here and wait, will the window pass? If I can go undetected for a few months, will my life return to normal?

I drag my finger over the circles stamped into my chest, and think of Dr. Andrews. The memory of his spilled blood floods my mind like a violent current breaking through a dam. The sound of sirens screams in my ears. Guilt wracks my stomach. I clamp a hand over my mouth and gulp down the bile that's racing upward. I killed someone. I *killed* Dr. Andrews. Can my life ever return to what it was?

I know the answer. I shove it aside, but it snaps at me. *Murderer*, it hisses.

I squeeze my eyes shut, and wrap my arms around myself. I wish my mother was here to hug me. Wish my father was here to stroke my hair aside and kiss my brow. I want to hear them say that they still love me, that they understand. . . . It was an accident. . . . I didn't know . . . Vanessa tricked me.

But they're gone. I'm alone.

I think of Lucas, guarding me in the hay shed, kissing me softly in Vanessa's cold, sterile barn.

He loved Spera, not me. He thinks she and I are one and the same, but he's wrong. We are nothing alike.

My father's dog tags rattle against Asher's mark as my entire body trembles. My mother's jet-black hair falls across my face. Dr. Andrews's blood clings to the underside of my nails—my kill, my fault. I'm *Tanzy*. Not Spera. What Lucas thinks he loves, what he's spent his life protecting, is a delusion. He'll realize that soon enough.

If we both survive, he'll leave me, too.

My head throbs. I clamp a hand against each temple, and lean against the wall. *What if I open the veil? Live forever? Fear nothing?* The questions whisper in my brain, caressing me like a lace curtain in a summer breeze, so simple, so lovely.

No.

"Shower. I need a shower," I mumble. I grab the towel and rush to the bathroom before the darkness gaining ground inside me has a second longer to spread.

I twist the nozzle and listen to the water pounding the basin. Steam builds in the tiny room. I peel off my clothes and step under the scalding spray.

It's not your fault, I hear my father say. But the voice is mine. It's easier to blame Vanessa and Asher and the transformation, to let go and wash away my guilt as easily as the dried flecks of ugly, crimson blood which swirl to nothing on the shower floor. But my guilt is my humanity, and owning it, preserving it, is the best way to fight Asher from afar. Still, a dark hole gapes at the base of me. A hollow place, wide and deep and endlessly black. A living emptiness. *What could possibly fill you*, I wonder?

Lucas's face flashes before my closed eyes, but he doesn't quite fit the gap I imagine within. Still, the constant patter of water hitting the floor is a bittersweet reminder of the rainy night I spent in his arms. The memory floats through my mind like wisps of smoke, vanishing the second the shapes become clear. I tug back the fragments, like plucking shards of shattered glass from the floor—waking from Spera's memories, the scent of straw and skin and the river ripe in the hay shed at Wildwood. Watching the glow of the sun come to life in Lucas's eyes. Learning the whole truth about what the Vessel must do, and what I must decide.

I don't want to die.

I don't want to live forever as Asher's Vessel.

I don't want to destroy my world.

I don't want to seal Lucas behind the Veil with Asher.

A sudden bolt of urgency belts through me. I have to free Lucas and get him as far from Asher as possible. That way, if I'm forced to the door of the veil and seal it, he'll at least have some distance. Some time. It's the only compromise I can think of, the only way I might be able to save my world *and* Lucas. To repay a debt I owe Lucas and Spera both. Maybe then I will be able to forgive myself for everything I've done . . . and they'll be able to forgive me for everything I'm not.

It's a Hail Mary, but it's a fighting chance.

With a start, I realize I've made my decision. If the moment comes, if the choice is to be made, I will seal the veil.

I fumble for the faucet and turn the water off. The silence is a vacuum, clearing debris from the rest of my brain. *I will seal the veil.*

The hole within me fills.

Surviving this life feels empty, temporary. So what if Reese manages to keep me hidden until the window passes? I'm still mortal. I will die, and all of this will begin again. The decision has to be made. I won't let another life roll around, another incarnation, another chance to be found—and fooled—by Asher. I will not let other families be torn apart and tormented—murdered—for Asher's quest.

My mother kept me in the dark. Now I know what's at stake, and my world is set ablaze.

This is *my* life, *my* choice.

I will not let the window pass.

ALLIES

I open the trunk, retrieve the first shirt and pair of jeans I find, and shove them on. My mind is already down the hall, through the slim staircase, out onto the beach, and then—

I pause.

And then what? I wonder.

My mind stalls. I haven't the slightest clue where to start my search for Lucas.

One foot in front of the other. My father's favorite line of encouragement repeats in my brain until my heart rate steadies. I close my eyes and force myself to take a long, slow breath. I can't save Lucas if I don't know where Asher is keeping him. I can't seal the veil if I don't know where to find it.

I grind my teeth, and fish through the pockets of Vanessa's pants for Spera's necklace. I fasten it around my neck and clutch the horseshoe charm in my palm. I'm in a house full of people who know infinitely more than I do about Asher and the prophecy. Why would I leave a library in search of a book?

I'll stay, I decide. Stay and rifle through Reese's research. I'll comb search histories and memorize earmarked pages. I'll train on the equipment in the room below my feet like a prized fighter preparing for a rematch. I'll pick the candidates' brains like a vulture, learn whatever I can, and slip away the moment something useful crosses my path. And I will start right now.

I move down the hall and slip into the living room. I'm cringing, I realize. My brow is bowed over my nose and my lips are pinched to a tight line. I relax my jaw and hope no one here is telepathic. It won't matter, one way or the other, if my plan is written all over my face.

Without warning, the front door swings wide and clatters against the wall. The room springs to attention, beastly reflexes reacting in synchronization. Claire, the girl who took my truck, blows through the opening and slams the door shut behind her.

"Turn on the news." She shrugs out of her jacket and flings it to the floor, revealing the upper arc of a single circle burned into her shoulder. The mark of a battle won in Asher's ancient arena. A scar carried over from a previous life. Like mine.

My lips part, and my fingers dart to my chest. She may not be one of the Artius Six, but she's an incarnation like me, dragged into the arena, preserved by Asher, reborn again and again. Our marks prove it. They bind us together, and will for the rest of time.

Someone has snatched up the remote and punched the power button. The boxy television buzzes to life. I peel my stare away from Claire's shoulder. My eyes wander over the rest of the girls now gathered around the screen. Some of their marks are visible, others are partially covered by clothing. The sense of belonging buckles into place, startlingly sudden and somehow familiar. The same connection I feel when I latch my legs over Harbor's saddle. These girls may be strangers, but they're candidates like me.

"That's Vanessa's house." Jayce's voice yanks my gaze to the television. The camera sweeps across the front of Vanessa's estate, which is lined with yellow crime tape. Police cars and sleek, black SUVs are parked, bumper to bumper, along the manicured drive. A police officer stands with his hat in his hands before a cluster of microphones. He gives an approximate time of death, and describes the horrific state of the crime scene, blanching further when he mentions the words painted in blood on the driveway.

I duck my chin, sealing my eyes to my shoes. I wrap my arms around my middle and squeeze, hoping that if I force air out I will be more likely to inhale again.

Do the other girls suspect me? I peer at Reese. She cocks her gaze to mine and shakes her head, discreetly, side to side. The movement is slight but deliberate. She knows I killed Dr. Andrews. She hasn't told anyone. Not yet.

How does she know?

The words *suspect* and *armed and dangerous* bleat from the screen. The officer's drawling accent echoes in my ears. Any second now, he'll say my name. Then everyone here will know what I've done, and Asher's heinous brand won't be enough to make me one of them any longer.

My pulse quickens, and my plan dissolves. Sneaking out of the house was one thing. But staying one step ahead of Asher and Reese *and* the cops will be impossible.

I force my eyes back to the television and blink. The officer is holding up a picture of Lucas, listing his features. The floor shifts beneath my feet. I stumble to the nearest piece of furniture and fold into it.

"Why would they think . . .?" I whisper, trailing off.

"Vanessa," Reese growls. "She's framing him. Now if he escapes—"

"He won't just have Asher on his tail," Jayce interjects. "He'll have the cops to contend with. He'll never make it to you if he runs."

I sink into the wicker couch, wishing the crevices between its wilted cushions would swallow me. Wishing I could disappear. Wishing the officer had said my name instead, held up *my* picture.

Reese crosses to me and kneels. "It means he's alive," she murmurs. "He's *alive*. Things could be worse. So snap out of it." She straightens. "What do we do, Tanzy?"

I gape. Is she serious? I'm not a leader here, she is.

The girls circle around me.

I clear my throat. If the cops are searching for Lucas, then there's no time to waste.

"Finding Lucas is my priority," I confess. "He could help us uncover the missing pieces of the ritual," I quickly add, and Reese nods.

She motions to the TV. "I see this as a message from Vanessa." The candidates murmur their agreement. "I think she wants you to find him, Tanzy. At the very least, she wants you to try."

"So, what?" Claire barks. "We're supposed to play straight into Vanessa's hand?"

I cringe. That's exactly what we're doing. It's a relief that someone else sees it.

"Doesn't matter." Reese's words are clipped and matter-of-fact. "Lucas vowed to protect Spera." She squeezes my shoulder. "He's one of us now. We take care of our own. So let's get started."

The candidates break into small groups, huddling together around computer screens. A laptop sits, unattended, on the coffee table. I press a key to bring it to life, then stare blankly at the screen.

The room falls quiet, keys clicking, girls whispering to one another. I tap my foot, unnerved by the sudden stillness. This already feels like a tremendous waste of time.

A girl drops onto the couch beside me. Her caramel skin is speared by two dark lines, a slight, sloping arc from tear duct to nostril. *Cheetah*, I decide, eyeing her slender, dappled neck, her long, spindly limbs. I wonder if she's faster than me.

"I'm Shaila," she says, glancing at the blank computer screen.

"Tanzy," I reply. "I guess you already know that."

Shaila shrugs. "It's nice to put a face to a name. We've been cooped up in this house for so long. Seeing you in the flesh has lit a fire around here."

She swats my frozen hands away from the keyboard and clicks open the internet.

"What are we searching for?" I ask.

"A needle in the haystack," she replies. "Anything out of the ordinary."

I give her a pointed look.

"I know, I know," she says. "It's not a perfect system. We look for patterns. Or something that seems to want to be found. Reese has one rule about research: If you think you've found something important, show her first. There's no reason to get everyone worked up if it's a false alarm. We've all had our fair share of disappointments."

"That's an understatement," I mutter, and consider the blank search engine staring back at me. I type in the most obvious thing I can think of: *Vanessa Andrews.*

The first few results tout her generous contributions to various charities, and show her in a series of long, glittering gowns from her attendance at fundraisers all over the country. Page after page sings Vanessa's praises—her philanthropy, her fashion sense. Older posts articulate her findings about lightning strike victims, and chronicle interviews with survivors, all of whom claim to have achieved some higher purpose with her help.

On a hunch, I Google the names of her former patients. Most seem illegitimate. There's no record of them at all, no phone book listings, no social media accounts, no birth certificates. It's as if they've disappeared, or perhaps never existed to begin with.

Only two patients have records beyond their interviews, and those records are obituaries. Both died by fire. Like Spera.

I backtrack and search for news clippings about the fire at Wildwood. During the investigation, traces of gasoline were found near the front of the barn. Arson was never ruled out and the horses' bodies were never recovered, leading some to wonder if a fire was set to hide a mass theft. One reporter dubs the incident the "Wildwood Horse Heist," claiming that the total value of all sixty resident and boarded horses was well over a million dollars.

Another columnist points a finger at my mother, citing that the barn burned to the ground on the eve of the anniversary of my father's death. I wonder if the writer uncovered that detail on his own, or if he was fed it by Vanessa's hand.

The evening blurs into screen after screen of research. Every now and then, a surge of energy zips through the room as someone lurches an arm into the air, summoning Reese, whispering feverishly into her ear. Pulses peak. The tangy scent of adrenaline rises. The clacking of keys ceases as everyone waits for Reese's judgement, and resumes at the dismissive shake of her head.

By the time night falls, I'm cross-eyed and exhausted, and I've got nothing to show for it.

"You ready to call it a day?" Jayce asks, appearing beside me. I look up to find that most of the other girls have left. I watch Shaila disappear through the door to the basement. I didn't even feel her stand up. My spine aches from leaning over the keyboard, and my eyes feel grainy after hours of staring at a screen.

I sigh. "I feel like the more I search, the less I learn," I say, and snick the laptop shut.

"Sounds about right." Jayce gives me a sideways smile. "I have a remedy. Come on."

She tugs me into the interior stairwell. We head down to the workout room where several other girls are taking turns on the equipment. Abby dangles from the rope ladder like an acrobat. Her blonde hair falls over her eyes. Claire does push-ups in the corner, clapping between each one.

Other girls are stretching. Shaila's sneakers beat over the belt of a treadmill.

Reese leaves her post by the weight bench and heads our way.

I pause in the landing. I might be willing to fumble around in the dark when it comes to research, but the idea of training in front of everyone makes my stomach drop.

"Come on." Jayce takes me by the elbow.

"I'm not really dressed to work out. Maybe I'll just watch."

"That might be hard to do," Reese winks. "Lights out, ladies." She reaches past me and hits the light switch on the wooden post. The room plunges into darkness.

For a moment, all I hear is the elevation of my heartbeat, the rasp of my breathing. Then the earlier sounds resume—Claire's palms smacking together, Shaila's soles thudding an even rhythm, girls grunting their repetitions, metal contacting metal. The others have continued with their routine as if nothing has changed—as if they can still see.

"Do you have some kind of night-vision equipment?" I whisper, feeling more exposed in the dark than I did in the light.

"They don't need it. Neither do you," Reese replies.

"I can't see a thing in here." I reach for the closest solid object so I can ground myself.

"Horses see in the dark." Reese's voice circles around me. "That means you can, too." Now her face is right in front of mine, her breath warm on my nose. "Your senses are keener than you realize," she says. "They'll align with your Vires blood if you let them, mimicking your match."

The black horse gallops into my mind, his coat shining on the beach in Spera's memory.

"Horses aren't like cats," Reese is saying. "It takes time for their eyes to adjust to the dark, and to the light. But they're very perceptive to movement. They have a wide field of vision."

Her voice is at my ear. I shiver away from it.

"They have two blind spots," Reese says, and taps the back of my skull, making me jolt. "One is directly behind them, and one is directly in front."

"I know all this already," I mutter.

Reese's mouth peels into a grin, her straight white teeth beaming against the black.

"Good," she says. "You need to remember what you're made of now, what instincts you answer to, and what abilities you can tap into if you try." Her voice slips behind me. She covers my eyes with her hands. The hair on the back of my neck stands on end and my legs tremble with the flood of adrenaline. I do my best to stay still, but it takes constant management to keep the wildness inside me in check.

"Now, don't think of the dark as an enemy," Reese instructs. "Don't search for the light. Allow your eyes to accept what's in front of you. Nothing more, nothing less."

She removes her hand from my face. The darkness is still there, unchanged, but I force myself to stop fighting it. One by one, shapes comes into focus. The instant someone moves, my eyes jump to their location. I can see enough to identify the form, and I can feel where each form is headed. Intuition trickles through me. The layout of the room becomes clear.

"I can see," I whisper.

"Good." There's a note of triumph in Reese's voice. "Let's get to work."

Jayce and Reese show me around the room, demonstrating quick repetitions at each station. Even though everyone else can see at least as well as I can, the absence of light makes me more willing to try.

I settle into the rhythm of the room, finding my place among the sounds. *Clap. Thud. Grunt. Inhale. Exhale.* Together, we're pushing forward.

Jayce cracks her knuckles. "Warmed up yet?" she asks.

"What's next?" My blood thrills at the question. At last, I have a place to put three days' worth of frustration. "Can I hit something?"

"It's about damn time."

She and Reese guide me to a heavy weight bag. I stand still and wait for instruction.

"Go on," Reese prompts.

"I'm not sure how to start," I mumble, the eager surge slipping away.

"We'll work on form later. Right now, I just want you to get everything out."

"Get it out?" I fidget in place.

Reese inhales through her teeth, rocks her weight onto her back foot, and explodes in a burst of movement, sending the punching bag sailing on its chain.

Jayce reaches out to steady it.

"So just hit it?" I ask, still unsure.

"Don't overthink it," Reese says. "Your fuse has been half-lit since the moment I met you. You need to burn it all the way out, finish it, before you can start fresh."

Vanessa's voice floats into my mind. Her face flashes behind my eyes, panic-stricken, the night we were attacked by the Unseen on Maris's property. *Finish him, Tanzy!* She'd wanted to set my instincts loose that night, to light my fuse and let me explode.

I press a finger to my chest, circling my innermost mark. My first kill. Vanessa's cries for help slice through me. Taunting me.

She thinks she's seen what I can do when I let go. . . . She has no idea.

The scream begins somewhere beneath my heart, rattling my lungs as it gains volume. Sound and motion become one as a rumble breaks through my mouth. My hands fly free, my shoulders and arms driving them harder and faster with every throw. I wait to tire, to feel empty, but each time my fist strikes the bag I want more.

The pressure builds by the second, and my strength doubles. Triples. *Thud. Thud. Crack.* Again and again. The chain groans for mercy. The sound of wood splintering barely registers. A loud crash doesn't make me stop, but there's nothing left to hit. The heavy bag is on the floor in the corner, surrounded by a scattering of free weights and what's left of the wooden rack they sat on seconds ago.

Somewhere in my mind, I'm aware the others aren't moving anymore. The dark around me is quiet and still.

It strangles me.

I scream, and break the silence too.

Someone sucks in a breath. Maybe this is what everyone expected—a broken, wild girl. But I don't feel like I'm breaking. I don't feel like I'm falling apart. I toss my head back and send my wildness, my violence, my sadness and anger and hate, shrieking into the sky.

I feel free.

BLOOD SONG

No one moves until Reese turns on the light. Even then, motion is kept to a minimum, eyes scanning from the floor to me, weight shifting from foot to foot. Nothing more. Jayce alone meets my gaze without balking.

"Get back to work, ladies," Reese instructs as she makes her way back to me. She picks up my hands. It takes every ounce of concentration I can muster not to swing again. My chest heaves at a steady clip, driven by the blood pounding through my body and the oxygen rushing in and out of my lungs. Every inch of me shakes.

"Do they hurt? You're bleeding," Reese says, voice low enough that only I can hear.

"No." The word trembles.

She turns to Jayce. "Will you grab a roll of tape from the wound kit?"

"Sure." Jayce hustles to the far corner of the room, bends to open a white, plastic chest, and returns with athletic tape. I stand as still as I can manage as Reese expertly wraps my knuckles and adds a supporting layer around my wrists. *She wants me to hit something else.*

"I can't control it," I whisper.

"No one can. Not at first," Reese murmurs. "Why do you think human blood is so weak? Human bodies are fragile . . . finite. Our bodies are different. We've endured incarnation after incarnation. It doesn't make us invincible. Vires blood is pure passion, pure instinct. It will drive you mad, if you let it. It's happened before. It will happen again. I can teach you how to control it, if you let me."

"Tell me what to do." My fingernails dig into my palms, a reminder to keep them still.

"Follow me." She turns on her heel, and slips through the blackout tarp, into the night. I cast a quick glance at Jayce, who nods in encouragement, and hurry after her.

Outside, the wind cuts through my thin flannel shirt. I wrap my arms around myself and scan the empty beach. Reese is nowhere to be seen.

Reflexively, I struggle against the new dark. The starlight overhead does little to brighten its pitch.

Reese's instruction slips into my mind. *Don't search for the light. Adjust.*

I blink. I'm trying to force the world around me into focus. It won't work. I soften my wincing brow and let impatience be speared away by the ice-laced breeze.

Slowly, the black becomes transparent. Still, the beach remains empty. I'm alone here.

"Be still." Reese's voice carries to me, curling over an arc of wind. One by one, I force my muscles to heed her. A frigid blast of air rushes in from the Atlantic, stealing my breath. I close my eyes against the spray of sand and shield my face with my hand.

"Are we safe out here?" I shout over the constant wail.

"Hope will hide us. We have a few minutes to work."

"I can't see you!"

"Find me another way," she calls, this time from the opposite direction.

My shoulders swivel to her voice, recalling how Harbor would twitch and jolt at every swish of a branch overhead, every crack of a twig underfoot. Every *sound*. Reese hums, the melody floating in from somewhere new. Her voice sends vibrations trembling over my Vires blood. I shift my foot ever so slightly toward her, paranoia preparing my muscles for flight.

She falls silent.

I take a measured breath, focusing on the sound as it moves in and out of my lungs. Then I allow my ears to search a little further into the steady roll of waves breaking on the beach. Dry grass cracks behind me as another gust whips through it. In the fray of movement, a new noise shuffles in, condensing my senses to a single focal point. Sand depresses, a slight movement, deliberately soft.

I drop my weight onto my back foot and swing right, bandaged hands tucked and ready beneath my chin. Reese's yellow eyes are within inches of mine, too close to strike. I startle at the nearness of her.

"How did you do that?" I ask, dropping my fists.

"We all have our gifts." She takes a step back from me. "Being difficult to detect is one of mine."

She motions for me to follow her as she walks closer to the ocean.

"I feel so far behind," I admit, jogging into the space beside her.

"You'll catch up," she murmurs. "One lesson at a time. Focus on balance, and the rest will come."

"Balance?" I say, peering up at her. The sand dampens and firms beneath our feet. Reese eases to a stop, and together, we survey the gentle slope and break of waves rolling over the sea.

"You are many things," Reese says. Her voice is low, the implication behind her words as powerful as an undertow. "You are Tanzy, and Spera. Vires blood rips through your veins. Humanity strangles your soul. You must find a way to be everything at once, to embrace all the pieces of yourself. To fully become who you were meant to be."

"There's not time," I whisper. "Lucas . . ."

"Have you started reading your mother's journals?"

I bristle. "No," I admit. "Do you think that I should?"

"I think when you're ready, they may offer some help." She tilts up her chin, eyes darting over the sky. "Our time's almost up."

She turns for the house, but I linger, listening to her retreat. Soles over sand. A whisper of sound, but I hear it clearly.

I scan the black horizon and wish I could sense Hope wrapping around me like a shield. But all I feel is the wind flapping against my ears, the sand scurrying over my ankles, the vibrations of the sea.

"How did it go?" Jayce asks when I reenter the house.

"Good. Fine," I mumble.

"You okay?"

"I think I need some air." I wave my hand in front of my face for added affect.

"You were literally just outside," she says. "You need water. And another shower. You stink."

I muster a grin. My sleeves are slicked to my skin by sweat and ocean spray. I strap my arms over my chest, shivering against the cold of my dampened clothes.

"You're right. I need water." I follow her up the stairs and into the kitchen. We each drain a glass, and fill them up a second time before heading down the hall to our room.

Jayce locks the door behind us and kicks off her sneakers. I sink down on my bed and pry off my shoes with my toes.

"You've had a long day." Jayce flops back on her pillow. Her eyes flick to the bare spot over my headboard and she daggers her brow.

"Did you tell Reese about Maris?" I ask before she can mention the absent poster.

Jayce nods. "I can tell she's worried, but she didn't say much."

"What do *you* think?" I push. "Do you think she's working with Asher?"

Jayce shrugs. "Reese will tell us when there's proof one way or the other. You don't have to figure everything out for yourself anymore. We're in this together. Try to relax."

I roll my eyes, and shift onto my back to stare at the ceiling. What if Maris fools Reese the way Vanessa fooled me? The way my own mother fooled me?

"Do you trust her?" I whisper?

"Maris?"

I shake my head, and Jayce widens her eyes.

"Reese? I trust her with my life. I'm not saying she's never wrong, but she doesn't lie."

I consider the difference between truth and honesty. My father always said he valued a person who admitted fault over a person who never made mistakes.

No one never makes mistakes, Tanzy. His voice sweeps over my ear.

"What happens now?" I ask.

"Dinner is on our own. Reese keeps the kitchen stocked, but it's too hard to cook a single meal for everyone. We each have our own . . . dietary requirements."

She waits while I absorb her explanation. Each of us is matched with an animal. Wild-born. Predator or prey. Tiger, cheetah, horse.

"Speaking of dinner." Jayce stretches her fingers over her middle, and her stomach growls. "Want anything?"

I shake my head, grateful for the prospect of a minute alone in our room. Jayce hops off her bed and strides through the door.

I ease to my feet and shut it behind her, clicking the brass lock into place. I place an ear against the wooden panels, listening as her footsteps grow faint in the hall.

I move to the wooden trunk and lift its latch, my movements over-cautious, as if something's waiting beneath the cedar lid to pounce out at me. But it's exactly as I left it. Clothes, dagger, journals, compactly arranged.

I pluck the top journal from its stack and settle into the back corner of my bed. I draw my denim comforter over my lap and drift my fingers over the supple, leather binding.

Are you here, Mom? Am I ready?

I thumb open the cover and begin to read.

Tanzy, I hope you never Read this. If these journals have passed into your hands, it means something terrible has happened. Asher has discovered you, despite my best efforts to keep you concealed, to hide you in plain sight. I've kept you in the dark, kept you unknown even to yourself. Now I have no choice but to bring you into the light. Otherwise, you will not survive.

Perhaps I've been a coward. Some will say I should have told you the truth long ago, but I Refused. What sort of mother makes her child choose one death sentence over another? I couldn't put that burden on you, Tanzy. Not while you were mine.

The tide is shifting. I feel him coming, closing in. Asher. Perhaps he's crossed your path already, though I pray his name is unfamiliar to your ears. These journals will explain what I could not. If you're Reading these words, it means he's close.

I pause long enough to scan the page for any mention of time or date, but there's no indication of when she wrote this passage. I continue on.

This world has its fair share of secrets. In these journals, you will discover mine.

There is an Unseen World where there is no birth and no death. Where life forms are stripped and Refined until they Reach their final states: sea and stone. Air and diamond. I am an Unseen creature. I came into existence beyond the veil. I have existed with my brethren since the very beginning. We were created as the earth formed, our energy too pure or too volatile to be fully absorbed by other elements.

I am a piece of wind and sky. I gave myself up for your father. Another story for another page. I promise I'll tell it to you. My love was my truth while I was with you Tanzy. There will be no more secrets between us. Not anymore.

I will say this much about your father—about the first time I laid eyes on him. He was Riding a horse across a field, his fiery hair every bit as brilliant as the autumn leaves burning all around him. I'd seen every blade of grass, every Ray of sun on the sea a thousand times over. Travis was somehow brighter, more beautiful. And then you came into the world, Tanzy. You were the grass, the sun, the sea, the air. You Restored every part of me. You made me whole.

Then Travis died. I wasn't prepared for the pain. Being Ripped from the sky was nothing compared to having him Ripped from this world. In an instant, his existence was everywhere and nowhere, all around me, suffocating me. Untouchable. Irretrievable.

The permanence of death is incomprehensible for someone like me, an Unseen. Perhaps even mortals cannot comprehend it, but I was in awe of you Tanzy. You were stronger than I was. Numbness was my only Relief, and I curled into it. I was selfish. I see that now. I hope one day you can forgive me.

A year has passed.

I think it's high time we make a new start.

The journal tumbles from my hands. *A year has passed.* She must have written this the day I ran from her. The anniversary of my father's death, when I sped blindly through the rain, back to Wildwood. Images whirl through my mind—white spears of lightning. Fire licking the sky. Lucas, Harbor. The fence cracking. Cats cackling. A flood of light. The hospital corridor streaking by on either side of me. Lucas in one world, and then suddenly, in another. *Be seeing you, Tanzy.*

Hot tears sear my eyes.

It should have been you in that river. It wasn't blame, wasn't a wish that I had drowned instead of my father. It was a warning: she thought Asher had caused the accident. . . . That it should've been me in the river.

I should have stayed home. I should have screamed at my mother, let her scream at me. Holed up in my room. Listened to the sound of her pacing in the kitchen below. Lightning wouldn't have struck me. Asher wouldn't have found me, wouldn't have transfused my blood. Wouldn't have unleashed his pet, Vanessa, on me.

I wouldn't be a killer. The veil, the prophecy of the Vessel, all of it would be nonsense to me.

My heart implodes and resurrects within the same beat. I choke on the aftershocks, swallowing roughly, grief and guilt pouring over my cheeks.

A draft ruffles my hair away from my face. I scrub the bleariness from my eyes and scan the room. The windows are closed. The door is still shut.

She's here.

A wordless lullaby drifts over my skin. A breath of air, warm and reassuring.

Heaviness settles upon my brow, bearing down upon my lashes, ushering in the shadows of sleep.

I close my eyes, and my fading mind surrenders to the dark.

GRAY

I swim toward consciousness, the thick dark dispelling a shade at a time as my mind reconnects with my eyes, and at last they flutter open. Our room is quiet and gray. Jayce's bed is empty, her comforter strewn halfway across the floor. Two pillows are stacked in the corner, as if Jayce spent the night upright; if she slept in here at all. I glance at the door, only now realizing I fell asleep without unlocking it.

My mother's journal lies face down on the foot of my bed. I run a finger along the leather spine. Even though I'll never see her again, I feel closer to her now than I have in years. The resulting ache in my chest is bittersweet.

Weak light brightens my curtains. I peel them back just far enough to peer through. The world outside is violet and black, awaiting the dawn. Maris said these hours were safest, but she didn't explain why.

Horses and the dawn. Asher's weaknesses. I file them away.

I change clothes and tiptoe down the hallway. Jayce sits perched on the breakfast bar, a mug in her hands and the blue glow of the television screen reflecting upon her face. Before I make myself visible, I scan the rest of the common area. It's empty.

"You're up early," I whisper, announcing myself as I move into the living room.

"It's my thing."

"Sorry I fell asleep with the door locked."

"No worries. Last night wasn't the first one I've spent on the couch."

"Where's Reese?"

"This is when she sleeps." She gestures to the blinds striping the windows. They're open for the first time since I've been here, revealing a frosty mist over the sea. "She usually goes to bed around four, wakes up an hour after sunrise like clockwork."

I file that away, too.

"You okay?" Jayce asks.

"Just thinking."

Jayce hops off the counter. "I know a better place to do that," she says. "Come on."

I follow Jayce to a hall closet, where she hands me a heavy coat and a pair of rubber boots.

"Where are we going?" I ask.

"The beach. It's wicked cold out there in the mornings, but it's good for thinking," she explains as she bundles up.

"We'll be safe out there?" I slip into my jacket and button it to the throat. It swallows me, the sleeves extending several inches past my fingers. The boots are two sizes too big. What if we're attacked, I wonder? How will I run or fight back? I can barely walk.

"As safe as we can get." She shrugs, and then gives me a once over. "We'll find something that fits you better, later. Let's get to the beach. We're wasting gray." She turns on a heel and heads to the basement.

"Do you have any sense of self-preservation?" I tromp down the stairs behind her, squirming in my gear. The noise we're making feels even more absurd than the risk we're about to take.

"Dude. Lighten up." Jayce practically skips across the floor of the gym and slips between the tarps. I grit my teeth and follow her through.

The beach sprawls before us, cloaked in fog and drizzle so thick I can't see the water. Jayce leaps ahead, disappearing in the mist. I can still hear her feet squeaking as she runs across the sand. Gulls call overhead. The ocean hisses each time little waves lap the shore.

"This is crazy," I whisper-shout. I turn in a circle, panic lacing my torso like a corset. "Is my mother casting a shield or something?"

"This," Jayce says, her grinning face appearing in front of me, "is the gray. We don't need a shield."

"This is fog. And a terrible idea, if we're out here with no protection." I turn back for the house.

"If you want any fresh air today, this is it. So take it or leave it. But I'm staying."

"You're impossible." I huff.

"You're no fun!" Jayce twirls, kicking off a boot. "Embrace the gray, Tanzy. The only time we get to pretend we're normal. Do you even know how to be normal?"

My mind travels a year in the past, and I see my mother standing at the kitchen window, staring at the dawn. Even on this chilly beach, I remember noting the worry on her face, and wondering what she saw on the horizon. *We are as normal as normal gets*, my father had said.

"So why do you call it *the gray*?" I ask, ducking the question while Jayce retrieves her shoe.

"Like we told you, Asher doesn't dig the dawn. He never shows himself on either side of the veil for about an hour before to an hour after sunrise. Even Maris confirmed this—that for centuries, he always disappears at dawn and no one knows where he goes. But he doesn't come here." She skips ahead.

"Asher isn't the only one I'm worried about."

"Vanessa could've made a move on you at her house. She didn't. She can't take you on her own and she knows it. They'll come for you eventually, no doubt. But not here, not now."

I trudge behind her, gnawing on a lip.

"Oh, that's a good one." Jayce crouches down so fast in front of me I nearly trip on her. She stands, her face bright with a smile, and shows me a bone-colored, twisted stone.

"Is it a rock?" I ask.

"Nope. It's what happens when lightning strikes sand. Didn't you ever see Sweet Home Alabama? Patrick Dempsey . . . girl, he only gets better with age."

"You're what, seventeen?" I ask, snorting.

"Dude. I'm reincarnated. I'm like *one thousand* seventeen. I'm a cradle-robbing cougar."

"Oh my God." I smile, almost laughing, and shake my head.

We reach the edge of the water. The fog is lighter here, giving just enough visibility to make me feel like I'll be able to see something coming in time to react.

Somewhere along the walk, I become accustomed to the way my rubber boots clomp on the beach. The oversized jacket makes a scratching sound when my arms brush my side, which happens with every step. This cacophony seems to have no effect on Jayce. She appears genuinely at peace out here in the open.

When did I last feel safe? I can't remember the last time I walked anywhere without imagining eyes on my back. Do I feel them now? I do my best to shut off my mind, to slow the blood coursing through my veins in fear I might miss the faintest sign of something coming.

"You're tense," Jayce says, breaking through my thoughts. "Your color is changing." She gestures to my hand.

I follow her gaze to my empty palm. "I can't see it, remember?"

"Have you told Reese that yet?"

"No." I can feel my cheeks flushing.

"You should."

I wriggle my fingers in the off chance the horseshoe mark is simply buried under my skin and needs a little movement to push to the surface. Nothing.

"Man, horses are drawn to you like moths to a light," Jayce says, bringing me back to the present. She points at a grove of tangled trees lining the other side of the dunes. Several horses watch us from the shadows, their ears pricked hard in my direction. One lifts its nose in preparation for a whinny, and drops it back down, tossing its head. Its long brown mane settles over its eyes.

I dismiss the sudden sensation of recognition. It's likely the black horse's blood in my veins recognizing one of its own, another wild-born horse, free as the wind.

"That's the horse that followed us on the way to the house. You've got an admirer," Jayce says.

I wonder how she can be sure. The horse's strong, stocky body and shaggy winter coat blends into its herd. Perhaps it's taller than the others, but beneath the cover of trees, it's hard to tell.

We return to the safe house in time for breakfast. I make a plate, and follow Jayce to the semi-circle of furniture they've made in the living room.

"Good morning, everyone," Reese begins, tapping a narrow stack of paper on her leg. "The last twenty-four hours have been interesting, to say the least. We have gained ground and lost ground. Tanzy is now among us." She opens her hand in my direction. "But Maris has disappeared."

Everyone shifts in their seats, myself included. Guilt circles my collar. I haven't thought much about her since we ran from the creek.

"Abby, I want you on this starting now," Reese instructs, and gives her a curt nod. Without a word, Abby excuses herself from the group.

Jayce leans in my direction. "She's the best we have in terms of research. She's found every major lead. She found you."

Found me? I assumed my mother told them what happened the moment she found me in the hospital. If so, why didn't they save me from Vanessa earlier? Then again, what were they supposed to do? Walk up to me and tell me I'm the Vessel, Unseen beings are hunting me down, and would I please come with them? Would I have believed them?

I want to think I could have seen the difference in a real ally had the option been presented to me earlier on. Deep down though, I already see how it would've turned out: Vanessa would've set me up to kill one or more of them and I would've done it. A shiver courses through my limbs. I fold my legs into my body and return my focus up front.

"Now then, fair's fair. Let's catch Tanzy up on the basics, starting with matches," Reese says. "Raise your hand when I call your name. Jayce, tiger. Claire, lion. Shaila, cheetah. Abby, wolf, Megan, cobra, and Iris, leopard." She pauses a beat, thumbing the corners of her papers. "And Tanzy, the black horse." She pauses and locks her eyes on mine. "Do you have any questions before we get started?"

More than I can count. I bite down on my lip, considering where to begin. "Is the species match enough or is the exact animal important?" I ask.

"Good question. With the Artius Six, the match is one of the most important parts of achieving a complete transition, aside from completing three kills," she starts. I hug my knees tighter to keep myself from shuddering. I am a kill away from a complete transition.

"With everyone else, it's anyone's guess. Take Megan, for example. She recalls being matched with a lion in her previous incarnation, but after Asher changed her blood in this life, she began manifesting signs of a very different creature."

I glance at Megan, noticing her long neck. It is remarkably slender from the side. Her face angles from her forehead and her chin, and her nose is small, turning up at the end. The skin running down the underside of her neck is several shades lighter than her face and what I can see of her arms, and even though it's near seventy degrees in the house, she's covered her lap and legs with two heavy blankets.

"Can everyone see the manifestation or is it limited to those who are also marked?" I ask.

Reese raises her eyebrows, impressed. "It is visible to everyone, but, as you can tell, the patterns are faint. We believe candidates see Vires markings more easily than regular people. Most of the time people don't notice unless they come close. We have plenty of cosmetics on hand to cover up should we travel in public."

This explains why Jayce had the compact mirror in her bag. I feel incredibly lucky that I don't have to worry about such visible side effects. My hair is longer, and has darkened from a flat brown to coal black in a matter of weeks. Structurally, the shape of my face has changed. My eyes are set wider apart and are larger than they were before, and my cheekbones are pronounced and high. Self-conscious, I run my fingers over my ears, which feel narrower at their tips. How far will the transition go?

"Now, I'd like to go over the descriptions of the veil and the Unseen world in detail. We could all stand a review, and Tanzy, I'm not sure what you've been told." She waits as if asking for my permission to continue.

"Sure." I scoot closer to the edge of my seat.

"Who wants to tell Tanzy something she needs to learn about the veil or the Unseen world?" Reese asks the room. Every hand shoots up but mine. Reese lets them take turns, and jots down a list of information as they describe the veil.

The Unseen world exists literally on top of ours, Unseen creatures passing by us every second of every day, and vice versa. An Unseen creature can create a window and peer through the veil to this side without crossing.

When it comes to traffic flow, Seen life gets the right of way. In most places, the veil is something only an Unseen is forced to physically acknowledge. There are two exceptions. First, there are many "pockets" below sea level, where rock has crumbled away on the Unseen side. When this happens, the veil barrier becomes something a human could touch, often mistaken for an unusual layer of quartz. This prevents Seen creatures from passing into the pocket, and Unseen creatures from rising out. Since Unseen things can't cross below sea level, these kinds of pockets are often used as prison cells for Unseens who have affronted Asher.

Second, there is a legend of a single door in the veil. Should the Vessel pass through, the veil would dissolve completely. If the legend is true, both worlds would become visible and accessible to everyone immediately.

"What would that look like?" I ask, imagining what kind of pandemonium would follow.

"No one can predict what we will see if the two realities collide," Reese begins. "But I can show you how this property appears on the Unseen side."

I straighten in my seat. "How?"

"Because I've been there." She flips over one of the pieces of paper in her hand. A pencil sketch outlines a break between still water and smooth stone. A narrow crevice runs about half of the page, denoted by a heavier coat of lead—a place to hide below sea level.

"How did you cross the veil?" My skin crawls with alarm.

Reese exhales and clasps her hands in her lap. "I belonged to Asher once. I am an Unseen."

I paint myself to the back of the chair. No one else in the room reacts to Reese's bombshell news. They know . . . *they know.*

My eyes fly back to the pencil sketch. Jayce's initials are in the corner of the paper. This safe house was a set up—and I walked straight into it. I jump to my feet, and my chair tumbles to the floor.

"Tanzy!" Jayce grabs my wrist. I snatch it away. My blood races in my veins, triggering every muscle in my body. I am bullet and trigger and finger all at once.

"Let me explain," Reese says without moving.

I back away, aiming for the direction of the door. "Do it fast."

"I completed my transformation twelve years ago. I belonged to Asher —lived with him. Loved him. Tried to find you."

I take in a breath and hold it.

"Every now and then, I would cross the veil to watch my family from afar. I have a twin sister, and to see her grow up in the Seen world was like watching what might've been. Back then I felt so lucky to have been chosen. To have more, to be more than my sister could ever dream of." She closes her eyes. I wait, rigid and silent, hearing her story like watching footage of an ambulance and a train racing toward an intersection.

"Once, Asher followed me there, to my family's home. He stood so close behind me I could feel his breath on my skin." She pauses and brings her fingers to the slope of her neck. Her eyes open. "Asher rarely crosses the veil—he only will if something matters, truly matters. I thought that something was me. But he looked over my shoulder at my sister, the two of us mirror images, and said: bring her home to me."

Pain and disgust flash in her eyes. In my mind, I can see it play out plain as day, just like in the cellar beneath the arena a thousand years ago, when Lenya told Spera that Asher fantasized about having them both. *His greed will be his downfall* . . .

"I actually thought about it," Reese continues, shaking her head. "The Unseen world values two things about all else: balance and choice. For Asher to have us both beyond the veil when my sister wasn't even a reincarnated candidate. . . . That flies in the face of honor and balance. I saw Asher for what he was, and I had to face who I had become, what we were doing, the wrongness of it all. I wish I could tell you I refused for the sole purpose of saving my sister, but that wouldn't be completely honest. I was . . . devastated. I felt used, betrayed. . . . So I left." Her hands fall to her sides. "But I had nowhere to go. I hid on this side of the veil for weeks before Asher found me."

"And he let you live?"

"He offered me a two-part deal. First, he sealed my past life inside of me. While you can speak of yours freely, I can't give anything away about mine, or anyone else's." She slips the collar of her sweater and shows me her back. The skin between her shoulder blades looks paper-thin, and the texture reminds me of oil-slicked Saran wrap: slick, shiny, and iridescent .

"Your previous life must've been pretty important then," I push. In an instant, her face is a portrait of lifelessness. I wait a few seconds, mystified and horrified at the effect. "I see," I whisper. Her expression relaxes. I don't give her a second to recover. "What's the second part?"

"I'm not allowed to cross the veil at all for now. But when the Vessel returns, I will return with you." She squeezes her eyes shut. "Permanently."

At last, Reese's real agenda. She doesn't want to return to Asher's possession, plain and simple. The pounding instinct to fight or flee leaves me in a single heartbeat. I deflate, leaning against the door.

"What happens if I seal the veil? Are you free?" I ask.

"No. If you seal the veil, all Unseen creatures are called home."

All Unseen creatures . . . Lucas, my mother, Reese, and Maris trapped for all of time with Asher because of a decision I will make—a decision I've already made. The weight of it is suffocating.

"Let's end there for now," Reese says, her eyes dull. "Tanzy, if you have any questions, feel free to find me." She stands, and disappears down the dark hallway.

Jayce is the first to approach me. The others mill behind the protective boundary of furniture.

"You said you didn't keep secrets," I mutter as soon as she is within ear-shot.

"I don't. It wasn't my story to tell."

"Is she ashamed?"

"She's not proud of it."

In this moment, I understand Reese and her fears better than anyone else in the house. Yet, if I succeed, her worst nightmare comes true.

TREADING WATER

In the wake of the confrontation between Reese and me, the living room feels like a battleground. The other girls speak in careful tones and avoid glancing in my direction. Even Jayce allows some distance, opting to claim a barstool across the room. Only Shaila treats me exactly the same, sliding into the seat across from me and promptly beginning her research as if nothing has happened.

A dull headache sets in. I press my fingers against my temples. Shaila chews on the end of her pen. The sound of her teeth gnashing the plastic cap is like nails on a chalkboard.

I clamp my hands over my ears, but it does no good. Since last night, my sense of hearing is too strong. I focus on reining my Vires instincts back in.

"So how bad was it on a scale of one to ten?" I finally ask.

"Three," Shaila says, her eyes still trained on her screen.

"Just three?"

"We all figured you'd flip when you found out. I did when she first told me. You didn't break anything and nobody's bleeding. So, three."

I scan the room. The stiffness. The silence.

"Are the other candidates . . . afraid of me?" I say.

Shaila hesitates. "You could take down Reese if you tried," she says quietly. "Everyone thinks so. That's what scares us. We don't want to lose her." Her head is bowed, as if she's talking to her keyboard.

Guilt snakes into my throat. I swallow it down. If I seal the veil, Reese will be absorbed by the Unseen world. The candidates will lose their protector, their purpose. What will happen to them then?

I don't want to think about it. I pull a laptop to my chest and begin to type Vanessa's name. *V-A-N*. My stomach protests, nausea coiling through me. I backspace, and scroll through images of Outer Banks horses instead.

An hour passes. The screen in front of me blurs, brown and bay. I scan through articles on wild-horse law until my eyes ache. I search the history of the Outer Banks ponies, sifting between the lines of legends, waiting for something, *anything*, to stick out. But nothing does. It's a dead end.

I push back from the little table and rub my face with my fingers.

"You ready for training?" Jayce asks, leaning away from her perch at the island. She smiles and winks, all prior tension forgotten. My muscles tingle at the idea of movement, and I am on my feet in an instant.

We change into workout gear and head to the room below the house. The other candidates are already shuffling in. Jayce points to a pile of extra mats in the corner, thicker than the rest, and says the entrance to the underground shelter I saw on her sketch this morning is hidden beneath them.

"It's narrow at first, but after about six feet it opens to a pretty decent cave. I'm sure we'll do another evacuation drill once the rain lets up. It partially floods during high tide and hard rain."

We skirt the edge of the training room and wait for Reese's signal to start—a flick of the lights. This time, I join in the regular rotation. Reese guides me through the first interval, and then reclaims her post in the center of the concrete floor as the second rotation begins.

There's no rest between sets. Instead we utilize varying kinds of cardio to keep up our heart rates in transition from machine to machine. By the fifth interval, Abby and Shaila have stepped out of rotation to stretch and cool down. I'm nowhere near ready to stop pushing. Jayce finishes her sixth interval and joins the others on the mat. By the ninth interval, I'm alone.

Reese keeps running me through as fury and violence flush out of my blood. At last, my burning muscles begin to slow. The faucet of adrenaline tapers off. Calm swaddles my body, and exhaustion numbs my mind. Reese arcs a brow at me, yellow eyes passing over my sopping hair and beaded brow, my sweat-soaked clothes and heaving frame.

I nod, reading her unspoken question. *I'm done.*

I join the rest of the candidates and begin to stretch the fatigue from my limbs.

"You did good," Jayce whispers, her cheek resting against her leg.

"I feel good."

Jayce smirks and switches sides.

We eat in silence at the bar while the others spill over the wicker furniture. Some read and others absently watch the evening news reel. David Andrews's murder and the search for Lucas replay. Lucas's picture flashes across the screen on a loop. I don't want to look at it, or at the crime-scene photos, but my gaze flicks back again and again.

Silently, I slip away from the others. No one stops me. I ascend the stairs and shut myself into my room, hand hovering over the little brass latch above the knob. I glance at Jayce's bed and decide to leave it unlocked.

I retrieve the open journal from its resting place on my bed and continue reading. My mother's script is faded and crinkled in places. Tear-stained. She must have been weeping when she wrote of my birth, of the first time I opened my eyes and stared back at her, the mark of the Vessel bright and burning beneath my irises. Spera's soul, a glittering, violet shade which only she could see. She calls it the color of stardust. I try to imagine what that might mean.

Her writing becomes tighter, the groove of the pen cutting deeply into the page as she chronicles the first time she caught Asher spying on me through the window of my childhood home in Vermont.

My breath catches. I never saw him, never noticed, but a vague recollection returns to me—my mother insisting we move. Swearing up and down that our cozy ranch and quiet neighborhood were no longer safe.

Her hand quivers over the memory of my father's alarm, his coddling and gentle confusion. The worry, and later, the pity, always etched into his face.

I kept Travis in the dark about all of this, too. I fell in love with him before he ever saw me. I was fully human by the time we met. I became human for him. And when I Realized our child was the Vessel, Spera incarnate . . . how could I tell him? How could I make him understand? I believed it was my Responsibility to shoulder the Unseen world; its prophecy and its secrets. I was sure it made me stronger, and made you both safer. I've never been more wrong.

When an Unseen forfeits immortality, the price is neither negotiable nor Refundable. I've heard legends of a Tribe of Five who can restore an Unseen to her immortal form, but those same legends warn of the high prices the Tribe will demand in Return.

That was the depth of my love for your father. I sacrificed my immortality. In the Seen world, life is never guaranteed. Existence is an unceasing battle. I could lose you as easily as I lost Travis. I could lose you to Asher and his Ridiculous quest for the Novus. I could lose you to the Unseen world and its greed. You're too high a price to pay for Tenix, Tanzy, but many of my kind would violently disagree.

Tenix is a wonderful thing and a terrible thing. It can be used to temporarily heighten an ability such as strength or speed, or other powers an Unseen might possess like telepathy or disguise. It can be used to join elements and create something new. As with anything, it has limits.

When Tenix is used to create something new, the creation immediately begins to expire, and Requires a constant supply of Tenix to maintain it. Purified Tenix is extremely Rare and even more powerful. In its purest form, it can bring forth what the heart desires most. This kind of Tenix is the most valuable, and the most dangerous.

As far as the Novus goes, I have mixed feelings. Many of us aren't sure there's such a thing as the Novus. How could we be when we've never seen one before? The words of the prophecy are carved in a circle on a diamond pillar. Although it's a stunning sight, its existence has caused so much ugliness, and the message is anything but straightforward. There's danger in such open interpretation. If memory serves, the words Read:

A sire's blood in a Vessel's heart, the first step for Unseen life to start.

The door and vessel, Vires blood and Vires soul, all must be willing to pay the toll.

Only then may the Novus take form, or be lost forever more.

Should the Novus come to be, first breath must be drawn among the Seen.

Light and dark, their balance the key, their match kept a mystery.

Six pieces show the story's core, the final piece will change the score.

I close my eyes against the crush of information. Prophecies, love, loss, doubt . . . and Tenix. *Purified Tenix.* . . . My eyelids fly open, and I search the room for Jayce's backpack from where I sit. It's still resting on the floor at the foot of her bed, where she'd dropped it the day we came. I wait, listening for any press of a coming foot in the hallway, but no one is there. I slip out of bed and unzip the little pocket where I'd stowed Maris's gift of purified Tenix, half expecting to find it empty. But there it is, the little stone vial, blacker than the night sky over the Atlantic, and just as cold as the water in winter.

I return to the bed, drawing my legs beneath me, and roll the vial between my palms, watching the flecks of mica in the stone sparkle in the fading evening light. What else could I use this for, if not to save Lucas? Maris had to know I would try.

A red glow warms my curtain, drawing my eye. The sun is setting. Another day is slipping away.

"I'm going to save him," I say softly. "Are you listening? I'm going to save Lucas. You'd do it for dad. Lucas would do it for me."

A balmy draft caresses my skin. It lifts my hair and fans through the pages of my mother's journal.

I don't know if she'll help me. But she's here. I know she's here. For now, that's enough.

I tuck the Tenix between my mattresses, lower my gaze, and read on.

CONFESSIONS

I'm standing at the center of the living room.

The other candidates are all seated in a semi-circle, staring at me.

Abby blinks from her perch on the wicker couch, feet flat on the seat cushion. A notebook is pressed behind her knees, a pencil tucked behind her ear.

Jayce kicks the legs of her barstool with her heels. She twists the fading pink tips of her hair between her fingers as she evaluates her new nail polish—Gun Metal Gray, she told me it's called.

I try not to squirm, but my heart is pounding. My bare toes curl into the carpet, and my fingers flex in my pockets. Over the past few weeks, each candidate has stood exactly here and shared their story for my benefit. I knew my turn would come. I thought about what I would say, but now, my mind is blank. Nerves strangle my throat.

Shaila adjusts the silk wrap that frames her hairline, the movement a temporary distraction. She catches me looking and gives me an encouraging smile. I'll watch her, I decide.

I open my mouth, but nothing comes out.

"You're fidgeting," Jayce murmurs between her teeth, as if the whole room can't hear her.

Someone giggles.

Reese has taken her usual seat in front of the back door. She clears her throat, and the room falls silent again.

I shove my hair over my ears and start mumbling about what I understand most—horses. I list their strengths and instincts, and describe the mirror effects on my body. My keen perception of sound, my strength. My increased field of vision. The endurance of an Energizer battery. But they know all this already.

Abby yawns. She drums her pencil on her shin.

I swallow, and my gaze finds Jayce, who nods, pale eyes newly soft. I straighten, and begin to describe the events of my eighteenth birthday, the rainbow sheen that swept across the Shenandoah valley, the sudden storm, the shadow on the trail, my father's horse bolting off the ledge, how big the river seemed when I looked down and found the brown, churning water void of any sign of my father or his horse.

I tell them about the moment I plunged beneath the surface. The freezing sensation reclaims my skin, and I shiver despite the vent blowing warm air into the room.

"Someone pulled me out of the river," I whisper.

Claire's brow stitches together over the bridge of her nose. Abby's pencil scratches feverishly over her page.

"Maris says she was the one who saved me. I'm not sure I believe her. I know how you all feel about her, but I . . ." I blow out a hard breath. "Well, that's neither here nor there. Anyway, the shadow on the trail was Lucas. He was trying to protect me." My voice breaks over the word. Behind my eyes, my father and Teague go over the ridge.

I clutch my fists. My breath has become uneven. I work to steady it, drawing in air, counting the seconds that pass as I exhale. The other girls wait, silent and still.

I clear my throat, and move on to the night I was struck by lightning. Waking in the hospital. Meeting Vanessa. Recognizing her voice from the radio . . . *A world in the clear.*

Memories rush back, overwhelming my senses. I recall the earthy scent of Lucas's flowers. The strength of his arms as he turned me into the sun. I don't tell the others about that. Those memories are mine. There's nothing of consequence to glean from them.

Jayce clears her throat, a signal I've stopped speaking.

"Sorry," I mutter, and clasp my hands together at my waist. The path I'm walking them down has arrived at the woods on the hill above Maris's tent. The night I killed an Unseen.

Should I tell them?

I glance at Reese, wondering how much she knows. Hoping for direction one way or the other. Her face is blank, her yolky eyes steady. This is my story. These are my secrets. The choice to reveal them is mine.

I stifle the urge to thread my fingers over the mark on my chest.

"Have any of you ever . . . ever killed before?" I say.

Half of the hands go up.

"A human?"

All of them drop.

Sweat slicks over my palms, and my fingertips tremble.

"Be grateful." My voice is barely a whisper. I can feel Dr. Andrews's clammy throat between my hands, the warm stickiness of his blood pooling between my fingers.

My heart sails over a beat and threatens to lurch through my sternum. I clutch my chest. Jayce leaps out of her seat, but Reese raises a hand to stop her.

"We're in a transient, undeclared war, Tanzy," she says. "People die in times of war."

"I can't kill again," I rasp.

"You won't need to," Jayce declares, her voice like a pillar, shouldering my panic. Lifting the weight of it away from me. The others are quick to agree.

I stare at them, stunned into silence. Their faces are hard and ready. Relief pricks the back of my eyes, threatening tears. I blink them away.

"What else?" Reese prompts.

Jayce returns to her stool. Abby flips to a fresh page in her notebook, pencil poised over the first empty line.

I relay what I saw of my life as Spera. Her last moments with Lucas.

I hesitate. It feels like a betrayal, somehow, to impart their tender, private moments in such a frank, clinical manner.

I tell them what came next: Asher shoving Spera into the pool of fire. Lenya, *Vanessa*, diving in behind her, what she said to Asher before she fell in: *you shall have neither of us.* She'd said more, but her other words are wisps of smoke compared to the inferno of memory. The fury which drove me to

Asher, and away from my guide. The moment I made contact with Asher, unintentionally revealing my future face.

"I never expected him to feel me. I didn't know it was possible to materialize in their reality."

I fall silent and glance at Reese. She folds her arms at her front.

"Time isn't linear when you travel between the planes. Did you touch Spera during your visit? Even accidently?" Her words are clipped, her face drawn.

I jolt at her tone. "Yes," I say, unsure why it feels like a confession. "My guide told me to."

Reese stiffens. "That is strictly forbidden. Touching Spera connected your bodies. Her soul has been waiting for you, Tanzy. It has not reincarnated, not once, until now. We've always wondered why. *This* is why."

Another trick. I shake my head. "But why?" I ask. "Why stall my soul's return?"

"I don't know." Reese's voice is grim. Her frown quivers slightly. Her features are stretched tight. "I'll find out."

Her words are a promise, her yellow eyes molten.

She rises, and tips her stiff gaze between the blinds.

Her quiet fury thrusts tension between us.

We shove out of her way as she exits the room.

SHIFTING SAND

Reese pushes us hard during workouts. She joins in the regular rotation for the first time since I arrived and matches me round for round.

Shaila's words cycle through my head. *You could take her down if you tried.* I don't know if I believe her, but my muscles thrill at the challenge.

After dinner, I collapse in a heap on my bed. Fatigue has pushed Asher and Dr. Andrews and Lucas to the far corners of my mind. We're no closer to finding answers than we were this morning, but for the first time all day, I'm too exhausted to care.

The door creaks. I glance up as Jayce slips into our room, her chin ducked to her chest. Usually, she bounds in and flops down on her bed. Tonight, her face is tight, her lips pressed to a line. She swipes her forearm over her face, scrubbing her sniffles away.

I sit up, alarm pinging through me. "What's wrong?"

"Nothing." She shrugs out of her sweatshirt and tosses it into her closet. Her face is drained of energy, the hollows beneath her eyes tinged purple as if she's been crying.

"You read a rhyme written in blood like most people would read a Hallmark card. Something is obviously wrong. But I can't read your mind. Not without the rings, anyway."

"What rings?" Her eyes narrow on mine and she sniffs loudly. "*Tanzy, what rings?*"

I shrug, suddenly defensive. I haven't been keeping Vanessa's rings a secret on purpose, but perhaps I haven't mentioned them before now . . .

"Tanzy," she hisses, her features moving center.

"Vanessa had two rings," I blurt. "She kept one for herself and gave the other one to me. When we wore them, we could communicate telepathically."

Jayce regards me, wide-eyed, and I draw my comforter up to my waist.

"What did your ring look like?" she asks. "Did you have any side-effects when you wore it? Redness? Swelling?"

"Well, yes, but I'm sensitive to metal. I don't usually wear jewelry." Heat crawls up the sides of my neck and tunnels into my ears.

"I wonder if that's why you can't see your elemental color."

"I don't . . ." I trail off. "I don't see anyone's colors anymore."

"What?" The single word fills the whole room, and her cheeks turn scarlet, her stripes nearly plum as the pigment deepens. "When did that start? Did you ever see the marks at all?" She leans in, teeth bared.

"Yes." I shut my eyes, remembering the glow, wishing I had one, too. The sapphire blue of Lucas's mark erupts to life behind my closed eyelids, pure and intense, sapphire and sky and tropical water all at once. I had never seen a color so vivid, so . . . alive. I open my eyes and blink the longing away.

"When did you stop seeing them?" she asks, softer now, her hand on my leg. Her touch is fiery hot even through the denim comforter.

"At Vanessa's house. Right after I started wearing the ring." Realization lights on my face. Jayce groans.

"She must've charmed it. Where is it? I might be able to tell what she did."

"I left it in Vanessa's yard." I lift my bare hands to her, as if to prove I'm telling the truth.

"We have to tell Reese everything. Right now," Jayce says.

"No, wait." I reach out and grab her wrists to keep her from prancing to her feet, but she slips through my grasp and gives me a pointed look.

"We have to fix this, Tanzy. We have to fix you, if we can."

"I don't need to be fixed!"

"What's the matter with you? Are you . . . protecting Vanessa?"

I reel away from the accusation, from her name. "That's the last thing I would want to do."

"Oh really?" She cocks her head. "Who are you protecting then? Me? Because this little secret of yours doesn't do jack for me."

"I'm keeping it for me!"

Jayce goes still, waiting, her level gaze burning two holes in my face.

"I know I'm not what you thought I would be—what you hoped I would be. Honestly, I'm not really what I hoped I would be either. What if everyone's wrong?" I look up at her and bring a finger to my heart. "What if Spera's not in here? Would you still help me? Help Lucas?"

"Lucas is important to you, so he's important to us. But he's not our main concern. You are, whether Spera is in there or not, because Asher is convinced she is. If something's not right with you, and this is not right, then it becomes the priority." She turns for the door. "So are you coming with me to tell Reese or not?"

I sigh and slide off the bed. I snatch a jacket out of my closet as we're exiting the room and pull it on. On the off chance Reese throws me out, at least I'll have something to shield me from the winter storm that has taken up residence in the skies above this tiny island for the last two days.

Jayce makes sure I'm still behind her as she marches up the hall to Reese's room. I muster a tight smile, grinding my teeth as she raps on the door.

We step inside. Reese is sitting cross-legged on her bed, a worn book tented over her thighs.

"Is there a problem?" she asks, glancing between us.

"I think so," Jayce starts. Her eyes dart from me to Reese and back again. "Do you want to tell her, or should I?"

You tell her, I want to say. But Spera would be able to open her mouth and speak the truth. Jayce was right—I owe them at least that.

I step forward.

Reese folds her hands in her lap. I tell her about Vanessa's rings, how we could communicate mind to mind when we wore them. How they mimicked the rings shared by Spera and Lenya, who used them to converse behind Asher's back centuries ago.

"There's something else," I say.

Reese remains silent.

My cheeks flush. Jayce grabs my hand and squeezes it. Then she turns my palm over.

"I can't see the elemental marks anymore."

Reese says nothing. She rises from the bed and crosses to a flaking, mahogany bookshelf. She slides her forefinger over the spines of various texts, then plucks one out.

"Would you recognize Vanessa's rings if you saw them again?" she asks me.

"I think so."

She fans through the pages, pausing when she comes to a chapter titled, "Portal Instruments," and turns the book to me.

The pages that follow are littered with sketches of rings. Most of them are ornate—fanged serpent heads and ruby-eyed lions with spectacular stones resting between their jaws. Others are made of impossibly slender twists of metal braided into intricate knots. Beside each picture is a brief description of how the ring is used. Most of them can absorb something from the wearer. One can actually allow two people to exchange physical locations.

"Are all of these real?" I ask as I scan one sketch after another.

"In theory. I've only seen a couple of them for myself, and they worked well."

The room dissolves as a picture of Vanessa's ring leaps from the center of the next page. It's simple in comparison to the others, a silver vine wrapping around a smooth, gray stone.

"There." I put a finger on the picture. None of us speaks as we read the description.

The book calls the ring a "Sorbeo" device, able to facilitate telepathy.

"It's primary purpose," Jayce reads, "is to absorb energy from one wearer and transfer it to the other."

"Was Vanessa trying to make me weak?"

Reese's face becomes pale. She shifts her jaw from side to side and glowers.

"These texts are very old," she says, her voice a near growl. "Energy means something different in this context. It means your essence. Your soul."

"My soul? But why . . . ?" The rest of the question evaporates as Vanessa's motive snaps into place. Opening the veil requires two things: my soul, and the black horse's blood from a thousand years ago. "The horse. They still have him. He's a stone statue, but . . . he's alive. They can probably draw fresh blood from him whenever they need to. You don't think . . ."

"I most certainly do," Reese growls. She snatches the book from my hands and slams it shut. We stare at each other, the realization paralytic. If they can't find me, can't convince me to open the veil, Vanessa will attempt to open it for me.

"Jayce, gather the others. We need to research through the night. Vanessa may not have what she needs to bring forth the Novus, but she could very well open the veil by herself if she learns how. I'm sorry, Tanzy, but our focus has to return to finding the pieces of the prophecy. If Vanessa took from you what we think she did, we don't have any time to waste."

I tighten my arms across my chest. She's right. I know she's right.

"Can we leave Abby on the Lucas detail?" Jayce suggests, glancing at me from the corners of her eyes. "She's the best researcher we've got, and I think it'll help Tanzy focus."

Reese nods her agreement and I breathe a sigh of relief.

"Thank you," I whisper.

"Of course," Reese replies, as if there was never any question. She turns her back on us to reshelf the ancient book. A dismissal.

Jayce ducks out of the room, but I stay behind. Giving Reese the whole truth about the rings and the missing mark has lifted a weight from my chest. I feel lighter. It's not just the heaviness of my secrets that has evaporated. I've been dragging distrust behind me like a ball and chain. It feels freeing to step out of those shackles.

"Can I ask you a question?" I say softly.

Reese pivots to me. "Sure." She temples her fingers against her chest.

"Maris . . . do you trust her?"

"Yes." Her response is automatic.

"Why?" I press.

She pauses. "I know her, Tanzy," she says. "Our paths have overlapped through the years. I'll tell you our story one day." She drops her hands to her sides, weariness creeping onto her face. "If Maris is working with Asher, it isn't by choice. I hope you can accept that, for now."

I nod.

Reese smiles and squeezes my arm. "I've been thinking about your guide," she says, and my ears perk up. "Do you remember what she looked like? Was her skin gray?"

"No," I shake my head. "She was the color of a pearl."

Reese's shoulders slump.

"What?" I say.

"Dead end," she mutters.

Her disappointment touches me, and I feel like I've failed her somehow. In the quiet of her shadowed room, my memory sends up a flare.

"There was someone who was gray. His name was Raffin. He was Asher's vizier."

Reese lights up, and her yellow eyes bulge wide. "Did your guide react to Raffin in any way?" she asks.

I recall her palpable hostility, and nod.

"It felt like she knew him," I say. "Like there was something between them. A history. I wish I could tell you more."

"It's a good place to start. Keep this between us for now. I don't have anything useful to report yet, and we must all abide by my rule. Even me." A grin appears on her face for a full second before her expression regains its usual neutrality. She steps ahead of me, and I follow her out of her room, catching myself smiling at her back. Reese is every bit what Jayce said she'd be and more.

"Get comfortable, ladies," Reese says as we emerge from the hallway. Her words evoke an immediate change in the room. Hope and panic sweep through in turns, each with its own taste and smell. I slide past her and take a seat on the floor next to Jayce.

Once everyone settles, Reese continues. "We need to uncover as much about the veil itself as possible. We're interested in any myths or legends about the Prophecy of the Vessel as well. What was important before is now very urgent. It has become clear Vanessa intends to open the veil in Tanzy's place."

Gasps and murmurs erupt. Reese lifts a hand. "We need to find out whether or not this is possible," she says. "You all know what to do. Abby, please come see me before you start. You have a different assignment."

Abby has already snatched up her notebook. She tucks it under her arm and scurries into the kitchen after Reese.

We assemble into our routine groups. I keep one eye on Abby, who nods eagerly at Reese and slides onto a barstool, concentration knitting her brow. She obviously enjoys a challenge, and Reese has given her one.

We work through the night, sleeping in four-hour shifts, shoving snack food into our mouths as the hours stack up and tumble away.

Sunrise burns through the dark, lighting the beach beyond our little brown house. We glance at each other. The sense that time is running short is ripe. Finally, I'm not the only one who feels it.

Vanessa has the black horse's blood. She has my energy; whatever rem-

nants of my soul she reaped from the ring.
And Asher has another day.

HIGH TIDE

The morning quickly grays as another front rolls in from the mainland. I stare at the drizzle through the slice of window peeking out from behind the drawn curtain.

A small herd of horses emerge from the woods and nose the soaked earth for new shoots of grass. Every now and then, one of them lifts its head and seems to stare right back at me.

The wet haze quickly turns into a downpour. Rain drums steadily on the roof and slaps against the beaded windowpanes. Gusts from the Atlantic thrust the storm sideways, slicing the glass with glistening streaks and making the landscape beyond appear bleary and bloated.

The drenched herd seeks shelter under the lip of our front porch, their furry coats damp and matted, their straggly manes slick against their skin. I shove off the urge to flip up my hood and dart outside, to offer them food, to stroke their long, tawny muzzles. It's illegal to approach wild horses in the Outer Banks, but that's not what stops me. The pull I feel, the subtle awareness of every darting eye and stomping hoof, unnerves me. I can *feel* them, huddled beneath us, flank to flank and shivering against the storm.

Awareness rakes through my blood. Every nerve inside me aches to dash into their midst.

I shift in my seat instead, and strap my arms around my bowed knees. I pretend to feel nothing, but I can't prevent myself checking the yard every few minutes. Glancing away from the white glare of my laptop, wrinkling my nose at the stale, warm air which circulates through the living room.

Outside, brackish puddles grow in the pits of uneven sand. By the middle of the afternoon, our front yard has turned into a lake. The idea of being surrounded by water makes me claustrophobic. I push back from my computer and walk to the kitchen. My muscles tremble with the desire to move, to run, to race. My lungs reach for the fresh air beyond our walls. My entire body begs for wide-open spaces.

I guzzle water, my eyes darting to the interior staircase and the makeshift gym beyond. Reese's instructions are strict and clear: research. I have a feeling she'll make an exception for me, but special treatment is the last thing I want.

I go to my room instead, hoping a change of looser clothing will relieve the trapped sensation taking hold of my nervous system.

The last of my mother's journals sits on the corner of my bed. So far, her words have been more helpful than anything I've dredged up online. I take a seat and open to the first page. My heart rate escalates as I catch sight of holes in the paper where my mother's pen broke through.

Where are you? I waited for you to come home. I called Dana. She said she'd go look for you at the farm.

I should call the police, but I don't want to draw any attention to you if you're hiding. If Asher has you there's not a thing the police can do about it. Where are you? WHERE ARE YOU?

I glance at my nightstand, where the journals I've read already are stacked. She wrote all of this in one day. My heart swells in my chest at the idea of my mother, frantic and pacing—and sober.

I wish she'd let herself have another drink.

I shake my head.

I wish she'd never gone numb in the first place. Wish Teague hadn't gone over the ridge, wish I'd never known what existed beyond the veil. Wish I'd spent my whole life wondering about a world in the clear and never learned the truth, never heard Spera's name, never laid eyes on Asher or Lucas or Vanessa.

I wish my mother had ripped the car keys from my hand the night lightning struck Wildwood. I wish she'd never let the churning rift between us grow so impassably wide.

I wish I'd never lost my parents. Never lost so much of myself.

I force my gaze back to the journal lying open in my lap.

I don't want to lead them to you, but I don't want to be too late. Not again. Not a day passes when I don't wonder what might have happened if we'd Recovered your father's body. I still wonder where he Rests. Could we have brought him back with Tenix if we'd found him in time?

I'm going to go check the farm. If you Read this, stay put. I'll be Right back.

I wrap my hands around my father's tags and squeeze them, stopping when the metal starts to bend.

She didn't blame me for his death.

She didn't blame me.

She blamed herself.

Every fight, every time she locked herself in her room, every drink—it comes back to me now bathed in a completely different light.

I draw a jagged breath, and have just begun to turn the page when the door flies open and slams against the wall. Jayce appears in the frame, her cheeks drained of color.

"It's Maris." She advances to the chest at the foot of her bed. "Your mom found her. It's not good. We've got to go. Now." She fastens a holster at her thigh and slides a knife inside the sheath. My blood responds to the urgency. I trade my mother's journal for her dagger and follow Jayce out of the room.

Reese stands by the main door, her jaw locked beneath her taut skin.

"Hope has located Maris," she says, her voice grave. "She's close, and she's in trouble. I have no doubt this is meant to draw us out, but I won't leave Maris to die. If we want to rescue her, we have to move now." She levels her gaze, somehow meeting all of our wide stares at once. "They know we're nearby," she says. "They must, if they've brought Maris here as bait. It's just a matter of time before they figure out our exact location. Shaila, grab a pack.

Pass out the masks. You, Jayce, and Tanzy, follow me. Abby, Claire, Megan, and Iris, wait for the gray. If we're not back by then, follow procedure."

Without another word, Reese turns on her heel and we follow her into the night.

A blast of icy wind snatches my breath the moment I slip through the gap between tarps. My pulse pounds in my ears, rendering me deaf. My other senses surge into overdrive. Every shadow moves with too much purpose, drawing my eyes in ten directions at once. *Is Asher watching us from beyond the veil?* I wonder. *Will Vanessa snatch us the moment we step inadvertently into her path?*

Reese pulls on a waxy, brown mask. Abby and Jayce follow suit. I shove mine down over my mouth, then lift it away from my lips, wincing at the faint taste of rubber and lead.

"What's with the masks?" I ask Jayce.

"They're like the tarps. Blackout material," she explains, her voice muffled by the thick fabric. "They make it harder for an Unseen spying from the other side to tell us apart," she explains.

"Why don't we wait for the gray?" I ask as we pick our way down the face of the dune.

Jayce peels her own mask up and leans in to my ear, her voice low. "Reese wouldn't bring us out here unless it was a matter of life and death. Maris hid Reese when she first left Asher. She saved her life. I'm not sure we'd be on this beach risking our lives for anybody else."

Realization slows my feet. Jayce tugs me along. How could I have thought I was the only one with someone I care about on the line? Asher would use any of our loved ones against us.

"There," Reese snarls, and points to a luminous object a couple hundred yards away. She starts to jog and we follow suit, making our way down the empty beach.

A vertical dune guards our left. The black sea roars on our right, making it nearly impossible to listen for anyone pursuing us.

Closer up, the glowing object takes on a rectangular shape. A box. *Or a coffin*, I think. It's large enough to fit a person inside.

Little beams of light shoot through rows of holes drilled into its panels. Waves roll over it, flushing water in and out of the pinholes, threatening to carry the whole box away with the tide.

"What is that?" Jayce asks. "And where is Maris?"

"Hope said she's inside," Reese answers, and breaks into a sprint.

The dune falls away as we pass onto the open beach. Paranoia raises the hair on the back of my neck as I am consumed by the chilling sensation of utter exposure. The others must feel it too. But we keep on anyway.

Reese reaches the box.

I draw my mother's knife, ready for whatever might materialize from the Unseen side. My pulse thrums against my palms, vibrating the blade. *Wound, don't kill,* I command myself, repeating the instruction even as my knuckles blanch white around the hilt. *Don't kill, don't kill.* But my muscles are quivering, my blood gaining heat and swirling through my veins.

"Tanzy, help Reese," Shaila barks, snapping the focus from my gaze. "I'll stand guard." She reaches out to me, palm open and beckoning. "Give me the knife."

"I'll be careful." My voice shakes with the flood of adrenaline.

"If it comes down to it, you don't need a weapon to kill. At least with your bare hands it'll take longer. You'll have time to reconsider."

I think of Dr. Andrews and swallow. Shaila meets my gaze and stretches her hand a little closer. My blood protests, hissing like steam, searing my veins as I hand her the knife.

"Maris! Can you hear me? Tell me what to do," Reese calls into the box. I step closer and peek through one of the holes. Maris is strung up by her arms with silver wire, her head slumped between her shoulders. Her skin is the color of ash, and has more cracks in it than I can count. Light beams from the fissures, setting her slumbering face aglow. Her dress falls away from her gaunt frame in tatters.

My gaze drops to her ankles, and I jolt, squinting against the glow. Her feet are gone. Vanished.

"Reese! Her legs!" I cry, and watch in horror as a wave rolls into the box, splashing Maris. She throws her head back, shrieking. Her pale-blue eyes roll in their sockets as pieces of her fall away, dissolving into water and sand. "What's happening? Why won't she phase?"

"She's bound to her physical form by Caro wire." Reese points to the silver ropes binding Maris inside the cell. "She can't phase completely, can't pass through the veil, can't *escape.*" She screams against a battering of wind, desperation spearing over her face.

I start to squeeze my forefinger through one of the pinholes. Reese snatches my wrist and thrusts me away.

I stumble over the sand and gape at her.

"The only person who can cut Caro wire is the one who sets it," she cries. "It's explosive. Human contact will detonate it." She makes a fist and smashes it against the panels. The box doesn't budge.

"What will happen if we can't get to her?" I ask, searching the inside of the box for any weaknesses.

"Elemental Unseens like Maris must return to their elemental forms once a day to survive on our side of the veil. They must be fully immersed in their specific element to return to it. She's obviously been kept from water far too long. She's entered survival mode, dissolving whenever and wherever the water touches her."

"What if she dissolves completely?" Jayce calls from behind us. "Will she be okay then?"

Reese shakes her head. "Not like this. Her pieces will be too diluted, too scattered. She might never reassemble."

"What if we can get the box into deeper water?" I ask, judging the distance.

Reese knits her brow, seeing what I see—the tide is low, the waves shallow around our feet, the box impossibly heavy.

"It's a long shot," she says. "But . . . she'd stand a fighting chance. We have to try. This way."

She rounds to the backside of the box. We line up on either side of her. Reese counts to three, and we throw ourselves against the panel. The box doesn't move. We go again, and again. My shoulder throbs from constant impact, muscle against metal, to no avail. The glow inside the box begins to fade.

I root my feet to the sand. "We're going about this the wrong way," I say, frustration billowing in my chest.

"And what would you propose we do?" Reese snaps. "I'm open to suggestions. Anyone?" She hisses against the frenzied breeze, all but baring her teeth at us.

"Give me a second." I step back. The black horse's blood, his instincts and strengths, are mine now. How can I use them? How would a horse break free?

A horse would pull. I've seen a tied horse pull free from the barn wall, taking a four-foot section of siding with it.

"I have an idea. Do we have any rope in the pack?" I ask.

"We should." Shaila slings her bag to the ground and retrieves a coiled length.

"Run the rope through the holes on either side of me, below my shoulders," I say. I back up to the front of the box. Reese and Jayce thread the rope while Shaila returns to her post. Once the ends are through, I tie them in front of my chest and test the strength of the rope.

"Okay, everyone slide under with me. On my mark, pull slow and steady, and don't you dare quit."

I give them a few seconds to position, then dig the balls of my feet into the sand.

I let out a yell as I throw my full weight against the rope. My body resists, shoulders straining against their sockets. The wind pummels me, snatching away my shouts of encouragement, my swears. It lashes my hair against my eyes.

Jayce is directly behind me, her breath hot on my neck, her grunts and groans growling against my ears. Slowly, the metal cage grinds an inch across the beach. Then another. I crouch deeper, working my hands under the rope, and drag the box to deeper surf.

A wave smashes into us, sending a plume of water into Maris's cage. I grit my teeth, expecting a wail of pain. Maris is silent, a far worse response. *Dig, Tanzy. Dig.*

Fear and rage climb my raw throat in a single roar. I summon every ounce of strength and lunge forward. The box jumps behind me. We use the momentum and run into the rope. The ocean floor drops off, and the water rises to my waist. I throw myself against the rope once more, and the cage slides down the submerged bank.

Water swirls around us, sloshing against our shoulders and plastering the box firmly in place.

"We have to tip it over!" I shout, and slip out from beneath the rope.

Jayce, Reese, and I scale the front of the box. I glance quickly at Shaila, who stands guard on the beach, my mother's knife gleaming in her hand.

Help us, Mom. Please help us, I beg. A new flood of strength rolls through me as I curve my fingers through the holes in the top of the box, careful not to graze the Caro wire inside.

"Now!" Reese shouts, and we heave ourselves backward. The cage sways, and gravity claims its weight. We throw ourselves to the side as it crashes into the surf. I thrust my face against the panels and see Maris inside, her chin hovering just above the sudden influx of seawater. Her skin is dry and granular, becoming sand.

A wave crashes over us, blurring my vision with salt and scattering us apart. We rush back to Maris's cage and peer through the little holes. The cage is dark and empty.

"Where is she? Where is her light?" Jayce throws her panicked gaze over the waves, but there's nothing. No flash of light, no gaping vortex. No Maris. Just a black, rollicking tide and an unsympathetic sea.

A sudden movement on the beach snatches my attention. Shaila is watching us from the shore, her shoulders slack, my knife dangling at her side. She doesn't see the crackling darkness that has materialized behind her.

I shout, waving her toward the water. She backs up instead, drawing her knife to her front. She thinks something is out here with us.

I race inland. I feel so slow, the water resisting every step. Shaila is almost close enough to touch when the form becomes solid and thrusts something into Shaila's back. She arches away, her hands snapping open, and my mother's knife drops to the beach. A blow from behind forces me to the wet sand. Reese lands on her knees in front of me. She struggles out of the sand and lurches ahead. I hear the dull thud of flesh on flesh as she makes contact.

The smell of blood fills my nose. I throw myself over Shaila's limp body. Her face is slack. A dark pool blooms around her, staining the beach.

"You!" The voice is unfamiliar and seething. It smacks me to attention. I spring to my feet, retrieving my knife from the sand, and stand guard over Shaila.

"She was supposed to be you," an Unseen hisses, female and charcoal gray. She points at Shaila with the dripping end of a silver staff.

My fist throttles the hilt of the knife. Worry belts along the edges of my mind. Where are Reese and Jayce? Have they been hurt, too? Are we outnumbered?

I can't see Reese, but I can smell her. Jayce appears in the darkness behind our assailant, easing across the sand. Prowling upon us like a cat. She must have run past her and circled back. Her light eyes glow against the dark, and her lips draw back. She nestles into her haunches and slingshots forward, airborne in an instant.

The Unseen twitches, narrowing her eyes at the awe beaming across my face. She drops a shoulder and lowers her staff for the next strike. Before she can shift her momentum, Reese explodes from the darkness and sinks her claws into the Unseen's hip. Jayce lands on her back, ripping the hair from her scalp with her talons.

The Unseen collapses to the beach, taking Jayce and Reese with her.

She kicks out, slapping and pulling at Jayce, who clutches her throat between her teeth. Between her fangs.

A blade glitters in Reese hand. She draws back and jams it swiftly into the Unseen's spine. The blade disappears, fully absorbed by gray flesh, and the Unseen goes limp.

I drop down next to Shaila and cradle her head in my lap. Her body is heavy, her limbs tumbling to either side.

"Shaila?" I place a hand over her heart. Her chest is still.

My chin quivers.

"I need Tenix!" I shout. I wrench my gaze in the direction of our house, where Maris's vial of purified Tenix is still sandwiched between my mattresses. The Tenix I was sure would be for Lucas . . .

Reese jogs to my side. "Unseens don't leave behind Tenix when they die," she says, panting. Her breath catches, and I feel her stiffen beside me.

Jayce kneels at my side. "Oh my God," she whispers. She clutches Shaila's wrist, then shoves two fingers against her throat, checking for a pulse. She tears her hands away and claps them over her mouth, sinking back onto her thighs. I look up at her, the order to run to the house and bring back the Tenix swells on my tongue, but I can't shove it out.

I brush the hair from Shaila's face, and force my gaze to the Unseen, glaring as it tenses and pales in the distance. Cracks spread across its surface. It begins to dissolve, crumbling away. Within seconds, there is nothing left of it but a rise of charcoal colored sand.

"Who sent it?" I ask, tightening my fingers around a lock of Shaila's hair.

"She was a Taigo." Reese sighs. "They're a faction of Unseen creatures who want the veil to remain intact."

"Like you," I growl.

"I want to *hide* you, Tanzy. I want to keep you safe. The Taigo believe it would be better to kill you and dispose of your body before Asher can burn your remains. They've put a bounty on your head."

"Why didn't you tell me?" I swipe at the tears running down my cheeks. "Shaila's dead because that *monster* thought she was me!"

Reese winces away from me. "I thought our location was secure," she says. "Shaila's death is on my hands, not yours." Her voice breaks.

"I have Tenix. In the house. Maris gave it to me," I whisper. "We can save her."

"She's already gone, Tanzy," Reese murmurs through her tears as she strokes Shaila's face. "Tenix might bring her back for an hour or two, but we would need more to keep her living and breathing. She's free now." A sob escapes her, and she inhales to steady herself. "Let's lay her to rest."

Reese scoops Shaila's legs into her arms. I cradle her head and shoulders and slowly rise, not wanting to jostle her. Jayce stands between us, supporting Shaila's middle. Tears shine on her cheeks, and air rushes through her clenched teeth.

Reese guides us back into the sea. We walk out as far as we can stand, and then begin to swim, towing her between us as smoothly as we can manage.

We take Shaila beyond the sandbar, then step off the sand shelf. The temperature drops, signaling deep water. The frigid chill makes my teeth chatter. It sends goosebumps plowing over my skin, but the affect goes no deeper. Everything within me is ablaze.

Shaila's complexion has become ashen as bone. Her hair cascades around her, fluttering as if in a breeze.

"May you find peace, my sister," Reese murmurs. "May your soul never return for Asher's purpose."

Jayce repeats her words, her voice clotted by sobs.

I say nothing. A flurry of ice combs back my hair, flecking my face with salt and seawater. I tip my gaze to the sky, wondering if my mother is with us. There's no way to tell. Shafts of wind tear in every direction, shredding the clouds, blotting out the stars.

Shaila's body becomes heavy as we cling to her, our hands trembling violently against the bone-rattling cold.

I feel Reese's eyes on me. Hear Jayce sniffling. But neither of them utters a word.

Shaila's chest heaves, rocked by the waves. The wind howls, a mournful lullaby.

"It should have been me," I whisper. "I'm sorry."

I glance at Reese, who shakes her head tightly. Jayce tilts her brow to my shoulder.

My breath shudders.

"Good-bye Shaila," I say.

And we let her go.

DARK

Jayce and I lay in our beds and stare at the ceiling. Our room is blanketed by the inky shadows of night. Every now and then, lightning spears the dark and brightens our tightly drawn curtains.

Rain thumps the walls. Thunder stampedes through the sky. The wind screams across the beach and rattles the shingles overhead, but the space between us is thick with silence.

Jayce shoves her blankets aside. Her mattress creaks beneath her as she tiptoes to my bed. I push up and slide over, patting the empty space, and she crumples in beside me.

"My mom thinks I'm dead," she whimpers. "I think about her all the time. How much pain she must be in." She curls into a ball, spine arcing against my stomach. I strap my arm around her.

She pauses to gather herself.

"I'd just come home from the hospital after, well, you can guess. That night, someone set our house on fire. Reese grabbed me before the firefighters came. I fought against her. She knocked me out cold, and took me."

Her body quivers, a sob wracking through her chest. "Tomorrow is the first anniversary of my death," she says. "Shaila is dead, *really* dead, and all I can think about is my mom. How much will she hurt tomorrow?"

"Honestly?" I ask.

She nods.

I roll onto my back. I can't look at her and be honest at the same time. "She'll probably have trouble catching her breath most of the day. She'll look at your pictures, and then hide them. She'll want to think about you every minute. She'll wish she could think about anything else. She'll visit you somewhere. She might take flowers. She'll probably pick all the petals off before she leaves. She won't mean to. It just happens."

My mind drifts to the day my mother sat in her wildflower garden and picked every petal within reach.

Jayce scoots closer, resting her head on my shoulder. "They had a memorial for me," she says. "She'll probably go there. Sit and talk to my plaque. Pretend I'm listening. It's not me. It's just a stupid piece of rock with my name carved into it." She shakes her head. "My dad was an Unseen," she says. "My mom never knew. He walked out on us. At least, that's what she always thought. Reese thinks something else happened to him. So do I, but it doesn't matter. She's all alone, Tanzy. I can't let her go through to-morrow *all alone*. Even if . . . even if she's safer this way. Safer without me." She exhales. "She's *safer* without me," she murmurs. I wonder how many lonesome nights she's spent repeating those words to herself. "Asher can't use us against each other if one of us is dead."

My skin burns at the mention of Asher. I slip my arm under Jayce's neck and tug her to my side, pinning our bodies together. "Maybe one day, when this is over, you can go back to her," I say.

"Will this ever be over?"

Sooner than you think. My heart surges at the idea of sealing the veil, at the vision of Asher's face twisted with rage and defeat. I may imprison every Unseen, but I will be setting every candidate free.

We wait out the darkness. The hours crawl by, and the silence between us resumes.

Jayce begins to snore softly. She calls for her mother, swallowing sobs as she dreams. Her tears dampen the pillow we share, but I don't shuffle away. I stay beside her, cheek to cheek, unable to sleep.

The storm lets up. Swiftly, its drizzling remnants are inhaled by the sky. Gray sneaks through our window. I glance down at Jayce, sure she'll want to take a walk this morning. Her eyes are closed, her lips parted. She looks peaceful.

I ease out of the crook of her arm, slide a pillow under her head, and slip from the room.

I'm not surprised to find Reese awake, leaning against the breakfast bar with a coffee mug between her hands.

"Any sign of Maris?" I ask.

"No." She sets the mug down and rubs her face.

I turn away and stare at the charcoal sea, the foam that collects in tufts along the shore. Somewhere out there, Shaila's body rests upon a soft bed of seaweed and sand. A watery grave, like my father's.

I slide into the seat beside Reese. "Last night didn't go the way I expected it to," I say.

"War is never what we think it's going to be. In the movies, the good guys always win. Sacrifices seem . . . worth it. The credits roll." She sighs. In this moment, she seems so much older than me.

"I know life isn't like the movies," I mutter. "I just hoped that . . ." *That what*? I wonder. That we'd rescue Maris? Save the day? That we'd all make it back to the safe house alive? It seems so naïve in retrospect. Childish.

My cheeks glow hot.

Reese blows the steam from her mug and gazes ahead of her, staring at nothing.

"Guard your hope, Tanzy," she says. "It's the easiest and most devastating thing to lose."

"But Shaila . . ."

"Is at peace," she interjects. "She can rest. This war is over for her."

I flinch. Is death the best we can hope for?

"Thank you," Reese says suddenly, dipping her yellow eyes to her cup.

I lift my brow, uncertain what she could possibly be thanking me for.

"You gave Maris and Shaila everything you had last night. Everything." Her voice is low and resolute. "When we find Lucas, I promise I'll return the favor."

I nod absently. Trudging home last night, my hands slick with Shaila's blood, my clothes sopping wet, I caught myself wondering if Lucas was already gone. For a second, I was relieved. He could rest. I could stop worrying about him. I could focus on protecting the other candidates.

I tip my brow into my hands, ashamed.

"Do you think Asher was watching us?" I whisper. "Do you think we should move?"

Reese shakes her head. "Not yet. Whoever strung Maris up in that box intended for her to suffer and die. Drawing us out was an afterthought. They would have attacked the house by now if they'd known we were here." She drops her voice. "What happened last night . . . I don't think Asher was behind it. I think it was . . . something else."

"The bounty."

She lifts her mug but doesn't sip.

"We can't just sit here and do nothing," I say.

"We're staying put. Strengthening our barriers and ourselves. That's not 'nothing.'"

I roll my eyes. "I don't mean to sound grim, but there are seven of us. If we're really facing a war, we're as good as dead."

"At last count, there were over two hundred living candidates," Reese replies.

I swivel back in her direction, my face a question mark.

"This is not the only safe house," she admits on a sigh. "This was the closest one to your last location. It's also the smallest, the most fortified, and the hardest to find. We limit this kind of useful information to the heads of the safe houses to keep everyone else as safe as possible. The more you know, the more Asher or the Taigo can use against you."

Pieces of recent conversations snap into place. The Taigo have gray skin. Someone with substantial power infiltrated my tour through Spera's memories, posing as my guide. Asher's advisor, Raffin, was steel gray from head to toe.

"You thought my guide was a Taigo, didn't you?" I ask.

"Either she is or she was," Reese concedes. "There's a hierarchy in the Taigo, and those with metaphysical abilities are at the top. Incarnation guides are renowned for those kinds of powers. Something tells me your guide and Raffin were both in the Taigo at some point, and your guide broke loyalties. The question is a matter of when. If we can figure out why your guide revealed your new identity to Asher, we'll have a better idea of whose orders she was following. I have a couple of contacts I can work for more information. Until then," she raises an eyebrow.

"It stays between you and me," I finish her sentence.

Jayce appears in the mouth of the hallway. Her face is puffy and her eyes are red. She glances dully at us. Then she crosses to the window and touches the glass with the tips of her fingers. A shiver passes through her, and I wonder whether she's thinking about Shaila or her mother.

The others file in soon after, wandering around the room as if they're somewhere they've never been before. Reese waits for them to settle, lifting her mug and replacing it, letting her coffee go cold.

"As I told each of you last night, we lost Shaila during the rescue attempt. We'll have a ceremony for her at sundown. As for today, I'd like to hold an informal class, then run drills in the gym. Nothing is required. Please mourn in the way you see fit. We'll resume our regular schedule tomorrow."

Abby raises her hand. "I'd like to continue research, if it's all the same to you," she says. Reese nods, and Abby excuses herself from the group.

The room falls quiet. Reese folds her hands in her lap, twisting her fingers together. "If you have questions, now is the time to ask them," she says.

Megan wants details about the attack. Reese recounts the ambush. I fight the urge to clamp my hands over my ears.

Claire asks about the Taigo. I straighten at that. Asher wants to enslave me for eternity. The Taigo want me dead. It's hard to know which is the bigger threat.

"The Taigo are made up of all kinds of Unseen creatures—elementals, mystics, common Unseens. Guards who deserted Asher and somehow managed to survive. When they cross to this side, they're always dark gray in color. They're smart, reckless, and passionate. They don't fear death."

"I faced a Taigo," I say in a rush, forcing my gaze from my knees. "At least I think . . . I think the first creature I killed was a Taigo. But he wasn't after me. He was after something Vanessa had."

"That doesn't surprise me. He may not have known your face on sight. The Taigo are as interested in spiting Asher as they are preventing any change in the veil, and now that we know Vanessa is acting as Asher's right hand, she would be a likely target. If war truly begins, they should not be discounted."

"How can they really wage war behind the veil?" I ask. "Only Asher can take a life on the Unseen side."

"Yes, but anyone can suffer." Reese blinks, pressing her lashes shut for a second too long. "And Unseens can force one another across the veil. Once on *this* side, anyone can die."

In my head, Reese's explanation paints a picture of utter chaos. The Unseen world would buckle at the knees should a civil war break out.

All the more reason to seal the veil.

I quickly derail the thought, worried it will reveal itself on my face. Once every question has been answered, we change clothing and assemble in the training room. Reese drills us on flexibility and defense, no doubt in response to Shaila's death.

I do my best to stay focused and motivated, but the previous night repeats in my head. Shaila didn't stand a chance against the Taigo that attacked us. There was no warning, nothing to defend. A shadow materialized in the black, silent and quick. She never saw it coming. None of us could have seen it coming.

Discouraged, I step out of rotation, briefly stretch, and gesture to Reese that I'm heading upstairs. She acknowledges my departure, the same frustration heavy on her brow.

I take a quick shower and slip on fresh clothes. Then I arrange myself on the bed, my back guarded by the corner and my mother's knife within easy reach. Once I'm settled, I draw in a breath, hold it, and count the beats as I exhale.

My mind quiets, and I start to read.

I've been speaking with other Unseens—my brethren, masking themselves on this side of the veil. They say the Tribe of Five is not a myth. It exists! I could track it down, but only if its members want to be found.

I've been given a lead, and a warning. The favor I seek will come at a high price. Whatever it is, I will pay it. The Tribe is my only hope of protecting you, Tanzy. Cost doesn't scare me. There's nothing I wouldn't pay to keep you safe.

I can practically feel the hope in my mother's entry. The Tribe of Five must have changed her back into an Unseen and demanded she sever her connection to me.

I slap the journal shut and beeline for Abby.

"Hey Abby. Any progress?" I ask.

"Not yet, but I'm switching search tactics. I have a good feeling about this." Her spine is arced over her keyboard. She works her lower lip between her teeth.

I pull up a chair. "Do you have any information on the Tribe of Five? My mother mentioned them in one of her journals."

She eases away from her laptop and stretches her arms behind her head.

"It's a group of five elemental Unseens," she says.

"Like my mom."

142

"Sort of. Each member represents the purest form of an element." She counts them on her fingers. "Air, fire, water, earth, and Tenix."

"Tenix is considered an element?"

Abby nods. "I've heard pure Tenix is like bottled lightning. It's as essential to life as the other four. At least on our side of the veil."

"What side of the veil is the Tribe of Five on?"

"Both. From what Reese says, you can't find them unless—"

"Unless they want to be found." My mother's journal entry echoes back to me.

Abby hums her agreement. "It's the only way they can protect themselves. When all five members come together, their power is complete. There's not much they can't do or undo. There are plenty of Unseens who would abuse that kind of power if they were able to control it."

"Like Asher," I muse.

"Exactly. We had a lecture on the Tribe months ago." She drums her thumb against the notebook tucked into her lap, its pages black with hastily scribbled script. "Asher captured them once. They either escaped, or were freed. Nobody knows how they got away." She frowns, as if the mystery irks her. Then she shakes her frustration away.

"The Tribe returned my mother to her elemental self," I say. "They forced her to renounce me."

Abby's face softens. "For an Unseen to become human in the first place is an epic violation," she says. "Shifting *back* into an Unseen . . . it goes against the laws of balance. The favor was steep, and so was the price."

"I could go my whole life and not hear the word *balance* again," I groan.

Abby shrugs. The gesture is slight and somehow, commiserating. "It's the universal law," she explains. "Sun and moon. Dark and light. Air and earth. Fire and water."

"What balances Tenix?"

"People have theories," she starts. "Mine is that Seen and Unseen creatures are the flip side. Tenix gives. We take."

I consider this, frowning as my head begins to ache.

"Thanks, Abby," I say.

"Sure!" she chirps. She plucks a pencil out of her bun, threads it between her teeth, and returns to clacking on the keys of her computer.

I go back to my room. Jayce arrives a few minutes later, fresh beads of sweat collecting on her forehead and a glass of water in her hands. She steps to her open closet and thumbs through the hangers.

"Aren't you coming to the ceremony?" she asks.

"I don't have anything to wear," I mumble, recalling the stack of barn clothes in my trunk. I won't go to Shaila's memorial in jeans and a T-shirt. It doesn't feel right.

"You can borrow something of mine, if you want to go," Jayce offers.

"Of course I want to go," I whisper.

"Here." Jayce fans through her wardrobe and withdraws a simple, white dress. Its sleeves are long and cuffed at the wrist. She holds it against me, and its hem skirts the floor. "White is your color."

She retrieves a turquoise dress for herself. "I'm going to take a shower. The ceremony starts in forty-five minutes. We'll say good-bye together."

She reaches out to touch my hand before she leaves.

I slip on the dress and study my reflection in Jayce's floor-length mirror. My face is gaunt and hollow, and my hair is tied back in a knot. I pull it free and let it fall over my shoulders, working through the tangles with my fingers.

When Jayce returns, I'm yanking at an impossible knot and swearing at my reflection.

"Whoa," Jayce says. "You kiss your mother with that mouth?"

I glare at her. She smirks.

"What's wrong?" she asks.

"I can't make it right."

"Here." She retrieves a hairbrush from her dresser and plucks a few bobby pins off her bedside table. She situates herself behind me and gently twists my hair into two long braids, fastening them together behind my back.

I relax the moment I see her handiwork. If Shaila is watching somehow, she'll see I tried.

We gather in the kitchen. Reese hands us each a piece of parchment. "For anything left unsaid," she explains.

I strangle my pen as I try to find words for the guilt and malice boiling inside me. At last I write down one sentence: *No one else will die in my place.*

Reese picks up a small, cedar box from the counter and leads us down the stairs.

I stiffen the moment we step into the open. The beach is bright and sprawling. Last night, its white sands were stained red. A battleground.

Jayce shifts her eyes skyward. "Hope will hide us," she says. "Reese won't keep us out here long."

I nod. I know she's right, but I can't help wishing I'd brought my knife along.

We walk in a single-file line to the water's edge and fan out in a semi-circle around Reese, who kneels on the ground. She pulls a little bottle of oil from her pocket and methodically covers every inch of the wooden box. Once she's finished with the outside, she lifts the lid and coats the interior.

Megan steps forward and places a picture of Shaila into the box. One by one, the other girls approach and set their notes inside. I save my message for last, pinching it between my fingers, trembling as I relinquish it.

This is a promise I will keep.

We follow Reese to the edge of the sea. She strikes a match, and sets the oiled cedar aflame.

We stand elbow to elbow, and send the burning memorial to the horizon in deafening silence.

Shaila is gone. Her battle is done.

But we are still here.

Together.

Smoke Rises
Before the Flames

Three days pass.

The rain pours, dark and unrelenting.

Morning phases fluidly to evening, like Maris phasing into the river. Like my mother's lithe body vanishing into the breeze.

We sleep, we rise. We read, we sleep. We gain no ground.

The beach just beyond our little brown house becomes a swamp. The storm makes the roads impassable. The thrashing wind beckons the tide and sends a violent surf slicing high across the sand.

We're trapped here, I realize. Dry and warm. Shackled together as we wait out the storm. Becoming restless. We tap our feet and drum our fingernails over our knees. We pace and pummel punching bags and barely eat.

The schedule drives me to madness. I am a hamster on a wheel. Round and round I go, pushing and racing, and ending each day exactly where I started. We cannot keep pushing the same way and expect new results. Isn't that the very definition of insanity?

We're guessing . . . Googling, for Pete's sake, about a prophecy that began at the dawn of time. We aren't going to stumble upon answers by luck and keystrokes. We need information as old as the prophecy itself. And I know of one place to find it inside these walls.

On the fourth day, I slip out of rotation, feigning fatigue. Jayce gapes, and Reese raises a brow, but neither one of them stops me.

I open the bathroom door and, without stepping inside, snick it shut again, in case anyone is listening. Then I proceed lightly through the hall and sneak into Reese's room.

I hunker down in front of her bookcase and fan through her ancient texts. My hand flutters absently over my father's tags as I scan through page after brittle, yellow page of legend and elemental theory.

I come to a chapter on weaponry and pause. Perhaps the silver staff is here, or my mother's knife with its gleaming, stone hilt.

I hover my eyes over a sketch of a spiraling disc, the *Solvo medallion*. When aimed properly, it can absorb an Unseen, trapping it inside.

I lower my nose to the page, furrowing my brow. A weapon that can be used *against* an Unseen? Against Asher? Why haven't we been searching for this?

I scan the medallion's lengthy description, committing three stipulations to memory:

The Solvo chant must be spoken three times without error to begin the absorption. There's no record of it. According to the text, the chant will lose all potency if it's ever written down. The disc can hold one Unseen at a time, and there's one Solvo medallion.

One.

Even if I manage to track it down, I'll have to find someone who can recite the Solvo chant and convince them to teach it to me. I'll have to come within snaring distance of Asher, close enough to point the medallion's spiraled face in his direction.

My shoulders sag. I stroke Spera's horseshoe charm between my forefinger and thumb and recall the moment Lucas gave it to me. The graze of his skin as he pressed it into my hands. "*Wear this,*" he said. "*If you need me, I'll know. I'll be able to find you.*"

I knit my brow, and thread my fingers over the chain. Lucas told me if I wore Spera's necklace, he'd always be able to find me. Is it possible her necklace could help me find *him*?

I thrust the book I've been reading back onto the shelf and dash my hands over wilted, leather spines, brow pressed low, searching . . .

"Is this what you're after?"

Panic seizes my heart, and my eyes leap to the door. Reese is leaning against the frame, her gym clothes soaked with sweat. She extends the book of portals to me.

Warily, I rise and take it from her.

"You could've just asked for it, you know." She folds her arms as I flip feverishly through the pages. "What are you looking for?"

"A portal instrument that can help me locate Lucas."

She sighs, and reaches over me, turning to an earmarked page. "I thought of that already," she says.

My eyes scan the various sketches of locator jewelry. Each description is essentially the same. They only work one way. If Lucas can find *me*, I can't find him. I slap the book shut and dig my fingernails into the binding.

"Easy." Reese peels the book from my grip. "These texts are delicate. They might as well belong in a museum." She tilts her gaze to my collar. "Lucas gave you something."

I frown, and stifle the urge to clutch the horseshoe dangling around my neck. If Reese finds out where it came from, *who* it came from, she might take it from me.

"Relax." She holds up a hand as if in surrender. "I know about the necklace."

"Jayce."

She nods. "There's something you should know. Something I've held off telling you. I'm not altogether certain I'm right." She hesitates, and temples her fingers against her chest. She's breaking her rule, I realize. Urgency wafts away from her. I can smell it, bitter and overripe.

"I think the Tribe of Five sent an impostor to pose as your guide. Someone wanted you to touch Spera, to reveal yourself to Asher. Someone who cares about you. Someone willing to pay a high price to ensure that you would return."

She pauses, as if waiting for the impact to dawn on me. I crease my brow, struggling to understand.

"It was Lucas."

I blink. My pulse stutters. I shake my head and retreat a step, my eyes going to slits.

"He arranged for the infiltration. The more I puzzle over it, the more the pieces slip into place. Your whole life, he's been guarding you, watching from the shadows. How could he have known who you were, unless—"

"Unless he saw me, too." The words tumble out of my mouth on a rasp.

"Asher's not the only one who saw my resurrected face."

"It makes sense," Reese says. "It's the only thing that makes sense. He wanted to make sure he could recognize you, protect you, even if it meant stalling Spera's reincarnation."

My pulse stops altogether. The void between beats is gaping and deep.

"No," I say.

"No?"

"It *doesn't* make sense. Lucas didn't want me to see my Origin at all. He warned me that it would be dangerous. He tried to stop me."

"You may be strong, Tanzy, but if Lucas had wanted to stop you, he would have. At the very least, he would've put up a good fight. Did he?"

I shake my head, remembering.

"Unseens enjoy their little games. And they're very good at them. Maybe he was trying to trick you."

Paranoia rakes over my skin. It enters my eyes, and in a flash I am my mother, staring warily through our kitchen window at the rising dawn. Wondering, I realize with a jolt, if someone is there, just beyond the veil, staring *back*.

"You're wrong," I whisper. "You said it yourself—Lucas is one of us. He vowed to protect Spera. He's on our side."

"Maybe," Reese allows.

"You promised you'd help him"

"I know what I promised."

"Will you take it back?" I force the question over my lips. Without Reese's help, my chances of saving Lucas are slim.

Reese doesn't respond. She presses the book of portals back into my hands. I clutch it to my chest as if it could anchor me, but I feel myself drifting away, swept into the undertow by shock, sputtering and spiraling.

"I think I found something!" a voice shouts out from the common area. Abby's voice. *Lucas.* I sprint down the short hall and burst into the living room. Abby is bashing her forefinger against her screen.

"Abby." Reese calls her name like a warning, but I've huddled over her shoulder already. The other candidates press around us. "What did you find?"

"I found a pattern in the county records. Someone's been buying up land in Carova for the last year. Whoever it is currently owns this entire end of the island, right up to the Virginia state line." She scrolls through page after page of tiny print, reciting figures as they appear to her. "They're paying double the estimated property value, so they're paying cash. No bank would agree to a loan for more than the property is worth."

Jayce slides off her stool and studies the screen. "Is there a name?" she asks.

"That's the thing. There's a name, but I don't think it's real." Abby points to the left-hand column. *Promes Cae.*

"It sounds Latin," Claire decides.

Iris grabs a book from the shelf and rips through the pages.

"Do you think the first word means 'promise'?" Megan chimes in.

Their questions fade as I stare at the screen. Jayce runs her fingers across the letters, and rocks back on her heels.

"It's an anagram," she whispers. "I know what it means." Her wide eyes pan from the computer to me. "*Come Spera.*"

Mine to Lose

Reese tips the laptop shut. She crosses the room and folds herself into her usual chair.

Jayce slides back onto her barstool. Abby tucks her pencil behind her ear.

I ease onto the wicker couch, and Iris ducks in beside me. Our murmurs cease, and we all stare expectantly at Reese.

Without a word, she's taken command of the room. But she says nothing. Her mouth twists with a sullen reluctance, and her promise bleats back to me.

She doesn't want to go after Lucas.

A ribbon of fury snakes through my middle. Reese's low voice renders it still.

"We'll send a team to search the property," she says. "If Lucas is out there, we'll do our best to bring him home."

The other girls nod.

"In light of this week's events, I will bring only those who choose to come. There's no shame in staying home. No one will hold it against you. I'll go, and Tanzy will go. We'll need one more."

She lifts her chin and passes her gaze over each of us, eyes finally falling to me.

"Do we have any volunteers?" she asks.

I don't blink. I don't breathe. The room shuffles around me. One by one, every girl raises her hand.

Reese straightens, pride billowing away from her in sheets. "Abby," she decides. "You grew up in Carova. You're familiar with the island."

Abby beams.

My eyes dart to Jayce. She catches my gaze and winks.

Megan fetches three packs from the hall closet and distributes them. I unzip mine and rifle through its contents: an empty canteen, matches, two flares, a tightly coiled blanket, a length of rope.

"We leave at four a.m.," Reese says. "I'll wake you. Get some sleep while you can. Wear something dark. No masks." Her jaw clenches. "Dismissed."

The other girls pile out of the room, patting my shoulder as they pass, or squeezing my arm. Murmuring good-byes. Things happened much more quickly when we set after Maris—a frenzy of activity, a blurred jog onto the beach.

I think of Shaila, her head nestled in my lap, her face pale and serene. I was *with* her, and even I was too late to say good-bye.

Jayce scoots in beside me.

"Come with us," I say.

"Reese has another assignment for me. Save your puppy-dog eyes." She shoves her shoulder against mine. "Think of it this way. I'll be safe and sound, ready to swoop in and save your ass when you do something stupid."

"When? Not *if*?" I ask.

She gives me a pointed look. "When, not if," she replies. Her mouth twitches, then breaks wide. It's the first time I've seen her smile in days, and it's contagious.

I grin. Jayce giggles. And then, suddenly, we're both laughing.

We crumple together, fat tears dragging over our cheeks, delirium rolling through our bones. We clamp our hands over our mouths to muffle the sound. Jayce snorts, and howls through her fingers.

My mind crowds with all the reasons I should feel angry, or sad, or afraid.

Something cracks behind my sternum. Happiness flushes through my veins. I haven't felt this good in weeks, in months even. For a few minutes, at least, all the ugliness inside me tumbles away.

WE EXIT THE LIVING ROOM, elbows linked. Reese is standing at the end of the hall. She motions for Jayce, who slips after her. Leaving me alone.

My smile flattens, dread returning to me. I hear Reese's lock click into place.

I go into my bedroom and stand at the center, hands on my hips, wondering what I should pack. I pass my hand over the journals stacked on my nightstand. My mother's last words.

I fan through the pages, then withdraw my fingers. There's no reason to bring them along. They're added weight, and anyway, I have a feeling she'll be with me. My guardian in the breeze.

Her knife glints up at me from the tray inside the trunk. I reach for it, fingers close enough to cast a film of vapor on the blade. My eyes catch on a brown-red crust that fills in the grooves on the handle. I snatch my hand away, remembering the way blood bloomed around Shaila's head when she fell to the cold, hard beach. Her blood is here on my mother's knife, and her warning is in my ear: *If it comes down to it, you don't need a weapon to kill. At least with your bare hands it'll take longer. You'll have time to reconsider.* I will not put another housemate in the same situation, where they have to coax this weapon from my hands, where their blood may stain the hilt alongside Shaila's. I leave the dagger where it rests and close the lid to my trunk.

Jayce swings through the door. "You packed yet?" she asks.

"Not at all."

She kneels by my trunk and sifts through my clothes. She flaps the wrinkles out of one of my T-shirts and holds it against her chest, wrinkling her nose. "Do they not have malls where you come from?" she asks. "Never mind." She shoves the shirt back into my trunk without refolding it. "You can borrow something of mine"

She crosses to her closet and starts to drape hangers over her arm. Dark, fitted layers.

I sit on the edge of my bed and fold my knees against my chest.

"What did Reese want?" I ask.

"She gave me a letter that I'm *only* supposed to read if you guys don't make it back alive."

I raise a brow. Jayce tugs a long, white envelope out of her pocket and slaps it against her palm. The seal is intact.

"You hate secrets," I say.

"It's a cruel, cruel world," she replies, and shoves the envelope back into her jeans. "This is one secret I can leave alone, as long as it means the three of you come home. So don't get killed, and for God's sake—"

"Don't kill anyone," I finish for her.

"I'm serious," she says. "Don't die."

"Not till it counts," I mutter.

"Hey." Jayce dumps a heap of clothes beside me and straps her arms across her chest. "I don't want a new roommate. And I don't want to go back to bunking alone. So come *home*."

I nod, and she turns off the light.

A SINGLE KNOCK ECHOES THROUGH THE DOOR.

"Time to go," Jayce says, and swings her legs to the floor. Her feet sound too heavy as they land, drawing my eye. She never took off her shoes.

I slip into the clothing she selected for me, tuck Spera's necklace and my father's dog tags under my shirt, and fit the pack close to my back. Jayce assesses me in silence, and gives me a nod of approval.

"You look like you know what you're doing."

"Good," I mutter, "because I have absolutely no idea."

She grins. I roll the tension from my shoulders and head for the door.

"Wait!" Jayce hisses. She darts into her closet and retrieves a shoebox full of pencils and paintbrushes. "I had a dream last night. About Maris. She crawled out of the sea and gave me that vial of Tenix." She kneels to her backpack and rifles through the pockets. "It's here somewhere. It has to be ..." She trails off and her brow knits.

"It's right here." I slip it from between my mattresses. A hum radiates from within it, filling my palm.

"What? You didn't trust me?" she feigns surprise, pressing her fingertips against her heart.

"I do now," I say.

Color touches her cheeks. "Keep it on you, not in your pack."

Jayce flips up the waistband of my leggings, revealing a small, zippered pocket at the hip. I secure the vial inside.

"Ready?" She turns for the door. I take a deep breath and follow her out.

The living room is full and silent. Reese glances at us, the last to arrive, and clears her throat.

"We should be back in twenty-four hours, maximum. If you don't hear from us, stick to the plan. Jayce will act as proxy in my absence. Should my absence become permanent, so will that role. Are we clear?"

I nod along with everyone else, as if I know what *plan* they're talking about. I peer at Jayce, who has paled and pinched her lips together in a line. Her gaze passes from Claire to Megan to Iris, as if wondering if Reese should have picked one of the other candidates instead.

"We'll come home," I whisper to her. "All of us." I tilt my head to Reese. "I won't do anything stupid," I add, wishing Jayce would smile.

She gives me a strained look instead, and says, "Do whatever stupid thing you have to. Just bring Reese back in one piece."

"Any questions before we depart?" Reese asks.

I glance around the room, wanting to see arms lurch into the air. The girls packed around us are deathly still, their faces grim and resolute.

"Alright then." Reese turns on her heel and disappears through the door.

I shift my pack on my shoulder and follow her, wordlessly, into the dark.

We pad down the stairwell and slip through the back of the garage. I glance over my shoulder at the little brown house. It blends seamlessly into the night. Every light has been snuffed out.

"What's the plan?" I ask as we make our way down the soggy dune.

"We'll keep to the beach, moving north, then cut inland in a couple of miles. The roads are flooded, so driving's out of the question. It'd be too easy to get turned around, and impossible to see what's at our feet."

"No, I mean *the* plan," I say. "What are the others supposed to do if we don't make it back?"

"Doesn't apply to you," Reese says. Her breath erupts in a cloud of fog, and her words snap against the cold. "When it does, you'll know. Until then, I think you have enough to worry about. Focus on Lucas."

We move directly across the beach, and don't turn north until we reach the water. We walk in the surf, our waterproof boots gliding easily over the firmer ground, our footprints washing flat with the tide.

I clasp my elbows with my clammy fingers and glance skyward. In the east, a line of charcoal gray marks the horizon. The temperature plummets, signaling the coming dawn. With any luck, Lucas will see this sunrise. With a miracle, we may see it together.

Heat zips across my shoulder blades, and the hair at the nape of my neck rises in alarm. *Eyes.* I can feel them trained on my back. I move to signal for Reese, but an earthy smell slips into my nose, warming my next breath, spinning me around. The outline of a horse emerges from the rolling dark.

"Reese," I hiss.

She moves back to me, and we stare out at the herd in silence.

"You feel it, don't you?" she finally asks. "The pull. The need to be among your match."

"Yes," I whisper.

A shaggy bay pulls away from the others. I can feel her pulse thrumming against my skin, though she's at least thirty yards in the distance. My own heart keeps the same time.

"I think she's waiting for you," Reese says, her voice low, her words hot against my ear. "Go to her."

My muscles ache to comply. A trap, my mind screams. *A horse created by Tenix. Another one of Vanessa's masterpieces.*

I shake my head. Will I ever be able to tell reason apart from my mother's paranoia? Still, reluctance seizes my body and anchors me in place. If I join the beckoning bay and her herd, I may never return.

"No." The refusal makes my legs buckle. "She's been following me for weeks. She won't stop now. Let's go."

I rip my gaze away from her laser stare and march on in the opposite direction. Reese hesitates, then falls in beside me. Abby, who has stilled ahead of us, resumes her long-legged gait.

"We're close anyway," she calls over her shoulder. Her voice is shredded to ribbons by the breeze.

We slink across the beach and into the dark cover of twisted trees.

I pause just beyond the tree line, my body sliced by the spindly shadows of bare branches. The forest feels . . . wrong. The ground is hard and flat beneath our boots, absent of pine straw and leaves, as if someone has taken a broom to the earth. Around us, the trees stand in tidy rows. A sour scent hugs the air, triggering my memory.

I close my eyes, sifting through the flashes of my Origin, breathing in deep. There's a reason this scent is familiar to me.

Lucas floats into my mind, grass stains on his elbows. Spera is beside him, blades of grass in her hair. Asher is seething. A sterile reek wafts up from the pool behind them. *Accelerant.*

Asher's hands thrust forth from his sides, a blur of movement. I stumble backward, as if he's shoving *me*. Spera's mark burns, raw and red where he's touched her. I clutch my own chest as her sun-stained skin crumbles to ash in my memory.

Spera flings herself into the pool. *Lenya's* pool. A splash erupts, and then the water detonates like a bomb. Flames heave up from the sloshing surface, setting Spera's body ablaze, burning her alive.

Lenya screams.

"Tanzy!"

Reese has clamped her fingers around my forearms. She shakes me free from the memory.

I blink, and curl my hands to fists to quell my trembling. "No flares, guys," I say, my voice too loud. "The water is laced with accelerant."

"I smell it too," Abby nods. She crinkles her nose.

Overhead, the wind blowing through boughs suddenly ceases. An unnatural silence falls heavy around us, walling us in. Asher. His name drums against my ribcage, matching my pulse. I can sense his presence at the depths of my soul.

I turn in a tight circle. Movement in the shadows catches my eye. Reese spears her gaze in the same direction. She lances an arm in front of Abby, but I push past them both. I won't let anyone else take a blow for me.

The bay emerges from the trees, striding toward us. She pauses, and bends her muzzle to me. I want to chase her away, but if I shout, or wave my arms, I might draw attention to our location.

Get out of here, I silently plead, and turn my back on her, ears primed for the clopping sound of her retreat.

We press on. Above us, the sky lightens to a silvery haze. I pin my eyes over one shoulder, then the other, back and forth, searching for any signs of Asher, wondering if this forest is as empty as it seems.

Reese snatches my arm and I jolt to a stop. Abby, whose been at our rear, walking backward, bumps into me.

Reese tilts her gaze to the ground, where a thin wash of brown water has softened the earth. It deepens as it stretches through the woods, an oddly still strait with a stagnant curtain of mist rising up from its face. It becomes a lake and consumes the woods, trees jutting out of the blackening depths ahead.

"Game for a swim?" Reese says, and slides off her pack.

"This feels like a trap," I say warily. I recall the massive stables Vanessa created with Tenix, the prison Asher carved out of a mountain for Spera. This is child's play by comparison.

"Of course it's a trap." Abby zips her jacket to the throat. Reese bends to fold her woolen socks over the brim of her boots.

"You don't have to do this," I say. "I can go on alone. You can wait for me here if you want."

I step to the bank. Abby strides ahead of me.

"Please," she says. "You've been stuck inside the safe house for what, a few weeks? I've been cooped up there for *months*. I'm done waiting around."

Reese arcs a brow, as close as she's ever come to teasing me, and the three of us wade into the water together.

The brackish marsh quickly rises to our shoulders. We shrug out of our packs and hold them over our heads. The accelerant in the water scorches my eyes and makes me reluctant to inhale.

"There were houses here before." Abby whispers, her wide eyes swiveling left to right.

"Asher must have torn them down," Reese replies.

"All of them?"

We squint against the murky distance.

"I'll climb up for a better view," I decide.

I schlepp to the nearest submerged tree and loop the straps of my pack over a low-hanging limb. Then I pull myself out of the water and yank myself skyward, branch over branch.

Beneath me, Abby and Reese flank the trunk, their bodies rigid, eyes pressed hard against the gray.

"There!" I say, shoving aside the thinly tapered, uppermost branches. "There's a watery clearing where the woods end."

"What else?" Reese calls up to me.

I roll my eyes at the massive white manor which seems to float above the water, supported by translucent stone pillars. "A house," I say. "About a football field from here. It's definitely Asher's style."

I work my way down the tree, pausing when I notice rings pulsing through the water. Ripples. The bay has trailed us through the strait.

Why are you so hell-bent on following me?

Suspicion blazes a path along my jaw. I pretend I don't see her and slide back into the water.

We take care to make our movements silent, gliding along as smoothly as we can manage. The bottom drops from beneath our feet, and we float from tree to tree until the waterlogged forest abruptly ends.

We each take a post behind the final curtain of trees. I submerge my shoulders and peer around a trunk, clutching the matted bark between my hands. The bank reappears, arcing around the clearing, creating a lake.

My brow leaps to my forehead. Bridget sits, cross-legged, on a wooden platform at the center of the lake. Her flouncy red hair cascades over her back. A quiver of arrows is perched at her hand, and a crossbow is slung over her shoulder. She's either guarding something, or bait. Perhaps she's both.

"Hurry up, Tanzy." Her voice rings out like a song, and I stiffen. Can she see us? "We don't have all day."

She doesn't crane her neck in our direction. Doesn't so much as flinch.

The water rustles behind us. Reese snaps her gaze over her shoulder. I swallow. *The horse*, I think. *It must be.*

Bridget peers from shoulder to shoulder. Her fingers walk a path to the arrows at her knee. I take a careful step backward, concealing my body fully behind the tree. I swallow, and let my lashes fall shut, and *listen*.

The dock creaks. *Bridget*, I decide, *turning in my direction*.

Something heavy drops and sends up a plume of water a few yards behind me. My eyes ping open. I fight the urge to whirl around, to see what made the sound.

Bridget's feet scuffle against the wood. Her bowstring whines as she pulls it taut.

I hold my breath and slowly press my back against the trunk, staring into the tidy maze of trees.

The bay breaks out of the shadows. I barely have time to breathe a sigh of relief before she's charging past me.

I bend out of her path, and tuck my damp pack into a low clutch of branches. One snaps, and I wince. Bridget's gaze whirls in my direction, searching for the source of smacking water.

I sink to my knees and let the water rise to my eyes. The bay drags her rib-streaked body over the nearest bank and begins to skirt the lip of the lake.

Bridget claps an arrow into her crossbow, then lets out a short laugh. She dismantles the arrow and slides it back into her quiver. "How did you get out? Dana should've had you all rounded up by now."

The bay whinnies and weaves back into the woods.

Bridget shrugs and resumes her cross-legged position on the dock.

"Not my horse, not my problem," she says to herself. "I'm not a damn stable hand."

Clearly, I think. The bay is wild. If Dana has horses . . .

My pulse quickens. It must mean the missing Wildwood horses are *here.*

Reese growls, and my focus snaps to the tree beside me. "I see Lucas," she says, her voice low. "There."

I follow her gaze to the dark water beneath the dock. A figure bobs beneath the wooden planks, strapped from head to toe in silver wire.

Dread slithers across my skin. *Caro wire.* The lake is loaded with accelerant. If I dash across the lake and grab him, the water will be set ablaze. Lucas will go up in flames. We all will.

I clutch my hands to fists and command my feet to be still. Everything inside me wants to belt after him, but I can't save him. Not that way.

"Ticktock, Tanzy!" Bridget sings out, her voice quivering. Reese presses a finger to her lips, and slips the pack from her shoulder. She drags up the zipper with maddening slowness, one notch at a time, careful not to make a sound. "Can you distract the girl without—" She slices a thumb over her throat.

I nod, banishing the uncertainty from my face.

"Good." Reese slides a hand into her pack. "Then do it. I have a plan."

I suck in a breath, then ease my head underwater and push off, into the dark.

PURPOSE

I stroke forward, panic shuddering through my body until my eyes adjust to the brackish water. I stay low, not wanting to ripple the lake, and push beneath the long shadow of the dock.

Overhead, Lucas's netted figure shimmers against the breaking dawn. I strangle the impulse to lurch upward, to rip away his bindings. If I even graze the Caro wire, the whole clearing will go up in flames.

I brace my boots against sand and mud and heave myself to the surface. I suck in air, and cast a wary eye at Bridget's feet dangling over the lip of the dock.

My gaze crawls over Lucas. He's tethered to the dock's weathered, wooden planks, cocooned by coiled silver.

They've wound him tight. His broad body seems lithe, pinched together by wire. He sways gently in the current I've created. Limp. If he isn't dead yet, he has to be close.

His face is submerged. Has he drowned already? Can he breathe?

Fury erupts at the base of me. The world flashes white. I grip the edge of the dock, nails gouging into the wood, knuckles-deep. My Vires blood swells, hot in my veins, and I swing my body out of the lake.

Bridget leaps up and whirls around, snatching an arrow from her quiver and pointing it at me.

"Thought you'd never come," she smirks, mouth quivering.

"Let's get this over with," I growl.

"Not quite yet." Bridget twirls the arrow over her fingers. I think of my mother, swirling her pen over paper. Of Abby, twirling her pencil between notes.

I lock my gaze on her face. I won't look for Abby and Reese in the water. I won't glance at the woods. I'm the distraction.

My lip curls, and I grind my teeth to keep from baring my canines. Beneath my feet, a wooden plank shifts and then steadies. Lucas's tethers have come loose. Reese.

Bridget plucks a lighter from her pocket. My stomach plummets. *Distract her!*

She sets her arrowhead alight like a torch.

"No way out, Tanzy," she sings.

"Careful," I say. "Don't chip your manicure."

She pouts a lip and sets the arrowhead against her nail beds, admiring the varnish.

"Unless . . ." I cock my chin, and Bridget glances at me. I scrunch my nose, channeling Jayce. "Are they press-ons?" I tsk.

Bridget scowls, and flicks the arrow into the pond.

I scream. A rush of heat and light explodes from below. Flames roll across the surface and race for the shore. Fire breaches the bank and licks up the trees lining the edge of the lake.

I lunge forward and then withdraw in one fluid motion, mouth gaping, eyes searching for Lucas and Reese. Did they make it to the bank? Have they been reduced to metal and ash in the burning water below?

"What? No more witty remarks?" Bridget crosses one knee-high boot behind the other. I watch her dancing closer and closer to the edge of the dock. "Where's your bodyguard? She's funnier, no offense."

We face each other from either end of the dock. Our skin flushes red as the lake blazes around us. One shove, and I could send her into the flames. Her lashes blink rapidly over red-veined eyes. Vanessa left her here to die. This time she knows it.

Bridget sweeps her gaze over the water, eyes burning amber and gold. "Poor lover boy," she says, and dabs an imaginary tear from her eye.

"I won't kill you, Bridget," I say. She glares at me, a real tear slipping down her cheek, and chucks her crossbow into the burning lake.

"You have to try!" A shout erupts from her throat. She plucks two arrows from the quill secured to her hip and charges me blindly, an arrow clutched in each fist.

On instinct, my body crouches, preparing to shoulder her into the inferno. At the last second, I sweep my leg in front of me, slinging my boots against her ankles, dropping her to her side.

She springs to her feet, limping slightly, and regains her footing.

"You're bait!" I scream. "What kind of person just waits around to die?"

Reese's words beam back to me. I could kill Bridget, here and now, I realize. Or Asher could make her *suffer*.

My mind blanks. My jaw goes slack.

Bridget comes at me again.

The lake bends around me, each crackling flame distinct. Bridget lunges. I feel the vibrations of her soles against the dock.

Her arm slices backward, muscles swelling as she whips a fresh arrow from her quiver. In a heartbeat, she'll make contact. I'll sidestep, and use her momentum to send her to the fire below.

We're linked, I realize—our lives inextricably bound. I'll belong to Asher if I kill her. She'll be at his mercy if I don't. He's controlling our fates already. There's one way this ends differently. So, I wait.

Her mouth gapes open the moment she realizes I'm not moving, not reaching to fling her from the dock. She brings her right hand down like a hammer, but her paralyzed stare never leaves my face.

She stabs the spiraled head of the arrow into the hollow plane beneath my collarbone.

Starbursts bloom red in front of my open eyes, and I stagger sideways.

It's only pain. I force the fact through every nerve in my body and close my hand around hers, which is still clamped around the arrow.

"What are you doing?" She twists against my grip, but I hold her fast.

"I won't kill you," I repeat. My jaw is clenched, so the words come out low and menacing. "You don't have to die." I glare against the shrieking gash in my chest, the warm gush of clotted blood that dribbles over my coat and sprays the dock when I cough.

"It's my purpose!" Bridget says, trying in vain to peel out of my grasp. "Vanessa said—"

"Vanessa says a lot. Dying is not your purpose. Your destiny belongs to *you*, and no one else."

"But she's right, Tanzy... she's right," she whimpers. "I've *seen* it. There's fire... just like this. And if I don't..."

"If you don't die for them, you get to live for yourself." My teeth begin to chatter, cutting the words to fragments as a chill rockets through my body. A flicker of movement draws my eye. Abby glides forth from the mouth of the strait, her movement fluid and silent. Behind her, strips of steaming water stitch a web across the burning lake. The fire has already begun to burn itself out.

"Is Vanessa watching?" I turn my gaze back to Bridget's colorless face.

"Yes," she whispers, trembling.

"Make it look good."

Confusion creases her brow.

Behind her, Abby clamps onto the dock and bursts upward. She smacks both hands over Bridget's mouth and heaves her backward, strapping her tight to her chest.

Bridget shrieks, a feral sound, and struggles against her.

Abby tightens her grip and plunges back into the lake.

I snap the feathered tail of the arrow off, desperate to yank the arrowhead from my chest, but it's plugging the worst of my wound. I stagger across the dock and drop over the side. Heat lashes every exposed place as I pass through the filmy surface and begin to sink.

I kick upward and beat my arms toward the strait. I reach a grove of gnarled trees, half-submerged, and latch onto a low-slung branch. I heave breaths, and will my spinning brain to slow, but it hurls round and round.

Reese's voice sounds above the pops of the dying fire. I strain my ears to make out her muddied tone, blinking the wobbling world into focus.

Something is wrong. I pass my bleary eyes over steaming, brown water and catch a flash of Bridget's red hair, vibrant against the blackened trunks of trees. She's kneeling on a shallow rise of sand, an embankment. Lucas's silver cocoon glitters in front of her.

I dig the toe of one boot, then the other, into the sunken floor, launching myself through waves of dizziness. The strait is shallower, the closer I swerve to the rise.

I catch my foot on a root and automatically throw a hand out to catch myself on the closest tree. Searing pain shoots from my shoulder. I clutch my arm, and bite my bottom lip till it bleeds to keep from crying out. My chin ducks to my collar. Nausea rolls through me at the sight of my impaled flesh.

My gaze dashes ahead. I squeeze my eyes shut, and my spiraling vision shutters still. I peel back my lashes. Reese and Abby are huddled on the embankment, their brown clothes blending them into the woods. Bridget is between them. Lucas's netted figure is still lifeless and limp at their knees. If Reese sees that I'm wounded, she'll make me the priority.

I yank my sweater over the broken arrow and zip up my jacket. I dunk my body to the shoulders, wincing as I scrub away the smears of wet blood on my clothes. I'm okay, I'll live. But Lucas might already be dead.

The strait dips, becoming shallower as I advance. I stomp to the embankment, knees threatening to buckle with every step, water smacking up in my wake.

"Tanzy!" Abby hisses. She stabs a finger in my direction, and hops into the ankle-deep water to help me up onto the rise. "Are you hurt?" she asks as she scans me.

"No. Not bad," I say, and force my arm to drop from its clenched position across my sternum. Bridget's eyes snap to the jutting arrow concealed beneath my coat. I meet her gaze and give a subtle shake of my head.

She presses her mouth to a hard line and turns away.

"How do we free him?" I ask, dropping to my knees beside the cocoon.

"Welcome to the debate," Reese growls, directing her answer at Bridget.

"What if it's not him?" Abby murmurs.

I stare at her, then turn my gaze to Lucas's wholly bound face. What if she's right?

"It's Lucas. I swear it." Bridget bows her head.

"If we get the wire off and it's not him in there . . ." Reese trails off, narrowing her eyes. "If it *is* him, and he's dead—we'll slaughter you."

I part my lips, and glance at Abby. Her eyes are pressed to slits. Focus pulses from her in beats.

"He's running out of time," Bridget interjects, her hands balling to fists. "You can't cut the wire. You have to let me."

"I'm not handing you a knife, you lunatic."

"Only the one who sets Caro wire can cut it," Bridget insists.

"I don't have to cut it. I can unwind it," Reese counters.

Bridget glances at the slender, copper watch on her wrist. "He's got less than two minutes. Can you untangle this wire from his body in two minutes? This wasn't for you, Tanzy. Yes, I'm the bait, but not in the way you think," she hisses. "This is the only way Vanessa could help Lucas survive

Asher."

"And why the hell would she do that?" Reese bears her teeth.

"Shut up!" Frustration flares in my head. The need to do something, anything, floods into my empty hands. I stare at the shimmering Caro wire, forcing my frenzied thoughts to order.

Bridget set the wire, she must have. She wouldn't offer to cut it otherwise, wouldn't risk killing me by detonating it. She struck my collarbone when she was in clear range of my heart because she wanted me alive, wanted me to strike back.

Vanessa is watching. Bridget is supposed to die, not me. I'm supposed to kill her. She'll be tortured by Asher otherwise.

Vanessa wants Lucas to live because if he dies they'll have nothing to lure me with.

It's all so simple. So brutally, horribly simple.

The pieces slip into place, winding together like locks of hair in a braid. I'm right. I'm sure I'm right. But Reese is right, too. Bridget stabbed me to bait me into returning the blow. If we put a knife in her hands, she might turn it on any one of us.

My Vires blood burns black, like the scorched bark on the trees still smoldering all around us. Something rumbles within me, thrashing to life. The same rage Bridget roused when she threatened Jayce with the crossbow.

This time, I recognize the dark. It's a part of me, not something I have to smother. I can control it now. I inhale, a long breath that hisses through my teeth. *I can control it.*

I wrap my fingers around Bridget's arm and squeeze, locking my stare with hers. "Reese, give Bridget the knife. If she even *tilts* the blade in anyone's direction, I'll rip her arm from its socket. You can live without an arm," I say. "You did this. Undo it. Now."

Bridget nods, and Reese hands her a dagger. She starts at the head of the cocoon, threading the tip of its blade beneath the netting. She delicately slides the knife down the length of Lucas's body. If she presses too hard, she'll slice him from neck to navel and back again.

Threads pop loose in a wave, snapping away from his center.

Lucas's face appears, deathly still and gray. I run a trembling finger down his cheek.

He's cold.

He doesn't flinch, or gasp for air. He doesn't react to my touch at all.

I'm too late. *We're* too late.

Another failed rescue mission, another body.
He's gone.

TENIX

He's *gone.*

A sob forces the air out of my lungs. He never knew I was coming for him. He died alone.

He's so cold. I ache to warm him. I lower myself toward the crook of his arm.

An unfamiliar hand catches my shoulder and hurls me away from him.

"What are you thinking?" Bridget hisses. "Just because it's cut doesn't mean it won't explode."

Vengeance snakes down my throat and bubbles inside of my ribcage, bathing my heart. My entire body convulses in response, and my eyes zero in on the knife in Bridget's hand, calculating how best to retrieve it.

Reese grips my elbow. "If it needs to be done, I'll do it myself," she murmurs.

She's right. *She's right.*

I'm in control.

I blink away the red.

"He . . . he had time left," Bridget stammers, and begins rising to her feet, her visible muscles coiling in preparation of flight.

I stare at her, unblinking. "Don't you dare run."

She looks down at Lucas's face, his sallow skin. "Vanessa told me—"

"Don't," I say, my voice scraping out of my throat. "Don't say her name."

"She *told* me exactly how long Lucas had. I was supposed to pull him up if you didn't come back in time. He should still be alive. I swear. Don't shoot the messenger."

"You're no messenger," Reese says through her teeth. She arcs her body over Lucas's torso and rests her ear on his chest. Disbelief touches her features.

"There's a heartbeat." She hovers a hand over his nose and mouth. "But he's not breathing. Damn it." She rocks back. "He's probably a minute away from dead. Did Vanessa give you any purified Tenix?"

"No." Bridget backs a step. Reese springs upright and lands on the balls of her feet, her spine curved low, her entire being ready to accelerate.

My hand flies to my pocket and the little stone tube. *You'll know what to do when the time comes,* she'd said.

"Maris gave me Tenix." I pull the vial from my pocket. "I'm pretty sure she said it's purified."

Reese's attention flies to my hand, and she stiffens. "Be very, very careful," she says, her eyes trained on the vial. "Don't move. Don't think."

I part my lips, but Reese shakes her head.

"Don't ask questions."

With a groan, she yanks the severed Caro wire from beneath Lucas, discarding it. Her yellow eyes bear into mine. Her face is grim.

"What do you want, Tanzy?"

I hesitate.

"Tell me. Quickly," she snaps.

"To save him?" My voice is uncertain.

"Don't ask me. Tell me," she says.

I find my voice, clutching the vial to my chest. "I want to save Lucas." My voice is louder now. "I want to revive him."

Energy shoots through my arms and pools in my fingertips.

"Good." Reese exhales, relief softening her face. "Tenix is absorbed through the skin." Using a single nail, she slices Lucas's shirt straight up the middle.

I stare at him, his muscled chest exposed, his skin striped by lacerations and oozing punctures.

"Massage the Tenix into his hands," Reese instructs. "Once his skin softens, move on to his face. Then cover his heart and work outward."

I carefully lower myself to my knees, slipping my hip into the arc of Lucas's flank. I feel the others staring at me, their eyes needling over my neck.

It's just you and me, Lucas's voice whispers in my head.

I jolt, sure I've imagined it.

"Can you give us some room?" I say, eyes darting over my shoulder.

Abby retreats to the lip of the embankment. Reese follows, dragging Bridget along by the sleeve.

Cold rises up from Lucas's body like a draft. I press closer, and slide my thigh over his waist, straddling his center. A painful blush blooms in my cheeks.

My heart pounds, throbbing against the wound in my chest. I set my jaw, twist the cap from the vial and tip a single bead of liquid light into Lucas's palm.

It doesn't splash or absorb, instead maintaining its shape. Before it can roll away, I press it flat with my thumb and work it over each knuckle and between his shriveled fingers. They soften, and his faint beat grows beneath his ribs.

Not a trick. The Tenix is working.

I snatch up his opposite hand and massage the Tenix into his skin.

I turn my attention to his face—his strong, scarred jaw, the concave slope of his cheeks. The valley between his closed eyes, the soft dip over his lips.

I pour Tenix into my own hands, crushing the beads to watery silk. I stroke my fingers over every ridge, every plateau, willing his lashes to flutter. Pressing the heat out of my body and into his.

A current builds between us. The Tenix becomes hot under my hands, begging me away, but I remain latched to him. I clutch his cheeks and pin his body between my hips.

A ragged breath drags up from the depths of me. I pass my fingers over Lucas's hairline, down the ridge of his nose, then over his mouth like a bow.

I trace a line from his lips to his heart. The current is stronger now, bristling, but his chest remains still, the slow beat of his heart like a whisper.

How long was he under the dock, bound and unbreathing? Is he too far gone? Can he make it all the way back to me?

The Tenix pours from the vial now. The beads have liquefied. A pool collects, warm and slick as oil, at the center of Lucas's chest.

I make a sweeping spiral with my fingers, spreading the glowing potion from his collarbone to his navel. I flinch over the lattice of wounds, not wanting to cause him any more pain.

Beneath my ministrations, the deep hue of his skin begins to return. The lacerations scar with stunning quickness, stitched together by ropes of white thread. I thrust my hands back to his center and begin again.

This time, the Tenix doesn't absorb. I press my ear to his chest, but his pulse remains faint. I douse him, emptying the vial, and repeat the spiral, sweat collecting along my brow. I push the liquid into his skin, but it rises up again and skims the surface, trailing along the groove between his ribs and dribbling to the sand.

I shove my hand into its path, catching the glowing stream before it can dampen the earth. The Tenix is lukewarm. Its light has begun to fade.

"No!" I shout. *No, no, no. He's not done. He's not back.*

I press my palm against his chest. His heartbeat is steady, but his skin is clammy. *I have to keep him warm.*

I shrug out of my jacket and yank my sopping wet sweater over my head. I toss them aside. Thick, dark red oozes from the tear in my flesh, staining my tank top.

The arrow juts from my chest, a pillar that will keep us apart. In one swift motion, I wrap my fingers around its neck and yank it out.

Air exits my mouth in a rush. I clutch the hole in my chest. Blood threads through my fingers, sticky and thick. I flatten my body to Lucas's torso and the blinding agony dulls.

I slide my hand out from between us and reach behind Lucas's head, offering a cradle from the earth. My cheek finds the flat bridge of his sternum. I tuck my brow beneath his chin. A rivulet of red trickles over the slope of his chest and pools in the hollow of his throat. My blood. My life draining away. I don't care. *Come back. Please, come back to me,* I beg.

Pain radiates across my middle. Heat spears into my stomach like barbs. I duck my chin, narrowing my eyes at the sliver of space between us, and gasp. The Tenix has become molten. It burns, brilliantly gold.

A swell of light engulfs our bodies. My memory churns. I've seen a light like this before, when Lucas transcended the veil..

Is he crossing again, or is he dying? Is his soul abandoning his physical form? I crush my eyes shut and press into Lucas. *I'm here, Lucas. I'm here. You're not alone.*

His chest heaves and he draws a labored breath. I hold him tighter as tremors roll through his body.

"I'm here, I'm here, I'm here," I whisper through gritted teeth.

A cry bellows from deep within his core. His limbs go rigid. His hands flex, and his muscles bow to the surface.

I lace my fingers through his. He jerks away, then squeezes back as a new wail of agony rakes through him. A shudder rips over his ribcage. He writhes on the ground and then, his muscles go slack.

I lift myself away from his chest and peer down at his face. His lashes flutter, his dark eyes rolling beneath them. His cracked lips move, but no sound emerges.

He's probably calling for Spera. Bittersweet relief makes my heart tight.

"Lucas," I whisper. At the sound of my voice, his eyes open, dilated and vacant. I blot the sweat from his brow with my fingertips.

"Tanzy?" he rasps, blinking. "Tanzy." He struggles to sit up but I stop him with a hand.

"Don't try to move," I say, choking on a sob. "Not yet."

I curl into his chest. He wraps an arm around the small of my back and combs his fingers through my tangled locks of wet hair.

"You came for me." His breath is warm on my neck.

"Of course I came for you. I'm so sorry."

He squints as if the shadowed embankment is too bright. Then he groans, lifts a hand to my shoulder, and pushes my body away from his.

"You're hurt," he croaks. I shake my head. "Tanzy, you have blood all over you."

I graze my fingers over my chest. The gaping hole has already scarred over. All that's left is a mottled scab, rusty streaks of dried blood and an oily, gold stain.

"That's purified Tenix." Lucas coughs. His eyes are wild. He reaches out and weakly grabs my hand. "Where did you get it?"

Dread creeps into my veins. "Maris gave it to me. It's how I brought you back."

He studies the scab on my chest, already flecking away. Ruby petals bloom from an unblemished center. He exhales, and lowers his body to the sand, staring up at the sky.

"Nothing comes without a price. Don't ever forget that. Tenix is currency in my world. I've never met an Unseen creature who will give something away for nothing."

"Welcome back." Reese steps into our midst. Bridget follows close behind. Lucas stiffens at the sight of them.

"They helped you," I murmur.

"Bridget . . ." he starts with a snarl.

I flush, and sidle awkwardly away from Lucas's bare chest. I reach for him, but he waves off my help and falters to his feet.

A strange distance swells between us, though we are a hairsbreadth apart.

I bow my head. Our shadows converge on the sand, and I remember the shadow on the ridge. *Lucas.* Teague rearing up on his haunches. My father going over the ridge.

My fault.

Lucas's fault.

I sidestep away from him, stifling the urge to reach for his hand.

"Where's Abby?" I stammer.

"She slipped off to scout a path from the bank to the beach."

Something whistles skyward. Red sparks trickle down like rain, reigniting little fires wherever they strike the strait.

I latch onto Lucas, my gaze jogging to his.

Reese swears and tilts her gaze to the clearing. "It would appear she's found something else. We need to vacate the area immediately. Bridget, you're with me. Tanzy and Lucas, stay together. Get to the beach if you can. If you can't, take cover and wait for the gray."

"Shouldn't we stay together?" I ask, peeling my fingers from Lucas's arm.

Reese shakes her head. "We divide, they divide. In fact, give me your sweater." I toss it to her and she pulls it on. "If they use scent to track you, hopefully this will slow them down."

"What about Abby?"

"She's on her own. She's tough and smart. She won't go down without a fight." She clenches her jaw. "Let's go. Now."

She drags Bridget back into the water, tailing her as they glide along the rim of the clearing. I glance up at Lucas. He peers down at me. We say nothing, and head in the opposite direction from the water, keeping to dry ground and the cover of the trees.

"Lucas," I say.

"Yeah?" he answers, too quickly.

Words tumble against my chest. I swallow them. "Nothing." He lifts a brow. "The beach isn't far," I mutter. "And the safe house—"

"Wait." He touches my arm and gazes into the forest.

A saber-headed creature emerges from the shadows, solidifying as it nears. Yellow eyes burn from its shadowy sockets.

"Lucas," I whisper on an exhale..

The beast hisses, and its yellow eyes narrow to slits.

Lucas grabs my hand. "Run," he whispers, and whirls away from the beast, thrusting me ahead of him.

We veer away from our path, ducking under boughs and tripping over roots, the shadowy Unseen at our feet. The forest breaks open in front of us, dunes rising one after the other in a rolling staircase. The trees thin. The sand pack turns loose under my feet, causing me to stumble. I catch myself on my hands and propel my momentum forward, and struggle back upright. The rise steepens, forcing me back to all fours. My breath heaves from me, and my chest burns with exertion. Windblown sand pelts the side of my face. The ground levels and I push up to standing. In front of me, the earth disappears.

"Lucas!" I shout, and yank him to a stop as he summits beside me.

Ahead, the dunes drop off. The Atlantic swirls violently, fifty feet beneath our feet.

A chuckle rumbles in our wake, a swirl of shadow lapping forth.

Lucas laces our fingers together. He squeezes my hand.

And we leap.

ALL THE
FRAGILE THINGS

The sand rips at my skin as we slide down the vertical drop. It fills my mouth the instant I cry out. I throw my hands out and grab at any kind of solid hold, but the clusters dissolve each time I make contact.

The ground rushes up, gaining speed. Lucas wraps his arm around my back and yanks my torso to his, dropping his body beneath mine the second before we break through shallow water and slam into the cold, damp sand underneath.

My ribs throb, the breath within them driven out by the impact. I roll over, squeezing my sides with my hands.

Lucas struggles to his knees and crawls several feet away. He grimaces, pushing himself upright, and scans the lip of the hill.

I follow him with my eyes, my body not yet willing to support its own weight.

"Do you see anything?" I ask between painful gulps of air.

"No." He makes his way back to the wall of sand and leans against it.

My entire body hurts, but everything moves when I ask it to. The world doesn't tilt. My legs don't quiver at the knee. I'm good enough to run again, if we have to.

I glance up at the unnatural peak. It's the sole dramatic rise on the beach as far as I can see. Did Asher make this, too? How could he have known the path we would take? Was *he* the shadowy beast?

"We need to find a place to lay low." Lucas searches our immediate surroundings, his back flat against the dune. "Somewhere below sea level."

I chew my lip. The shelter beneath the safe house is the only place I can think of.

I tilt my gaze skyward. The gray is gone, replaced by tufts of white clouds and sunny blue. If anyone is spying beyond the veil, they'll see us clearly. They might follow us to the little brown house, to the candidates waiting there. To Jayce.

I glance at Lucas. His breathing is labored and quick. He's alive, but he's nowhere near full strength. Neither am I.

Take cover. That was Reese's instruction. *Wait for the gray.* But there is no cover. Nowhere to hide. And the Unseen, whoever it is, might soon be at our heels.

"I know a place," I say, and push off the wall of sand. "Follow me."

Lucas staggers a few steps before establishing a normal gait. Our hands brush, but we don't join them. We're both on guard. We'll need both hands free if the beast catches up to us. One wasted second spent untangling our fingers could make all the difference if we're attacked. That's what I tell myself, anyway.

We hurry on, hugging the dunes. The sliver of beach broadens as we advance, pushing us farther and farther from the water's edge.

The safe house appears more quickly than I expect. We skirt along the siding, eyes peeled for any rippling shadows. For any sign of the advancing Unseen.

I guide Lucas into the training room. His gaze passes over the blackout tarps, the exercise equipment, the socks and sweatbands crumpled into a hamper in the corner.

"How did you find this place? Who brought you here?"

"Help me move these mats," I say, avoiding the question.

"Tanzy." He bends his brow.

"Please. We might not have much time."

He helps me shove the mats aside. A hole stares up at us, carved into the floor, large enough for one person to fit through at a time.

"Tanzy, whose house is this?" Lucas asks, his tone clipped and low.

"Mine," I say, and drop into the hole before he can stop me.

The fall is short, and my feet land square on the slippery surface. In the darkness, I can just make out the line where the stone floor ends and a pool of water begins.

My pulse staggers as I scan the pool's quivering surface, deeply black, almost velveteen. Something about it feels endless and beckoning.

Lucas drops beside me. Heat rolls off him. In the meager light filtering in from the gym, I can see his rigid profile tilt up to the ceiling.

Above our heads, footsteps skitter over linoleum. My ears hone in on the location, the pattern of movement. Not the training room, I decide. The kitchen. Sneakers. *Jayce.*

Lucas's gaze darts to mine, reading my eyes. "You're not alone here," he says.

"It's a safe house for candidates." I gulp as panic seizes me. What have I done? If we were tracked here, the other candidates are as good as dead. We should have warned them. The Unseen will rip them to shreds.

I lurch back into the dim circle of light beneath the hole, but the tunnel is narrow and slick with no handholds. There's no way I can crawl back up, no way to let them know . . .

"Hoist me up on your shoulders," I say. With Lucas's added height, I should be just able to reach the lip. Lucas doesn't move. I whirl around to face him. "Help me," I say.

He swallows and shakes his head, *no.*

"It'll kill them!" Why doesn't he understand? "If it followed us, if it tracked my scent—"

"It won't kill them," Lucas says. "Not if it kills us first." Urgency deepens his voice. He throws his gaze to the open mouth of the tunnel, as good as a buzzing, neon sign. "We've got to cover the hole," he says.

"Jayce," I murmur. "Iris, Megan." He doesn't know their names. It doesn't matter. I have to go back, I *have* to.

Lucas yanks me into the shadows, pinching my arm. "We stay alive, Tanzy," he whispers. "*You* stay alive."

I shake my head.

"You said this was a safe house. It's meant to keep you safe. *You*, Tanzy. Isn't it?"

It's not a question. I nod, and he nods. Reason settles over my panic. I cling to it, remembering the way I used to hug my father's quilt around my shoulders, as if it could smother my sorrow, my guilt.

There's no way to ascend the tunnel without Lucas's help. If my scent dead-ends in the training room, maybe the Unseen won't go further, won't search for me upstairs.

I'll keep myself safe and Lucas safe. It's the most I can do.

Lucas narrows his eyes on the hole, straining for something. His breath becomes shallow in his chest. Urgency billows away from him, rendering me silent. Seconds pass. He heaves an exhale and swears. Then his eyes flick up, whirling left and right. He sniffs the air, and his breath catches.

He leans close to me and runs his thumb along the back of my neck. I stiffen at his touch, and my stomach dips.

"This should be enough," Lucas says, stepping back. His palm is aglow with a smear of Tenix. To my dismay, he takes my hand and carefully transfers the Tenix to my palm.

"What am I supposed to do with it?" I plead, reaching back to him. *You do it*, I want to say. Reese isn't here to guide me this time, and the hole is much too high. Impossible to reach.

"I can't think straight when I'm around you!"

"What are you talking about?"

He clenches his arms at his sides. "I can't be sure what I want," he growls.

Every inch of me goes still.

"What do *you* want?" he asks. "More than anything else. Right now." His voice is strangled. I imagine the Unseen padding after our scent, misting into the training room, descending through the tunnel in a shaft of smoke. Solidifying. Snapping Lucas's neck.

"I want to close the hole," I answer.

"Concentrate on what you want, and lift your hand toward the hole like this." He spreads his fingers as wide as they'll go."

I mimic him, but I can't look at him.

"Don't think about me," he says, reading my face. "Focus on what you want, and will it into existence."

I stare at the bright spot above us. I stretch my arm to the ceiling and imagine the rock growing together. An iridescent light blooms in my hand and shoots at the opening. It fades as quickly as it came, and we plunge into a void beyond black.

Lucas fumbles for my hand. I let him take it, but I don't return the squeeze.

"You said you can't be sure what you want. What aren't you sure about?" I ask the nothingness.

"When I'm with you . . ." He sucks in a breath. "I can't always separate what I want from what's best for you. Tenix delivers the truest desire of the blood—what you want most in the moment. If you aren't absolutely sure, it won't work. Or worse, it will fulfill a desire you never intended to act upon." He pauses. "You're not like Spera," he says. "You're so sure and decisive."

I glare, even though he can't see me. But maybe his night vision is better than mine.

"She seemed pretty decisive to me," I remark. My brow lifts as memories from my Origin flip through my mind like a highlight reel: Spera reaching for the boy as he slipped over the cliff. Spera pulling the lever in the arena. Spera refusing to bow, refusing to eat. Risking everything for one shot at freedom.

"That's because in an Origin, you see decisions," Lucas explains. "You don't see the struggle that precedes them. Spera had a habit of making up her mind at the worst possible moment."

Understanding rises within me, transient and vague. Impossible to ignore. Something I know deep within the recesses of my soul.

"Her last moments in the garden," I say. "When Asher set her on fire."

"He didn't," Lucas replies. My eyes have begun to adjust. I can just make him out, bowing his head. Remembering. "He touched her with Tenix. He wanted to know the true desire of her blood. Her heart answered," a shudder passes through him, "so steadfast and sure that the Tenix made it so."

"What did it say?" I ask him. Faintly, words are circling my brain. I already know.

"*Release me.*" He drags the words out of his throat. "She asked for death, Tanzy. She wanted death, and the Tenix made it so."

"That's not what happened," I stammer. "He burned her. Asher burned her. She sought refuge in the pool, and it went up in flames. It was laced with accelerant."

I shake my head, remembering. My mind screams—*Asher's fault. Asher's fault. He killed her.*

"You can feel it, can't you?" Lucas says. "Your soul is your own. I see that now. But it belonged to Spera once, and this was her most precious truth."

"You were barely conscious," I argue. "You didn't see what I saw!" But he's right—somehow, I know he's right. My heart drops into my stomach. My words echo and are absorbed by the silence of the cave. Shivers take hold of my body. Nothing inside of me is warm enough to repress them.

"She'd said it once before," Lucas murmurs. "She whispered her truest desire to the wind."

His voice is a rasp. My mind conjures the memory of Spera, trapped in Asher's tower. Leaning through the stony arc of a window. Shifting her weight onto the balls of her feet. Closing her eyes, hair swept away from her face by the breeze.

Release me.

I stagger away from Lucas, one step, two. My knees buckle at the edge of the pool.

I steady myself. A tear burns a trail down my face and drips from my chin. It splashes into the shallow water beneath me, a hollow sound, too loud. Its ripples glow turquoise and spreads across the pool, illuminating the boundary between sea and stone.

Lucas reaches for me, pulling me into his arms. He braces our bodies against the cave wall as the water churns in a lazy spiral. The light grows. A brilliant blue emanates from the surface of the pool, and at last I recognize its shape. *Maris.*

I drop to my knees and draw a spiral on the surface the way Jayce did when she called Maris forth. The glow intensifies, and then subsides. She must not be strong enough to take solid form yet, but she's alive.

"Maris," Lucas whispers. He crouches beside me and stares into the shimmering pool. "I trapped her in a pocket once," he says. "She spent thousands of years in a space smaller than this."

"Why would you do that?"

"Asher asked me to. Back then it was reason enough." He studies Maris's glow, his face changing in the transient light. "I confronted Asher soon after Spera's death. I sought him out on this side of the veil, and I attacked him." He glares at his reflection in the pool.

"What happened?"

"He dragged it out, let me almost close on him over and over. Let me catch my breath between blows. It was a joke to him, Tanzy. I was a joke. He was taunting me. I'm no match for him. Nothing is."

He grinds his teeth. I can hear his molars scraping together.

"I realized he wasn't going to kill me," he mutters. "He knew I'd suffer more if he let me live. *She left you*, he said. *Why on earth would you forfeit eternity for her?* It didn't make sense, not then. It makes sense now."

He shakes his head as alarm skitters up my spine.

"He laughed at me," Lucas continues, weariness edging into his tone. "I charged him. He deflected me. Then he just . . . strolled off. He knew—"

He curls his fingers to fists. "He knew his words would haunt me. And they did."

He glances at the shimmering pool. "Years passed. I found Maris, and she led me to you. Before we parted ways, she told me the truth of Spera's death."

"The truth?" I ask, the words trembling over my lips.

"Do you want to hear it?"

I hesitate. Uncertainty bathes my skin and makes me shiver. "Yes."

Lucas exhales, and slides down the wall, settling on the damp, stone floor.

I stay standing. Somehow, looking down on him makes me feel brave.

"Asher was returning from an excursion with his vizier when he came upon Spera in the garden."

"Raffin," I say, remembering the gray Unseen. The Taigo.

Lucas nods. "They'd tracked down a source of purified Tenix. Asher wanted to learn what Spera would choose should her blood affect the veil. He'd doused his dagger in Tenix. He meant to gather a few drops of her blood and bring it back to Raffin for interpretation. The blood oath, the kiss," he cringes, "all of it was a ruse."

I inhale, remembering Spera's quivering resolve. Her palm, tense as she'd placed it over Asher's. The wet sound of a blade shoving through flesh.

"The Tenix slipped into Spera's veins. A drop at most, but it was enough to manifest her deepest desire."

"Freedom," I breathe. "Release."

Lucas unfurls his fingers against my chest, mirroring the way Asher touched Spera the moment before she dove into the pond. "He covered her heart like this," he whispers.

"I remember." I rest my hand on top of his and press it into my skin.

"Her mark began to burn before he ever touched her." His eyes are black and vacant. He stares at my chest, at the rise and fall of my lungs. His fingers curl beneath mine.

Grief presses down on my sternum, and my hand closes around Lucas's. "Maris wasn't there when Spera died. How does she know what happened?" I ask.

"She was sent by your mother to an Oracle to learn everything about Spera's life and death. I think your mother hoped to arm herself with history. She was shown Spera's last moments. When I found her, she passed the truth on to me."

"Why?" I ask. "You told me Unseens never do anything for free."

"We reached common ground." He stares at the silvery-blue gleam of the pool. "I gave her the Solvo medallion. It's a weapon, one of the only ways to eliminate an Unseen on our side of the veil."

"I know what it is," I hiss. "You were hoping she'd do what Asher wouldn't. You wanted her to use the medallion . . . to use it against *you*. Why didn't you use it against Asher when you had the chance?"

"Because he is the only creature in two worlds who could bring you back."

I suddenly see his stare for what it is. *Longing.* Spera is gone. Maybe he thought she'd eventually return. That my darkened hair and honeyed skin were signs of her reclaiming this body. But he was wrong.

I'm not Spera. I'm not enough.

He doesn't want to live in a world without her.

How romantic, my mind scoffs. *You coward,* I want to say. The word is ripe on the tip of my tongue. I bite it back.

"Dana was searching for something," I say, "in the creek bed behind Vanessa's house. She was searching for the medallion."

"Probably," Lucas says.

"What would have happened if she'd found it?"

He shrugs limply. "Maybe she would've done what Maris refused to do."

I gape at him. Anger sizzles inside me.

"I've done terrible things," Lucas says. "I've been alive since the dawn of time, and I've used the eons of my life to cause so much suffering, so much pain."

"This isn't about your regrets, Lucas," I growl.

"I've suffered," he says. "You can't know how I've suffered."

"Guess what?" I snap. "I'm suffering too. And I'm not looking for an easy way out. I'm going to seal that veil, no matter what it costs. No matter how much Asher hurts me, no matter how many of the people I love are ripped away." My eyes glass over, but my voice remains strong. "I need you, Lucas. I need your help. So get over yourself, because I can't do this alone."

My words echo in the stone enclosure, beaming back to me. I hadn't meant to speak my decision aloud. Will Lucas try to stop me, now that he knows my plan? Will he let himself be sealed forever on the Unseen side of the veil?

I swallow, and pass my gaze over his hollow eyes, his sunken shoulders. My father is dead, my mother is gone. Dr. Andrews's body is in a grave somewhere. Shaila's body is at the bottom of the sea.

Spera is never coming back. In her heart of hearts, she didn't want Lucas. She wanted to be free.

My face softens. Will we ever be able to come to terms with the people we've lost, I wonder?

I settle beside him and hold out my hand. He takes it, twining our fingers together over his knee.

"Asher has no idea who he's up against," he says suddenly. He turns to me, brushing a twist of hair from my face. "I've never believed anyone could defeat him. Not until this moment." He clenches his jaw. "You don't need anyone, Tanzy. Least of all me. But I'll stand by you anyway, if you'll let me."

I settle into the crook of his arm. The uneven wall digs into my back. I tilt my gaze to the ceiling and wish Reese had told me the backup plan. Is there any escape from these caves? There must be, but I don't know it. How long will we be trapped here?

What will the candidates do if the gray arrives without us? Will they think we've been killed, or captured? Will they leave us behind? Somehow, we have to alert them to our presence.

"How do we make the seal disappear?" I ask.

"It'll dissolve on its own in a few hours," Lucas replies.

Tenix runs out. The realization hits me like a freight train.

"The Tenix I used on you . . . will it dissolve too? Is its power the only thing keeping you alive?"

"I wasn't dead, Tanzy," he says. "There was a sliver of light left inside me, winking out. What you did for me . . ." He trails off, and shrugs away from the heaviness of it, forcing a grin. "It was like jumping a car battery," he explains. "But what you did there," he nods at the ceiling. "You created something new, which requires a continuous source of Tenix to be maintained."

Overwhelmed, I wrap my arms around him and blink back the burning in my eyes. My heart is a pendulum, swinging from one reach to the other, unable to settle somewhere in the middle. Lucas is here, solid and real. He won't crumble away. But the image repeats in my mind, the Taigo reducing to nothing but ash on the beach. I clutch onto him.

"I'm right here," he murmurs into my hair. "I'm not going anywhere."

He might not be, but I am. When I seal the veil, I will disappear forever. Lucas will be alone, without Spera, without me.

A wave of doubt rolls through me, dark and cold, pressing goosebumps over my skin.

There's no other option, my mind argues. *This is the only way.*

"What are you thinking about?" Lucas asks.

"Nothing."

"You're lying," he says.

"Yes."

He draws me closer to him, clouding my senses with the feel of him. His hand cradles my head against his heart. The beat of it counts a rhythm like a clock.

Ticktock.

Our time is running out.

"You need to rest while you can."

Lucas's voice breaks through my mental fog. He tucks a lock of hair behind my ear.

I give him a pointed look, and he warmly smiles, mouth bowing upward, a teasing light returning to his eyes.

"You're safe here," he says. "I'll wake you when the Tenix dissolves."

He tugs me closer, and I curl into his arms.

I want to argue, to tell him we'll take shifts. I don't even know if Unseens sleep. The dim light lulls my eyes shut like a lullaby. The weight of what I must do wraps around me like chains, so heavy. Soon, the bond that stitches Lucas and I together will be ripped apart at the seams.

"Shh. Sleep, Tanzy," he croons in my ear.

I cling tightly to the sound of his voice, to his smell, and let go of everything else.

EMPTY

My mind swims toward a spider web of red light. It bends and blurs, making me dizzy.

It's okay. You're waking up. It's just daylight, my mind reassures my pounding heart.

Daylight. The word charges through every cell in my body, shaking me to attention. I thrash awake. Something strong holds me down. I dig my nails in and try to pry myself from the restraint.

"It's alright, Tanzy." The voice is familiar, the arms wrapped around me muscled and warm. *Lucas.*

I stop fighting and relax into his chest.

"Didn't mean to startle you," he chuckles. "Breathe."

I draw his arms tighter across my body and hold them there.

The pool of water has receded. Maris's light has vanished beneath the dark.

My eyes move to the growing hole over our heads. Gray light filters through thin cracks in the dissolving stone. It's not yet big enough to pull myself through.

"How much time do we have?" I ask.

"Ten minutes. Maybe less." He fiddles with the horseshoe on my necklace and brings the clasp back to the nape of my neck.

"You told me if I wore this, you'd always be able to find me. How does it work?" I cradle the charm in my palm.

"My blood," he says. "I hollowed out the horseshoe and filled it with my blood. Then I sealed it inside." He flips the charm over and shows me two places where the metal bubbles up in a hard glaze.

"And you can . . . smell it?" I ask.

"No," he grins. "Unseen blood is different. It's as eternal as I am. It doesn't dry up and fleck away like mortal blood." He brings the horseshoe to my ear, turning it gently over and under. If I listen closely, I can hear the liquid sloshing inside. "It's still a part of me," Lucas says. "It calls out to my body."

Like a horse to its herd, I think. It makes perfect sense.

My heart sinks. I left the wild bay to fend for itself. I never asked Bridget where Wildwood's stolen horses were being held.

"Did you hear anything about the horses Asher took?" I ask.

Lucas shakes his head. "I didn't see much of Asher," he admits. "They kept us in a cellar. Most of the time, we were completely alone."

"Us?"

"There was a girl in another cell. She slept a lot. Refused to speak. Probably another candidate."

"What makes you think she's a candidate?"

"Asher locked her up, which means two things: she's not on his side, and she's valuable. Otherwise, he would've done away with her. Although," he glances at me, "it didn't seem like Asher was the one calling the shots."

"Vanessa?"

Lucas nods. "She can work Asher like I've never seen. It makes it easier to accept the fact she fooled me."

"She had us all fooled," I mutter. "Do you think it's possible she has Asher fooled, too?"

"Before yesterday, I would've told you absolutely not. She seems to enjoy torture as much as he does." His jaw shifts beneath his scarred face. "The night before you rescued me, Asher came to my cell. He said he planned to destroy me. Vanessa stood between us and told Asher if he didn't let me live, he'd be sorry. Here I am."

"Here you are." I tilt my cheek to his collarbone, listening to his heart thrum steadily beneath his chest, and wonder what Vanessa gained by keeping him alive.

Lucas eyes the gap in the ceiling. It's doubled in size. "Come on," he says.

I stand and he lifts me to the mouth of the tunnel. A thread of nerves pulls tight along my spine as I claw my way to solid ground. Lucas springs through the hole, his formidable body nimble as a deer. A new wave of appreciation for him warms me, beginning in my cheeks and spreading through my middle.

I cross to a window and pull open the tarp, relieved to take in the soft, safe light of the gray. "Ready to go up?"

Lucas gestures for me to lead the way.

We climb the interior stairwell. Lucas steps carefully, guarding me from behind. I can feel his focus pulsing in the narrow space between us.

I reach for the doorknob, but it resists turning.

"Is it usually locked?" Lucas asks as I jiggle it.

"Not during the gray. Maybe it's a precautionary measure." I press my ear against the door and rap gently on the metal panels. Nothing stirs from the other side. "Maybe they're all still asleep," I whisper. The moment the words leave my mouth, I'm certain they're not true.

"Should we break the door down?"

I knit my brow, studying the frame. "Reese designed these doors to be as sturdy as possible." I listen again. Nothing. "Wait here. I'll go around front and open this door from inside."

Lucas shakes his head. "I'm not letting you out of my sight. Especially now."

I slide past him, hurry down the stairs, and slip through the maze of tarps until I find the garage. The Jeep is parked in its usual spot, the hood cool to the touch.

I take the stairs two at a time and wrap my fingers around the handle. The door creaks open the moment I touch my fingers to the knob.

I withdraw a step, my heart pounding in my chest. Lucas arrives at my side and tips the door wider, peering inside.

It's empty. Reese isn't here, *no one* is here. The candidates are gone.

I take a nervous step across the threshold. Lucas creeps in behind me. The television is off, the lampshades dark. I pass my hand over the coffee table, then drum my fingers atop the island, brow lowered with thought.

In the kitchen, beads of water persist over dishes in the drying rack. The faucet drips—Reese's rule to keep the pipes from freezing.

I glance at Lucas, my face tight with confusion. *Where is everyone?* Reese said to wait for the gray. They should be here.

A sudden draft gusts through my hair and rattles the blinds. My muscles tense. I block my torso with the kitchen counter and scan the common area from corner to corner.

The windows along the back of the house are wide open. Another breeze rolls through and knocks a slender table lamp from its perch beside the wicker couch. With a start, I realize all the other surfaces are bare. No books, no laptops.

I hurdle the counter and sprint down the hallway to my room. The door is ajar. I shove inside, and my skin crawls. The floor is clear of laundry and crumpled paper, Jayce's usual debris. Her bed is made, pillows neatly stacked and quilt tucked in tight. Her bag is nowhere to be seen.

Is this a part of the backup plan, I wonder? Did she evacuate?

My eyes land on the photo of Jayce and her mother still propped atop her bedside table, and I frown. Jayce wouldn't have left it behind unless she planned on coming back. Or was taken by force.

"All of the other rooms are empty," Lucas says from behind me.

"This is a message, but I can't tell who left it."

I search the rest of my room for clues. The trunk at the foot of my bed is closed. I can't remember if I left it shut. I ease open the lid. The trunk is empty except for two words carved into the cedar planks. *Promes Cae.*

I recognize the handwriting. Vanessa's perfect script.

I slam the lid shut. "Vanessa was here. She has Jayce. She probably kidnapped Iris and Megan, too. My friends," I add when I realize Lucas is staring at me. "Other candidates." He nods. "Damn it." I slam my hand down on the closest surface. "This was all a setup. Bridget must have let her in." Dread pummels through me, shortening my breath. "What if she came last night? What if I lead her straight here?" My voice quavers. I swallow to steady it.

"There's nothing you can do about that now," Lucas says. "She probably took everyone to the cellar where she kept me. It's airtight, Tanzy. Holding cells, guards."

I swing my gaze to his, desperation wild in my eyes, and he stiffens his jaw. "We can be there in twenty minutes if we run," he says, and I nod.

He turns on his heel.

"Wait." My stomach clenches with guilt. "You don't have to go back there, Lucas."

He straightens. "This isn't about me, remember?" He reaches out for my hand. I link my fingers with his.

We leave the house just the way we found it, slip through the tarps covering the garage, and turn north. I pick up a run, and we weave through the twisted forest. Vanessa has extended a personal invitation, and I doubt she'll send anyone to interfere. If she wants me to knock on her door, I'm happy to oblige.

A dark place between two trees solidifies in front of me, too quickly. I crash into something—*someone*—heavy, hard, and the color of steel.

Recognition tears through me, every fiber tensing in its wake. My body reacts like a machine. The balls of my feet plunge a layer deeper into the mud and catapult me directly backward, landing me a step from Lucas's shoulder.

"Taigo," Lucas growls as the gray figure refines and the Unseen takes a male shape.

"Traitor," the Taigo hisses in response.

"You're a fool to face us alone," Lucas rumbles. A vein swells along his neck. His heart beats a furious rhythm against his skin.

I jog my stare between them, a strange thrill licking my spine. Negotiation isn't part of the Taigo agenda. This exchange won't end until I'm dead, or he is.

"I'm not alone." The Taigo grins. His gaze lifts and makes a wide scan of the forest. A rustle of movement rises up from the wooded crescent around us. Every dark place shifts—every shadow solidifying into another Taigo.

"Stay behind me and let me clear a path," Lucas orders under his breath. "The closer we can get to Asher's house, the less likely they'll be to follow. If a Taigo reaches you, don't hold back."

I glance at him from the corners of my eyes. "Are you sure?"

"They won't let you take another life. They'll end their own lives first as long as you give them the opportunity," he explains in a rush.

A chill of fear touches my skin as more Taigo gather in a solid ring around us. Each of them holds the same kind of spear used to kill Shaila. I have nothing but my fists. My third kill is no longer my foremost concern; what if the Taigo succeed right here, right now?

Behind me, a wailing note punctures the air. The Taigo respond together in a uniform cry, clapping once, twice. My muscles draw tighter as I scan their line. They are now stationary, but there's nothing still about the waiting Taigo. They quiver with anticipation, and descend.

Lucas explodes into motion, shoving his fist through the chest of the leading rebel before it can aim its spear. The steel form dangles from his arm for a full second before dissolving into sand, and litters the ground behind him in a charcoal trail. Lucas's jaw unhinges with a roar so forceful it rattles my bones. His entire body coils, and he blasts into motion again.

He dismembers his next target so quickly, I can't tell which limbs he severed first. Warmth grows in my middle as I watch the utter destruction he renders, marveling at how deadly his hands are in contrast to how carefully he handles me. If this is Lucas in a Seen form, how strong is he behind the veil? How strong is Asher?

How strong would I be as an Unseen?

My pulse hammers in my ears. My blood longs to be a part of this chaos, to fight alongside Lucas, to defend him. How strong am I *now*? I've never been tested, not like this. Not when it counted.

Something shuffles at my side and I whirl into the sound. Three armed Taigo rush us. Lucas thrusts his knee forward, and the first of them drops. The second takes aim at Lucas's center, snaring his attention as the third springs over his shoulder, directly in front of me.

He levels the tip of his spear at the hollow place at the base of my throat. Reese's training takes over, and my leg extends in a roundhouse kick, heel burying itself in the Taigo's firm flank the same instant his metal staff cracks across my cheek.

I stumble sideways, reeling from the blow. Blood fills my mouth with the tangy taste of copper. White spots pollute my vision.

A ringing erupts in my left ear. The ground crunches beneath the Taigo's feet as he rights himself.

Desperation burns in my chest, and the world around me tilts. I reach down for a fistful of sand to throw, and close my fingers around a rock instead.

The Taigo lurches at me. I whip my blurring focus from his chest to his leg, and hurl the stone at my mark. The thud of contact is followed by the crunch of yielding bone, and the Taigo collapses to the sand. His hands open to catch his fall, and his spear flies free.

I dart forward and snatch up the weapon, half expecting it to turn to ash in my hand. It's light as air and solid. Relief surges through my limbs.

I glance at Lucas. He flips a Taigo from his bloodied back, and drives his elbow into the next gray figure that advances on him.

I throw my focus straight ahead. Two more Taigo are crashing toward me. One swings high as the other jabs low. I jerk my knees to my chest and block the spear that jabs forth, mere inches from my face. They trade positions and come again, striking in synchronization.

I leap backward and their spears collide with such force, I feel the impact in my teeth. They come again, and I advance in a slide, taking out the legs of one Taigo as she extends her arms, preparing to swing.

The other lunges, and I deliver a crippling blow to his hamstring. He bellows and grabs his leg, crumpling beside me.

I draw my hand back, momentum guiding my spear. Before my elbow releases, the closest Taigo buries her spearhead into her comrade's chest. His body spasms once before dissolving into sand.

For less than a second, I cannot move, spellbound and mystified and horrified. An eternity forfeit, just to keep me from reaching the veil.

Another wave of gray crashes around me in an arc. I leap to action, heaving breaths. The constant smack of spear meeting spear makes a jarring cadence. My arms tremble with exertion. Each exhale roars from my open mouth. The Taigo gain ground, taking turns to preserve their energy. There's so many of them, striking forth in clusters, and only one of me. I'm not sure how much longer I can hold them off.

A flash of movement draws my eye to the left. At the same time, a Taigo's staff whistles through the air and impales my right side. I grunt and double over. The rest of my breath is trapped somewhere between my lungs and my throat.

I shake the stars from my eyes. My kneecaps bleat back at me, submerged in the cold, hard earth. A Taigo's shadow extends over me, bathing the sand in black. I watch as it raises its spear for the kill, and coil my muscles, readying myself to drive straight on, latch onto the Taigo's waist, and throw him off-balance.

The spear peaks and descends.

I leap to my feet.

A guttural shout sounds from above me, and sand sprinkles down like rain.

A sudden rush of footsteps breaks the eerie quiet, wrenching a final burst of adrenaline from the depths of my battered body.

I spring to standing, thrusting my hands to fists in front of my chest.

The clearing is empty, not a single Taigo in sight.

Lucas races to me. Relief makes my entire being sag. I slump against his solid form and clutch his bare, torn back. Behind him, a thick dusting of charcoal and ash paints the wood. Otherwise, there's no sign of our fight. Its remnants will soon be swept away by the breeze.

Lucas buries his face in my neck and draws me close, eliciting a fresh burst of bright pain from the wound above my hip.

He kisses my throat, his lips full and hot against my skin.

"I thought I was going to lose you, Tanzy," he murmurs.

My name . . . he said *my* name. Not Spera's.

"I'm not going anywhere," I whisper. "Not yet."

I stand on my tiptoes and tilt my mouth to his. He surges upon me like an ocean swell, powerful and reckless.

The taste of him floods my senses. Waves of eagerness rock through me. My fingers fist in his hair, pulling him closer. Wanting more of him.

"Lucas," I rasp, and he withdraws a fraction. He peers down at me, tracing my lip with his thumb, watching my eyes.

I stare back into his, endlessly dark.

He presses a kiss to my forehead, another to my hair.

"Come on," he says, his voice hoarse. "We have to move."

I nod, but we remain still, locked to one another, unwilling to part. Lucas passes his hands over the small of my back, curling my shredded shirt in his fists. "Never thought I'd say this," he mutters, teeth clenched, his thin smile grim, "but we need to get you to Asher."

ASHER'S MARSH IS GONE, reduced to puddles. The dock becomes visible. The exposed pilings are striped with stains of water and char. There's no easy way into the house from this side. Lucas steers us around the close corner, keeping low as we maneuver in and out of the brush, our boots sticking in thick, black mud. The front of the manor comes into view. We press close to the wall and slow our movement. I guard every exhale, ensuring its silence, and peer across the width of the house. Clear stone pillars support the awning over a curved front porch. The exterior is lined with floor-to-ceiling windows, which are shrouded with silver drapes. A curtain quivers, and suddenly, the sprawling veranda is bathed in soft, yellow light.

Lucas pulls me flat against the white siding, one finger pressed to his lips. We wait, but no one emerges from the ornately carved entry. No eyes press against the windowpanes. None that we can see.

"I'm going in," I say. "Alone."

"No way. You're hurt. I saw you limping."

"Asher wants you dead."

"There are worse things than death. Tanzy, he could do worse things to you."

I graze my hand over my hip, where blood has plastered my shirt to my skin. The wound is shallow and already scabbing over with spongy flesh.

"I'm safer in there than out here," I reason. "If Asher wants me to open the veil, he needs me alive. He needs me . . . compliant."

I might be lying. I might be expendable, now that Vanessa possesses a piece of my soul and the blood of the black horse.

I don't tell him that. Instead, I press my hand to his cheek, tracing his scars with my thumb.

He exhales, uncertainty passing over his face like clouds. Then, his shoulders give. He sighs through his teeth. "Break a window if you need help," he relents. "You're good at breaking windows."

I muster a smile. My gaze flicks over the property, then slides back to him. "Be seeing you, Lucas," I murmur. *In this lifetime or the next.*

If You Remember Nothing Else

Vanessa already knows I'm here. I'm sure of it.

I creep anyway, ascending the veranda on the balls of my feet, cringing when the wooden stairs protest beneath my weight.

The door is ajar, beckoning me to slip inside.

I've had enough of bait. I don't bite. Instead, I shake the dread from my hands and hover my finger over the doorbell.

"Tanzy!" Vanessa beams, swinging the door wide before I can ring. Her voice is like honey. Her eyes are eager and bright. "Welcome! I expected you hours ago. Rough trip?" Her eyes dart to my chest, where my mark is covered.

Anger swells between my bruised ribs. "Slight delay," I reply, easing sarcasm into my tone. "Nothing we couldn't manage."

She lifts a brow and skims the property. I chastise myself for letting it slip I'm not alone, but there's nothing to be done about it now.

"Come in, come in." She steps aside, bidding me to enter.

"I'm good out here, thanks." I rock back on my heels.

"Well you're not dressed for company, I'll give you that." She tips her gaze over my soiled clothes, my muddied boots. My bruises and shredded skin. "So uncouth," she tsks.

"Well, you look lovely," I say, my voice dry.

"How kind of you to notice," Vanessa replies. She's dressed in a white, button-down shirt and a crisp pair of jeans. Her blonde hair is pinned back in a bun. She taps a manicured finger against her chin. "That's why I like you, Tanzy," she says. "Always so polite." She waves me inside. I remain firmly planted just beyond the threshold. "Have it your way," she says.

"Wait!" I brace a hand against the door before she can snick it shut in my face.

She steps back, heels clicking against the marble floor. A hollow sound. "Have you changed your mind, then?" she snarls. "Will you grace us with your presence?"

I stiffen my jaw, and nod.

"Wonderful!" A smile leaps across her face. She claps, and I glare at her. "Honestly, Tanzy, don't look so glum. You're my guest of honor!" She latches onto my arm. "Now I hope you don't mind," she yanks me into the foyer, "but I *will* have to lock you up in the cellar for just a little bit." She wrinkles her nose, pretending to wince, though her smile persists. "Don't worry. You'll have plenty of company."

"Who's down there?" My throat constricts.

"Everyone," she says. "Everyone is down there."

I swallow, goosebumps piling over my skin. My gaze leaps to the marble, and I imagine my housemates, my *sisters*, shackled somewhere below.

I level my eyes with Vanessa's. "Take me to them," I say.

She squeals, and links our arms at the elbow. "I thought you'd never ask," she grins.

She tips the door shut behind us with her heel.

The foyer is expansive and gleaming, its windows trimmed in floor-length, lace curtains. My gaze flicks to a large, metal door at my left. A beam rests across its middle, held in place by wide, metal brackets.

At the center of the foyer, a crystal vase bursting with frost-white roses has been perched atop a mirrored table.

Each corner of the room opens to a hallway.

I peel away from Vanessa's grip, my eyes jogging from corner to corner, searching for guards. For Asher's lackeys. For *Asher*. But we're alone.

I curl my bloodied knuckles to fists as nerves and excitement trip through me. "You're feeling brave," I remark.

200

"I have friends and you have friends," Vanessa replies. "Kill me, and my friends will kill your friends." Her voice is like a song, taunting me. "Speaking of our friends," she says, dragging me back to her side, "mine tend to get a bit testy when they're bored, and they've been waiting all morning to meet you."

She guides me to the metal door and heaves up the beam. I suck in a breath at the staircase that drops steeply in front of us. A murmur of hushed voices floats up the narrow passage. They fall to silence as Vanessa nudges me lower.

We arrive at a tight, stone-walled landing. The cellar. I squint my eyes against the darkness, searching for the hulking figures of guards, but there's no one here.

"Where are all your friends, Vanessa?" I growl.

She leans her painted lips against my ear. "I lied," she whispers, and shoves me ahead of her, through a hall lined with sleek, black bars. "I brought something for you," she calls, her singsong voice flooding the stagnant enclosure.

Reese peers out from behind the first web of metal. She catches sight of me and deflates, her hard, determined eyes snapping to dull.

Behind her, Bridget and Abby are huddled together in a corner. Anger flashes through me, but tapers as I catch sight of the terror in Bridget's eyes, the exhaustion pulling at her cheeks. Abby drapes an arm over Bridget's shoulder, and her fingers trail the slope of her forearm, comforting her. They watch me pass, wordless, their faces stunned and utterly still.

"Tanzy!" Jayce calls from the back of the cellar. I jog down the short aisle and crouch in front of her cage. She waves her hands as if to shoo me away. "Don't touch the metal. It's like Caro wire on steroids," she says. "Even the Unseens can't touch it."

"Why don't you two catch up?" Vanessa sneers, and pulls on a pair of silver mesh gloves before unlocking the cell.

Jayce bares her teeth, and her anxious eyes dart to mine. I shake my head as if to say, *not yet*, and slip into her cage.

Vanessa slides the door back into place and snaps the lock shut. "I'll be back soon. Don't do anything I wouldn't do," she purrs, and glides from the cellar.

I listen for the sound of her heels clacking over the staircase. The whine of the metal door on its hinges, the thick beam clunking into place. Then I latch onto Jayce's wrists, scanning her from head to toe. "What happened?"

She chews her lip. "I didn't stick to the plan," she says. "We came to find you guys, and we split up to cover more ground. I doubled back to the house. Vanessa must have followed me. This is my fault."

She glances in Reese's direction, as if anticipating some scathing admonishment, but Reese offers none.

I chew the inside of my cheek. *It was me*, I think. *If the shadowy beast was Vanessa, then I led her straight to our door.* "Where are the others?" I ask.

Jayce shakes her head. "I don't know. Maybe Hope found them."

"Lucas is out there," I offer. "If he sees them, he'll keep them safe."

"I'm afraid not." Reese gestures to the first cage on the opposite side of the hall. Lucas lies there, crumpled against the far wall, hand outstretched.

"Lucas!" I shout, nearly grabbing the bars. Jayce hooks an arm around my waist, catching me before I make contact. "How did they get him in here? I just left him."

"There's a trap door above his cell. We heard a bang, and there he was," Jayce says.

My mouth parts with disbelief. "She's always one step ahead of us," I mutter.

I pass a hand over my brow. The promise I made to Shaila repeats in my head, the scrap of parchment I placed in her little cedar box on the beach.

My gaze darts over the cellar. I'm surrounded by my own failure. Everyone here has suffered in an effort to keep me from Asher. Everyone here will die because of me.

No.

"Asher! I'm right here! Let's get this done!" I scream.

"Asher is mine. Not yours. Mine," a voice croaks. I hurl my gaze to the sound. A girl crawls to the front of her cell. Three empty cells stretch between hers and mine. She stops inches shy of the bars.

Blonde, dirty hair is matted around her gaunt face. The neck is torn out of her T-shirt. Her jeans are coated in streaks of black and brown.

"Asher is mine." She stumbles over the words.

"Fine," I say. "He's all yours."

She blinks, confusion fluttering over her features. "What time is it?"

"I don't know," I answer. "Morning."

"Did you feed the horses?" She rocks back to sit on her heels.

I straighten. "What horses?" I ask her.

"I'm not talking to you." She frowns. "I had the strangest dream," she mumbles, and presses her forehead into her hands.

"Where are the horses?" I demand, raising my voice.

The girl scowls. "I'm not talking to you."

"Who are you talking to?"

"Lucas. Lucas, did you feed the horses?"

"Why would Lucas feed . . ." My voice trails off as my eyes adjust to the shadows. Now that she's sitting up, I can see more of her shirt. Half of Wildwood's logo is visible where the fabric has been torn.

I blink, and my heart accelerates. Those T-shirts were only handed out to staff of Wildwood Farm.

"We should ask Dana," I say. "Dana will know if the horses have been fed."

"No!" the girl hisses. "No, no, no." Her voice deepens to a growl. "Asher is mine," she says again, and snaps her teeth at me.

"She's struggling with the change," Reese whispers from down the aisle.

"Change?" I peer at her through the bars.

"She's not handling the blood transition, clearly," Reese explains.

"I don't think so. She worked at Wildwood." I point at her shirt. "Maybe Dana kidnapped her to care for the stolen horses. Maybe she's been, I don't know, brainwashed or something."

"Then why does she know Asher?" Jayce counters.

I consider this, twisting back around to study the girl. Her eyes ping in every direction. Terror rattles over her fingers. She latches them together and shoves them into her lap.

"Who's Asher?" I ask her.

"A man. A beautiful man," she whispers and wrenches a hand free to twist a lock of matted hair. "Too beautiful to be real. I think I may have dreamed him."

I stiffen. "What else did you dream about?"

"Get the horses out! The barn is burning! Help! Is anyone here?" she screams. Her cries echo in the narrow space, her panic tunneling through my bones.

"Are you talking about Wildwood?" I plead. "Were you there when lightning stuck the barn?"

"It wasn't lightning. It wasn't lightning. It wasn't lightning."

"It was!"

"They're gone! Where are the horses? Where are the horses? Help!"

"What's your name?" Reese asks. Her voice is low and calm. It ripples over me like a sigh. I peer back at the girl, who's scrubbing her cheeks with her sleeve as if she's been crying.

"Kate," she whispers. "Kate. Kate. My name is Kate."

Recognition lights my eyes. "Kate," I murmur, covering my mouth with my hands.

"You know her?" Reese asks me.

"She was a new trainer at Wildwood," I explain in a rush. "She came on after my dad—" The words screech to a halt in my throat. I shove past them. "I never met her. Dana told me about her."

"What else do you remember, Kate?" Reese says.

"The stalls are empty. All the stalls are empty. Somebody's truck is in the parking lot. They shouldn't be here. I've never seen that truck. There's a storm coming."

"She's talking about the barn fire that happened the night I was attacked," I say quietly. "But lightning struck the barn. I saw it."

"The whole barn shook," Kate whispers. "But that's not how the fire started. It started in the front. Raced down the aisles, lit every door frame. Dana was there. Dana didn't help. Dana smiled. She called me a name. . . . She . . ." She hugs her knees to her chest and begins to rock. "I'm not just Kate. I'm . . . I'm . . . I can't remember. I'm not Kate."

My chest constricts at the sight of her. I didn't even know she was in the barn that night. Lucas never mentioned her. Did he know? He couldn't have known.

"She's seen her Origin," Jayce speaks up, moving in beside me. Breaking my train of thought. "We need to know what she saw."

"Give her a second," I say.

Jayce ignores me. "There was a crowd, wasn't there?" she asks, and Kate nods.

"They were shouting."

"What did they say?"

"Jayce, let her rest." I glare at her, but she repeats the question.

"A name." Kate clamps her hands on her ears, no doubt besieged by a cacophony of sounds from inside her own mind. The memory of her Origin. She grits her teeth and lets out a growl of frustration.

"Say the first thing you can think of," Jayce prompts.

"Jayce!"

"Spera. They were chanting *Spera*. Over and over. But she didn't kill me. Lenya killed me. A spear came so fast . . . so fast," Kate moans.

Bile rises in my throat. I swallow it down.

"She's one of the Artius Six," Jayce gasps. "They won't let her go."

"What makes you so sure?" My eyes dart from Jayce to Kate and back again.

Jayce raises a brow. "There's only been one Spera and one Lenya," she reminds me. "Let's make sure her mark matches." She pulls her messenger bag into her lap and retrieves a pen and piece of paper.

"Vanessa let you keep your bag?" Suspicion skitters over my spine, twining with doubt.

Do you think she has Asher fooled too? I recall Lucas's answer, as good as a yes.

"She took out all the good stuff." Jayce makes a face, and sets the paper on the floor between us. At the top, she writes *Tanzy* and *Vanessa*, and draws three rings above our names. Beneath them, she makes two empty lines, each with two rings above them.

"Who goes there?" I point to the empty lines.

"No one. None of the Artius Six will have one or two rings. It's impossible. Vanessa's first battle was against her sister, and she obviously won." She fills in Bridget's name at the bottom and draws a circle with a line through it. No circles for Bridget. No kills. "I faced you first, and it didn't go so well for me." She gives me a wry smile and fills in her own name. "Now, if Kate heard the crowd chanting for Lenya and Spera after she died, then it sounds like she fought you next. Poor girl. At least it was fast."

"Spera didn't kill her," I whisper. "Lenya did. She threw a spear from the stands."

"Why the hell would she do that?" Jayce murmurs. We glance at Kate, who's staring back at us through the bars. Jayce shudders, and fills Kate's name in the bottom slot beneath mine and draws a single circle above it.

"So, if she is one of the six, she will have a single circle mark," I say, studying Kate.

"What mark?" Kate asks.

"It will be on your back." Jayce pulls down the neck of my sweater to show Kate the top of my brand.

Kate cranes her neck over her shoulder. "I don't see anything," she whimpers.

"Turn around. Let's be sure," Reese interjects. "Lift up your shirt."

Kate obeys, and we all stare at her bare back, where a single circle is branded to the left of her spine.

"We're sure, all right," Jayce mutters, and makes a little check beside

Kate's name. A new wave of dread rolls through my stomach as I scan the list.

"That's five," I breathe. "Five of the Artius Six, all under one roof." *What will happen if Asher captures the sixth?*

Jayce is nodding as the pieces slip together. "Whoever's left won't have a mark," she muses. "It was a go-big-or-go-home generation, huh? She would've faced Vanessa—*Lenya*—in the arena and lost in the second battle. Not surprising." She rolls her eyes. "If we know anything about Vanessa . . ."

"She's one step ahead," I finish grimly. "She probably already knows exactly who the sixth candidate is. And where to find her. But then, why isn't she here?"

I glance at Reese, who shakes her head, stumped.

Jayce crumples her paper in her fist and chucks it into the corner.

A low moan rumbles through the hall, familiar and masculine. Lucas rolls over in his cell.

My heart doubles its speed. "Lucas," I call, and dart closer to the bars. An electric current hums through the metal, charging the air.

"Don't touch the bars," Lucas mumbles, slowly pushing himself up by his hands.

A whine erupts from overhead, the cellar door straining on its hinges.

We all fall silent. I ease to the front corner of my cell for the best vantage point. Gleeful footsteps clip-clop down the stairs. Vanessa emerges from the shadowed landing, a triumphant smile splitting her face in half.

"You." Vanessa points to Kate and strides to her cell door. "You're first." She arcs a thin brow at me, daring me to protest.

I glare.

"Are we going to feed the horses?" Kate perks up, her face a hopeful question mark.

Vanessa pins her lips together, her smile becoming serpentine. "Yes, dear. That's exactly where we're going," she says.

"So you know where they are?"

"Of course." Vanessa croons, her voice sickly sweet. "I always know where everything is."

Everything, I think. *Including the sixth.*

"I'll go," I offer. "Take me to the horses." I do my best to sound bored, and shift onto my throbbing hip.

"Not yet. I'm saving you for last," she winks, and ushers Kate up the stairs.

"What was her name?" Lucas groans.

"Kate. She worked at Wildwood. She said she was there the night of the fire," I answer.

Lucas frowns. "I never saw her. I would've . . ."

He trails off. He abandoned a barn full of horses to come after me that night. Would he have done it if he'd known Kate was there? Would he have left her behind?

Something inside me says *yes.*

And I'm angry.

I shouldn't be. He saved me. He saved *one* of us. He could only save one.

He didn't know Kate was in the barn. He never got the chance to choose between us.

It doesn't matter. Kate was an innocent girl, and now she's a wreck. Not because of Lucas.

Because of me. Because of Spera, choosing forfeit over suffering. Because of Asher and his quest for something that might not even exist.

We stand in silence, our eyes and ears trained on the ceiling. The pair of footsteps echoes over our heads and fades into a farther region of the house.

"What's happening up there?" I whisper to everyone and no one. I can't decide what's worse, the unknown, or the fact we're all waiting to find out. Either way, it's maddening.

"Well she's definitely not taking that poor girl to *feed the horses,*" Jayce scoffs. She pulls a clean sheet of paper from her bag.

My whirling brain needs something to focus on. I settle on the floor beside her and watch as she begins to sketch.

Her pencil skates over the paper, swift, clean marks. She smudges a line into a shadow with her finger. The black-and-white chaos starts to resemble the outline of a horse, but the feel of it is all wrong, violent and furious. The gray strokes outline its head and neck in jagged, frantic pieces. Its ears are flattened with rage, and its nostrils are flared above its open mouth.

She flips the paper around so I can see it right-side up. "It's something I keep dreaming about," she says.

"I wonder where they are," I whisper and run a finger down the broken crest of its neck.

"You should ask Vanessa when it's your turn," Jayce snorts, her voice callous with derision.

She might be joking, but it's exactly what I intend to do.

More footsteps lumber down the stairs, heavy and rushed. Two guards file into the cellar. One of them I recognize from Spera's life. His name is Calen.

Traitor. I saw you call Lucas your brother.

He ignores his old comrade, tugging on a pair of gloves and skimming his gaze over the cells.

"Bridget," he says, and slides her door open, cocking his thumb to the hall. We don't offer her any consolation as she bows her head and slips through the bars. Abby's the only one to sigh at her departure, but even she says nothing to stop Calen from jerking her along.

Guilt barbs through me. Bridget's not one of us, I tell myself. She only helped us revive Lucas because she was outnumbered, because Reese threatened her and meant it, because it was an easy way to be taken captive instead of executed. Her fair-weather loyalty is a farce. If Vanessa hands her a match, she'll burn this whole place to the ground.

More time passes. We don't speculate anymore as to what might await us upstairs, or how many of us they'll take. Every few minutes I exchange a glance with Lucas.

Calen returns, this time calling out for Reese. She glowers at him. Fury ropes around her arms. Her claws descend from the tips of her fingers.

"Reese, no," I plead. It's a risk in more ways than one. I won't have her sacrifice herself for me.

She grinds her teeth in her skull and narrows her eyes at Calen. "I will obey the one true queen," she snarls, and I jolt. Even Calen seems taken aback.

She cocks her head over her shoulder and winks at me. What game is she playing? I'm the candidate's burden, not their queen.

The fewer of us there are, the smaller the cellar feels. Calen comes for Jayce next. "Leave the bag," he barks.

"Make me," she says, and curls her fingers over the strap. Calen yanks it from her arm, and she bolts from the cage.

"Jayce, stop!" I leap to my feet sprinting to the far end of the cell. I thrust my arm between the bars to catch her sleeve.

She goes deathly still. Calen's eyes press wide. The bars are a hairs-breadth from grazing my arm on either side.

"Let go of me, *carefully*," Jayce hisses, but I hold tightly.

"Do you remember what you said to me, back at the house?"

"Tanzy."

"What did you say?"

She huffs. "Don't die," she answers, grimacing.

I give her a pointed look.

"That'll be a little hard if you blow us all up," she whispers dryly.

"Fair point." I release her, drawing my arm back through the bars. Calen exhales, his gaze darting to Lucas, and I wonder . . .

He heaves the cell door back into place and latches onto Jayce, hauling her along by the elbow.

"Keep her safe," I growl, and he pauses.

He tilts his gaze over his shoulder. "Make me," he murmurs. Something desperate glares bright as afternoon sun in his eyes, and I realize in Calen's eyes I am royalty . . . and if memory serves, Calen can be swayed by a queen.

Torture Comes in Many Forms

I pace my cell until the door groans open again. Then I freeze, waiting for the heavy plod of Calen's boots. The passage leading into the cellar is silent. I glance at Abby, who is staring at her knees. She knows Calen will take her next.

Something rustles in the landing, silk over stone, and I start. Vanessa emerges from the shadows like a lioness. She's changed her clothes. A gold, form-fitting slip barely covers her curves. A small, shimmering vial dangles from a thin chain loped around her neck. How she managed to walk down the stairs without making a sound or tumbling in her needle-slim stilettos is beyond me.

She clears her throat, and Calen's boots thump into the landing. He pauses just behind Vanessa's bare shoulder.

His gaze flits to me, and then to the floor. Dread fills me from my middle to my mouth.

"Her," Vanessa hisses, breaking the silence as she points to Abby. "And for heaven's sake, bring her outside. Smoke is so hard to get out of the furniture." She crosses her jeweled arms and tips her smirking gaze to me.

"Smoke?" I murmur.

Abby presses her body into the corner, color draining from her cheeks.

"Oh my God," she breathes, and clutches her chest. Her eyes dart to the ceiling and then to me, pleading, and I remember: the souls of the candidates must be released by fire to return whole in the future.

"No!" I scoop up Jayce's bag and smash it into the bars. Sparks fly from metal, copper rain skittering across the concrete floor. In my head, Jayce's skin peels away, and Reese is consumed by flames.

I shield my face and throw my body into the bars. They bow to the pressure, absorbing the blow. Ice and fire tear through my veins. I charge the cage front again, biting my bottom lip against the pain. "Calen, please!" I gasp.

Vanessa sighs, bored with my tantrum, and snaps her fingers at Calen. "Go. Now," she says.

He squares his jaw and unlocks Abby's door. He shoves it aside and sidles in.

Abby cowers in the corner, and I gape. I've seen her run drills, seen her bash a punching bag with her fists. Now I watch, horrified, as panic glasses over her eyes. She shrinks to her knees. Calen drags her up, then straps his bulky arms across her chest when she twists and shrieks against him.

"Fight, Abby!" I scream, but she is fighting. Her cheeks are purple, her voice is raw. She wrenches her body back and forth, but it gets her nowhere.

Calen's eyes drift briefly to mine and he sighs. Then he forces Abby from her cage and up the stairs. Her cries reverberate in the stairwell, lingering in the dark air even after the metal door swings shut.

Vanessa chuckles and sweeps her fingers through her unbound hair.

I drop to the floor, all of the air leaving my lungs in a hard rush. Red welts cover my hands where the current must have penetrated Jayce's bag. The burning sensations crawling across my back are alive, chewing on my flesh and licking my bones.

"Stay awake, Tanzy," Vanessa croons. "I haven't told you a bedtime story yet."

"Go to hell," I rasp.

"Now that's no way to talk to a dear friend, is it? We're practically sisters." She kneels beside my cage. Goosebumps rise on my flesh where her breath trails over my skin. I push myself up by my hands. Fresh pain rockets through my body and a strangled gasp escapes my mouth.

"I love surprises," Vanessa is saying. "Especially when they're for you."

She twists the top off the vial hanging from her neck and slides a finger inside. When she pulls it out, her fingertip is glowing, coated in Tenix.

My eyes press wide.

"Do you know what this is?" She pauses to twist the vial closed with her clean hand. "Of course you do, or else Lucas wouldn't be alive." She lowers her voice. "That was quite a show you gave us on the embankment, Tanzy. Tantalizing."

"You watched us?" Blood rushes into my cheeks.

"I watched *you*," she corrects me, "sliding onto his chest." She bites her lip.

"He had hypothermia," I stammer, and she laughs.

"I don't blame you, darling." A smile slithers over her jaw. "I wanted a taste once, too. And I always get what I want. Don't I, Lucas?" Her green eyes go dark in an instant.

"Vanessa... It was *you*?" Lucas's voice scrapes over his throat. "Let me tell her."

She flutters her fingers at him. "Hush," she purrs, and his eyes become vacant. In an instant, his parted lips are as rigid as stone.

"Now then. You've clearly seen a teeny, tiny bit of what Tenix can do, but you have no idea what it's capable of in the hands of a true artist."

"Get to the point," I interject.

"No." She giggles. "I like to be a little ... theatrical." She claps her hands, making my eyes move from Lucas's frozen face to her glowing fingers. They move in a sweeping motion, painting a circle at the center of her chest. "Feel free to guess any time," she chides, and paints a second circle.

My eyes lower. To my mark. She's painting the mark we share on her chest. Why would she, when Asher burned the same mark into her back? She completes the third circle, closes her eyes, and steps away, arms outstretched. Her skin darkens to the color of cinnamon. She brings her hands to the crown of her head and runs them down the length of her blonde hair, which turns coal black the moment her palms pass over the strands. Then she covers her face with her hands, pausing for a few seconds before dropping them to her sides.

I retreat a step. Vanessa's ivory, heart-shaped face has vanished, replaced with gaunt edges and wide-set eyes. Even before she opens them, I can predict what color they'll be. Gold-flecked amber, the color of Spera's eyes.

"It's amazing, isn't it? See, a little bit of Tenix and a little bit of Asher's blood, and you can change into whatever, or whoever you want. Can't you,

Lucas?" Vanessa's voice, dripping like honey from Spera's mouth, makes me sick. She saunters over to his cage, and slips on a glove.

My stomach drops as she slides open the door.

"*Enervo*," she croons. Lucas's chin sinks to his collarbone. He remains standing, but his body relaxes and his lashes seal shut.

She picks up one of his hands and runs it down the slope of her waist. "He missed Spera so much," she pouts. "He'd searched for her for nearly a thousand years. I had to bring him a little comfort." She steps closer to him, sweeping her glittering gown behind her, and presses her body into his. "I've never been kissed with so much desire before. He was so hungry. He devoured me." She brings her free fingers to her lips and traces the curve of her neck to her shoulder.

I clutch my own throat. "Why?" I demand, my voice trembling with anger.

Vanessa shrugs, and releases Lucas's hand. It collapses to his waist.

"He sang like a bird for me, Tanzy. Told me everything he knew about the veil and the ritual. To be honest, it wasn't much. At least we knew he didn't have any information we needed, and we knew your pathetic little soul hadn't made an encore appearance." She glides from his cell and locks it behind her. "You should have seen his face when my little Spera disguise dissolved into a shadow. It's like he witnessed her death all over again."

The sound of Lucas's cage door rattling shut fades away as my mind conjures the image of Vanessa and Lucas together. Something breaks between my brain and my body, numbing every inch of me.

"What's wrong, Tanzy?" Spera's face comes into focus within inches of mine. Emerald green bleeds into her gold eyes, and the skin surrounding them lightens a shade at a time. Vanessa purses her lips and reaches through the bar to run a gloved finger down my face. The moment she makes contact, my heart slams into my ribs, forcing hot blood through my shriveled veins.

"You're worse than I ever imagined," I say through my teeth.

"I know, right?" She grins. "And lucky you. It's your turn. Calen!" she calls.

I crease my brow and scan the hall, eyes darting to the stone floor and then overhead. Aside from the dark hole above Lucas's cell, there's no way out.

My gaze snaps back to Lucas, still motionless.

"Oh, relax," Vanessa scoffs. "Your boring boyfriend will snap back to his boring self eventually."

Calen shuffles into the space beside her.

"Finally," she snaps, examining her nails. "What took you so long?"

"The fire . . ." Calen trails off, peering in my direction. Stomach acid rushes into my throat. I swallow it down, doing my best not to gag.

"Save it." Vanessa holds up a hand. "Shackle her."

Calen removes a pair of chain-linked cuffs from his belt and walks to my cell.

I suck in a breath, standing obediently as he claps me in iron, and force myself to giggle.

Vanessa glances up, her interest piqued.

"Something funny?"

"You're afraid of me," I say matter-of-factly.

She barks a laugh.

"No one else needed shackles," I reason.

"You, Tanzy, are not like everybody *else*. Take it as a compliment." She flips her blonde hair over her shoulder and bats her eyes at Lucas, tracing her top lip with her tongue.

"Don't," I say before I can stop myself.

Vanessa grins. "Don't worry. I won't. Been there, done that," she winks.

The image of Lucas giving her a thousand years of pent up desire makes my gut clench with disgust. He would have called her *Spera*. He would've been devastated when her warm skin disintegrated to shadow. When Vanessa's laughing eyes shone out of the face of a monster.

"How could you do that to him?" I say on a breath.

"Haven't you figured it out by now? Eternity gets boring if you always play by the rules."

Calen tugs me out of my cell. I glance at Lucas. His body is still slack, his eyes moving from side to side. As I watch, his breath quickens and he slumps against the wall. Muffled sounds leave his lips as Vanessa's paralytic weakens.

"Lucas, blink once if you can hear me," I call. My insides tie into knots as I wait for a reaction.

His eyelids drop slowly, purposefully, and remain closed for several seconds before reopening.

"Are you okay?" I ask.

He squeezes his eyes shut again. Guilt darkens the ridge of his brow.

"None of it matters, okay? Look at me, Lucas. She tricked you. She tricked all of us."

He tries to speak, but it's as if his tongue is swollen. I can't make out the words.

"You saved me," I whisper, and he shakes his head, *no*. "You've always tried to save me. Vanessa will get what she deserves. I promise."

"She promises!" Vanessa pretends to wipe tears from her eyes. "Upstairs," she yawns, and motions to Calen.

Calen thrusts his hand against my back, steering me past her, into the landing. His fingers soften the moment we're out of Vanessa's sight. I stumble over the first step, and he steadies me.

"Change her into her dress, then take her to the solarium," Vanessa calls, lingering behind us in the cellar. "I have a few final preparations to make."

"What dress?" I whisper. "What's happening?"

Calen shakes his head stiffly. He might not know. He might be afraid to even guess aloud.

I duck my chin, my mind circling Vanessa's words, searching for the answer.

You, Tanzy, are not like everybody else.

I pause. Calen clears his throat and nudges me through the metal door. She won't burn me.

I'm not just a candidate. I'm Spera incarnate.

Vanessa may have a shadow of my soul and my match's blood, but it won't be enough. If there's a sliver of fairness in all of this, *it won't be enough.*

She's taking me to the veil.

THE GIRL IN THE MIRROR

Calen leads me down a narrow hallway with windows on one side. I stare unseeing through the glass. In my head, Jayce screams for her mother as her pink hair burns to oily black. I shake the image away, and try to think of anything else. The veil. Lucas. *Nothing.*

"This way." Calen pushes open a door and nudges me ahead of him.

I step into a small, square room. A floor lamp stands in the corner, shining light on an antique chaise lounge. Several pieces of jewelry glitter from the rich fabric. A white gown runs the length of the seat. A pair of gilded sandals is neatly tucked beneath its hem. A small metal bowl filled with water rests on the floor, two white towels folded over the lip.

I do my best not to shake as I extend my shackled wrists to Calen, expecting to be released so I can change.

"Afraid not," Calen grumbles, his cheeks warming. "Step out of your pants, please."

I balk. Calen drops his eyes to give me a shred of privacy.

Heat crawls up my neck. Fury pounds through my entire body, making my lips twitch and my fingertips quiver. I wriggle out of my leggings and kick them aside.

Calen draws a short dagger from his belt, and my muscles tense.

"Don't move," he says. His cheek flinches where my gaze burns a hole.

"Did they suffer?" I shove the words between my teeth.

Calen pauses, hand suspended within inches of my waist.

I draw in a measured breath to steady my pulse. The stench of char lingers on his skin. "Abby and Reese and—" *Jayce.* I don't trust myself to say her name. "Did they suffer?"

"I didn't—" he starts to say. He ducks his chin, stiffens his jaw, and starts again. "Abby." His voice falters over her name. He clears his throat and lifts his gaze to mine. "No," he says resolutely. "It was instantaneous." A tremor ripples over his bicep. He trains his eyes on his dagger, tightens his grip on the hilt, and tips the blade to my skin. "Now hold still."

He slides the knife up the seam of my tank top, severing the neat row of stitching. Then he cuts each strap and pulls the fabric away. I cross my shackled wrists over my chest, shivering as damp air creeps across my bare skin.

Calen crosses to the bowl, chooses a towel and dunks it. He wrings out the excess water, and raises his brow to me.

"It's cold," he says, his voice gruff and somehow, apologetic. He scrubs my cheeks with the moistened cloth, then cleans the layer of grit from my arms and washes my back

He hesitates, examining the shallow laceration at my hip, the plum-colored bruises leaching upward. Then he refreshes the towel and presses it tenderly against my throbbing ribs.

He repeats the gesture once more before exchanging the wet towel for a dry one. He pats down my skin, gentle, though his hands are callous and heavy.

Against my will, my body relaxes. Calen slides the lily-white dress over my head. The floor-length hem settles just passed my ankles. He secures the halter straps behind my neck.

My gaze darts to the plunging neckline, then away. *Typical Vanessa,* I think. She must have known how this would humiliate me.

Calen retrieves the jewelry from the chaise and clamps a serpent-shaped cuff over each of my forearms. His large fingers move to the metal clasps at the nape of my neck.

"No!" I clutch the horseshoe charm and my father's dog tags in my fist.

Calen's voice dips into the recesses of his throat. "If I send you to Vanessa with these, you'll never see them again," he says

I exhale a shaky breath and obey. Calen tucks the necklaces into his pocket. My neck feels bare without them—the only remnants I have of my father, and of Lucas.

Sorrow surges through me. I peer at Calen.

Murderer. Vanessa's dog.

My last link to the Seen world, if sealing the veil destroys me.

"Will you tell Lucas good-bye for me?" I say, forcing the words, though my hate-filled heart tries to wrest them back.

Calen whispers, his breath warm on my ear. "Should the time come, I shall honor your request."

My body tenses again as Calen pulls my hair into sections and begins to weave the pieces together into a braid. In my head, I call out for Lucas, for Iris and Megan and Claire. For my mother. But no one comes.

I am the final piece. I am the only piece. Spera's words float back to me like a warning, too late. This path is only wide enough to walk down alone.

"You were always most stunning in this dress," Calen says, breaking me from my trance.

I glance down at the shimmering fabric. The long lines of stitching cascade over my breasts and hips as if tailored to my exact measurements. Something about the gown feels familiar, though I'm sure I've never worn it before.

"This is Spera's dress," I realize. My insides knot as my memories converge with hers—Spera leaning out of Asher's tower, bathed in white satin, a braid draped over her shoulder and these same bracelets adorning her arms.

Release me. The little prayer must have left her lips a moment after my guide dissolved the scene before my eyes.

The same two words echo in my mind, but I press my eyes shut against them.

Not yet, I tell myself. *Not until it counts.*

I curl and flex my fingers, desperate to distract myself. Calen retrieves the sandals and slips my feet into them. His fingers are featherlight as he laces them up my calves.

"You don't want any part of this, do you?" I ask, staring at the top of his head.

"It's not my place to have an opinion."

I have to strain to hear his words. He glances over his shoulder, as if

Vanessa might be listening. Then he rises to his feet.

"Are you ready?"

I close my eyes and nod my head.

He guides me from the room, stiffening noticeably as we enter the hall. He squares his shoulders and plasters his focus straight ahead. I lower my eyes to my feet. If Vanessa hasn't foreseen Calen's turning heart, I won't be the one to give it away.

The hallway ends at a copper gate. Calen raps on it twice before shouldering it open. He leads me through the entrance and steps aside as Vanessa spins to face us.

Her black dress is identical in cut to mine. Silver cuffs band her arms, and a dainty crown adorns her hair. She's the spitting image of Lenya.

I glance down at Spera's dress, a glaring waterfall of white. We look like royalty. Like queens.

Around us, the room is just as grand. White stone columns stripe the glass walls, rising up to support an atrium ceiling. Black and white crystals drip from a ring of six chandeliers.

A fire roars in a quartz pit at the center of the circular floor. I cringe and turn my face away from the crackling flames, averting my gaze to the far side of the room, where an easel and a stack of blank canvases are propped against the wall.

A girl I've never seen before stands beside them, a length of black silk in her hand. She quakes, mumbling.

My gaze travels back to Vanessa's ivory face. We lock eyes briefly. She smiles. I shiver.

"Spera," she says, her voice dripping with delight. "So good of you to finally show up." She glides across the marble floor and wraps her chilly arms around me. She kisses the air on either side of my cheeks.

My fingernails dig into my palms until they sting.

Vanessa withdraws a fraction and mopes. "Come now, Tanzy," she says, "this is a special occasion! Smile."

"You killed them." The words are hollow in my throat. "The others. My sisters. Calen burned them because of you."

She rolls her eyes. "Sisters," she mocks. "We all know I have made a habit of killing mine." She sighs, as if I'm being exceptionally tedious. "But I did nothing of the sort."

My heart leaps against my chest. *It's a lie*, my head says. *Another trick.* I recall the smell of smoke on Calen's skin. But I can't banish the hope from my eyes.

Vanessa giggles. "Maybe I eliminated *one* of them," she shrugs. "But it's not as if she's gone *forever*. Her soul is, I don't know, flopping about somewhere in space."

My mouth goes dry. "Whose soul?" I hiss.

Vanessa taps my nose with the tip of her finger. "You'll find out soon enough," she sings. "But first, you and I have business to discuss. There's a deal I'm willing to make with you. Do you want to hear it?"

A bark of a laugh escapes me. "No."

"Have it your way. Since we're such good friends now, I feel inclined to inform you not all of your beloved *sisters* turned me down so quickly." She whirls away from me, swishing her hem over the marble, severing the conversation. A curt response forms on my lips, but I yank it back. There's no way any of the girls from the house would be foolish enough to make a deal with Vanessa.

Vanessa's hand flirts with the train of her dress. I've never seen her so excited, so eager. It's not a good sign.

"Calen, will you bring me my little mouse?" she calls across the room.

Calen retrieves the slender girl standing beside the easel and leads her to us. She clutches the black silk in her hands so hard her knuckles blanch. Her chest rises with a long breath, and her face snaps to mine. Her blind eyeballs shudder side to side, washed in a milky blue.

If she's the mouse, then I'm the snake.

I recoil like I've been struck. I won't kill her. If my transformation has to be complete before I seal the veil, I'll find another way.

"What's wrong, Spera?" Vanessa mocks.

"I won't hurt her," I choke.

"Oh please." Vanessa rolls her eyes. "You're the one in handcuffs, princess."

"Leave us," the girl interjects, her nimble fingers playing notes only she can hear along the length of silk.

"You didn't ask for time alone with the others," Vanessa counters.

"She is unlike the others, is she not?" The girl turns her pale eyes in Vanessa's direction.

Vanessa scowls. "Fine," she says, her voice clipped. She backs away a few steps and gestures for Calen to do the same.

I blink. I've never seen Vanessa relent to anyone before. Who is this girl? What has she done with the other candidates? What does she want with me?

"I require more space," the girl calls out, her unseeing stare locked on me. Displeasure crosses Vanessa's features before she whips the train of her dress around and stalks to the fire. Calen backs to the entrance and leans against the frame, watching us with wary interest.

The girl steps to me, her right hand open. She slides her palm up my arm. My flesh tingles as her fingers pass over it, her touch smooth as the morning sea. She warms a trail across my collar, pausing a hairsbreadth from Asher's mark. Her face tightens with concentration.

"Finding them is the beginning," she whispers, dipping her mouth to my ear. She withdraws, then drips her icy fingertips, one after the other, over my bare back. "Nothing can cross below sea level. You'll need the sea to set them free. They're running, running. Running out of time."

Her breath sparks goosebumps on the nape of my neck. I smother a gasp. She's talking about the horses, I realize. Asher must have trapped them on the other side. If I seal the veil now, they'll be stuck there forever.

"Enough," Vanessa snaps, storming across the marble floor.

"I won't do it." I raise my chin.

Vanessa narrows her eyes at me, then purses her lips and lifts the black fabric from the blind girl's hands.

"I want to paint a little picture," she purrs. "Something for Asher to remember you by, just in case."

"In case what?" I hiss.

"He's so certain of how this little game will play out," she muses, ignoring my question. She pops the length of silk between her hands. "Men always think they know best, don't they, darling? But I always know better."

She's always one step ahead of us. All of us, even Asher.

I grind the truth of it between my teeth.

She raises the silk to my face and blindfolds me, pitching my vision into the dark.

"Bring the others," she calls out.

My ears perk at the hush of doors sweeping open. Uneven footsteps erupt from all directions, echoing across the atrium.

I take a measured breath. If any of the steps belong to the other girls, I'll recognize them.

I close my eyes behind the blindfold, sifting through the varied gaits. One cadence is light and swift, the footsteps barely audible. Another is heavy and drawn out, as if whomever it belongs to is being forced to movement. A third, erratic rhythm catches my ear. Short, nervous steps. Behind them, a pair of heels, steady and somber.

Jayce, Reese, Kate, Bridget.

Alive.

Hope rushes into my eyes, searing and wet.

"Calen," Vanessa says. "Follow the Mouse's instructions. Turn your back when she tells you to do so."

"Yes, my queen."

She snaps her fingers. "Lower guards, you are dismissed."

I hold my breath and try to count the number of guards by their steps as they exit. They march in time, too synchronized to tell apart.

Once they've left, the Mouse beckons Calen, who shuffles closer. She utters short orders—*Move her here. This one next.* Arranging us.

I strain for confirmation. A pair of light, agile footsteps advances. I tap into my other senses, inhaling deeply, my pulse springing to life at the scent of pencil lead. *Jayce?* Calen's heavy soles accompany her, depositing her at my left. Over and over, he retreats and returns, till I can feel a line of bodies beside me.

My right side remains empty. Too empty, somehow, like the crumbling edge of a cliff.

A series of quiet taps and strokes fills the lofty room. Horsehair swishing over canvas. Brushes swirled in water and tapped dry. *Painting. Someone is painting. The Mouse? Or Vanessa?* The noises bounce off every wall and bleed into each other in the dark.

Minutes creep into hours. Below my knees, my legs begin to go numb. How much time has passed, I wonder? The urge to tear the blindfold from my face is maddening.

At last, the room falls still and quiet.

"It is complete," the Mouse announces.

Vanessa's pin-prick heels strike the ground, pausing a few feet away from me. Then she marches in the direction of the blind girl's voice.

I roll my shoulders, wishing I could rip my arms wide and tear my shackles apart. The backs of my knees ache, and my wrists are sore where the heavy cuffs press into my skin.

Murmurs fill the silence. I squeeze my eyes shut and bend my ear toward the sound, but I can't make out the words.

A clap smacks over the atrium. *Definitely Vanessa.*

"Calen, reward the Mouse for her hard work. Give her anything she wants," Vanessa squeals.

I follow the sound of the Mouse and Calen until they disappear somewhere to my right.

Vanessa lets out a terse laugh. "Sing a song of six souls, one body full of fate," she says.

Whoever stands closest to me sucks in a breath.

"You should see yourselves," Vanessa continues. "Pouting. Scowling. So much time spent with your noses in books, and I just swoop in and steal your hard-earned discoveries." She cackles gleefully. "You're pathetic, all of you. I didn't *steal* that piece of the ritual. I wrote it, and left it where I knew you would find it. Let that be a lesson to you. This is my game. You play by my rules. You move when I tell you to, how I tell you to, even if you never hear my voice. Do not think for one moment your actions are your own. When you leave here, you leave because I will it. Now, take off your blindfolds. I want to see your faces."

My fingers itch to snatch the slip of silk away. I force calm from my knuckles to my nails. My hands are steady and controlled as I lift them to my face and slide the blindfold down over my nose, letting it droop beneath my chin.

My eyes object to the sudden flood of light. I drop my gaze to the smooth ground and blink as they adjust. Out of their corners, I spot Reese and Jayce directly beside me. A large gap separates Jayce from Bridget and Kate, probably where Vanessa stood. Our dresses are identical, each of us in a unique color.

"Let's have another little lesson, shall we?" Vanessa croons from the front of the room. "The ritual of the Veil and Vessel was divided into six equal pieces. True or false?"

"Trick question. No one can be sure," Jayce growls.

Be quiet, Jayce. I cast a sideways glance at her.

"I like you!" Vanessa chirps. "You're feisty. You're also wrong. I can prove there are six pieces to the real ritual, because I'm looking at them. At us, to be precise." She scans the line. The silence in the atrium hangs over us like a guillotine. In my mind, the rope suspending the blade begins to snap a thread at a time.

Vanessa grins. "How do you keep a ritual concealed and protected, always moving and equally accessible? How far do you go if your lives depend on keeping it hidden? You require a ritual to read the ritual! It's brilliantly twisted. I must admit, I'm impressed. The pesky council etched it into six marked souls and required they be united side-by-side, in the correct order, for the ritual to appear. Then, the council took one more step and protected the image of the ritual from any eyes that can actually see. It takes the cake, as far as rituals go. So many rules and requirements." Weariness edges into her voice.

"Too bad you don't have the right six," Jayce quips.

"Wrong again." Vanessa glances at Reese. "Did you ever just want to scream at them?" she asks. Her voice is airy with awe. She saunters to Reese, a smile slowly spreading from cheek to cheek. "What morons! They *died* searching for you, and you were right in front of their faces the whole time. How dreadful, to be cursed and surrounded by idiots."

"She's the sixth," I say under my breath.

"Bravo, Tanzy," Vanessa jeers. "Six special souls and a blind Unseen." She dances her tongue over each word as if it's a nursery rhyme. "What do I have?"

"You have the veil ritual," Reese growls.

"I have the veil ritual."

My eyes jump to the front of the room. The stack of canvases is nowhere to be seen.

Vanessa snaps her fingers. "Pay attention, Tanzy."

I chew the inside of my cheek. She has the horse's blood. She has a piece of my soul. She has a sacred message painted by an unseeing immortal. She has everything she needs to open the veil. We're out of time.

Vanessa glides toward me. I count each hollow click of her heels.

"Tanzy." She repeats my name, her voice like honey. "I know your plans for the veil differ from mine. Did you really think you could pull the wool over my eyes?"

My mouth hardens in a line.

Vanessa tsks. "The final piece, the only piece." She rolls her eyes. "Spera was always so self-absorbed."

"You're one to talk."

Her lips push into a smug smile. "Tanzy, dear," she says, "you're *not* the only piece. I don't need you. No one needs you. You're a pawn, and your time on the board is almost up."

"Why are you telling us this?" I ask.

"Because it's more fun to win in front of an audience. There's also one last little caveat to the ritual. It will appear once. Even if you could recreate it, which you can't, it will never reveal itself again." She beams.

A fit of laughter, bitter and cold, comes from further down the line. The sound of it is so unfamiliar I have to look to determine who made it.

Jayce straightens in her place, still chuckling, and rolls her eyes before casting them to the ceiling.

"What's so funny?" Vanessa glares, crossing her arms.

"The council created a ritual to read the ritual, and you think whatever message the blind chick painted won't be protected by some kind of code? They guarded it with their eternal, ritual-loving lives. They wouldn't write it down in plain English. If anyone's a moron, it's you."

"Sweetheart, I'm six steps ahead of you," Vanessa seethes.

Jayce's eyes narrow to slits. Reese studies the floor. Bridget trembles. Kate's wild gaze roams the room. Her muscles seize every few seconds, jerking her limbs on her frame.

Defeat settles over me, heavy on my shoulders. Vanessa is beyond six steps ahead of us. How do we begin to catch up?

"What's with the long faces? I gave you the entire ritual for the ritual. No, you'll never be able to use it, but think of how much you learned today! Now then, I'm sure they'll have a funeral for the council, and I'm not properly dressed."

I crinkle my brow. *A funeral for the council?*

Of course. Their lives are dependent on purpose.

I part my lips.

Vanessa glances at me. Before I can utter a word, she blows me a kiss and vanishes to the other side of the veil.

WE ALL HAVE A TRUTH TO BEAR

Reese stands in the center of the atrium, silent and shaking. "I should have known it was too easy," she mumbles to herself. "She has everything she needs. I've failed. I've failed . . ."

"Where's Abby?" Jayce asks, scanning the room.

I don't want to be the one to tell her, but I don't want her to have to ask again. "Vanessa ordered her soul released," I answer.

Jayce's expression turns to stone and the color leaves her cheeks. She walks to the fire still burning in the center of the room. Her gaze travels upward, tracing the path of the smoke as it dances in the air and escapes through an opening in the ceiling.

"Abby died for nothing," she hisses under her breath. She glares over her shoulder at Reese, her lashes damp with tears. "It took you over a year to track down *one* part of the ritual, and it was all a setup. We can't win this. You couldn't even tell us the truth."

"I wanted to." Desperation shines in Reese's eyes, and she opens her mouth to keep speaking, but Jayce lifts a hand to stop her.

"I'm done," she says. I'm going home. My real home. If we're all doomed,

I want to spend the time I have left with my mom."

"If we fail, she dies," I murmur. Jayce's wide, angry eyes lurch in my direction. "You're right," I start before she can lay into me. "We can't win. Not the way we thought we would. We need a new plan."

Jayce snorts derisively.

I latch onto her wrists. "They have everything they need to open the veil, *except the veil*. So I say, let's beat them to it, and I'll *seal it*."

Jayce pauses, her body tensing. Her lips part, but she doesn't speak.

Reese stiffens. "Tanzy's right," she says.

Surprise jolts my heart against my chest.

"Allowing the window to pass isn't a permanent solution. We'll all come back. This . . . all of this, the suffering, the death. It will all start again unless we take action now."

I exhale, relief surging through me as the secret I've kept lifts away. My gaze follows the smoke as it twirls into the vent. "There are two things I need to do first," I say.

"Name them." Reese raises her chin in salute. I study her for a moment, searching for any sign of reluctance. She's our sister, part of the Artius Six, but she's also an Unseen. When I seal the veil, she'll be absorbed by the other side, barred forever from the Seen world.

Reese's eyes remain firm on mine. She holds her head high, her entire body ready and resolute. She's our sister first. Everything else is secondary.

"The horses," I say. "We have to find them and set them free. I think they're in one of those pockets on the other side of the veil."

"Of course," Reese says.

I glance at Jayce. I don't want to do this without her.

She sighs. "What else?" she asks.

My pulse hums in my ears. I force my gaze to stay level, though it threatens to drop to my shoes. "If there's a way to save Lucas and Reese," I begin, "to keep them on this side of the veil when I seal it . . ." The impossibility nearly renders me silent. But if there's the slightest chance, we have to try.

Jayce nods, a curt, decisive gesture. "If there's a way, I'll find it," she says. "For Abby."

Reese murmurs her agreement. If Abby were here, this task would go to her, hands-down, no questions asked.

"We probably should've figured out what to do with Crossbow Barbie before we had our big climactic moment," Jayce quips, and points at Bridget with a thumb over her shoulder.

"We leave her here, somewhere below sea level." I glare at Bridget, and the taste of metal warms my tongue. The color leaves her face and she backs away, but she doesn't leave. I wish she would run. My muscles thrill at the idea of a chase.

"Tanzy . . ." Jayce's voice steers my attention to her. She tilts her chin, and her blonde brows furrow over her eyes. "She's still a candidate."

"I—" Bridget starts.

"She's a Trojan Horse," I growl, cutting her off. "Taking Bridget with us is playing right into Vanessa's hand, again. She's not even running away, even though she should really be trying to right now," I say, directing my voice in Bridget's direction without looking at her. "I think Vanessa's plan all along has been to make us take Bridget hostage."

"I'm not saying trust Bridget," Jayce says with a harsh laugh. "I'm saying trust me. Trust us. Trust yourself. Even if she's planning on trying to destroy us from within, we won't let her. We are better. We are stronger. And she's like a walking playbook on the mind games of Vanessa Andrews." She glances at Bridget. "Do we need to give a speech about what we'll do if you try anything, or are we good here?"

Bridget scowls at the marble floor and cups her elbows with her opposite hands, hugging her arms to her front.

"Looks like we're good to go. So, what first, fearless leader?" Jayce asks. "Any idea how to get Lucas out of the cellar?"

"About that," I say, and she lifts a brow. "I've been wondering the same thing."

Jayce rolls her eyes, then snaps her face to the open gateway. The sound of heavy footsteps echoes in the hall.

Tension whips through the room. We all snap to a fighting stance. All but Kate, who quivers violently.

"What's the plan" Jayce whispers.

I turn my ear toward the threshold. Whoever's coming isn't doing a thing to muffle their approach. "I bet it's Calen," I decide. "He'll probably take me first. I'll put up a fight once I get him downstairs. Give me a few seconds, and then get out of here. I don't think he'll kill me, but he might kill one of you."

I hurry to the front of the group, remembering the promise I made Shaila as the footsteps become louder and closer. A guard's lumbering form takes shape in the dimly lit archway. Light spills across his face, revealing two scars running down his cheek.

"Lucas," I say on an exhale, leaping into a sprint before his name has completely left my lips. Warmth swells within me with each step I take.

Lucas swings his head from side to side, scanning the width of the atrium. Then he breaks into a run. His arms encircle me, clutching me to his chest. His mouth finds my hair.

"Tanzy," he breathes. He tips his brow to mine, inhaling deeply.

"How did you get out?"

"Calen." He shakes his head in disbelief. "He came to the cellar. Said something about Vanessa leaving me to rot. Then he made a show of hanging his keys on the wall right beside my cell and just . . . walked out. All the power went dead, even the electricity in the bars. I grabbed the keys and unlocked my door. I was sure it was a trap." His gaze drifts over me. "You look . . ." He withdraws a fraction, as if he recognizes the dress. "What's going on?" he asks. "Are you hurt? Was Vanessa—"

"She's gone," I say, and he stares at me. "She . . . *left*," I amend. "Lucas, she has all the pieces of the ritual. She has the horse's blood."

"She doesn't have you." He presses his hands over my shoulders, stroking me to my elbows and latching on tight. My gaze collapses to the floor. Lucas tucks a finger beneath my jaw and tips up my chin. "She doesn't have *you*, Tanzy," he says again. "That's all that matters."

I shake my head. "The ring she gave me, she used it to steal a piece of my soul."

I watch his throat move as he swallows.

"I should have known," I say.

"No," Lucas interrupts me, shaking his head. "You shouldn't have. There's no way you could have known."

"Not to rain on the reunion," Bridget calls, her voice mockingly sweet, "but why, exactly, would Calen just let you go?"

"I have no idea," Lucas admits. "But if they're abandoning this house, so should we."

Silence claims the room. Everyone looks to Reese, seeking direction. Everyone, I realize, except for Jayce. Her eyes are still trained on the ribbon of smoke over the flames.

"Let's move," Reese says.

"Wait." Jayce takes a step closer to the fire pit. "We should say good-bye."

I pull myself out of Lucas's embrace and join her. She doesn't look at me. The red flames reflect in her eyes.

I take her hand, locking our fingers together.

Reese moves into the space beside her. Lucas comes to stand beside me.

We form a ring around the stone pit and stare into the glow. Out of the corner of my eye, I see Bridget bow her head.

"This ends with us," Reese says, her voice low.

"With us," I whisper.

Jayce nods. "With us." The words slice over her tongue like a swear.

In my head, I remember Abby stretching her hand high in the common room, volunteering to rescue Lucas, striding past me into the strait.

Thank you, I mouth the words. Beside me, Jayce's lips are moving, too.

I squeeze her hand. Lucas squeezes mine. And one by one, we exit the room.

Stepping through the front door and into the sunshine feels like coming up for air.

We follow Reese across the lawn and into the cover of trees.

Quickly, the blue wash of sky is snatched away by shadow, and the suffocating wood threatens to yank us into the undertow again.

My skin crawls up my neck and pricks my hairline. Every sense is piqued, straining for the first signs of an attack. For beasts lurking in the branches. For pillars of mist and smoke that might mold into spear-wielding Taigo.

Overhead, the bare boughs intertwine, weaving together and sealing out the afternoon light. Soon, we are shadows ourselves, cloaked in shifting panels of gray and black.

Reese pauses, holding up a hand, and we gather around her.

"What's the plan?" Jayce asks, her voice barely more than a whisper.

"This is Tanzy's call," Reese says, and levels her gaze at me. "From here on out, we follow her lead."

Nerves slosh at the pit of my stomach as every pair of eyes turns to me.

"We split up," I decide. "Reese, I'm sure you want to find the others. Iris, Claire, Megan. If you have any idea where they might be—"

She cuts me off with a nod.

"Good," I say. "I'm going after the horses."

"I'm with you," Jayce pipes up. "If Asher's hidden the herd with Tenix, I'll be able to see right through it."

"I'm coming too." Lucas steps to my side, bathing me in his solid, sprawling shadow. In the scent of him.

"Bridget, you're with me," Reese says, and inwardly, I thank her. "We'll check on the safe house," Reese continues, "but we're abandoning it as a residence for now. I'll send word with Hope of our new location once we've established it. Do your best to be there by dark. And Tanzy," she turns to me, and lowers her voice, "we monitor Asher's usual haunts. He hasn't made an appearance since you arrived. Whatever he's planning, we won't be able to warn you against it. Be safe."

"We will," I confirm, straightening.

She links her arm with Kate's, and holds a hand out for Bridget, who huffs in response. Then the three of them depart, their footsteps fading to silence as they move deeper into the trees.

"Let's get this show on the road," Jayce says. "The sooner we rescue these horses, the sooner I can get out of this freaky dress."

I can't help but smile as she plucks the silk away from her waist. Of all the things we've been through, a form-fitting gown proves too much for Jayce's prickly constitution.

"Where do we start?" I ask.

"Didn't the blind girl tell you where to go?"

"No. She said the horses were hidden in plain sight. That they couldn't cross over because they were below sea level. I'm assuming they're blocked by something Asher made with Tenix, which is where you come in."

"I can't sense Tenix, I can only see through it," Jayce reminds me. "You've got to point me in some kind of direction."

"Right," I say. Doubt trickles through me. *What if I can't find them?*

Lucas ducks his cheek against my hair. "Close your eyes," he whispers. "Concentrate."

I obey, and draw a long breath. My brain breaks down the information in the air. Distance to the ocean. The mix of fresh water in the brackish sound. Mud and sweat and rain-soaked bark.

One scent rises above the rest—lathered horses, panicked and tiring. I spin in the direction of the smell.

Lucas and Jayce fall in step behind me. We move through the trees, back the way we came, and skirt the sodden edge of the lawn.

The scent intensifies, compelling my legs to move faster. We round the opposite side of the house. There, in the cover of brush and low trees, stands the horse who has followed me since the moment I set foot on this island.

It's caked in sweat and dirt. It raises its nose and inhales, testing the air for our scents, its nostrils flaring.

I signal to the others to wait.

"This horse again," Jayce grumbles as its tidy gait breaks into a trot. I crinkle my brow, studying the graceful sweep of its hooves over the earth, the long reach of its forelimbs, the curve of its neck as it drops its head into its supple frame.

Its every gesture is polished, so at odds with its scruffy, unkempt coat. Its steady gait slows, and then it ducks its copper muzzle to me.

My breath catches. Nothing about the way this horse moves is wild. "Jayce," I say on an inhale, "tell me what you see."

"The same gray horse that's been harassing you for weeks," she says.

Gray?

Hope lights in my chest. I lift my hand, pressing my trembling fingers flat. The little red pony nuzzles its brow against my palm. "What else?" I ask, my voice faltering.

Jayce shrugs. "Black tail, really dirty," she replies.

Gray horse, black tail.

"Harbor?" I rasp.

She whinnies and nudges my chest with her nose.

Lucas steps into the space beside me. Harbor snorts, and I almost warn him away. He sifts his fingers through her mane before I can stop him.

"She liked you," I remember. "You took care of her after . . ." *After my father died. After my mother begged me to stop riding. After grief and exhaustion crippled me, braking my truck again and again at the edge of Wildwood's drive.*

"Tenix," Lucas says, but I already know.

"It's her."

Harbor nickers.

"Smile, Tanzy," Lucas murmurs, and I do. I *laugh*. Tears roll, fat and warm and happy, over my cheeks.

My trembling hands automatically grasp the side of her face and rub along her cheekbones. She snorts and buries her nose in my hair.

Guilt punctures the elation bubbling inside of me. She's been following me for weeks. Why did it take me so long to recognize her? I close my eyes against the burn and stroke a long line down the center of her face where an ash-white blaze should be.

Hidden in plain sight. The Mouse's words come roaring back to me.

"Vanessa must have used Tenix to transform all the horses from Wildwood. To disguise them as Outer Banks ponies." I glance at Lucas. "They're protected by law. I can't bring her home looking like this. We can't bring any of them home."

Behind us, Jayce sighs. "If Maris were alive—" she starts, and I whirl on my heel, startling Harbor.

"She *is* alive," I say. I reach for Lucas. "We saw her. She's weak, but she survived."

Jayce's brow leaps to her hairline.

Guilt tugs into my chest. "I should have told you."

"Hey." She holds up her hands. "It's not like the world is ending or anything. You got distracted. Happens to the best of us."

"After the rescue, Lucas and I hid in the shelter beneath the safe house. That's where we saw her. If Vanessa followed us there . . ."

"What? You think you're the reason she caught me? This is Vanessa we're talking about. She always gets what she wants."

"Not this time," I say.

"Not this time," she nods. "We'll find the horses, then we'll find Maris. We *will*." She claps her hands onto my shoulders and looks me straight in the eye. In an instant, she's the old Jayce again. I realize suddenly how much I've missed her, how much I've needed her.

"Harbor will lead the way," I say. "We can ride her together. I think she's been trying to tell me where to go all along." I run my fingers through her coarse mane and automatically work to free a snarl in her straggly hair. She paws at the dirt and shakes her head, eagerness wafting up from her skin.

"No way," Jayce says, and I glance at her. "I've ridden a horse all of one time and it ended in a dirt facial."

"The faster we move, the faster you can take that dress off," I bargain.

Jayce glances at the deep valley of her neckline and straps her arms over her chest. "Fine," she relents. "What about puppy-dog eyes?" She nods at Lucas. "I don't think there's room on that pony for three of us."

"I could shift," Lucas says.

Dread tightens my brow. If he shifts into the frenzied shadow form of an Unseen, Harbor won't like it, and neither will I.

"I could take the shape of an island pony," Lucas suggests. "You could . . . ride me, if you wanted."

Jayce balks. Then she tightens her arms over her bodice and dissolves into laughter.

Mortification creeps up my spine. Beside me, Lucas's cheeks flush red.

"I'll ride with Jayce," I mutter, glaring at her. She scrubs her hands over her eyes and bites back her grin.

Lucas shifts slightly away from us, leveling his gaze on the sunny horizon. Focus bends his mouth to a frown. I watch, spellbound, as fissures web across every inch of his exposed skin. Then his body blurs to black.

A horse's shape takes form, transient and quivering against the frost-laced breeze. Four legs descend and two sculpted ears emerge at the height of the living shadow. A tumbling black mane whips into the air, its ends stained red by the sun. A wide chest and deepsprung ribs solidify.

"Lucas?" I gasp.

He bucks his long muzzle skyward, and the hazy gray surrounding his transformation dissipates.

"Damn," Jayce says, and I elbow her. "What?"

"He's just a horse," I mutter. *Violently pure, quick-tempered. Beautiful.*

He lowers his jet-black eyes to mine.

Loyal. Fragile, I think. *A prey-animal relying on muscle and speed to keep himself out of harm's way.*

I scan the places he's most vulnerable. His wide, open chest. The jugular vein running down the underside of his neck. His flank, where a Taigo's silver spear might easily penetrate his vital organs. Even his legs, powerful and dangerous, will be his undoing should one break or become ensnared.

I swallow, and Jayce smirks.

"Shut up," I say, and weave my fingers together to hoist her onto Harbor's back. She adjusts her seat across his spine and grips her mane, scanning the woods from her elevated position.

"Not so bad?" I ask.

"Not terrible." Despite the quiver in her voice, she sits tall, and straightens her shoulders. She scoots back, making room between her body and Harbor's withers, and coughs when she catches me staring at Lucas again.

I quickly look away, and pull myself up. Jayce wraps her arms around my waist, and I nudge Harbor into a trot.

"You okay back there?" I call over my shoulder.

"More or less." Jayce draws her lips into a tight smile, and yelps when a shallow groove disrupts Harbor's mirror-smooth gait.

"Serves you right," I chuckle.

Jayce gasps her mock-dismay. "I'm not the one making moon-eyes at horse-boy," she replies, and I grin.

"Try to relax. Think about moving *with* her instead of trying to stay still," I offer.

Jayce shifts, awkward and over-cautious. I glance past her, trying my best to be discreet. Lucas's sleek, black body ripples with strength, and his ears swivel back and forth, absorbing sounds from all directions.

Harbor steers out of the trees and onto the beach. Once the footing levels, she breaks into an easy canter, elongating her stride to cover more ground. A head wind blows my hair behind me as her steady rhythm devours a stretch of flat sand. I close my eyes and breathe in the salt-choked air, pretending for a moment I'm simply riding. Pretending, for a brief, stolen fragment of time, that I'm not merely surviving from one minute to the next.

"I see something!" Jayce's cry yanks me from my false, flimsy peace.

"Where?" My eyes fly open and I scan the barren horizon. The beach is empty. No houses with windows where someone might see us. No lone soul wandering along the shore. No witnesses.

"There's a glow on the sand, straight ahead." She points. The empty beach juts into the ocean, creating a narrow crescent about a football field in length. Waves tear at the bank, sand reluctantly sliding into the ocean with every swell.

He's buried them. In my mind, the horses strain for air and paw fruitlessly at a coffin made of sand. The bitter taste of fear works its way down my throat like bile. For weeks, my heart has centered on this task—*find the horses.* But the Mouse was right. Finding them is only the beginning.

I urge Harbor faster, each second more precious than the last. Behind me, Jayce lets out a gasp as we leap ahead and race down the beach. Lucas pulls alongside Harbor's shoulder, and together we gallop to the mouth of the peninsula.

A shallow crevice runs the length of the crumbling bank. I hop off Harbor and shove my hands into the crack. "There's nothing here," I cry, digging out a handful of sand. Wet earth slips into the hole I've made. Within seconds, it's barely visible.

Grief squeezes my heart, stilling it in my chest. Beside me, Lucas phases back into his human form, and crouches down to inspect the gritty earth.

"It only appears that way," Jayce says, her lips pressed into a firm line. "They used Tenix to make something. They wouldn't waste it as a decoy." She slides clumsily off Harbor's back, and walks along the edge. "There's a pocket under here. I can feel it."

"How do we get them out?" I ask. As if to answer, Lucas reaches down and shovels out a chunk of sand. We can't possibly dig to them, but he understands better than any of us how our worlds coexist and how the veil divides them. So, I cup my hands and match his movements.

Jayce's fingers curl to claws and her face tightens with purpose as she joins us, tunneling to whatever she senses below.

We work in silence, the ocean quick to reclaim the sand as soon as we clear it away. A spray of water crashes ashore, flooding the hole. Sunlight fractures on the shallow pool, casting a rainbow above the puddle.

"Look," I whisper, terrified I'm imagining it.

"We're almost there," Jayce grunts without slowing.

The glow remains, hovering above the wet sand. I can't see the horses, but I can feel their hearts beating in a frenzy, taste the sour panic rolling off their skin. My blood surges with the sense of belonging. I draw in air until my lungs protest and rocket my hands to the earth. My fingers crash into an impermeable surface. I yank them out and shake away the sting.

"She found it." Jayce grins, and instantly resumes clawing away wet clumps of sand.

"Found what?" I press my throbbing hands against my chest.

"The veil." Jayce's expression rounds in awe as she clears the last layer of grime from the quartz-like surface. "Remember from class? The veil is tangible when there's empty space on the Unseen side and something solid on ours. This is our way in," she says.

"In?" I stiffen. "Don't you mean out?"

"We can't get them out from this side. We can dig down all we want, but they won't be there. They obviously can't find this portal on their own. Lucas will have to cross the veil and show them the way out."

"No." The word snaps over my tongue like a rubber band. Jayce shrugs apologetically. I whip around. Lucas's eyes remain low. "You can't go in there. Are you crazy? What if you can't get back out?"

"As long as the portal stays above the water, I'll be able to cross back over," he says to the sand.

I shake my head. "I've come *this* close to saying good-bye to you too many times. I'm not letting you cross."

"If you want to set the horses free, this is the way it happens."

"Look at me." I choke on the words.

Lucas's dry, steady eyes lift to mine, gentle and devastatingly certain. "They'll starve to death in that pocket if we don't get them out soon," he says.

I suck in a breath.

Jayce sits back on her shins and glances warily at the shimmering seal.

"Time to steer, boss." She dusts the sand from her palms. "Word has it you're pretty good in a crisis. This is a crisis."

She's right. They're both right. My blood turns to ice water in my veins. "Okay," I say, exhaling shakily.

"Tanzy—" Lucas starts.

I shake my head. *Don't say good-bye. Don't say it 'just in case.' Don't say it.*

I level my gaze with his. "Go," I say. "But just long enough to see if they're there and whether anyone's guarding them. Then come back and tell me what we're up against."

He nods. Before I can say another word, his form dissolves to black, and disappears altogether.

Helplessness seizes me. He's gone, just like that. And I'm stuck here. If he's hurt, if he's captured again by Vanessa, I'll never know.

"How long will this take?" I ask Jayce.

"Hopefully not too long." She glances at the crumbling edges of the island.

"Can you see anything?" I plead.

"No more than you can, now."

Within seconds, the air around us crackles. I jump to my feet, forcing myself between the rising shadow and Jayce, bracing myself for a Taigo.

Lucas appears. "The pocket is the exact same width and length as this island. The horses are down there. Dana is with them." He turns to me. "She's using a whip to make them run. The vibrations are making the walls crumble. It's almost like . . . " Lucas doesn't finish.

Like the horses are moments away from a grave of water, or a grave of sand.

"Is there any way for them to run up a wall?" I ask, going down a mental checklist.

Lucas shakes his head. "The walls are all practically vertical. There's a hole in the floor. Dana is guarding it."

"How big is it?" I ask.

"Big enough for them to fit one, two at a time max."

"Is it the only way?" I bite down on my lip.

"Yes. But Tanzy, it might not be a way out."

I draw in a measured breath. "We send them down the hole," I decide. "We have to. If we don't try something, they'll die, and there's nothing else to try."

It's a terrible truth.

Lucas nods, his face grim.

"You'll have to subdue Dana first."

"Gladly," he says.

"Then herd the horses toward the hole. If they get frenzied, they'll scatter. Move slow and steady. If one tries to break away, lean toward it, but don't get too close."

"What if this doesn't work?" Jayce interjects.

"Then Lucas gets out." My voice cracks. Behind my eyes, the walls cave in and the horses are trapped. I clear my throat and shove the waking nightmare aside as Lucas moves back to the portal. Tension ripples across his shoulders. Everything inside of me screams out to stop him.

"Lucas," I catch him by the sleeve, curling my hand over his muscled arm. "Come back," I whisper.

"Always." He runs a thumb down my cheek.

His skin begins to fade, his body blurring into the breeze. And then, before I can change my mind and say good-bye, *just in case he never comes back*, he's gone.

To Hell and Back

"We've got a problem." Jayce rises to her feet. I follow her gaze inland, and my breath leaves my lungs. Our strip of land is now an island, a channel of water growing between us and the beach. We're drifting out to sea.

If what's happening here is mirrored on the other side ...

I swallow.

Harbor paws at the ground and spins with nervousness, clearly sensing the danger. She trots the length of the island and raises her nose in the direction of the beach.

"Can horses swim?" Jayce asks, staring over the wild surf.

I nod. "If the island goes, we'll all get to shore." My voice is more certain than my pulse. If the island goes under, will Lucas be able to cross back? Will he be stuck below sea level on the other side of the veil?

"Lucas," I breathe, cold desperation stripping the sun from my skin.

Jayce drops to her knees and brushes more sand away from the portal. I crouch beside her, and we stare blindly at the jagged prism beneath our hands. Seconds pass. Then a full minute. Two.

"What's happening down there?" I force my words to steady.

Without warning, the island quakes beneath us, throwing me from the portal. Harbor leaps into the air. She takes off across what remains of the island and throws herself into the ocean, powering her way to deeper water.

"Jayce!" I turn my head in her direction. Her hands are buried in the sand, clinging to anything dry and solid. Another tremor rocks the ocean floor. A violent spray of water rushes across the slip of land, taking too much ground with it as it slides back to the sea. We're losing. Fast.

I spit the salty grit from my mouth and inch toward Jayce, who is furiously swiping at the covered portal.

A deep groan echoes from somewhere below. We lock eyes for the briefest of moments before a roar behind us snatches our attention. The sea pulls away like an army in retreat, revealing the rolling ocean floor.

My brain kicks into overdrive, sorting through the broken puzzle pieces. Is this Maris? Asher? Something new? I peer into the smoky crystal, furious I can't see through. *If the pocket floods, will Lucas lose sight of the portal?*

"What do we do?" Jayce pleads.

Frustration rushes through me. I close my fist and strike the quartz surface. Blood splatters from my split knuckles, emitting a ruby glow wherever it touches the veil. The chaos around me blurs. My blood can open the veil. It can seal it. Will it let me reach through?

"Jayce, hold onto my leg," I order.

She freezes, searching my face. "What are you doing, Tanzy?"

"Don't let go," I say, avoiding the question.

She nods, and fastens her hands around my ankle in a vice grip. Claws shoot from beneath her fingernails, biting into my calf. I reach down to the punctures she's made, collecting more blood on my fingers. Emulating the same spiral I made with the Tenix to bring Lucas back from the edge of death, I rub it into the surface of the portal. The stone beneath my fingertips softens, giving in to the pressure. I land another punch on the portal's rock-hard outer edge, bringing fresh blood to the surface, and use my fingers to coat my hands in it.

"Only reach in as far as you have to. You may not get back whatever goes in," Jayce shouts.

I shove my hand through the portal. It passes through with little resistance. A tingling sensation buzzes beneath my skin, as if I've reached inside a wasps' nest. Within seconds I'm sure my flesh is peeling away from the bone, but I can't see it.

I let out a scream of anguish and will my throbbing hand to search the pocket below. Water crashes against my fingertips.

"It's flooded," I yell. "I think the ocean is draining into the pocket."

"Keep trying, Tanzy. You can do this," Jayce calls back.

Coarse hair passes beneath my fingers. I reach out for it, but I'm not fast enough. I press my body flat against the stone surface. Blisters ignite wherever my bare skin comes into contact with the spots of plasma. Something ice cold and smooth as glass bumps against my hand. New pain makes my arm jerk straight, an electric current burning a path up my limb. *Lucas.* I wrap my fingers around the solid object and pull.

The weight is tremendous, impossible. My damaged arm trembles with exertion and my grip begins to slip. A grunt of effort leaves my throat as I slide my other hand through the veil, wedging it in beside the arm I'm not even sure is wholly attached to my body anymore. Talon-like fingers close around my arm, forming a lock. I tense every muscle in my body, preparing for one last pull. Either he's coming with me, or I'm going in.

Jayce's rips her claws from my ankles and latches onto my shoulders instead. She plants her feet on either side of me. Her grip tenses, ready.

"Don't you dare quit," she growls in my ear, echoing the instruction I gave the night we saved Maris. A scream tears through my mouth and I throw myself backward. She catches me as my feet slide close to the portal, and digs her heels into the sand. My arms inch upward, the skin passing back through the veil charred and cracking.

"Come on, Tanzy!" Jayce shouts, heaving us away from the portal.

I close my eyes and fill my mind with Lucas's face. Fresh adrenaline charges through my body, numbing the pain gnawing on my arms and filling them with one last surge of strength This is it. This is everything I have to give.

I draw my knees underneath myself, suck in a breath, and pull.

Lucas's fingers appear first, clamped around what's left of my wrist. His head surfaces, his eyes fixated on something still beneath the veil.

"Pull," he moans. Two black-tipped ears emerge from the plasma, and the rest of the horse's head bursts above the surface, cradled under Lucas's other arm.

The moment the horse inhales, water explodes through the opening, flinging Jayce and me to the side. I crash into the sand, losing all orientation. The ground bucks with another tremor and the island splits down the middle. Horses and ocean erupt from the chasm. The surge of water overtakes me in an instant, tossing my body into the gray abyss.

Horses' legs thrash above me. My mangled hands reach for the surface, where sunlight plays on the liquid ceiling. I kick my way through and draw in a haggard breath before sliding beneath a swell.

I reemerge, heaving again, and whip my head around. I should hear splashing hooves, panicked whinnies, but instead, there's silence. Nothing but the wind whipping the sea to froth.

A short blast echoes over the water. Harbor's pony form moves steadily in my direction, her dark head protruding from the sea. All around her, shimmering ribbons of light dance below the surface. My breath comes faster as my heart pounds in my chest. Something is stalking her, no doubt whatever has made quick work of the other horses.

And Lucas. And Jayce.

A sob cripples my throat as Harbor nears. I need to touch her, to rest my fingers against her nose and be sure she's solid. As if reading my mind, she stretches her short neck out across the water, straining to reach me. The light surrounding her intensifies. Copper rays pierce the surface of the gray water, swaying side to side like searchlights. One of them spirals around my legs, warm and slippery. I kick it off and propel myself with my feet, my arms unable to fully extend.

Harbor lets out a frantic whinny, and tosses her head. Her eyes roll in their sockets and a squeal erupts from her gut. The bands of copper lace across her back and coil up her neck.

"No!" I flop uselessly on my side. *I have to touch her. I have to. She's so close.* I swing my arm out for her. My fingers trail her shoulder, and slip beneath the water, unable to close to a grasp.

Before my eyes, her coat becomes translucent, the same copper shooting up from the water now emanating from her skin. Her brown eyes find mine and a strange calmness settles across her rugged face. A riptide sweeps my feet from underneath me, pulling me into her side. Even though every inch of her glows, she is solid where my body bumps against hers. The metallic bands loop around my legs and claim my torso. At least this way, we'll go together.

I wait to be yanked under, for Vanessa's face to appear from out of nowhere, smirking victoriously as the last breath is whipped from my lungs. Instead, a haunting voice drifts from somewhere very far and very close at the same time, calling out for Spera. Peace spreads inside of me, bursting forth from my core, flooding my veins and releasing the iron grip my muscles have on my bones.

"I can set her free." Maris's voice circles the air above my head. "Stop fighting, Tanzy."

Her words cradle my mind. I thread my fingers through Harbor's hair and press myself into her shoulder.

Before my eyes, Harbor and I dissolve into beads of copper light. We are neither attached nor separate. We are not water. We are not air. We are not whole, not broken. We are the current, the pull of the moon on the tide, the force behind a sudden gust of wind. In this moment, I am certain we're all here, my light joined with the glowing ribbons crisscrossing the ocean. I can feel Lucas, Jayce, and every single horse Asher took.

The sea propels us, the underwater wave building faster and faster. We gain strength. The Atlantic blurs by, a menagerie of grays and blues streaked with sunlight and glittering in our wake. We change course, the movement as natural and fluid as breathing. The light binding us together intensifies, and I see it—my eyes taking shape inside of my solidifying skull. My arms ache to life, my fingers clutched around a bright ribbon sailing in front of me. A long neck and sculpted head emerge from the shimmering blur. Harbor's head. Her true face. My hands take a fistful of her tidy, black mane.

The joy is short-lived, the burning in my lungs devouring all distractions. I will my heart to slow down, but it beats wildly. Starbursts explode in front of my eyes, rapid, dizzying blooms. *Don't pass out,* I tell myself as the air thins and my skull begins to feel light.

Harbor leaps forward, her hooves catching on sand. I use the momentum to swing a leg over her back, and press my chest against her outstretched neck. She powers off the ground and a new current lifts us to the surface. We burst through the marbled ceiling at the crest of a wave. I gasp for air and then rock my body back as she descends the rolling curl.

She catches her weight on her front legs and springs ahead, the water shallow enough she no longer has to swim. My eyes move beyond her and scan the beach for any sign of Asher. All I see are beings of pure light rippling in the waves. I watch, spellbound, as the light turns to form, and form turns to horseflesh, galloping free from the surf.

Sand and spray shoot in every direction, kicked up by hundreds of hooves. The horses race ashore, white, gray, brown, bay, black, paint—all of them in their true forms. Harbor's body has returned beneath me, the contour of her spine and the slope between her withers and her barrel all familiar, her dappled gray coat gleaming in the high sun.

Horses pound the empty beach in an endless roll of thunder. I relish the sound. The power.

Ahead, houses are perched just beyond the dunes. Maris must have swept us several miles south during the transformation.

Lucas strides out of the ocean. Sunlight catches in the water dripping from his skin, making his damp body shine gold. The need to touch him barrels through me. I slide from Harbor's back and start limping to him.

He stiffens, and his attention jerks in the direction of the shallow tide. "Jayce!" he bellows, springing into a run as her name leaves his mouth.

I whirl around. Dana stands behind Jayce in ankle-deep water, the rope end of the whip wrapped around Jayce's neck.

I take off at a sprint, the world around me slowing. Jayce's legs wobble. Dana's arms pull harder. She growls, her face contorting so much she barely seems human. She shoves Jayce beneath the surface and plants a boot on her back.

"What will you do here Tanzy?" she sneers. "You can't save her unless you kill me."

The words register with Lucas first. He jolts to a stop and braces an arm in front of me, barring my path as my Vires blood begs me to action.

Dana chuckles. "Good boy." She wags the handle of the whip at Lucas. With her free hand, she pulls a copper medallion from beneath her soaked shirt. The metal piece glows in the light. "Another step from either of you, and it's all over for Lucas."

The spiraled face of the medallion makes my heart stop in my chest. It's a spitting image of the Solvo medallion in Reese's book. I glance at Lucas. His jaw flexes, confirming my suspicion.

Jayce's limbs thrash in the water. I want to tell her to be still, to preserve her oxygen, or pretend she's dead. My mind spins, searching for a solution that saves us all.

Lucas's fingertips slide over my palm. I make a fist around them and squeeze. Without a word, we charge ahead.

Dana's face is the portrait of surprise. She recovers in less than a second.

"Everlasting, ever mine. Elements I call you, five by five," she says into the wind. Lucas crumples like he's been struck. I drop to my knees beside him and raise his head above the surf. He spits out water and sits up, fighting for breath.

"I can keep going if you want. Your call." Dana shrugs.

"What I want?" I shout. "What about you, Dana? What do you want? Do you really want to take orders from Asher and Vanessa for the rest of time?

Do you want to offer yourself as bait any time they need a fresh body?"

Her mouth tightens in a line. The hand closed around the chain of the medallion quavers ever so slightly She shifts a fraction of her weight from the foot pinning Jayce underwater.

A sudden drumming sound gains volume behind me. I stifle the urge to whip around. I can't give Dana an advantage, not when Lucas is too weak to stand and Jayce is struggling for air beneath her boot.

A gray blur shoots past me, leaving a trail of sand and heat. *Harbor.*

"No!" I shout, but she doesn't stop, galloping flat out toward Dana like a runaway train.

Dana twists away. Her form begins to blur as she hastens to phase. Harbor leaps into the air, mouth open, black eyes wild and rolling, ears pinned back. She chomps her teeth shut on Dana's cheek and flings her head backward, tearing flesh from bone. Her hooves punch through Dana's chest and pummel her beneath the shallow surf. The dull popping sound of crushing ribs fills my ears. Bright pink tinges the water as Harbor plunges deeper still, Dana tangled beneath her churning legs.

I sprint the short distance to Jayce and hoist her head and shoulders to the surface. She sputters, gasping for air, and claws at my arms, her eyes unseeing.

"It's me! Jayce, it's me," I cry, and hold her fast until she recognizes me enough to stop fighting. My disbelieving stare swings between Harbor, who circles back to shore, blood streaking her face, and the gray sea, which has completely swallowed Dana. Guilt and shock roil at the base of me, one hot and sticky and horrified, the other cold and quiet.

I should go in after Dana.

What if she's not even there?

What if she phased or passed through the veil?

What if I touch her and she still dies? Would it count as a third kill? I can't risk it.

She deserves to live.

No, she doesn't.

I'm the kind of person who would save her anyway. Aren't I?

I can't answer myself. So, I watch the water roll.

Lucas staggers to where we crouch and helps me take Jayce farther up the shore. Every few seconds, I glance back at the sea, sure Dana will break the surface. She doesn't. Even the spill of crimson has faded into the gray.

Above us, a small cluster of people gather at the top of the sand dunes.

They point at the horses, their mouths agape. What all did they see? How will we explain it away?

"It was a setup," Lucas growls. "They had to be sure." He inspects my arms. The skin is gnarled and twisted with scars like the weather branch of an old, rotting tree. Maris must have healed the wounds during our transformation.

I pass my exhausted, salt-stung eyes between his dark glare and Jayce's pale, pained expression.

"Do you have any idea what you did today?" Jayce whispers, her teeth chattering louder. "Your blood affected the veil. You proved you're the one true queen. You're the Vessel. Now everyone knows it."

HOMECOMING

I can't hear. I can't speak.

Vanessa wasn't convinced I am the one who could open the veil. She needed proof. So she orchestrated a perfect test. Now she's sure. So is Asher, and he's coming. I can feel it. My heart pounds. My mouth shrivels.

The spectators descend the hill in a messy line. My hands tingle at my sides. Any of them could be Asher. Or Vanessa. I search my surroundings with new awareness. One of the people descending the hill catches my eye. It's the affect she has on the others I recognize first, humans sensing her presence as she approaches from behind, and stepping, with the smallest nod from her, stepping aside to yield the better path. Reese.

Reese tilts down her sunglasses and sweeps her yellow eyes across the beach, changing course the moment she catches sight of us. Her stride lengthens. One by one, she touches a stranger on the elbow, gives them a smile and a polite nod. One by one, they step back, waiting for her to go ahead.

"Tanzy?" she asks once she reaches me. Her face is a question mark.

"Dana is dead. I didn't do it," is all I can think to say.

"Okay. We'll take care of everything from here," Reese says. Together, she and Jayce form a wall in front of me. Then they allow the siege of people to advance.

The artist in Jayce rises to the occasion, and she paints a vibrant story as onlookers press for details. She explains we attended a wedding the night before and spent the night on the beach. Yes, we know it's illegal. No, we won't do it again. We saw the horses swimming off shore, and a couple of them seemed like they couldn't move. We swam out to help. They were tangled in an old drag net. No, we can't believe it either. Yes, someone above was looking out for these horses.

Police and animal control officers are called to the scene. They rope off the beach on either side of the large group of exhausted horses, pushing everyone else outside the perimeter. No one asks us to leave, moving almost as carefully around us as they do the herd.

We're given spare jackets and bottles of water. Lucas throws his hood up immediately, and keeps his face tilted to the sand. I stiffen and note the proximity between Lucas and the handful of officers on the beach. If they watch the news they've seen his picture. I touch my tongue to my top teeth, aware that I'm counting their guns and batons.

"Go wait down by the water," I murmur. He presses his lips in a hard line, runs his thumb down the small of my back, and walks out of the fray.

I finally remember to ask Reese about my housemates. She tells me they're safe. My mother had found them and will shield their route to another safe house. Bridget agreed to travel in guarded custody. Still, Reese's face draws tight with worry.

I catch fragments of conversation, mostly speculation as to how the domesticated horses came here, six-figure show horses strewn across the beach like dazzling sea shells left behind after high tide. The real feral ponies of the Outer Banks are nowhere to be seen, which is for the best. Two separate herds meeting for the first time wouldn't be a civil affair.

Two officers make their way to us, maneuvering through a cluster of horses that have formed a ring around us. Reese relays the story this time, her tone matching theirs in authority. I catch myself nodding along, committing the details to memory in case someone asks me anything specific. Jayce slips behind me, drawing her hood around her face to hide the stripes on her skin.

One of the animal control officers makes notes on a pad of paper. He glares skyward as a news helicopter whirs overhead. The beating of the blades startles the horses, and they whirl in a tight formation, searching the flat sand for a safe place. Harbor emerges from the group, studying my face.

Is it Harbor? Lucas changed into a horse. Who's to say Asher or Vanessa wouldn't do the same? This Harbor killed someone. She charged Dana the moment her loyalty to Asher seemed to falter. She tore off half her face, knocked her to the water, and trampled her. *Harbor's always had a temper, but she wouldn't attack someone. Would she?* The uncertainty makes me dizzy.

Harbor snorts, tossing her head in the air, and trots forward. My hesitation must be contagious. She stops and paws at the sand. She won't come closer, and neither will I. I don't know what to do. How can I be sure of anything anymore?

"Where are we going to take them all?" one of the officers mumbles, scanning the crowded beach.

"We contacted a couple of farms on the mainland. They can shelter them till we get a search database up and running."

Shelter. They have to take all of them to a shelter until they're claimed by their owners. Panic floods my mind. There's no way I can prove whether or not the horse standing in front of me is Harbor. There's also no way I can prove she's mine.

"Where do you think they came from?" The other officer asks.

"They were stolen," I blurt, and step out from behind Jayce. "These horses were stolen from Wildwood Farm in Virginia."

"The Wildwood Horse Heist? I heard about that," the one with the notepad says, straightening. "What makes you think so?"

"I can name at least half the horses on this beach. The farm was my father's, the gray mare is mine," I say. I sound entirely more sure than I feel.

The officers look from me to Harbor and back again. "Way to bury the lead. You're telling me you happened to be walking on this beach and saw a bunch of horses in the water, and one of those horses happened to be yours, and that all of these horses were stolen from your farm in Virginia?"

"Yes." I stare him straight in the face. "What do I have to do to get her back?"

He studies me for several seconds. "In order for any of these horses to be claimed, the owner has to present some sort of paperwork. A bill of sale, or registration papers. The latest Coggins test and a couple of current pictures would probably work, too." He tilts his head to the side. "You have any of those things?"

"Yes," I lie, my eyes narrowing on the angle of his nose, the roots of his hair, the dull flecks of blue in his eyes—anything that might suggest he's Asher in disguise, digging for information.

"Here's my card." He pulls one from his wallet. "Give us the day to get all of these guys to shelters, and call me tomorrow. I'll need any contact information you have for other owners, and I'll tell you where she is."

"Can I go with her?" My voice cracks.

He shakes his head. "I'm afraid it's not possible. We've got five stock trailers on their way now. If you'd stay and help us get everyone on board it'd go a long way toward my future generosity. It would also give me a chance to see if the gray horse knows you." He raises an eyebrow.

I want to say yes immediately, but a dagger of fear pricks my heart. What if he's trying to keep me here a little longer so something unseen can unfold around me? I examine my surroundings as far as my peripheral vision will allow. Horses mill around their temporary pen, sniffing and pawing at the sand. People stand in clumps along the edges. Some take pictures with their phones. I nearly smile at the idea of Vanessa taking a selfie with a horse.

"So, will you help or what?" he asks.

"I'm staying. I'll help," I stammer.

"Sit tight. It's going to be a while before we can do much." He scratches the pencil along the notepad once more.

I nod, absently studying my hands.

Both officers stare at me for a second longer, and then turn their backs on our little group. I can hear them discussing the likelihood of our story. Part of me wants to knock them unconscious, swing aboard Harbor and run far away from here. Deep down I realize how futile that would be. Even if they give her to me, I'm not sure how long I'll live. *At least I can make sure she goes to a good home.* New tears prick my eyes.

"You need a break," Lucas says in my ear.

"You were supposed to stay by the water," I whisper.

"Come sit on the beach with me. There's more room to breathe."

I let him guide me closer to the ocean. Sunlight glitters on the surface, but it's the dark places that transfix me.

"What happened in the pocket?" I ask, keeping my eyes on the sea.

"Once the water came up through the hole in the ground, I couldn't remember where the portal was. I knew if I could help one horse find the way out, the rest of the herd would be able to follow. It was filling up so fast. I was sure we wouldn't make it. Then I felt your hand."

"And I felt yours," I say. *Your real hand.* His clawed, marbled fingers were the size of my forearm. I stare at the scars and pocked places on my forearms, and the notch of flesh and skin missing behind my wrist like it was dished out with a spoon. He casts me a sideways glance before staring across the ocean.

I follow his gaze. A flash of copper in the new wave catches my eye. Dana's medallion washes ashore alone. It skims the thin sheet of water and catches on a rise of sand at my side.

Lucas leans away from it but does not object as I pluck it from the beach and turn it over in my hand. "This is the Solvo medallion, right?" I ask, settling back.

He nods. "I can't believe Asher gave Dana the first lines of the Solvo call. I hope she didn't have the whole incantation. He's more reckless than I remember."

"Do you know it?" I ask. I may finally have an upper hand on Asher.

"Yes. But I can't risk saying it out loud while we're this close to it."

"Is it safe for me to keep this?"

"Safer for you to keep it than to leave it," he says.

"Animal control wants to talk to you," Jayce announces from behind us.

I slip the medallion over my head and stride toward them with new confidence. If an Unseen is hiding as one of the officers, I feel certain the Solvo pendant will make them reconsider any rash moves. The officers' hushed conversation evaporates the instant they sense my arrival. I look from one to the other, waiting for them to ask me what happened, who I really am.

"The gray mare has been watching you all afternoon," one of them says, nodding to Harbor.

"Looks to us like she's yours, but we still have to follow protocol."

"Sure, of course." I drop my gaze, and let it wander to Harbor. I start at her hooves and work upward, examining her front legs for two telltale scars: the notch above her left knee where she put it through a chicken wire fence as a yearling, and the crescent moon of shorter hair stamped into her right shoulder by another horse in the field. They are there, and they should be proof enough, but the storm of doubt rages on.

"You seem to have cooled off on her since we first got here. Are you having second thoughts?" he says.

"It's just hard to believe," I say. "It's been over a year. I thought I'd never see her again."

"You're in good company there," the other officer says, his face softening. "The trailers are almost here. Why don't you go take a good, hard look.

Let me know what you decide, and I'll see what I can do."

Can I trust what I see? Can I trust what I feel? My heart and my eyes have both led me astray in recent months. Still, my feet move forward.

Harbor tosses her head as I approach. Her dark eyes assess my face, take note of my hands. I raise one, palm up, and let her sniff my skin. She nuzzles my fingers and drops her forehead to my chest. Her black-tipped ears feather my chin. She's perfect—every hair, every dapple, every mannerism. It's not enough.

She bumps my side with her nose, lipping at my empty pocket where mints should be. I suppress a smile. Harbor would do anything for a mint. My father taught her how to take a bow using nothing more than a handful of peppermints.

My heart leaps at the memory of the day Harbor arrived at Wildwood. My father and I were alone in the barn. He turned Harbor loose in the indoor arena; he said it was important to find out what motivated her. Some horses like praise, some like freedom, some like to play. Harbor was simple: she liked mints. Within ten minutes, he could tap her behind her left shoulder and she'd drop to one knee, straightening the other leg out in front of her in a deep bow. She waited with her nose tucked to her chest, her eyes following the crinkle of the wrapper.

Would she still remember how? I draw in a long breath, willing away the ache in my stomach. It's such a little thing, a nudge on the tender place where her front leg descends from her girth. Victory will be quick. So will failure.

I step to her side, leaning a little weight against her barrel. She swings her head around, expectant. My hand closes to a fist and I bring my knuckles to the smooth dip in her skin, applying a moment of pressure. Her left leg drops back, and for a second I think I've lost. Then her weight shifts to her hind end. She drops her left knee to the sand, her right leg extended in front of her, and her nose tucks to her chest.

A bittersweet torrent roars through my body. It's her. Painful, perfect, and the last piece of my father, of myself, I have left.

FOUND AND LOST

"I'm sure it's her." The words feel so good coming from my mouth, even though I'm not sure what will happen to either of us in the coming months. The certainty it's really, truly Harbor is enough.

The animal control officers take what little information I can give them. I'm reluctant to provide my name. I don't have an address or a phone number. They ask me another question I can't answer, and then scrawl their cell phone numbers on a piece of paper and make me promise not to lose it.

The first of the trucks arrive, pulling open-air stock trailers behind them. More officers come, equipped with halters and lead ropes. As soon as a trailer is full, it pulls away, heading for a farm on the mainland. Since the horses are all considered part of a criminal investigation, the police officers want to keep them in as close proximity to one another as possible.

People have stopped asking me what happened or how I think the horses came to this stretch of Swan Beach. Theories mix with Jayce's earlier answers, the mystery turned into myth inside of a single afternoon. We leave it alone. There's plenty to keep our bodies moving and busy. I wish I could say the same for my mind.

Harbor keeps my shadow good company, standing next to me as I halter the next horse, and waits beside the makeshift rope gate while I walk up the dunes to the lone stretch of asphalt exiting the four-wheel district. The newfound certainty between she and I makes what's coming harder. She will have to get on a trailer, bound for somewhere unknown.

Lucas keeps a steady eye on me, finding a way to touch me when he can see the grief roll in. He halters a horse and we walk side-by-side to the last trailer in silence. His presence helps, warm and constant. We hand the horses off and head back to the beach. There are a few left to load on the trailer. Harbor is in the last group.

"I have to go say good-bye," I whisper. Lucas squeezes my hand. His face is full of anguish, I'm sure a direct result of whatever he sees in mine. Time will tell if this is the right move, if at last I've made a decision without springing a trap for someone I care about.

Lucas lets go of my hand. "I'm sure you don't want anyone putting her on the trailer but you."

"No, I don't." I start down the hill, but he catches me by the wrist, turning me into him.

His face is a storm cloud, dark and expectant. "Harbor will be safe. You have my word," he says, and brings his lips to mine, quick and tender. "Now go," he whispers into my hair, letting his arms fall from my back. I steal one last glance of him, and jog down the hill to my horse.

She nickers at the sight of me slipping beneath the rope fence, and trots to my side. Then she pushes her sculpted head into the cradle of my arm. Heat pricks the corners of my eyes. I ignore it. This is a good thing, the best thing. I am not safe company.

A hand too small to belong to Lucas takes hold of my shoulder. I spin around and bat it away.

"Sorry." The animal control officer lets me go and takes a step back. "I didn't mean to scare you." He's holding one of Wildwood's lesson horses.

"You surprised me," I recover, and pet the horse's shoulder to mask the tremble in my arm.

"I have the address of where your horse is going." He hands me a piece of paper with the information for a farm in Camden. "I can write a letter on your behalf if you don't have paperwork. I'll tell anyone what I saw today. I've been with Animal Control ten years and I've never seen a connection like what you have with your mare."

"Thank you. I thought I'd never see her again." I shift my eyes to Harbor—the sight of her whole and unharmed keeping me glued together. "If you don't hear from me in the next couple of days, will you contact a man named Russ at Hideaway Farm in Kentucky? He was my father's best friend, and he'll take good care of her. If something happens, will you make sure she gets to him?"

"What are you worried about happening to you?" he asks, his brow creasing with concern.

I blink, trapped. With each passing second, his face hardens. "Well, you never know what might happen, right?" I manage a laugh and gesture at Harbor.

"I reckon so." He frowns, and scrawls Russ's information on his notepad. "If we don't hear from you, we'll call him."

"Thank you." I exhale. Harbor bumps my shoulder with her nose. "I guess she's ready."

We follow the officer up the hill. I swallow the lump in my throat and cluck to Harbor as I step up on the trailer. For the first time in her life, she balks and backs away. My stomach knots and adrenaline pumps into my veins. What is she afraid of? What is she trying to tell me?

She lets out a shrill whinny and swings her head down the hill. I follow her gaze across the sand, and catch sight of a huge, well-muscled chestnut horse galloping wide open toward the street. His copper-colored coat gleams in the sun, and his white legs churn beneath him in a rhythm that accelerates with every stride.

The officers jump into a line, waving their hands to stop it from running onto the main road. The horse wheels away from them, floating across the asphalt in an extended trot, its tail arched and proud, and its nostrils flaring. Two men close in behind him, lead ropes taut in their hands.

"Wait," I order in a low voice. "You see how you're holding yourselves? You're crouched like predators. Don't make it a fight. Just walk up to him."

They react immediately, straightening from their crouched positions, and move calmly toward the huge horse. He stands completely still while they fasten a halter and clip a lead rope under his black chin.

"Well, he settled faster than I expected," one says, and walks the big chestnut to Harbor's side. As soon as he reaches her, Harbor hops onto the trailer and looks back at him. He follows her up before his handler can even get a foot inside the rig.

"Let him go. I'll grab him," I say, and catch the horse by the halter. He and Harbor touch noses, greeting each other without a typical squeal of protest. She snorts, satisfied, and listens to the bustle of final preparations taking place outside the trailer.

The chestnut's eyes are dark, flecked with embers of gold. He turns them to Harbor, watching her, and then peers deeper into the trailer. He's comfortable inside, clearly a horse who has logged a lot of miles on the road, and he certainly looks every bit the part of a show horse. Dad would say this guy has an old soul. I catch myself smiling at him, glad he will be along to keep Harbor company for the ride.

"Take care of my girl, handsome," I say, and rub his shoulder. Before my conviction falters, I jump out of the trailer and help them secure the metal doors. They clang shut, loud and final. One officer slaps the back of the rig. The truck rumbles to life and pulls away.

I watch the trailer until it disappears around a curve. Loneliness tunnels beneath my skin. The sound of Reese's clipped voice is a welcome distraction. She and Jayce crest the hill. I study the rise behind them, waiting for Lucas's dark hair to become visible, and for the warmth of him to be beside me.

"We need to leave as soon as possible," Reese keeps her voice low so the lingering spectators and officials don't hear them.

"What's going on? Where's Lucas?" A new wave of alarm draws my blood to the surface like the moon to the tide.

"He's not with you?" Jayce asks, her face a mirror of the panic growing inside of me.

Without answering, I jog to the crest of the dune. A few people mill around the stretch of flat beach, gathering the ropes used to fence in the horses and toting orange barrels up the hill. None of them are Lucas. I turn in a slow circle, searching for any form I've seen him in, but he's gone.

A door bangs shut on a squad car, making me jump. Did they discover Lucas? Do they have him in custody? I strain to see any shapes or movement in the darkened interior of the police car.

"Excuse me, miss?" a voice prompts my ear and a hand brushes the back of my arm. Another officer peers at me, his hand outstretched.

"Yes?" Every muscle across my back catches, ready.

"Your friend had to leave. He asked me to give this to you." His eyes drop to the folded piece of paper clutched in his fist.

Vanessa. Her love of life-altering notes makes me immediately certain a new message from her awaits me.

"Thank you," I mumble, taking it from him. My mind races ahead, assembling a thousand nightmares one word at a time. I squeeze the note until the officer steps far enough away.

My entire body reacts to my first glimpse of the writing, not at all Vanessa's textbook script, but neat, simple lettering: *Be safe. I'll keep an eye on Harbor. Hurry back, Lucas.*

The sight of the chestnut horse galloping up the sand dune roars back. The deep quiet in his eyes. The way Harbor greeted him like she knew him. Lucas wanted to make sure she'd be safe, so he followed her where I couldn't.

"He went with Harbor." I stare down the empty stretch of asphalt. Why wouldn't he say good-bye? Why wouldn't he say something? Anything? "He left," I say, bewildered.

"He probably did what was safest." Reese peers at me over the top of her sunglasses. "Something's come up. We really need you right now. Don't worry, I told Lucas where we're headed." She takes a step closer.

I tuck his note in my pocket. "What do we need to do?"

"The coast guard pulled a girl out of the ocean," Jayce says, leaning in. "Alive."

"Another candidate?" I ask.

"Or Abby," Jayce says. Her gray eyes are bright. She bites down on her lip in a grin. Even here on the beach, I can smell the lingering smoke on Calen's skin, see the ash on his hands. My heart sinks, pulling at the base of my throat.

"That's . . . highly unlikely," Reese mumbles.

"It's not impossible," Jayce counters.

"Let's go. We'll talk in the car," Reese says, casting her eyes along the horizon. The open stretch of sand feels too interested, the dwindling number of people too many and too close. Jayce and I fall in line behind Reese and follow her to the black jeep. Jayce climbs into the back seat and hands me a change of clothes.

Reese cranks the engine and turns up the radio before she speaks. "I heard about the rescue on the scanner. The coast guard pulled an unconscious Jane Doe out of the water this morning. She doesn't have any identification and she's wearing a dress."

"Definitely sounds like a candidate," I say. Even if she isn't Abby, she needs us.

"While you were loading horses, Reese called the hospital to see if she could get any information, and they said she's stable and awake. This is the kicker: Jane Doe says she'll only speak to Spera." Jayce grips my headrest.

"That's impossible. We've named all of the Artius Six."

"The final six, yes." Reese pauses, scanning her mirrors. "But Asher always starts with more than he needs. If I remember correctly, there were over twenty candidates in our group at first. If any of them died by fire, it's very possible they could come back."

"Or it's Abby, and she's trying to catch our attention," Jayce says, too much hope in her voice. Reasons it can't possibly be Abby gather on my tongue. Jayce needs to know—to be prepared for walking into the hospital and not seeing her friend, not finding what she's lost. It's better to be ready, to accept what is in front of you, even if you don't have proof . . . Just like Mom at the river, desperate for some sign of Dad's fate . . . I close my eyes against the sting of memory, her tear-streaked face glowing in the sun. I remember the day I tried to tell her Dad was dead, believing in the idea that accepting his death would heal her, would move us forward. Instead, it tore us apart. Hoping for Abby's return for a few more minutes won't do Jayce any harm.

"What do you make of this?" I ask Reese.

Her mouth pulls into a line. "I'm not sure. I'm going to attempt to claim her either way. Will you speak with her?"

"What makes you think she'll talk to me?" I ask.

"When's the last time you checked a mirror?" Jayce chimes in.

"Before Shaila's memorial." I bring my fingers to my face. Its edges are barely covered by a layer of tough skin. My eyelashes are thick and long, and the slope of my eyes is deeper, wider. I reach a wary hand for the visor mirror and flip it down. Spera's amber eyes stare back at me. I lean away, waiting for them to change. They don't, instead narrowing as if to dare me to doubt them a second longer.

I blink, breaking the spell, and examine the rest of my face. Its shape is not mine, but it's not entirely Spera's either—her features emerging like peaks from the softer curves of the face I used to call my own.

"Amazing, isn't it?" Reese says quietly, as if not to startle me. "The new cells your Vires blood makes have less and less of your original DNA. Do you remember how Spera changed once the horse's blood took over?" she asks.

I nod, remembering the first time I saw Spera once her blood had been replaced. These features don't belong to Spera. They belong to the black horse. When people see Spera in me, they are features we share, not features I took.

"Okay," I say, and close the visor. "Take me to her."

"What if it's a trap?" Jayce asks.

I pause, considering the possible outcomes. They all arrive at one conclusion. "Then I go in alone."

Jayce and I lock eyes in the rearview mirror.

"Never going to happen," she says.

THE LION AND
THE LAMB

I step over the threshold into the hospital lobby. It's not the same facility I recovered in, but the smells and sounds are identical. Blood and disinfectant, hushed voices slipping out of cracked doors. The sudden squawk of monitors. Orders blaring over the speakers. Tapping shoes and the inconstant trill of nervous heartbeats.

Reese and a silver-haired doctor lead the way through a pair of double doors guarding the Intensive Care Unit. Jayce slinks beside me as we make our way down the hall. Her ivory fingers wrap around the Solvo medallion. I insisted she wear it when she refused to let me meet Jane Doe alone.

"She's in here," the doctor says. He pauses with his hand on the door. "We had to give her a sedative a few minutes ago. We use it as a last resort, but she became very combative with the nurses. I expect she'll be out for at least another hour. We're hoping you can identify her for us."

"We'll do our best," Reese says. I wonder if they ever had to sedate me, if there are periods I don't remember from those early days in the hospital when my body or my mind fought back against the foreign blood.

"Are you ready?" Reese asks me.

"Yes," I say, and we all step into the room.

It's not Abby.

Jayce drops her chin to her chest, blinking rapidly. She clutches her fingers to fists at her sides, and then shakes them loose. She forces her gaze back to the stranger in the hospital bed and draws in a hard breath.

I'm not sure whether to be relieved or devastated. *Abby could still be alive,* I want to tell Jayce. *Just because this isn't Abby doesn't mean she's not out there.* The shred of hope comes from some tiny, fragile, recovering part of me. I marvel at the warmth of it and allow it to spread a little farther. If Calen let Abby go without Vanessa catching on, he would have every reason to lie about it.

We crowd into the narrow space beside the girl's bed. Her eyes are closed, her black hair fanned across the pillow case. Angry, red lines stripe her arms. The doctor tells us they're likely from jellyfish, but we know better.

"It's her." Reese swipes behind her glasses at the dry corner of her eye. "That's Genesis." Clearly, Reese's talents are not limited to combat. I train my gaze on the floor so I don't ruin her performance.

"An unusual name. It suits her though," the doctor says, studying the steady rise and fall of the sleeping girl's chest.

"Yes, it does," Reese says. Her smile touches the corners of her mouth without affecting the rest of her face. I wonder if some small part of Reese hoped we'd see Abby, too.

"If you all will follow me, I'd like to get some information about her and contact information for any family she might have." He moves to the door and waits for us to follow.

"We'd like at least one of us to be here when she wakes up." Reese hesitates at the foot of the bed.

"I can't allow you to stay in here alone. The patient, sorry, Genesis, has made it clear she refuses to allow any visitors except someone named Spera."

"I'm Spera." I think it's the first time I've said it, and it's the first time I've fully believed it.

The doctor takes me in as if seeing me for the first time. "I'd ask for identification but you look just like her." He moves to my side and opens the folder in his hands. "We assumed you were a figment of her imagination, maybe something she'd hallucinated from exposure." He turns the folder where I can see it and flips through a stack of paper, drawing after drawing of Spera. "You're all she can remember so far."

"Is it okay if they stay?" Reese asks as I struggle to maintain my composure.

"I insist." He motions to the chairs and turns his attention to me. "Do you want to have these when she wakes up? It might help." He gathers the drawings and holds them out for me.

"Sure." I take the folder with numb fingers.

"She may not be the Genesis you remember. It'll take time for her memory to come back, her personality. She's been through a lot. You should prepare yourselves. She may never be exactly the same."

I am more prepared than he could ever imagine. My doctors said similar things about me when I was the one lying semi-conscious on a hospital bed. Sympathy washes through me for this girl. I don't know a thing about her, but I understand her—at this moment, maybe more than she will understand herself.

"Of course," I say, absently resting a hand on Genesis.

"Please have me paged if she wakes up while you're here." He holds the door open for Reese. Ever cautious, she scans the room once more before leaving us.

"Is her name really Genesis?" I whisper. I turn my gaze from her drawings to her hands, the ends of her fingers still smudged with silvery lead.

"I doubt it," Jayce says.

I set the folder down on the foot of the bed and move beside the sleeping girl. I wish I could tell her to sleep as long as she can. Once she wakes up, her life will become exponentially harder.

"It'll be nice to have another artist in the house. Is she any good?" Jayce picks up the folder.

"Her drawings remind me of yours." I glance at Jayce, and then peer down at the girl. *This will be the hardest thing you've ever done, but you won't go through it alone.* Out of curiosity, I ease my hands behind the girl's shoulders and peek at her back. My mind and my eyes clash: this girl has two rings. This girl, who called out for Spera, who drew my face half a dozen times, has two rings.

"Something is wrong." I jerk my hands from under her and fumble for the nearest drawer, searching for anything I can use to defend us should the need arise. "How would she know Spera if she has two rings?" My fingers clasp around a pair of long scissors.

"These are my drawings," Jayce mumbles as if she didn't hear me.

The girl explodes into motion, something silver glinting in her hand. Jayce drops the folder, and the drawings scatter at her feet. My muscles bunch and propel me toward the meager space between them. Before I reach the foot of the bed, the girl's eyes train on Jayce's center, soft and exposed, and she drives the silver blade into her belly.

Jayce grunts, unable to cry out. The light leaves her eyes in an instant, and she crumples to the floor.

"Jayce!" The scream is mine, but it's a stranger's voice in my ears, the sound of someone breaking in two. Pure instinct descends upon my being and tells me what to do. There's no further thought. Nothing else to consider.

Asher will regret the decision he made to buy my third kill with Jayce's blood.

His sacrificial lamb simply closes her eyes as I draw my hand across my body and shove the blunt-nosed scissors through her sternum. Her heart shudders to a halt, a tiny quiver runs up the blades. The air rushes from her mouth, and a tremor rocks her body. She collapses to the hospital bed, her waist twisting unnaturally from her hip, and her eyelids ricochet open from the impact.

The floor beneath my feet begins to tremble. The air fractures. Colors bend and bleed, separating into particles, brilliant and intense. They spin faster and faster, combining into hundreds of thousands of colors I've never seen—never even imagined before.

I'm falling but I'm not, suspended as the world around me blurs to static, and refocuses once more. A high-pitched whistle cuts through the roar. The ground stabilizes and the noise evaporates. Rock, smooth and polished, is under me. Light from above condenses into a single source, reflecting off the stone. I shield my eyes from the glow and peer across the glittering landscape. Rainbows grow like trees from the glassy floor as far as I can see. They are dazzling, blinding.

My mother's description of the Unseen World haunts my mind; the land of sea and stone, some of it polished to its hardest form: diamonds.

This is the other side of the veil.

I've imagined the Unseen world, but my mind never created anything like this. It's beyond words, beyond beauty. Perfection. My grief and rage evaporate in the incredible light.

I reach out, half expecting to meet an invisible resistance, or for the spellbinding scenery to dissolve into Asher's desert. Nothing happens. I take a step and reach further. Why do I look the same? Shouldn't I be . . . different?

A shock zips through my palm and down to my elbow. I retract my arm and glance at my hand. A small, shallow horseshoe is carved into the center of my palm. Blood trickles down my wrist and drips to the iridescent floor. The moment it makes contact, light erupts from the laceration, a silvery lavender: the color of lightning. At last, I can see my mark.

The open skin seals in a scar, and the color dims, but remains present. I close my hand and open it again, testing to see whether my mark will stay. It does. My first instinct is to tell Jayce. The fresh memory of her face going slack makes me double over. I clutch my fists against my middle, gasping for breath.

The air around me crackles. I snap upright as a frenzied black blur distorts the brilliant glare.

Asher.

I drop my weight to my back foot and twist my torso to the side, guarding my vital organs from a direct attack. It's the last step backward I'll willingly take in this fight. He will pay dearly for taking Jayce's life.

"You sure don't waste any time," I growl at the transitioning shadow. The shape is wrong, shorter and leaner. The eyes materializing are bright yellow instead of Asher's frigid white. Reese's dark features form around them, her mouth hanging open. Blood covers her shirt. It's still liquid on her hands.

"Reese!" I start for her. Guilt slows me; I am the reason she's here.

She trembles, clearly disoriented as she surveys the dazzling surroundings.

"What happened? Are you hurt?" I reach out my hand, but she doesn't step closer.

"Jayce . . . she's . . . why am I here? What happened when I left?"

"The girl killed Jayce. I'm so sorry. Reese, I'm so sorry." Under her gaze I feel small and childish. The vengeance I allowed to propel me to murder minutes ago shrinks away.

"Jayce isn't dead. They were putting her on a stretcher. They were doing chest compressions. I helped them." She trails off and stares at her glistening hands. "They were taking her to the operating room. I was running after them. Then everything went black," she mumbles. "Why am I here? This wasn't part of the deal." Reese clasps her elbows, her face rounding with disbelief as she turns in a circle. "She swore to me I wouldn't have to come back."

"Reese, what deal? Tell me you didn't make a deal with Vanessa," I half demand, half plead. *This isn't happening. This can't be real.*

She chokes on a sob. Her stare falls to the glittering floor. "When Vanessa and I were alone, she offered me a bargain."

"And you took it?" I try to breathe but I can't. My heart is numb, my lungs two stones in my chest.

"The writing was on the wall, Tanzy. The second I set eyes on you I knew you'd kill again. Vanessa said she could undo the oath I made with Asher if I did her one favor. All I had to do was take you and Jayce to the hospital when a new candidate arrived. I had to tell the doctor her name was Genesis. Then I would never have to come back here."

"How could you?" I rasp. "You made a deal with Vanessa, and Jayce could die for it. I killed again for it."

"You killed again for yourself. Why didn't you check Jayce first? You left her there to bleed to death. Why was your first instinct to take another life instead of helping Jayce? If she dies, it's on your hands. She loves you like a sister. Don't you dare judge me. You're so hell-bent on sealing the veil you don't care who you hurt in the process. You declared war, Tanzy. Do you have any idea how many creatures will suffer? How many will die?" Tears roll down her face. "Did you think for one second what would happen to me before you took your third life? Or is there no stopping you now? Who's next, Tanzy?"

Reese sucks in a hard breath. Her eyes are wide, darting from side to side. She takes a step back, her legs quivering beneath her. *She thinks I'm going to attack her next . . .*

"Reese, I won't hurt you," I sputter, and reach out a hand.

She spins on her heel and takes off at a dead sprint across the dazzling landscape.

"Reese!" I shout.

"I'll catch her for you if you want me to," Asher's voice fills my ear. His breath paints the back of my neck. "A homecoming gift for my queen."

The sounds in my head evaporate and leave a single, piercing note: the whistle of a wild stallion challenging another. I don't turn. I don't say a word. A ribbon of salty air races past us, tossing my hair over my shoulders, and I close my eyes.

The black horse swells within me and screams again, a thousand years of confinement at last breaching every wall. My heart responds like drumming hooves.

My promise is silent, a whisper repeating endlessly in my head.

I may be a queen, but I will never be yours.

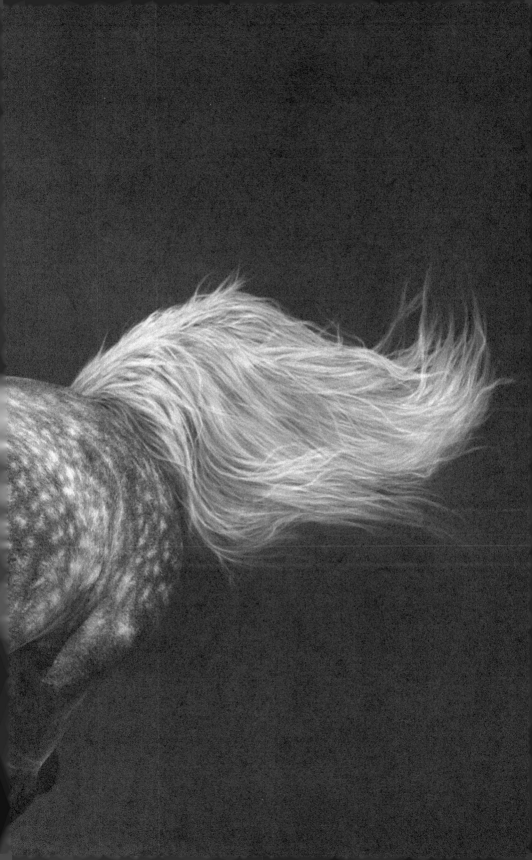

THE HIGHTOWER TRILOGY

WILDWOOD, BOOK ONE
AVAILABLE WHERE BOOKS ARE SOLD

ABOUT THE AUTHOR

Young-adult author. Equine professional. Southern gal. Especially fond of family, sunlight, and cookie dough.

I wrote my first book in seventh grade, filling one hundred and four pages of a black and white Mead notebook. Back then I lived for two things: horses and R.L. Stine books. Fast forward nearly twenty years, and I still work with horses, and hoard books like most women my age collect shoes. Its amazing how much changes... and how much stays the same.

Tanzy Needs You!

Did you enjoy Windswept? Reviews keep books alive . . .
The Unseen world will collapse unless you leave your review
on either GoodReads or the digital storefront of your
choosing.

Tanzy and Lucas thank you. . .